PRAISE FOR
THE MEDEA COMPLEX

"An utterly chilling experience. Roberts leads the reader on a harrowing trip through the dark corridors of a Victorian asylum and the unexpected twists of relationships that are as complex as they are compelling. Nuanced and mesmerizing, it is a gripping tale from first page to last with an ending that left me reeling."

—Deanna Raybourn, *New York Times* bestselling
author of *The Dark Enquiry*

"A riveting debut novel filled with psychological suspense and dark, unexpected twists. In its chilling and compelling narrative, it manages to be both pull-no-punches historical fiction and a story so modern it could have happened yesterday."

—Simone St. James, author of *The Other Side of Midnight*

D0055076

The
MEDEA
COMPLEX

Rachel Florence Roberts

 NEW AMERICAN LIBRARY

New American Library
Published by the Penguin Group
Penguin Group (USA) LLC, 375 Hudson Street,
New York, New York 10014

USA | Canada | UK | Ireland | Australia | New Zealand | India | South Africa | China
penguin.com
A Penguin Random House Company

First published by New American Library,
a division of Penguin Group (USA) LLC

First Printing, June 2015

LIBRARY OF CONGRESS CATALOGING-IN-PUBLICATION DATA:
Roberts, Rachel Florence.
The Medea complex/Rachel Florence Roberts.
p. cm.
ISBN 978-0-451-47414-8 (paperback)
1. Commitment (Psychology)—Fiction. 2. Mental illness—Fiction.
3. Psychological fiction. I. Title.
PS3618.O31588M43 2015
813'.6—dc23   2014046877

Printed in the United States of America
10 9 8 7 6 5 4 3 2 1

Set in Bulmer MT
Designed by Spring Hoteling

To Peter, my one, and Sebastian, my only

ACKNOWLEDGMENTS

First of all, I have to thank my agent, Stephanie Kip Rostan, for giving me the chance of a lifetime. I am privileged and humbled to be working with you—thank you for your insight, expertise, and honesty. Thanks to Jim Levine and Daniel Greenberg. Shelby, thank you for your many lovely e-mails and your continuing support. Thank you to everyone else at Levine Greenberg Rostan Agency.

To my brilliant editor, Danielle Perez—your input, advice, and wonderful suggestions made this book the novel it is today. Your patience is second to none. Thank you for letting me bounce ideas back and forth and for answering all those silly little questions. I appreciate it more than you know.

To everyone at Penguin Random House—thank you. Dan Larsen, thank you for dotting my I's and crossing my T's.

A huge thank-you to all of my readers—both old and new. Thank you for your wonderful and helpful feedback. Thanks to those who read the earlier version and loved it—I can't tell you how much your kind comments mean to me. I hope you enjoy this version! Thank you to all the bloggers and beta readers—namely, Caroline Barker, Lauren Becker, Tracie Podger,

Acknowledgments

Kellie and Natalie, Auggie J, Jessica Ramirez, Fizza Younis, Rosie Amber, Ailyn Koay, Gin Oliver, David George, Mark Wilson, Shane Morgan, Wendy Ewurum, Lauralee Jacks, and many, many others. You know who you are.

For my historical question regarding debentures, thank you to David Nash at Oxford Brookes University. Thank you for your expertise and guidance on the subject.

To my grandmother, Florence Wright—thank you for unknowingly passing down the writing gene! To my father, Roland Roberts, thanks for hiding those adult murder novels from me when I was ten years old. I found them. To my mother, Deborah Roberts, thank you for your ongoing love and support.

To Peter—husband, what can I say? I'll never forget the rain. Thank you for encouraging me to follow my dreams. Thank you for your never-ending, somewhat blind faith in my ability to write a novel. Thank you for putting our son to bed whilst I wrote till the early hours of the morning, for dealing calmly with my many tears of frustration and anger during the writing process. Thank you for laughing when I cried because I ordered a whole cow's worth of beef for dinner. Thank you for the three computers I word-processed my way through. Thank you for helping me get out there. I couldn't have done any of this without you. Your cuddles are the best in the world. Thank you for being the One.

Sebastian, you have grown into an amazing, kind, intelligent little boy, and I am so proud of you. I love you with all my heart. Soon enough you will be a big brother, and I just know you'll be the best. Look after your little sister always.

To all mothers out there—you're doing a great job. Keep going.

The
MEDEA COMPLEX

HOW THE BASTARDS DID IT

Anne
October 11th, 1885
Unknown location

What I really want to know is how the bastards did it.

It's the blackest part of the night, and I've woken on a bed of straw. However, I quite clearly remember falling asleep on a mattress stuffed with *horsehair*, same as I do every night.

I sit up quickly.

Well, then. Someone has stolen it.

I must see what else they have taken: my jewelry, my bonnet, my books . . . all ripe for oiled little hands; why, they may even have stolen my hairbrush! They could, at this very moment, be making ladders out of the strands from my very head! To think—something tickles my foot, probably an insect; straw breeds the damn blighters—yes, to think, somebody or *something* crept among the shadows into my room and simply took my bed! While I slept! I push the blanket away— blanket? A filthy, dirty, stinking, thin, scratchy, awful *blanket*?

They stole my quilt!

"Beatrix!" I call, struggling to free my legs. I kick the coverlet off and shuffle to the edge. I must get help, quickly. The thieves won't be too hard to find if we are fast enough: A mattress is not an easy or sensible thing to walk along a road with, even under the cover of night. I stretch my feet, wiggling my toes searchingly. They scrape against the floor and I move them around, wincing at the coldness. Where are my slippers?

"Beatrix! Wake up, we've been robbed! They've taken everything!" I bend over and reach down toward the floor, my hand clinking against my chamber pot. Damn, damn, damn—where are they? This is wasting valuable time. How did the men get past the butler, the hall boy, the maids? How was I not woken? Why would they steal *my* mattress, when there are plenty of empty guest rooms they could take one from? I stand up angrily, annoyed now.

Why am I standing on a cold floor? Where is . . . ?

They've done away with my Ambusson rug!

"Beatrix!" Where is she? "Come in here and light a light, will you?" It is too dark. I'm cold. I can't see the door. No matter. I need my shawl. I raise my arms in front of me and swing my hands back and forth as I head toward my wardrobe. I have no need for light; I know this room well.

I take a few quick steps and walk straight into a wall that shouldn't be there.

What the . . . ?

I run my fingers across it. The wall is cracked and in a dire state of disrepair, and I pull my hand away.

This is *not* my wall.

A fleck of paint flakes off, making a soft *pft* sound as it hits the floor. Something cracks inside my mind.

This isn't my bedroom.

I've been kidnapped.

No, no . . . stumbling backward, I look around me—it is so dark I don't know if my eyes are open or closed. I hold them open with my fingers for a moment, but it makes no difference.

There must be a logical explanation for this. Perhaps I hit my head falling from my horse again. Perhaps I am still asleep. I pinch myself, yet the pain that shoots through my hand is suddenly over-taken by a horrible ache inside my breast: a hot, tender, bruised, strange sort of yearning.

I am fearfully, horribly awake.

Where am I? I dare not breathe, but somehow I do. I have to.

"Beatrix!" I say quietly. The sound of nothingness buzzes inside my head.

What time is it?

I must move.

Reaching out, I walk slowly at first . . . cautiously searching for something, anything that might inform me as to my location. As my panic increases, so does my pace. I must find a lamp, a door. A dress-ing table. However, I brush nothing but air until I hit another stone wall. Placing my back against it, I follow it quickly with my palms until I reach a corner. I continue onward, repeating the motion, until I real-ize I have counted four corners and effectively walked in a square.

I'm in a room.

A *small* room.

A small room without a door.

As horrendous a prospect this may be, I duplicate the process, carefully searching for any grooves or handles that, in my haste, I may have missed the first time. I kick my feet outward, hoping to knock over a chair, or a hat stand. Yet frighteningly, other than the bed, noth-ing of sufficient prominence or irregularity strikes me. I walk diago-nally across the room; I walk in circles. Nothing.

I sit on the floor.

How is this possible? Every room has, at the very least, a door. Even if a person is poor, he still has doors!

I don't know how long I stay like this, thinking of everything and nothing. Scared to call out, too frightened to move, and yet terrified not to do both. I close my eyes for just a moment.

When I open them, a small pool of light rests on my arm.

I lift my head.

A small, square window hangs roughly twelve feet above the floor. Unusual, vertical lines cross its pane. I squint. What are they? Cautiously, I rise, intending to investigate, when a loud bang reverberates from somewhere nearby.

I shriek, and run toward the bed that I can now see, albeit faintly. I grab the blanket off the floor and leap, pulling the cover over my head. I hide myself deep and pray they won't notice me.

They.

My heart is beating too fast. I can't breathe under this insect-ridden material, and it smells. A piece of straw pokes me in the back, but I resist the temptation to move.

"Lady Stanbury?"

Who?

"Anne?"

Me?

Oh, it's Beatrix, dear-hearted *Beatrix.* I push the cover away from my face and ready myself to jump into her arms. "Quick, Beatrix, come inside! Quickly, now! What has happened to my bed? Where are we—"

A familiar scratching sound: the lighting of an oil lamp. Held up to a woman's face.

A face that is not Beatrix's.

I scream.

She is wearing a white uniform complete with a starched collar: a strange wraparound dress slightly reminiscent of my maid's yet, bewilderingly, somehow subtly and grossly different. Her vast body fills the doorway, illuminated by an unknown source of light. She stands still for a moment, assessing me, as another insect crawls up my leg.

Doorway?

There is a *doorway*?

"Now, now, Lady Stanbury," she says, bosom heaving, "I don't expect any trouble from you, especially not at this ungodly hour. Here is your breakfast."

I flick at the spider and push myself as far up the bed as I possibly can—away from her. What has she done with Beatrix?

"Where is Beatrix?" I say, my voice rising, wavering. She puts a stinking tray on the floor next to my bed and peers at me as if I were a specimen.

Who in hell is this damn fiend, and how does she imagine I will eat my breakfast . . . off the floor? I may be sleeping on straw, but I am not a pig!

"Beatrix will be along momentarily, my lady," she says. Smirking, she steps away from the bed. Before I realize what she is about to do, her hands move toward her fat hips—oh God, she has a plank of wood in there; she is going to beat me to death; she must have killed Beatrix—and with a small incline of her fat head . . . she performs a wobbly, insubordinate imitation of a badly executed curtsey. "I am your *maid* now." She spits the word into the air.

I could kill her.

I *will* kill her.

"Leave at once, intruder! I certainly did not employ any more maids—you liar!" Leaping off the bed, I run to the other side of the cell. Where is Beatrix? She is dead. I know it. "Father! There is a thief in our house!" Where is my riding crop? I shall beat her senseless. I whirl around to find it, but wait—this is not my room. I have been kidnapped!

What *is* this accursed place?

"Calm yourself."

"Father! Beatrix!" Spots of black float in front of my eyes. Lord, if I faint in this monster's clutches, I'm doomed. She might try to eat me.

Until Father or Beatrix arrives, I must find something with which to hit her. An object to defend myself. Yet, sadly, there is only the thin mattress on which I woke, atop of which lies a brown blanket. Whose blanket is that? No matter, it is useless. Even the bed frame looks affixed to the floor. The room is roughly eight feet squared and, unfortunately, sparse. Not even a wardrobe to topple. The floor is as bare as my toes, and somebody stole my rug.

Heavens.

And the window! It has bars across it! I have been thrown in a cell! Lord, have mercy on my soul! This is an exercise in utter futility. There is nothing to make a weapon of here. My safety is a thing of the past.

"Our Father, who art in heaven, hallowed be thy name . . . ," I mutter, searching the room. I wipe my hands across the floor, picking up dust and throwing it. God will help cast out this devil.

In my haste to find a dangerous object, I fail to notice a lone flagstone in the floor, which has risen above its neighbors. The one-inch jut is adequate enough to trip me.

As I land on my head, pain shoots through my brain.

"Doctor!" Doctor? Does she imagine she can dupe me into believing I am in a hospital? This cell does not resemble a place of rest! I consider the wall opposite me as I lie on my face, my cheek quickly becoming numb. It is a sickening yellow in need of a paint—who paints their walls yellow? Don't they know this is the year of green?—and somebody needs to fix this floor. And what is that smell? Twisting my head, I raise myself onto my elbows and look back at the offending slab. It mocks me, and threads of green grace its edges. Green. I smile. But wait . . . how . . . what is that on my legs? What am I wearing?

This is not my nightgown! They have stolen my beautiful Parisian beauty and replaced it with an awful linen *thing* that trails beyond my feet.

The reason I tripped! The hem must have become stuck on the slab. This gives me a sense of satisfaction. It is simply my clothes conspiring against me as opposed to my own unwieldy awkwardness. I point at her—you supplied me with the wrong-size gown! A manic laugh resounds inside my head, and I chuckle. This is evidence of her stupidity—if she cannot judge the size of my frame, then she will surely make a further mistake, which, I am certain, will allow me to escape.

I am happy. Tomorrow she might give me the jailer's keys for breakfast and put the bowl of porridge in her pocket. That would serve her right. Suddenly dizzy, I roll onto my stomach. She can have a view of my behind. She doesn't deserve my face.

"Why is she laughing?" A man's voice.

"How am I to know? But she has fallen, there is blood everywhere, and she has urinated upon herself!"

There are two of them? If this situation weren't so dreadful, it would be almost comical. And *who* has urinated upon herself? That is disgusting. Splayed in a most undignified manner on the floor, dressed in an appalling linen gown with blood trickling out of my head, I contemplate which is more worrisome: the state of my cell, no fit state for a lady, or the fact that a man has an open view of my unmentionables?

My head does not bother me, the warmth of the blood rather soothing.

"Pervert!" I shout.

The floor is comfortable. I don't want to get up.

Rustling and hushing from behind me.

Before I realize what is happening, I am hauled into a sitting position. I squirm in a pathetic attempt to stay where I am. What impolite, rude behavior!

"My father will not give you a solitary farthing!" I say, looking into the face of the "doctor" holding me. "Unhand me at once and let me go home, you, you . . ." I struggle to find an insult strong enough. "You utter, foul sod of a *rotter!*" My voice breaks. Ashamed and astounded, I start to sob.

"Lady Stanbury, look at me," he says. I refuse, and moan into my gown. He is not talking to me. He *can't* be talking to me. I am not who he thinks I am—and yet he continues. "I am a doctor. My name is George, Dr. George Savage. I am the chief medical officer here at Bethlem Royal Hospital. I assure you, you are safe. You have not been kidnapped. The courts simply requested that you were sent here until we can make you well again. I give you my word that you are not a prisoner. You are a patient." He attempts to rub my arms and is rewarded by a smack in the face.

This is outrageous. They have the wrong person! My name is not Lady Stanbury, nor do I know of any person by that name. Safe? They steal everything I have, even my own body, and then they try to assure me I am "safe"? I don't believe a word he says! Blood runs into my right eye, making it difficult to assess him in any detail, but I can see enough to know he is nothing but a charlatan. A long brown beard and a well-fitting suit—no doubt swindled from some innocent gentleman.

How dare this degenerate masquerade as an eminent doctor?

"My name, if you please, is Lady Anne. You have kidnapped the wrong woman. I have never seen you in my life! Incompetents!" Suddenly, the reality of the situation claps me on the back. This is hilarious.

I laugh.

"Chloral?" asks the enormous example of a human by his side.

"No, no," he says. "We only dose them as a last resort. It is better to let her rest awhile, see if she comes to her senses somewhat by noon. Get the new attendant to come and clean her up."

I blink with panic as they move away from me.

"Don't you dare leave me alone in this place!" I jump to my feet and almost faint. Swooning, I run after them, but I am too slow—they are at the door. The "nurse" winks at me and slams the door: a yellow door that matches and blends perfectly with the imperfect walls. They leave me standing and for a moment, I sway . . . not sure where to go, what to do.

Eventually, I sit on the bed and sob.

BEHIND A BEAUTIFUL SMILE

Dr. George Savage, M.D, M.R.C.P
October 12th, 1885
Bethlem Royal Hospital

Preparing for my next entry, I scan through Lady Stanbury's admission notes. Her life reduced to one page of tick boxes and yes or no answers, filled in by a person who surely never met her before. Age. Weight. Height. Personality. Risk.

Crime.

Before.

After.

For a moment I find myself taken by her photograph. Such a normal-looking woman. Demure. Soft. Kind.

Her eyes stare at mine and I close the book, pushing it away.

Unfortunately, insanity is scarcely recognized until it interferes with the law in some way, and Anne's crime certainly brought attention to hers. As a father, I find that the knowledge of what she did scratches at my heart, yet on a professional level I understand she is blameless. Given time, I expect her to recover completely as do most patients of this type, but sometimes I wonder if it would be a mercy for her if she did not. I remember all too well the screaming crowd outside the hospital on the day she arrived. Men, women, and even children armed with placards, many shouting for death, all demanding justice. In their minds, there was no excuse for what she did.

But it is rarely that simple. Yes, society is scared of that which it does not understand—the man who mutters to himself on the street corner, the woman who flings herself off a bridge: liars, thieves, prostitutes, vagrants, murderers, homosexuals—those whose mannerisms and deeds portray a deviant mind, an immoral life. It's my job—no, my *role* in life, not just to heal the sick, but to enlighten the general public. To inform them that many who are frightening in their appearance, deceptive in their actions, defective in their life, are just . . . broken. Lady Stanbury's crime is widely—yet wrongly—viewed as the worst a woman could ever commit, and I suspect only one reason for this: Women are, quite simply, unable to forgive one another for transgressions. How dare she scratch the dazzling surface that reflects the perfect image of the angel in the house?

Men will forgive what women will not.

I pull the casebook toward me, licking my finger and flicking through it until I reach the next blank page. Picking up my ink eyedropper in one hand and a pen in the other, I carefully fill it without any spillages. I smile. Preparation is everything. I do not want to run out midsentence.

It has now been little over a week since Lady Stanbury's admission to Royal Bethlem Hospital and as yet, no discernible progress has been made. Despite rest and recuperation, everything of which she suffered on admission is still very much established. There are no longer any doubts or questions regarding the initial diagnosis.

Patient is violent, and as a direct consequence of this I am unable to do a complete physical exam. She is still lactating and remains amenorrheic. Friction of the breasts with salt and castor oil has, as yet, proven impossible.

There is no sign of mastitis.

She remains flushed in appearance.

Enhanced state of excitement. I am in full agreement with Dr. Goldenheind and Dr. Johnson: the two physicians who signed the first certificates of insanity. Their reports adequately reflect the behavior I have since witnessed.

She remains in isolation for her own safety.

Commissioners duly informed.

I read over what I have written, and carefully correct the bottom curl of a *y*.

There.

At this time, Lady Stanbury is certainly a person who should be deprived of her liberty, as much for her own sake as for that of society. She is not the first woman to be admitted to my asylum on this charge and will not be the last.

Behind her beautiful smile lies the diseased mind of a lunatic.

FISH-EYED FIEND

Anne
October 13th, 1885
Bethlem Royal Hospital

Last night I was kept awake by a woman weeping: an awful, incessant, irritating sound that rose steadily in pitch and prolongation throughout the night. Covering my head with the flimsy blanket proved useless. "It's difficult enough to sleep in here, you fiends!" I cried, hammering at the handleless door that confuses me so: the yellow metal gateway that separates me from freedom. It does not even have a keyhole for me to peer through. I don't know if something worse than incarceration awaits me on the other side, but there is not much in this world more terrifying than ignorance.

I *do* know that I'm at the mercy of my captors if I can't find a way out.

Damn them all, the bunch of goats. I roll over and try to get comfortable. An errant strand of straw pokes me in the eye. Giving up, I push myself onto my knees and try to stem the tears that pour from my injury as I think of my family.

Father must be frantic, and what of Beatrix? I hope they are both safe and well and haven't been abducted too . . . No, no doubt they have contacted the police and everyone is busy searching through fields and rivers looking for my body. Indulging myself in this moment of self-pity heartens me, and I close my eyes. I can smell the water and touch the sky. Surely, my incompetent kidnappers left clues that will lead my family to me.

Yes!

But . . . what if they didn't? What if I am left here—forever, and nobody knows where I went?

I blink. I want to see my eye—how badly injured is it?—but then I suppose I should be glad I am without a mirror. Surely, I resemble a lower-class prostitute, since I can't remember the last time my hair was brushed, my face washed, or my fingernails filed. I haven't had a warm bath in days. My eye releases more tears when I think about the feel of warm water on my skin.

As the darkness of my cell begins to fade, I get out of bed and move toward the window. I raise myself up until I am standing on the tips of my toes, and listen closely for any sounds the dawn may bring. I stand here for a long time, and it occurs to me that no church bells toll the hour.

I must be somewhere in the countryside.

I keep listening—for how long I don't know—until my suspicions are eventually confirmed with the rewarding crow of a cockerel. I have no way of telling the time in here: No clocks adorn the walls, and I wonder idly whether my captors might be kind enough to supply me with a stick. As I consider my plight and troubles with keeping time, my cell door creaks open, disturbing the quiet. The fat woman who appears every morning is hovering in the doorway, holding my breakfast tray. I don't know why she hesitates there, every day. It is as if she is teasing me, or goading me: I don't know which.

I hate her for it, for confusing me. I hate the way she stares, as if she knows something I do not.

I hate the way she watches me.

Well, at least she doesn't want me to starve to death.

"What unsolicited advice do you have for me this morning?" I say as she moves wordlessly into the room. She normally comes armed with a prepared speech regarding my behavior: Stop banging, stop shouting, stop crying. She ignores me and bends, putting the tray onto the floor. My breakfast unsurprisingly consists of a single bowl of thick, tasteless, glutinous porridge, a vast and sad difference from the perfectly golden, buttery toast to which I am accustomed.

"I said—"

"Yes, Anne, I heard you. Just as I heard you screaming in the night." She doesn't bother to look at me, busying herself with my breakfast.

I walk around to peer at her large behind. The fabric is stretched tight across her buttocks. If she bends forward any farther, she is liable to rip open the seams.

"Were you trying to kill someone last night?" I ask, licking my lips. I can't help imagining all the sorts of wonderful foods that she eats in the mornings. Bacon, eggs, fried tomatoes, sausages . . . all piled high on beautifully polished silver plates.

"No, Anne, I wasn't."

I shuffle. "I'm sorry. You wasn't what?"

She turns to look at me, a frown on her fat little face. "That's the answer to your question."

"What question? I didn't ask you a question."

What is she talking about? Is she purposefully trying to confuse me? "You asked me if I was killing someone last night," she says. "I wasn't."

Oh, that.

"You were," I say. I pick at my nails.

"I wasn't."

She's such a dirty liar! I resist the childish urge to stamp my foot. "You most certainly were. I heard you. I heard the shouting. I couldn't sleep! You could have at least killed the woman silently! Why did you have to make her scream so? You are cruel. Cruel, and stupid, and you eat too much. I think you have a problem. I think you eat and eat and eat and forget that you are eating, so much that you keep eating and eating and eating more. Look at how tightly your dress clings to your bosom. It's disgusting."

She stares at me.

"Look," I say, pretending to be nice. Polite. "Can I have something other than this slop for breakfast?"

"No."

"Have you ever read *Oliver Twist*?"

She mutters under her breath and stands, turning as if to leave.

"May I have a stick to tell the time?" I say, quickly, not wishing to be thwarted so soon. She spins and looks at me as if I am mad, and I back away from her until I hit the wall.

"No, Anne. I dread to think what might occur if we gave our inmates sticks. Full-out war, I expect. And how do you suppose a stick will help you tell the time?"

Inmates?

"Well, you place a stick in the ground, upright—normally easier if you have a bit of soil, which I don't, but I'm fairly sure I can make it stand up somehow. In that porridge, most likely. Anyway, then, when the sun hits the stick, you look at the shadow as you would imagine a clock face, and—"

"Anne, stop. The only times you need to know are those of mealtimes. In fact," she says, and I hear the sneer in her voice, "you don't even need to know the times of those! You are to remain here, alone, inside this room." She pauses and looks about her, before walking over to me. I huddle into the paint, but she brings her face close to mine. Foul breath invades my nose, and panic wells up inside me. "Do you need to be somewhere?"

"Well, yes, I—I need to be at home," I stutter. The stench of her essence blocks my voice.

"I will bring you your food for now. When, and if, you are eventually allowed out into the hospital freely, a bell will ring at the times of breakfast, lunch, and dinner." She shakes her head. "A stick—Lord have mercy!" As she opens the door I run and try to peek around her.

It's no use.

She's too fat.

And yet . . . any human contact is better than none.

"I want to observe the body," I say, enticing her to stay.

"Oh, Anne . . . I told you, I didn't kill anyone last night. I never have." Her fat chins ripple as she closes the door. At the last instant, she pokes her head through the small gap and stares at me. I have the urge to slam it against her head. "Yet, Anne. I haven't killed anyone *yet*." She closes the door, and I am reminded of the red jelly Mrs. Cook used to make for me when I was a child.

I shudder.

I don't think I will ever eat it again.

No matter.

I leap onto the floor and search the porridge with my fingers.

No keys.

Dejected, I sit with my back to the door and watch the sun rise in the sky through the window. I ponder nothing for a while, but quickly tire of thinking. Everything bores me. I'm bored of everything. The days in here are long and utterly pointless, and nothing holds my attention. Not even my thoughts.

Eventually, dawn turns to noon as the yellow fireball peaks at the uppermost part through the bars, and at once my stomach grumbles. It has learned that lunch will be delivered soon after the sun hits that particular spot in the glass. There is a crack in the window at that exact point, and I wonder why. Was someone here before me? Did they throw something at it in an effort to escape? Did the sun burn a hole through it? Will I soon be freed? Will we all melt away?

Suddenly, my dull mind is racing with more thoughts than I can control.

What do they want with me?

Do they intend to harm me?

Who are "they"?

And where is Beatrix? I miss her. Nobody else here speaks French, and if I don't practice, I may forget how to speak it. I hope that my confidante, my best friend, is outside these four walls discussing my freedom with my kidnappers. It is lucky my captors are not French, though, as Father would be absolutely hopeless in any sort of foreign negotiation.

A tickling sensation in my hands. Looking down, I find I am holding a pile of yellow paint chips. I must have spent my morning picking them off the walls, but I don't remember moving from the door. I brush them away, scattering them onto the floor.

The fat woman in the apron returns right on time, but she is not alone; instead, she is accompanied by a younger, slimmer version of her foul self. They are wearing identical aprons, so no doubt this newcomer is a lying, thieving fiend too. This new one reminds me of a rat: all teeth and bones. Her eyes protrude from her face.

My, they do employ the most graceless women.

"I don't suppose you speak French, do you?" I say, staring at the newcomer hopefully. She shakes her head and remains silent, looking at the floor and twiddling her key chain.

"Does she even speak English?" I say pointedly to the fat one.

"Be quiet," the fat one replies. "Today we are going to take you for a walk. God knows, I shan't be taking you alone. You'd like that, I imagine?" She nudges Rat Face in the side, who startles before scuttling over to me. She grabs me by an arm, and I ignore the urge to smack her.

"I thought you said I couldn't leave the room," I say. I lean as far away from Rat Face as possible.

The fat one snorts. "Yes, well . . . the doctor has decided he wants you out for a while. Might drive you crazy if you stay in here too long." She slides a look at Rat Face, who sniggers, and this time it truly takes all of my self-restraint not to hurt her.

"Oh, how wonderful! Yes! I would love to go for a walk!" I smile innocently. I almost clap. Bastard, only letting me out for a "walk" like a dog. If a fair opportunity arises, I'll give them both the slip. Aha. *That* would surprise the "good doctor," wouldn't it?

"Let's get it over with, then," the fat one says. She grabs hold of my other arm, and the two of them pull me out of my cell into the longest corridor imaginable.

Light!

One side is made almost in its entirety of large windows—as far as I can see. Sunlight pours through the glass: shining stars and whorls up the walls. Wooden benches run along both sides of the passageway at regular intervals, and potted flowers bloom under the golden rays. It is incredible. It is almost beautiful. The twitters of canaries comingle with the sounds of doves cooing, emanating from ornamental birdcages scattered everywhere on small wooden tables.

And people! There are other women! This fact delights me for a moment and I almost jump with joy, until I remember that I am a hostage and whoever my captors are, they must earn a fortune in ransom money if I am not the only one here. I am smiling and frowning at the same time: a stifling, rumbling pot of contradictory thoughts.

As I am flanked on either side by my two captors, escape is imminently futile. I have no choice but to follow wherever they lead.

"Thieves, robbers . . . ," I gripe quietly under my breath, loath to make my feelings known in case I am marched back to my cell but unable to suppress them completely. I stay alert for signs of an exit while letting myself be maneuvered down the corridor.

As we make our way through the hallway, we are forced to slow our pace by a woman curled up in the fetal position, moaning and crying on the floor. We stop just in front of her, and my fat captor nudges me in my side with a surprisingly knobbly-feeling elbow. The woman is laid at another's feet: those of a handsome, fair-haired woman who is leaning forward, stroking her face. She is dressed in the same apron as my captor, but she seems different.

She looks kind.

"Anne," the fat one says, "do you see this woman?"

"A little hard to miss, seeing as if I take one more step I shall trip over her," I say.

"This is your body."

"Pardon?"

"The body you presumed had been left after the alleged murder last night," she says, grinning at me. She elbows me again in my ribs. I wince. "I told you nobody was killed. The patients can be noisy, that's all."

"Oh." I am momentarily lost for words.

"This is another patient, just as you are a patient. Her name is Grace."

"Miss Grace, could you kindly move your body off the floor so we may walk by?" I say, studying her. Grace stops sobbing and looks up at me. I smile, but this is wasting time. I need to find an escape.

"Don't be cruel," says her captor, who stops stroking her head for a moment to look at me. "This is Grace's spot. She stays here all day, and she's been here much longer than you."

"Her family hasn't paid the ransom yet?" I shake my head sadly. Then I tut and waggle my finger. "Shame on you. Shame on *all* of you. Cretins." I am rewarded with a curious, questioning glance.

"She thinks she's been kidnapped," says my fat jailer.

"I have been kidnapped," I say assertively. I nod to emphasize my point.

"Oh, this is the one, who . . . you know . . . ," says the nice-looking jailer, her eyes widening as she flicks them over me from head to toe.

"Yes," says the fat one.

"Pardon? I'm the one who what?" I'm confused.

"Nothing of your concern at present," says Rat Face. "Now come on, we can walk around Grace and continue on our way." She starts tugging at my arm, but the fat one pulls at my other arm in the opposite direction. We're not going anywhere unless they both pull me one way or the other. Rat Face gives up the fight and lets go of me.

I turn to the fat one. "Are you taking me home?"

"No. I'm taking you for your salt and castor oil rub. You're leaking."

"Leaking where?" I look down at myself. "What do you mean?"
She sighs. "Forget it, Anne."

I do. "Well, then . . . can I please have a stick?"

"No."

"But I asked nicely!"

"No."

I sigh and turn to the fair-haired woman. "Do you speak French?" I raise my eyebrows pleadingly as I am pulled past her.

"Oui."

That one word gives me the hope and courage I need to smile and let myself be dragged onward.

"What is your name?" I say as my fat jailer leads me back along the corridor. We had a not-so-nice walk up and down the corridor—for an hour. I know because I counted the steps in my head. Rat Face scuttled off somewhere halfway through, on step three hundred and eighty-seven: possibly to find some cheese or a dead body to chew on.

"My 'name'? Oh, dear Lord . . ." She starts to laugh and wipes a tear from underneath a fat eye with a tubby finger. Somehow she manages to keep one hand shackled firmly around my upper arm. "My name is not the one that should be of importance to you. It is your own."

"What?" We reach my cell door and she hands me over to a nearby woman, asking her to keep hold of me for a second while she unlocks it.

What does she think I am, a donkey? To be tethered to a lamppost at will? The girl holding me is wearing a nightgown identical to my own. However, it strikes me very quickly that she is worryingly bald: outrightly *denuded* of hair, and two large, water-filled blisters bulge as oversize slugs sucked onto her head. Her eyes are devoid of human emotion, and her eyelashes are gone. I yelp and kick her in the shin, and she lets go of me with a cry.

I start running down the corridor, the sunlight burning flashes in my vision as I pass the windows at the speed of a gazelle. The sound of a shrill whistle being blown momentarily startles me, but I ignore it, keeping my momentum. I revel in the fact that my feet are taking me far away from here, leading me home. I'm free—I'm *free*; there's no way that fat woman can possibly catch me. People jump out of my way, tables crash in front of me, a birdcage tips over, and as I look behind me, I see a dove soaring on its own way to freedom. It is a funny sight and I giggle, just as a familiar cramp hits me in the side and I am bowled over by a man.

"Nurse Ruth!" he shouts, in a loud and authoritative boom. The buzz of activity I've incited during the past few minutes stops. The only sound is that of someone faintly laughing, and the dove's wings as it flaps ineffectually against the glass in a fatalistic attempt at freedom.

I know just how it feels.

Just as someone catches it in a net, the man catches me and as we are both being led back to our cells in opposite directions, the bird's little black eyes meet mine. It stops struggling for a moment, looking at me.

What happened? it says. *We were almost there.*

I know, bird. I know. I'll ask them to give you extra feed tonight for your trouble.

But it's not really good enough, is it? I hate you, it says.

I shrug. *Qui onques rien n'enprist riens n'achieva,* I say to it.

"Nothing ventured, nothing gained," I repeat aloud, in English.

The man deposits me back outside my cell, and the fat one comments on how "mad" I am, glaring at me as she holds the door open. The doctor tries to push me through, but I thrust back. Most unwomanly, but I don't care.

"They're all mad, Nurse Ruth, or have you forgotten where you work today?"

"If only," she harrumphs, practically farting out of her mouth.

"You never answered my question," I say. My principled display of nonconformance continues as I advance through the doorway: inch by excruciating inch. He is stronger than I am, and it annoys me.

"What question, Anne?" she says, idiotically, as she watches me with her ever-present smirk.

"You could at least employ someone intelligent," I say to the man, who I realize now is the "doctor." "I asked her name, about four minutes ago, and she's already forgotten about it."

He looks at me and offers me a small grin. For a second—less than a second—I feel a brief sense of solidarity. It quickly disappears when his fish eyes goggle at me.

"My name isn't the question, Anne, and my memory isn't the one in dispute here; *yours* is. Lady Anne *Stanbury*," she says.

I could scream; I really could.

So I do.

And then, with a lack of any other options, I sit on the floor in the doorway. The "doctor" lets go of me.

"Oh, how frustrated you people are making me! I've told you before, and I'll tell you again: You have the wrong woman! My name is Lady Anne, yes, but my surname is Damsbridge: D-A-M-S-B-R-I-D-G-E. Just in case you're having difficulty understanding that, I thought I should spell it out for you. But are you illiterate? Yes, I suppose you probably are. Again, Damsbridge. My father is the Earl of Damsbridge. The name of Stanbury is not mine. I have never heard of it, and I don't even know anybody by that name!"

"Anne, her name is Ruth," says the "doctor." "Ruth" farts again, and the doctor turns to her. "Well? There is no harm in her knowing your name. She should, anyway—you're supposed to be building a relationship with the patients. I've told you this before."

Ruth makes another sound, and I ask her whether she just farted out of her bottom or out of her mouth. "For when you talk, it's nothing but a lot of smelly noise," I tell her. "Your breath stinks. I noticed the other day, but decided to be polite about it and not say so."

Her face turns a deep shade of pink. "But . . . she's so . . . so . . . stubborn! Doctor, she won't do hardly anything I tell her. She—"

"There is no such thing as a 'stubborn' insane person, Nurse Ruth. A man or woman bereft of reason is perfectly incapable of such. The only stubborn people of the world are sane; your job is to understand this. Now, leave us alone for a minute. Seeing as how I am here, I may as well use this opportunity to try to assess Anne again." Large hands push against my back amid a muttered apology for doing so, and I am finally forced inside my cell.

"You shan't be assessing anybody, least of all me," I say. I leap to my feet and run away from him. I stop at the opposite end of the room. "And I'm not bloody well insane!" As I raise my voice, Ruth leaves, slamming the door behind her.

Ruth.

Fat Ruth.

It has a certain "ring" to it, or "roll." A dumpy, lardy, big Fat Ruth roll.

"Put out your tongue, please, Anne," the "doctor" says, approaching me slowly.

"I don't want to, you beast," I say. I'm really in trouble here.

"Anne. You must show me your tongue. I am a doctor."

"My tongue is perfectly fine, you fiend. The only thing wrong with my tongue is that it has to be used to talk with you," I say. I close my mouth and purse my lips together tightly.

He sighs and looks about him, before making his way over to my bed. He sits on it and puts his head in his hands.

"Yes, you may very well cast your eyes upon the ground, you despicable creature. How dare you lock a lady in a cell, and pretend to be a doctor, in order to look upon her tongue?"

He moves to pull something out of his pocket, and I move quickly: far too fast for him to catch me.

"Anne—"

"Aha! You never imagined this did you, you wobbly-eyed fish!" I am over to the *other* side of the cell now, facing him, brandishing my chamber pot. I hold it above my head. "It is full—stinking, filthy, dirty *full*—and I shall throw it upon you unless you give me the key."

His puffy fish eyes wobble a little more, practically standing on stalks out of his face.

"I can smell them," I say. My arms are starting to ache. I am malnourished, no doubt, from tepid, thick, nasty porridge.

"Smell what?"

"Your eyes, you sea creature."

"My eyes?"

"Yes, your *eyes*. Your horrible, beady *eyes*. Fish eyes. I should imagine you'd like to cut mine out and make chairs out of them. I simply *refuse* to put my tongue out." I can hear my own voice, and it sounds slightly hysterical.

He starts writing on a long, slender notepad, evidently that which he had pulled out of his pocket before I retrieved my weapon.

"Can you stretch out your arms for me instead, then, Anne? Perhaps wiggle your fingers a little?"

While I'm holding a chamber pot? Either he thinks I am stupid, or he is stupid.

"No. I shan't do anything you ask of me. Is that my ransom note?"

"No, Anne. It is—"

He is a liar.

"It is. I know it is. Why else would you be writing upon a pad? I hope that the ink leaks out of your pen, all over your disgusting, cheap-smart clothes."

He frowns, ignoring me, continuing to write, occasionally wiping an invisible piece of dust from his lap. "Have you ever taken any morphine, Anne?"

I ignore the question.

"Give me the key."

"No, Anne. I can't give you the key."

"Give it to me!" My voice rises; my throat starts to close. "Give it to me right *now*, give it to me, give it to me! Give it to me, give it to me—"

The door opens with a bang, hitting itself upon the wall. Some yellow paint falls onto the floor in a pile. I want it.

"Doctor! What on earth is she up to now—"

I launch my chamber pot.

Time stops for a moment.

I giggle.

"Oh my!"

The "doctor" runs to Fat Ruth's aid.

"Doctor! Ohhhhhhh, oh, oh, oh, ohhhhhhhhh!"

I am in hysterics. The laugh simply won't stop and it comes with force, pushing my voice up my windpipe and out into the air in dancing, happy tones. It forces me to bend over, such is its vigor, and—wait, something is shining next to my foot.

A shard.

Before I can grab it, hands pull my arms behind me sharply and I am thrown to the floor. My giggle stops in a huff sort of sound, and I can't breathe right. The odor of feces invades my nose.

"Nurse Ruth!"

"What, Doctor? *What?* You want me to let this little wretch hack us both to death?"

"Be careful with the patient. There is no need for such violence!"

"There is. She was going to stab us! Why on earth is this lunatic not at Broadmoor?"

"Because of her father, Nurse Ruth . . ."

My father? Broadmoor? Lunatic?

The hands let go of me, and they, as well as I, are covered in my filth.

"Get the gloves, Nurse Ruth," he says, wiping at his trousers. I laugh; now they have something on them to be wiped off.

"How about the dress?"

"Yes, fetch the dress, then. Right away."

What are they talking about? The "doctor" looks at me forlornly from a few feet away, blocking the door.

"I am sorry to have to do this, Anne," he says, leaving. Fat Ruth comes back, holding a brown sack.

"Do what? What is that?"

"A restraint. For imbeciles like you," Fat Ruth says, and launches herself upon me with astonishing speed. I wonder if, earlier, she just watched me run for amusement.

"Let me go, let me go, let me *go*!" I shout and I shout and I shout. My voice is heard by everyone but acknowledged by no one.

PRESUMED CURABLE

Dr. George Savage
October 13th, 1885
Bethlem Royal Hospital

There is nothing in the world more soothing than a strong cup of coffee coupled with a light read. I consider the newspaper in front of me longingly for a moment before pushing it aside, and open Lady Stanbury's case file.

> *Emotional side of Lady Stanbury uncontrolled, a tendency to mood swings, verbal and physical violence, marred by restlessness. Hallucinations ceased, yet delusions very much in force. Attempted to escape this morning, disturbing other patients and frightening staff. Threw a full chamber pot of feces over an attendant. Reached for a broken shard, unknown whether she harbored intention to do harm. To remain in isolation until behavior improves. Currently restrained in strong clothing for as short a period as necessary, while she is a danger to herself and others. Lunacy Commissioners informed.*

The law requires that, during the first three months of a patient's admission, I make an entry into this book every week. After that, once a month, and after *that*, once every three months. However, given my newest patient's current behavior, I find myself writing inside it much more often than required—I do not wish to incur a twenty-pound fine.

Gone are my mornings of a good, hearty breakfast accompanied by news of lighter matters.

I finish the paragraph and blow on the paper, the ink drying perfectly. That should make the commissioners happy. A tidy read portrays an organized hospital.

I tap my pen against the desk, thinking.

Prescribing Croton Oil.

Attention to the bowels can be of great service to these particular patients, though, in Lady Stanbury's case, I am eager to examine her uterus. Yet . . .

Patient will not let me perform a physical assessment.

A loud knock on my office door startles me, and I drop my pen. "Yes?"

"Doctor?" Nurse Ruth leans through the gap. "Sir, Lord Damsbridge and a Mr. Stanbury are here."

"Send them in, please, and bring the tissues too, as this will stain." I've asked her before to knock more quietly.

She peeks at the widening ink stain and grimaces before turning on her heel and exiting the room. Seconds later, the aforementioned gentlemen enter.

I glance at the paper. If I am unable to read it, it can still be put to use.

I throw it over the ink stain. "My lord, Mr. Stanbury. Good morning to you both."

"And to you, Doctor," says Lord Damsbridge, shaking droplets from his umbrella. His eyes search my office.

"In the corner—"

He deposits it in the stand before I can finish.

The recently bereaved husband stands back and off to one side with his hands in his pockets. His face is as grief-stricken and apt to the occasion as his stance as he glares stoically at the certificates on my wall.

"Mr. Stanbury, I don't believe we have met."

"Indeed not, and I must say I would rather have preferred it stayed that way." His gaze moves toward me as he answers, but his body remains still.

Generally, people dislike meeting me. The policemen because they believe I "save" guilty men and women from the gallows. The patients because they are terrified I'm going to throw them in a cell and let them starve. The relatives because they don't understand why their loved ones are locked away from society. Other doctors, who sneer in disdain at us "alienists" while considering us little better than those that we treat.

I am sure it would affect a lesser man than I.

"I agree," I say. "It is most unfortunate that this has occurred, and I offer you my most sincere condolences."

He grunts in acknowledgment.

"Excuse my son-in-law's rudeness, Doctor," says Lord Damsbridge, helping himself to a chair. He gestures to the seat next to him. "Stanbury, sit."

"Oh, I'm not at all offended, my lord—"

The earl interrupts me. "Well, you should be. A true gentleman should know how to act despite, or perhaps *because* of, his grief." He stops and peers around his chair. Mr. Stanbury is still standing. "Stanbury . . ." He trails off, turns back to me, and offers a small shrug. "I keep telling him, Doctor—an attitude like that doesn't exactly inspire endearment from others."

Mr. Stanbury shoots a look of confusion toward the back of his father-in-law's head, but acquiesces.

Grief. It will make enemies of even the closest friends.

"My apologies," Mr. Stanbury says, his voice wavering. "I fear I am not myself. My wife murdered my only child less than two weeks ago, so you'll have to excuse me."

"Completely understandable, Mr. Stanbury. Now, could I offer you gentlemen a coffee?"

"Yes—"

Lord Damsbridge interrupts his son-in-law. "Something stronger would be more appropriate at this time. Whiskey, perchance?"

I glance at the large grandfather clock, left here by my predecessor. I assume he's referring to the meeting's impending subject matter as opposed to the hour, as the hands show only nine and twenty.

"Well, of course. I'm sure Nurse Ruth can fetch some; that woman can find anything given half a chance. She should be back momentarily, as I spilled . . ."

I stop.

It's best I keep my inherent clumsiness to myself.

"You were saying, Doctor?"

Opportunity presents itself in the personification of my attendant, as she knocks on the door and looks questioningly at me through the gap.

"Yes, come in, Nurse Ruth. I was saying, gentlemen, when you let women into a man's domain, they tend to get carried away with their curiosity. Take this one here, for example. . . ." I nod toward Nurse Ruth. "Liked the look of my pen and decided to write a note to her husband with it!" I remove the newspaper with a flourish. "Look what she did! This is solid oak, gentlemen. Ruined . . . by romantic sentimentality. In a flash." I press my finger into the ink pointedly.

Nurse Ruth's mouth drops open, but she quickly recovers.

"Yes, I am such a stupid woman," she says, the sarcasm lost on the two men but not on me. She shakes the tissues in her hand and advances. "Here, let me clean that."

I wave her away.

"No, Nurse Ruth. I shall buy a new desk." I crumple the newspaper into a ball and hand it to her. I lean back—the king of my domain. "You can repay me by finding our gentlemen here a bottle of our finest whiskey."

She narrows her eyes and takes the paper. She knows full well I have neither the funds for a new desk nor a secret stash of "finest whiskey."

"Certainly. Lovely to meet you, my lord. Mr. Stanbury." She curtseys and leaves the room quietly, closing the door with a small click.

"Women," I say, laughing.

"Quite," says Lord Damsbridge.

I reach into the desk and pull out Lady Stanbury's folder. "Gentlemen. I requested your company today so I may learn more of Lady Stanbury: her habits, friendships, personality, et cetera, in order to start appropriate treatment. This is a two-way discussion, and I welcome any and all questions from you both." As they nod in synchrony—Lord Damsbridge more so than the other—I continue onward with the speech I give to the relatives of every new patient admitted.

"Let me allay any fears you may have with regards to Lady Stanbury being in, dare I say it, a lunatic asylum." I raise my eyebrows in an imitation of mock horror. "Forget the histrionic stories that old wives exchange on street corners about madmen being chained to the walls. This is the nineteenth century, gentlemen, and modern asylums differ little in their constitution and management from ordinary hospitals. Our field of expertise is much more advanced than that which prescribed the inhumane and inexperienced treatments of yesteryear."

"Though it remains true that the people in here are lunatics, does it not, Doctor?" Mr. Stanbury says.

"Well, yes—"

"So I don't understand why I am even talking to you. My wife is *not* a lunatic."

"Your wife—"

"Is *not* mad. She just made a mistake."

"I—" I splutter, speechless for a moment. "Mr. Stanbury, your wife was declared clinically insane by at least two doctors—not including myself—and admitted directly into Bethlem Royal. She wasn't even fit to stand trial, such was her madness. Why—the crime *itself* is proof of her insanity!"

"This is all just a big mistake, a mix-up. They don't really know her. Nobody does. I would like you to review my wife, and release her."

"We don't make errors, Mr. Stanbury—"

"Surely, she could recover at home?"

I take a deep breath. "Mr. Stanbury, I hate to be the bearer of bad news, but in this particular case my hands are tied. Your wife was ordered here by the court, and until I see an improvement in her mental state, there is nothing I can do."

He opens his mouth as if to interrupt me, but I wave a hand. "Please let me finish. You may feel better about her being here if you do. Bethlem *is* a lunatic asylum, yes, but it is also a place of rest where *anyone* suffering mental deficiency can come to be treated. We even have people admit themselves." I sift through the drawer of my desk again and pull out a form. I put the paper in front of the two gentlemen and reach for my pen. Ah, it is covered with ink. I fumble discreetly for a spare while the men read over the sheet. "Cast your eyes over the writing at the top." Aha. A pen. I pull it out and tap it over the paragraph I want them to read. "It says: 'All persons, of unsound mind presumed to be curable, are eligible for admission into this hospital for maintenance and medical treatment.'"

"Presumed 'curable'?" Lord Damsbridge asks, eyebrows raised.

"Yes," I say, pleased he focused on that word. "She can be cured completely."

Mr. Stanbury gestures to the paper. "So, correct me if I am wrong here, Doctor . . . but what you are trying to tell me is that relatively normal people who just need an extra bit of 'help' can admit themselves?"

"Yes."

"Absolutely of their own free will?"

"Yes."

"And that my wife can be cured?"

I nod.

"So in that case, Doctor, my wife is not a lunatic. I knew it. There has been a mistake." He leans back in his chair and I despair at the look of satisfaction on his face. The man is in absolute denial about the whole situation.

"That doesn't mean she can just go home with you," I say, choosing my words carefully. "You need to understand that she committed a very serious crime, and there is a system, a specific set of guidelines and assessments that I must abide by and laws I must adhere to." I gather the papers together and put them back in the drawer, deliberately taking my time. *Think.* "Lady Stanbury must be of sound mind, cured completely, before I release her anywhere."

"Cured of what, precisely? What is wrong with her, if not the consequences of a mistake? Tell me why she killed our eight-week-old son. She wouldn't have done what she did; it had to have been an accident."

A knock on the door.

"Didn't they tell you what was wrong with her at the trial?"

"They did, but I don't believe it. I want *you* to tell me what is wrong with her. I want to hear it from your mouth while you look me in the eye and tell me the truth. I'm sick of being lied to." He stares at me, and the very room seems to inhale, holding its breath.

Another knock at the door, louder this time, impossible to ignore, but I do so.

The clock ticks loudly.

Mr. Stanbury's left eye twitches.

"Mr. Stanbury, before I answer your question I first need you to answer mine. Then I can give you my opinion." I smile at him. "Would that be all right?"

"Fine."

The room exhales, and so do I.

"Did Lady Stanbury ever act strangely in any way, or was it only after having the child she became unstable?"

Mr. Stanbury hunches over. In the silence that follows, a third knock on the door disturbs us and at his next words, I am grateful for the relief.

"Nothing seemed amiss until she killed him."

"Good choice," I say as Nurse Ruth makes her way inside carrying a sliver dish. Atop is a crystal decanter, three glasses, and a bottle of Tullamore Dew. I have no idea where she got it from, but it certainly raises my suspicions about the attendants drinking on duty

"Good choice *indeed*," Lord Damsbridge enthuses, lifting the bottle appreciatively. "Eighteen sixty-five." He reaches for the glasses and pours two generous measures, hesitating on the third. "For you, Doctor?"

"I prefer coffee, my lord. I only drink on special occasions—Christmas and such."

He frowns disapprovingly but continues to pour a third measure, oblivious of my refusal.

"Well . . ." I watch in horror as he fills the glass to the brim, loath to taste that which leads to perversion of the mind, yet I am unable to refuse his smile as he hands it to me. "Well, I suppose I do enjoy a little indulgence from time to time," I lie. As I lift the contents to my mouth, I note that Mr. Stanbury has already drunk his fill, eyes fixed longingly on the bottle. I sip my liquor tentatively and try not to heave, mentally filing the information for later.

It travels down my throat like liquefied nails.

"Your wife is suffering from a mental illness called 'puerperal mania.' I believe you both heard this term during her first assessment, shortly following her arrest on October fifth, 1885. I stand by that diagnosis. Puerperal mania, in Lady Stanbury's case, is the *cause* of her insanity. Just as others go mad because of epilepsy or alcohol or fever, pregnancy and childbirth have caused Anne to become temporarily insane—"

"She is not—"

"Please, Mr. Stanbury. I need to ask a few questions first."

I make a note.

Husband is in absolute denial that there was ever anything wrong with his wife. Refers to the murder of his son as "a mistake."

"Mr. Stanbury." I place my glass on the desk, and his eyes follow. "To return to the question—your wife must have displayed some signs after giving birth, *before* she killed your son. Please. If you really do want her to come home with you, you have to answer me—and answer me honestly. You are not helping her by being obtuse."

He addresses the whiskey. "I don't mean to be, Doctor. It's just . . ."

"What?"

"Can I have another drink?"

"Certainly. My lord—" I stop. Lord Damsbridge is already filling it for him.

"Thank you." Mr. Stanbury raises the alcohol to his mouth and takes a big swig. "Look, Doctor, I'm not quite sure what you mean by altered behavior. I mean, every woman changes a little after she gives birth, doesn't she? She . . ." He coughs, slaps his chest. "After our son was born—" He coughs again and places the glass down with a bang, the cough quickly turning into a choking hack, and he stands up, kicking the chair onto the floor. He turns away from us and flees to the corner of the room, shoulders shaking.

Crying.

Lord Damsbridge sits stock-still, staring at me as if his son-in-law does not exist.

"My lord?" I roll my eyes toward Mr. Stanbury, who is now bent over, hands on knees, trying to catch his breath.

Lord Damsbridge ignores the gesture and merely pours himself and his son-in-law another drink. "Well, I barely saw her during her confinement, Doctor . . . though I hear she kept well enough. It's not for a father to intervene in such matters, now, is it?"

Apparently not. Why does he not feel compelled to assist his son-in-law? Is he truly so—unemotional? So closed off to the feelings of others?

A few minutes pass.

"Sorry." Mr. Stanbury returns to the table and picks his chair off the floor, his eyes swollen. "That happens to me sometimes. I don't know why."

"I understand," I say meaningfully as he sits. "I mean, I really *do* understand." I hold his gaze until he nods.

"Please continue, Doctor. I'm perfectly fine now."

Sweat drips from his brow.

I consider calling the meeting to an end, but he senses my hesitation.

"Truly, I'm well. You were asking me how my wife was after our son was born, correct?"

"Please."

He looks to his knees, nods.

"Honestly—she changed. And I mean, *immediately* after the birth. She—"

"I thought you said that she *didn't* change until after your son was born," I say gently.

"She didn't. I mean, I thought it was normal—you know, for a wife to not be quite the woman she was before having a child. Having a baby alters everything, Doctor, but that's normal, isn't it?"

"It can be," I say warily, fiddling with my pen.

"Exactly. And now you're asking me whether she changed, and I suppose she did, but at the time I never perceived any of the changes in her behavior as abnormal. For example, she never wandered in the night before John was born, but afterward she had a legitimate reason to do so. I too took to walking the corridors as the clock struck all hours of the night—it's very difficult to sleep with a new baby, Doctor."

"I understand, Mr. Stanbury."

"And so here I am, explaining to you the banalities of having a new child. Don't misunderstand me, Doctor. When I say that she both did and didn't change, I mean it. It's only with the negligible value of hindsight that I can sit here and say to you now—honestly—that yes, she changed. But I didn't see any of that at the time. How could I? How does anyone see the wind from the eye of the storm?"

Interesting choice of words.

"So yes, there may have been issues to which I was blind at the time. I knew she was checking on John and that was *normal*. She seemed constantly afraid that something bad would happen to him, and again, *that was normal*. Occasionally—"

"You say she was afraid? Of what?"

"I . . ." Mr. Stanbury blinks, falters. "I don't know. Sometimes she would wake him up—I told her not to—just to check that he was still breathing. She . . ." He opens his mouth to say more but stops midsentence.

"Yes?" I prompt him.

He fidgets, running a finger around his neck and tugging at the collar. "I'm having difficulty saying these things, Doctor. Anne was very protective toward John, and I don't wish to speak badly of her. I *know* she didn't mean to do what she did; I know in my heart that this is all some sort of tragic mistake. But now, sitting here and talking to you, and thinking . . ." He breathes in, a deep, shuddering sigh. "I felt ostracized at times. She barely let me hold him. It's almost as if she was afraid of me, of . . . oh, I don't know. Afraid of the world. I don't profess to understand such matters. I know women have this—attachment—

to children, but . . . I suppose she was the mother, and it was her duty to look after our son. Not me. I don't like it, but I understand. What I *don't* understand is how . . . It doesn't make sense . . . that a woman, a mother, could change so quickly—from being so *over*bearing and affectionate to . . ." He clears his throat, and I worry he is about to have another coughing fit. "To being the person to cause him harm! She worried about *dirt* hurting him, for heaven's sake!" Now there are no attempts at hiding the tears that well in his eyes, though he discreetly removes a handkerchief from his top pocket. "She couldn't have done it, Doctor—at least, not on purpose. She, a mother, would *not* hurt her own baby. I know this. How could she? Answer me that!" Almost angrily, he dabs quickly at his face, the white handkerchief a startling contrast to his ruddy complexion. "Why? Tell me why!"

"Quite," Lord Damsbridge adds, drumming neatly manicured fingers against the edge of my desk. "That's the part we don't understand. People go insane all the time, but they don't go around killing others, least of all their own flesh and blood."

How differently these two men hide their grief. One behind denial, disbelief, and tears; the other behind a shadow of calm indifference.

No wonder they are at odds with each other!

"Puerperal mania," I say.

"Pardon?"

"Puerperal mania. I believe you both heard this term before, shortly following her arrest, during her first assessment."

"I did, Doctor," Lord Damsbridge says. "I don't know what my son-in-law heard, though; he's been in denial the whole time."

I write a note.

"Haven't you, Stanbury?" he continues, nudging his son-in-law. It is almost as if he is trying to provoke him into some sort of reaction. "Doctor, I don't mean to sound awful, but I find it most exasperating. It's as though my son-in-law believes my daughter simply slipped on spilt milk and accidentally dropped the baby on its head. Denial, denial, denial. His only solution to this situation is a marvelous amount of self-pity, and I don't need to tell you where he finds it." He nods pointedly toward the now-half-empty bottle of whiskey.

"How dare you!" Mr. Stanbury springs from his chair. "You always treat me as if I am something, something . . . *less* than you—"

"Gentlemen—" I stand up.

Lord Damsbridge holds up a hand.

"No, Doctor—he needs to hear this. The reality, Stanbury, is that my daughter killed your son—"

"And where were you? You think that with your fancy house and your fancy clothes—"

"She *killed* your son, Stanbury—on purpose—yes, the truth is hard to bear, but there it is, and now he is dead and buried and there is nothing neither you nor I can do to bring him back. But we can bring my daughter back—with the good doctor's help. Thus, I won't have you persuading him that this was some sort of accident, or that she was sound of mind. All of these things you describe—her wandering, not being able to sleep, being overly protective and frightened—these are not the actions of a sane woman. Of a normal mother. It is natural to worry about your baby, Stanbury, but Anne was excessive. You *must* accept this, because if you don't, there are others who might question it. My daughter is the most precious thing in the world to me—greater, in fact, than my 'fancy house' and my 'fancy clothes,' as you say—and I will *not* see her brought to greater harm from your inability to accept the facts."

Mr. Stanbury stops, stares at him.

"I am simply doing what is best for my daughter. You may find me unemotional. You may think I am a complete bastard—and I freely admit I am both of those things, but above all else, I am practical. I have complete faith that the good doctor here is the *only* one that can help her, and he requires total honesty to do that. The doctor wants the facts, Stanbury, as he himself said, not a pitiable version of events. It took a great deal of effort on my part to have her admitted to Bethlem as opposed to Broadmoor, and you would do both her and me a very great disservice by continuing to insinuate that there is nothing wrong with her. Isn't that correct, Doctor?"

My sense of pride battles with my intuition.

Something is wrong here.

"Yes, my lord," I find myself saying confidently. "Your daughter *is* responsible for killing your grandson. I'm sorry, Mr. Stanbury, but you do need to accept that your wife killed your son and that she is a criminal lunatic: It was no 'accident.'"

PUT IN A SACK!

Anne
October 13th, 1885
Bethlem Royal Hospital

My arms are pinned to my sides; my hands stuck inside deep, itchy
pockets. I can't straighten my fingers, and my long nails dig painfully into my palms. This thing must be made of stout linen—or possibly wool, for it is tough and unyielding. I lean against the wall and
rub my body up and down limb by limb: right arm, left arm, stomach, back—ah. It brings me welcome relief for roughly two minutes
before the itching starts up again.

Are there insects in this thing?

Oh, woe is me. There are insects everywhere. I can hear their little mouths chewing, munching on my skin.

I try to yank my hands upward and outward as hard as I can, but
this only makes me almost topple over backward. Where are the buttons, or laces?

I must be able to get out of this—somehow.

This is harsh punishment *indeed* for simply throwing a chamber
pot at my captors. What did they expect me to do? Let them carve out
my eyes? I'm not sorry for doing it, though I am regretful to be re-

strained because of it. They don't seem to take too kindly to my defensive strategies. However, they must understand that they can't just go around the world, taking people from their homes in the middle of the night and putting them in cells.

Perhaps the best thing I can do is stay quiet and wait to be rescued.

I shuffle over to my bed and lie down awkwardly, not sure how I'm going to stand up again but not caring. I close my eyes and try to imagine what must be happening on the outside, back at the Manor. What I wouldn't give to be back at home, among the people who love me.

I must have dozed off, because one minute I'm sitting in my father's library, my favorite place in the whole world, and the next I'm being poked by a fat finger telling me to get up.

"And quickly about it!"

Another poke.

"Wha—"

"Now!"

I'm still sleepy when Fat Ruth lifts the brown sack over my head, accomplishing in mere seconds what I failed to do given hours. Unfortunately, she mashes my face into the mattress as she does so without a care nor thought for my well-being. The smell of feces invades my nose as she sits me up, and I can't help gagging.

"My arms have gone numb," I say, swallowing vomit. "Can't you open a window?"

"It's your own fault your arms are numb, and no, the windows don't open. People would fling themselves out of them," she says, throwing the tangled sack into a corner by the door. "And if you hadn't emptied your chamber pot over me, we wouldn't have to restrain you, would we?"

I wonder briefly why people would be compelled to throw themselves out of a window—why on earth don't they just ask for a ladder?—but become distracted by Fat Ruth bustling about with another porcelain jug while keeping it discreetly out of my reach. I smile a little at that, until she dips a sponge into the water and wrings it out over my head. I utter a few profanities. When I'm all soaked through, she pulls the sodden nightgown off me and I sit there, naked and ashamed, on the edge of what has become "my" bed, trying ineffectually to cover myself with crossed legs and folded arms. She starts washing my feet.

"Ah! Wash my stomach first. I was asleep, you bloody degenerate! You are going to destroy my circulation!"

She ignores me.

"You're absolutely filthy. You are a disgrace." She repeats the motion over and over again, adding some foul-smelling soap into the mix, rubbing my arms, legs, back, face, and last of all, my stomach. Now all of my blood that has been involved in digestion is bound to stay there, and I shall feel sluggish and woeful for the rest of the day. I suppose that's how the lower classes wash themselves, which explains why she's so fat.

"Aren't you going to wash my hair?"

"As you please, my *lady*."

The rest of the dirty water in the jug gets poured directly on my head. She starts roughly drying me with a towel produced from somewhere, turning my skin pink.

I tell her not to rub so hard. She tuts and finishes up, ignoring my request.

"You are supposed to delicately *pat*, you bloody imbecile!"

She stares at me for a moment, and I wonder if she feels guilty.

"My God, you're leaking *again*. Wait a second." She disappears out the door in a rush and comes back in with a bowl. Dipping her hands into it, she grabs hold of both my breasts.

I shriek.

"What on earth are you doing!" I scream. I try to push her off me, but she holds on tight and starts squeezing and rubbing them. It hurts.

"It's salt, Anne. Just salt."

"Dear God! You foul, immoral horse!"

"Oh, be quiet," she says. She lets go abruptly and picks something up from the floor. "Now, put these on, and be quick about it." A clean nightgown is flung onto my lap as she bends down to pick up the empty jug. I stare at the top of her head and consider staying naked for a while: putting my shame to one side just to offend her.

"I'm going to have you arrested," I tell her. "You just abused me."

"Anne, the doctor is coming," she says, ignoring my threat. She stands. "Do you want him to see you like this?" Her keys jangle as she makes her way over to the cell door. "Do you know what men do to women who are exposed in such a manner?" She leaves with a smile, slamming the door.

I dress quickly, scoot myself over to the wall, and start picking the paint.

YELLOW PAINT

Dr. George Savage
October 13th, 1885
Bethlem Royal Hospital

Leaving my office, the three us make our way to the female ward. The earlier dispute echoes in my mind as our footsteps clack a staccato against the floor and I marvel at how one woman can have two men, so wildly different in temperament and class, fighting each other over her innate inability to care for herself. There is a reason that the excess of women in Bethlem is regular, and constant: For all their charm, they are all too often more hassle than they are worth.

Every now and then the gentlemen stop, and I am forced to wait while they stare at the patients. I try to neither acknowledge nor judge Mr. Stanbury's horrified gaze and Lord Damsbridge's sharp intake of breath as we pass through the asylum. One woman is banging her head against the floor, another chewing the skin off her hand with her teeth. And here, we pass by Esther Base, another case of puerperal mania, rocking and singing nursery rhymes to a ball of paper.

Esther threw her nine month-old-baby out of the window.

Thankfully, decades have passed since the public was allowed—indeed, *encouraged*—to darken the asylum's gates twice a week to study the oddities within. My predecessors were under the rather unfortunate impression that the monetary value gained in handing out sticks at the door, and allowing the public to literally poke the patients, outweighed any ethical concern they may have had with injuring their fellow man. Although naturally, I understand the nature of human curiosity, I have never subscribed to the principle of *schadenfreude*—pleasure derived from the misfortune of others—and strongly detest those who do.

"I don't see the benefit in my wife being here," says Mr. Stanbury as a woman runs past us, shrieking down the corridor. We all turn to watch her. "I—oof!"

"Sorry, sir!" shouts an attendant as she bounds past us in pursuit, white hat hanging askew from its pins. "She's got the iron again. She's all charged up and a thunderstorm is coming!"

Mr. Stanbury rights himself, rubbing at an elbow.

I shake my head.

"That was one of our chronic patients—don't worry. She's usually segregated from the other patients. She's one of the incurables. Perfectly harmless, though, except in an electrical storm."

I look out the window. Black clouds loom.

"Why? What does she do?"

"Finds an iron wherever she can, and stands on it. She rubs the back of her head for hours at a time to carry off the electricity with which she believes she is 'charged,' stuffs the left side of her nostril to prevent the electricity from flowing to her . . . uh, her private parts, and when a thunderstorm comes she runs around the ward electrocuting everyone."

The men stare at me, openmouthed.

"Oh, don't worry!" I say. "It's all in her mind, of course. It doesn't actually work. Why, if it did, we could use her to power the whole building, couldn't we? The danger is that when she thinks everyone is dead, she runs out into the garden with a big metal pole to finish herself off. Here, gentlemen." I deflect the subject by diverting their attention. "Do you see this?" I stop and gesture to my left, where a doorway opens up into a large, high-ceilinged room. Patients and attendants alike lounge on couches, sit at tables, lie on the floor. "This is the female dayroom, where certain patients are free to roam, sit, and pass the day at their leisure. At Bethlem we strongly encourage moral activities: sewing, drawing, singing—"

"Old maid!" somebody shouts, and I smile at the ensuing round of applause.

"—and cards, as you can see. The capability of imbeciles for pleasure is, perhaps, not very great or varied, yet when I see their faces light up with joy and gladness, I would say that their enjoyment is very real."

"It's a bit noisy in here, though," Mr. Stanbury says.

"Oh, it is—I agree! But don't worry; the patients who are free to walk around are equally able to take a stroll in the garden. It's much quieter out there. Come, there is more to show you."

We continue onward. The floors are clean, the windows sparkle in the sun, and the sound of simple laughter drifts in the air. As always, I get an innate sense of pride to see the cogs in my machine running to perfection.

"The asylum is rather impressive, don't you think?" The words are out of my mouth before I can think.

"Indeed it is, Doctor," says Lord Damsbridge. "You are obviously very committed to your work."

"Thank you, my lord."

We continue down the corridor until it turns sharply at the end into another. Here, I have the opportunity to introduce the gentlemen to Grace, another one of my incurable patients, obscuring the pathway in her usual spot. An attendant is bent over her, stroking her hair gently.

"Good morning, Grace," I say. "Good morning, Nurse Agnus."

"Good morning, sir," the attendant replies cheerfully, standing up to offer the two gentlemen an outstretched hand. Despite her newness and social awkwardness (a woman should never shake a man's hand, for one!) she is an absolute delight to work with. Dedicated and gentle, she is well on her way to being one of my best nurses, despite coming from some obscure background with no experience in the field.

Mr. Stanbury grasps the proffered hand firmly, pumping it with the first genuine smile I've seen all day.

Lord Damsbridge merely sniffs and flicks a look of disdain.

"Will you excuse me for a moment, gentlemen?"

The attendant moves away from Grace as I momentarily bend down to touch the patient's forehead. Hot. I twist my hand and press down hard with my thumb on the supraorbital notch: a bony little arch in the center of the eyebrow. No response. I ceased writing notes regarding this patient a long time ago. She is, sadly, now nothing more than a pet. I turn to the two men. "As you can see, a most sad case indeed. This is a true incurable, gentlemen. Utterly unresponsive." I stand up and flash them a smile. "But, as you can see, we take great pride in treating everyone as a human."

We come to a halt outside Lady Stanbury's room and I detach the large metal ring from my belt. "This is one of our most prestigious rooms, utterly private." I flip through the keys, searching for the right one. "The room is south facing, so Lady Stanbury has the enjoyment of daylight. I do believe there is something in the sun, gentlemen, that contributes to health. Perhaps one day, somebody will prove it."

I find the right key and slip it into the lock. As the bar disengages it clicks loudly, and I place my palm against the heavy metal, ready to push.

"Is that locked?" Mr. Stanbury asks suddenly.

I hold my weight steady. "Yes."

"Can she get out?"

"Well, when we *unlock* it, yes," I say, inwardly cringing at the sarcasm that seems to have unwittingly seeped into my voice. I know well enough that I would never answer Lord Damsbridge in such a manner, and it shames me.

"Do you mean," he says, his voice wavering, "that you have my wife locked up like some common criminal?"

The door thumps against its frame as I remove my hand. "No. This is common protocol for patients whom we deem to be dangerous. Your wife is delusional, and as such, is treated with an appropriate level of caution. If she were being treated as a 'common criminal,' as you say, she would have been placed in the jail and forced to work the crank wheel." *Or hanged,* I refrain from adding.

"Dangerous? Doctor, in our travels to this room we've come across at least one deranged woman who was—quite clearly—dangerously insane, yet you deem her not to be so and she was running free—"

"That patient was not dangerous. She has never harmed anyone."

"—running *free,* yet somehow you judge my wife to be worse. Are you insane?"

I almost laugh at the pun.

"Not yet, Mr. Stanbury." I cross my arms. "Your wife is not here simply for a *rest.* She did not admit herself freely. She is a criminal lunatic. *Criminal.* That means she committed a *criminal* offense. The woman to whom you refer, though steeped inside her own world, has never touched a hair on anyone's head. Except her own. Appearances can be deceiving."

Mr. Stanbury still squints at me, waiting, not understanding.

I pull the key out of the lock and sigh. "We don't treat *any* of our patients like criminals, Mr. Stanbury. You don't have to worry. In fact, we don't even have the facility for them anymore. All of the patients who had committed criminal offenses were moved out of Bethlem twenty-one years ago, when they opened Broadmoor."

"Then why is she here—"

Lord Damsbridge interrupts. "She's here because I paid for her to be here, Stanbury. And very highly I paid for it too."

"Why—"

"To keep her safe."

"Thank you, my lord," I say, pleased that he should choose Bethlem above all others.

On entering, we find Lady Stanbury sitting on the far side of the bed, hunched over. Her shoulder blades work up and down as if she were knitting—though I know for a fact that she is not; she is not allowed needles—the bony prominences of the scapula clearly visible through the thin gown. At the sound of the door opening, she stills.

"Good morning, Anne," I say.

She lifts her head slowly, without turning. "Go to hell."

Both men gasp, and I quickly usher them into the far corner of the room. "Do not be too alarmed at her behavior," I say quietly. "She is delusional and doesn't know where she is, or who she is. She will likely say things that you have never heard out of a woman's mouth before—never mind a lady's. She may scream and cry out, and even throw things. Be careful: As I said earlier, appearances can be deceptive. This is not the wife and daughter that you both know and love."

"What are you whispering about, you fiend?" Lady Stanbury shouts. Mr. Stanbury's hand brushes my own as he jumps, unprepared for the sudden intrusion.

She has moved from the bed and is now standing upright, facing us. Her hands are cupped around something and as we watch, she opens them to reveal a pile of yellow.

"What the . . ." Lord Damsbridge trails off, leaning forward, transfixed by the spectacle of his mad daughter.

"Father!" Her nose suddenly scrunches in delight, and she scatters the yellow to the floor, where they settle like yellow petals, torn from a flower by an errant child. She runs toward him. "Father!"

"Paint flecks," I tell him, gesturing toward a patch of wall where she has exposed the stone.

"My love!" Mr. Stanbury suddenly leaps forward, embracing her tightly before any of us realize what he is about to do.

"Let go of me!" Instantly, Lady Stanbury becomes wild. She brings up a knee and sharply hits him between his legs. He howls in surprise and bends over, protecting his manhood.

And that's when she punches him in the face.

"Dear God!" she cries, breathing hard. "Who on earth is that madman?"

I look down at Mr. Stanbury. "That's your husband, Anne."

"I don't have a husband."

"I *am* your husband," Mr. Stanbury groans from the floor.

She pushes his chest with a foot. "I don't remember you."

"That doesn't change the fact that I am still your husband."

"Oh, doesn't it? No, don't get up or I swear. I will hit you again." She pauses. "Thank you. Now, sir, answer me this: If a tree falls in the woods, and nobody is around to hear it, does it make a sound?"

"What?"

"'The trees are in the garden no longer than while there is somebody by to perceive them.' That's what."

"What?"

"It's pardon, Stanbury, not 'what,'" Lord Damsbridge interjects. "Please, you're not a commoner anymore."

"I have no idea what she's trying to say to me!"

"I believe she is quoting Mr. George Berkeley," I say, momentarily fascinated. "A rather poignant philosopher from the early eighteenth century, I believe."

"But what is she *saying*?"

"She is saying that you are only her husband if she recognizes you as such." I scratch my beard. There is no way a woman could know of such things. "I think. Or it could, of course, be another insane rambling. Have you ever heard of George Berkeley, Anne?"

"Who?"

"There." I can't help smiling. "She didn't mean anything by it, after all."

She smiles back at me, a glint in her eye. "Father, how much do they want? They kidnapped me and threw me into a sack full of insects."

Lord Damsbridge looks at her. "A sack?"

"Ask him." She points at me with a yellow finger. "Ask the fish-eyed man, the lying thief who wears cheap-smart clothes. Ask him what his little bitch did to me this morning." Lord Damsbridge turns to me, confused. "Ask *him*," he says.

"Part of her delusions," I say, deciding that now is not the time to discuss the use of mechanical restraints. "She doesn't know what she's talking about."

"Anne, why are you speaking so . . . so *commonly*?"

"Because they locked me up!" She gestures to the door in emphasis. "How would *you* like to be locked up? Ask him about Fat Ruth, Father. Ask him about the woman who lingers outside the *locked* door, day and night, but hardly ever lets me out. Ask him about all the other hostages. Ask him what my name is."

"Your name?"

"Yes, my name!"

"What is her name, Doctor?"

"My lord, this really isn't—"

He lowers his voice. "Humor me, please. I want to see for myself what is wrong with my daughter. She is desperately ill—I am ashamed to listen to her."

I swallow. This is a most unusual situation.

"Ask him!" she screams.

"Lady Stanbury," I say, my voice betraying a calm I do not feel. There is something about this woman—about the whole family, the whole situation—something . . . wrong. I have never been so instructed in my care of a patient.

"Pardon, Fish Eyes? What is my name?"

"Your name is Lady Stanbury," I say, louder.

"Anne—"

"You see? Father, it is a simple case of mistaken identity!" She skips toward him and encircles him with her arms. "We can go now." She clasps his hand in hers and pulls him toward the door. Lord Damsbridge stands still. She tugs harder. Harder still. "Father? What are you doing? Why aren't you taking me home? Why haven't you punched this man in the face already? Why are you standing there like an *idiot*, when you could be—?"

Lord Damsbridge pulls his daughter back to him. "Compose yourself, Anne. Do you hear me?" He shakes her gently. "You are safe here. I will get you home, I promise. Have I ever broken a promise to you?"

She stares at him.

"Well, have I?" He lets her go and she sways for a moment, silent.

"Have I, Anne? Have I *ever* put you in danger, in harm's way? Would I ever sit by and idly watch somebody hurt you?"

She whispers something.

"Pardon, Anne? I can't hear you."

"You did, once. That's why I'm here."

"I—" His face crumples, and he pulls his daughter to him, cradling her head against his chest. He starts to rock her gently, back and forth. "I am here for you, Anne, always and forever. I am your father, and I love you."

"But—"

"You haven't been kidnapped. You must get that thought out of your head—do you understand?" He pushes her away slightly and places a finger underneath her chin. "Trust me. If you don't trust anyone else, trust *me*. You have not been kidnapped. If you had been, I would be walking out that door with you right now. I wouldn't just punch the 'fish-eyed' guy in the face; I'd shoot him where he stands."

Something passes between them, a flicker below the surface of her features, a ripple across his. A mutual recognition. It disappears as quickly as it has appeared and she frowns, rubbing her hands together, turning her face away from him.

She chuckles and steps over Mr. Stanbury, who is still lying on the floor.

"You see? That's my girl. You are your father's daughter, Anne. Don't you ever forget it."

A CURIOUS THING

Edgar
October 13th, 1885
Bethlem Royal Hospital

"Here." The doctor hands me a cold compress, which I press gingerly against my nose. "No, press harder, Mr. Stanbury."

I wince.

The two of us are sitting in his office, Lord Damsbridge having left abruptly to attend some business matter.

"She doesn't know who I am," I say, voice muffled. "How can that be? I'm her husband." I remove the bloody compress. "I can't believe she hit me."

Dr. Savage leans forward in his chair, his expression earnest and penetrating. Is he searching for signs of madness in my own face? The muscles around my mouth tremble as I try to relax. What must it be like to spend every day of your life questioning the sanity of those around you, forever taking temperatures and blood and photographs and history? Does he query every turn of a hand, every glimmer in an eye?

"I think you may have a nasal fracture, Mr. Stanbury."

"Wha—pardon?"

"Your nose. It's broken."

"I . . . oh." I push the compress back against my face. "It hurts."

"Nothing to be done for it, though. Bust noses are one of those things, like broken toes, fingers, and ribs. Nothing to be done for any of them. I expect you will wake up tomorrow with two black eyes."

I squeeze my eyes tight for a moment.

"Doctor, the pain in my nose is nothing compared to the pain inside my heart."

"I can imagine."

"Can you, though? Really? I've been denying her culpability for quite some time—my father-in-law was right when he said so. He didn't see her as much as I did and I tell you, she loved our son. I told myself she would never, ever have hurt him, but . . ." I trail off awkwardly, searching for the right words.

"Take your time, Mr. Stanbury. I understand what a strain this is for you."

"I—" I take a deep breath. My mind is a mess of images and thoughts. Anne, covered in blood. My baby; too pale, too small, too still. Too cold. The doctors, the neighbors, somebody crying, screaming. A hand, dragging me away.

"I also believed that she would never hurt me."

The doctor nods minutely. "And yet she did."

I look at the compress. "Exactly. I never believed the truth until she hit me in the face with it. And now I don't know what to do."

"First, you have to put that back on your nose. Yes, that's it. Second, you have to understand puerperal mania. Just as others go mad because of epilepsy or alcohol or fever, childbirth itself caused Lady Stanbury to become temporarily insane. I am sure that she loved your son with all her heart and never meant to harm him, Mr. Stanbury. That is why—medico-legally speaking—she is guiltless. *She never meant to do it.* Third, you need to understand that loss of memory is very, *very* common; these women rarely have even the smallest recollection of what has taken place. Forgetfulness is a defense mechanism. Can you imagine the pain of knowing that you killed your own child?"

"No. Of course not."

The doctor nods gravely. "Many of these women kill themselves, Mr. Stanbury, when they realize what they have done. The agony of remembrance is simply too much for them."

"I—" No, she cannot. I don't want my wife dead. I love her. "I don't understand—" I can't seem to stop shaking my head, my whole body trembling.

"Don't worry, Mr. Stanbury." He waves a hand in my direction and rises from his chair. Reaching into his bookcase, he takes out a large volume. "Here, take this. Read it. It may help you come to terms with this awful situation." It lands on the table with a dull thump. "*Insanity and Allied Neuroses*, wrote it myself. You won't find a better source of information."

I run a palm over the leather cover.

"You will see that I have dealt with dozens of cases such as this. Let me assure you: I will try my very best to cure your wife. If, and when, she does remember what she has done, both the attendants and I will keep a very close eye on her and offer her as much support and consolation as she needs."

"How . . ." I think I need a drink. "How long will it take?"

He shrugs. "A lot of it depends on her, though normally I see complete reversion to sanity within a matter of weeks."

"'Normally'?"

He steadily holds my gaze. "You do need to understand one last thing, Mr. Stanbury. Some women remain permanently feebleminded. Unless she rather quickly remembers you, her child, and what she has done, I'm afraid she may never be cured."

"I—" I falter, pick up the book, and walk out of his office without a backward glance, intent on seeing a lawyer. As I walk out into the sunshine and down the gravel path, a man runs past me and dives into a bush, muttering something about finding himself.

He's not the only one.

INCOMPETENT FOOLS

Anne
October 17th, 1885
Bethlem Royal Hospital

Since the sack incident, I've been on my best behavior, and they've decided to let me attend a dance. Accompanied—of course—by one of the jailers, but at least this time it is the nice fair-haired woman: Agnus. Fat Ruth is part of the band. Imagine.

"What is the point of Grace attending this ridiculous ball when she can't enjoy the music?" I say, stuffing another sandwich into my mouth. I realized Grace was deaf by shouting into her ear one morning and getting no response. Swallowing back a lump of ham and cheese, I wait for Agnus's reply, but none is forthcoming.

She has dressed Grace in a beautiful silk dress, pinned her hair into a French pleat, and sat her onto a chair, but it all seems rather contrived and pointless. I get the impression Grace doesn't much care as to how she appears, nor where she is. In fact, I'm certain she would rather be back on the floor in the corridor.

"And I don't know why you bothered yourself to dress her up, really. She still looks like my grandmother. And dressing her in silk?

She cannot dance in that, even if she actually wanted to, or could," I say. I pick up another sandwich.

"Anne, please don't eat so fast—those sandwiches are meant to last. And will you kindly stop being rude about Grace?"

"She can't hear me," I say. "Though perhaps you imagine that dressing us up in such mock finery will entice us all to beg our families to pay you the ransom—is that it? Well, I'm just here for the free food." I purposefully pick up another three sandwiches and stuff them all in my mouth at once. "You told me to eat as much as possible—so that's exactly what I am doing."

"Anne . . ."

"Schsmsugfh," I say, showing her the contents of the half-chewed-up bread.

I swallow.

"I can't imagine why they bother. Did the ransom money pay for such a mockery of a feast? And the band is truly terrible," I say, watching them. Five idiots: all liars, thieves, and robbers. None can play a tune. "I hope for your sake that their hostage-taking skills are better than their musical talent."

"Anne, remember what I told you?"

"What?"

"You have not been kidnapped!"

"I—" There is indeed something I am supposed to remember. But I can't remember exactly what it is. Something about my father. He came to visit me; he left without me. Why? Oh, bother. I don't care. Without finishing my sentence, I turn my back to Agnus, pick up another four sandwiches, and make my way over to one of the longer trestle tables, atop which stand dozens of bottles containing various-colored liquids and towers of cups. I fill two with something brown and bubbly and pour one into a nearby potted plant. I wait a moment. Satisfied, I drink the remaining cup quickly and ditch both empty cups onto the floor underneath the table. The squashed sandwiches in my hand meet the same fate, making a sad-looking picnic indeed. I didn't really want them.

There must be thirty-some people in here, possibly even forty. Difficult to tell, as everybody is moving, dancing, walking, mingling, making my eyes cross and blur. They are all dressed in various states of eccentricity: Some are still in their green linen gowns, and others are wearing "normal," nonconvict clothes. Some must be drunk because they keep falling over, and shouting. Bewilderingly, a cup flies past my head and I duck, looking around to see who the perpetrator of such a pointless exercise could be, but see no one.

Loath as I am to admit it to Agnus, at this point in time I'm rather unsteady on my feet. The confusion generated by not knowing who is who hurts my head, yet I am becoming aware of something.

This ball is a perfect opportunity for me to escape! For most surely, if I am unsure of who *they* are, they must equally be confused as to who *I* am.

Incompetent fools. Why hold a ball for your hostages? Serves them right if all of us escape.

Aha!

A plan forms inside my head.

I think back to the window in my cell, the one with bars across it.

I look at the windows here, in this large room. They don't have any bars. But even if I managed to smash one of them, at least twenty jailers would be on me before I could make a move toward freedom.

Hmm. Weapons seem to be inconspicuously absent, but there must be one somewhere.

Pretending to be absorbed in the music, I stand at the side of the room, humming to myself: making it appear to all who might be watching me that I am simply observing the dancers. I put a smile on my face— essential wear, after all, for a ball. Without turning my head away, I let my eyes wander farther. A few more birdcages, some useless plants. Same as the corridors. No, I cannot attack anyone here. I would be swiftly thwarted. What would I do anyway, release a lark to fly into their face?

"Missus, would ye do me the honor t' dance with me?" A man emerges from the crowd and stands in front of me. Bending forward in a respectful bow, he motions to me with a slight movement of his right hand. He no doubt presumed I was waiting to be asked: poor, deluded creature. I am inclined to refuse his invitation—his obviously common accent doesn't help matters—yet maybe . . .

Could he help me?

And anyway, it *is* bad manners to mar the pleasures of others, and he *is* dressed beautifully—from his black waistcoat, tailored trousers, and white vest, down to his black cravat. Though by no means handsome, he could be a diversion.

"With pleasure, sir." I hold out one of my gloved hands, and he elegantly takes it, leading me onto the dance floor.

"Me name's William. William Smith. Nice t' meet ye acquaintance." He places a hand on my waist, and I incline my head a little to the left.

"Anne. Just call me Anne."

He starts to tell me about all the dances he's learned while being here. "I bin' taught t' polka, t' gallop, and the waltz!" he declares, a little too proudly.

"How about the polka mazurka?"

The resulting confusion on his face makes me feel rather guilty, so I shake my head slightly and offer him a rueful smile.

Halfway through our dance, our eyes meet and he smiles at me. In them, I see recognition of a fellow comrade.

"How do ye like t' drinks?" he asks, performing a perfect two-step and engaging me in the prerequisite small talk of ballroom etiquette.

"Rather unpleasant," I say, matching his dance but not really wanting conversation. I'm too annoyed at trying to pull my skirt out to the side when I'm not wearing one. Apparently, my behavior has not been "good enough" to earn some proper clothes, and I'm stuck in this horrible bloody linen *thing*. "I much prefer root beer."

"Coca-Cola, they're calling it. Developed by some quack called Dr. Pemberton."

I snort, the sound lost under the screeching death of a violin.

At this point, I suggest making an escape.

"Aye, I would love to," he says. "The damn idiots in here keep makin' me miss me train. Do ye know, I have tried *ten times* to get out of this place?"

Another song starts and we continue to dance.

"How did they kidnap you?"

"Kidnap? Lady, me family put me in here. Damn them."

Interesting. Perhaps they paid the captors to take him? But what possible reason would they have for this? Wait—what is that music?

I recognize it.

"That's . . . that's 'Ride of the Valkyries'!"

"Who?"

"I *know* this song! Oh, but how do I know it? I think I know how to play it!"

"You know how t' play this?"

"I do! Do you think they will let me play it, if I ask them nicely?"

"Not a chance."

"Oh, all right. Well, then, please carry on. Tell me how you possibly failed to escape on ten separate occasions." Perhaps I have not picked the best fellow to aid me.

"Well, the first time I broke me hand tryin' t' break a window," he says, blushing. "It's the first thing ye try in here—break a window, and freedom is yours. Not so."

I feel a little idiotic for falling for the same sentiment. I stay quiet.

"Second time, I picked a lock with a hairpin I'd found on the floor. I managed to open the door but ran straight into a bunch of orderlies." He laughs. "That got me put into a cold sheet for two days—to *cool* my hot temper, apparently. They put me on my bed, stripped me naked, wrapped me in wool blankets, poured water all over me, and left me for hours. No matter. Third time, I went on hunger strike, and when they tried to put the tube down my throat I grabbed it . . . and, well, not much happened. The tube went down my throat. That was a plan without much foresight, really.

"Fourth time I hid behind my cell door and punched the orderly when he entered. Knocked him clean unconscious, I did, but then I tripped over him and unfortunately knocked *meself* out too on the doorframe."

I giggle.

"Aye, very amusin'. Sixth time . . . sixth?"

"Fifth."

"Ah. Righto, so fifth time, I put a piece of thin wood I'd whittled down out of the workshop into the side of the doorframe. The plan was that when the door closed the lock wouldn't be able t' engage. It fell out, and that was that. Sixth time was a plea for release really, which fell on deaf ears, so not sure if that really counts as an 'escape attempt.' Seventh time I crept into the kitchen and started a fire, but they apprehended me minutes after; the cook spied me immediately." He sighs.

"You're not very good at this," I say.

"Why should I be? I'm just a tobacco merchant." We dance a quick step silently as a jailer walks past us.

"So, eighth time, I tried to seduce one of the female orderlies and was rewarded with a squeal, a slap, and isolation for a month. Sexual predator, they called me. Ninth time, I tried to seduce a male orderly. Got stuck in the hole for that, and almost ended up back at court. Did ye know it's illegal for a man to lie with another man, but in Persia he can have sex with a goat? Anyway, tenth time I tried to poison myself with weeds from the garden, but simply ended up vomitin' for a week."

I feel sad for him. "Didn't your family pay the ransom then?"

He squints. "What?"

I frown. Why does everyone act idiotic when I mention the ransom? Is it such a verbal faux pas in here? Why am I not allowed to state the reality of our affair?

"Anyway, darlin', whatever ye think, I'm definitely interested in

attemptin' escape number eleven, with such a bonny face as yours."
He squeezes my hand.

"You know, on the outside, I am a lady," I say, slightly taken
aback. "I know that much."

"Doesn't matter in here," he says, "though I s'pose I should beg ye
pardon. Sorry. But the reality, me lady, is that we're all trapped. What
difference does rank matter? Hey, if I get ye out of here, maybe p'rhaps
ye could invite me to one of ye fancy dinners. I ne'er been to a lady's
manor before."

"Certainly. If we ever get out of here, I would even pay you handsomely," I say. "I'm simply loath to pay these foul thieves and robbers
a single penny. They can snatch it out of my dead hands. I do have
some moral standards."

"I don't quite understand ye, but I do understand ye sentiments,"
he says. "Righto. So, what do we do now?"

I can't think. Oh, but I must. There has to be a way out of here.
"Can you recognize any of your male jailers?"

"Jailers, ha-ha. Ne'er heard that one before. Yes, of course I recognize the male orderlies. That one o'er there is George Davis, damn him.
He gave me a bloody nose once. The ot'er one's John Wilson. Bastards."

"What are they wearing?"

"Same as me. Though, of course, no way near as handsomely."
He chuckles, then stops and looks at me. "My lady, I do believe ye just
hit upon a potential plan in that pretty head of yours."

I am glad to know he's thinking the same thing.

"Ye askin' me to pretend to be an orderly, right?"

"That I am. And I will be the 'disorderly' captive."

"Patient?"

"Pardon?"

"Ne'er mind. Captive it is. Oh, I always dreamed of taking a lady
captive, taking off her corset . . ."

I raise my eyebrows.

"Sorry, me lady. Me thoughts do run away with themselves. Me wife wouldnae b' 'appy. Righto. I suppose ye must act disorderly, then. What do ye suppose ye can do?"

"I could have a fainting episode?"

"No. They would come running over to check if ye were alive. Not a good thing."

Hmm.

"This will never work. How about we just steal a bunch of keys?" I say.

"And how, pray tell, d' ye s'pose we do that?"

"How about you seduce a female 'orderly'?" I suppress a smirk.

He grins. "Aye, at least someone in here has a sense of humor. God forbid, I thought it had been banned from t' entire human population. No, I already told ye, they seem strangely immune to my charms. Did I tell ye I murdered me wife, by the way?"

"Pardon?"

"Just jokin'. Ye should have seen the look on ye face. Here, I know what to do." With that, he pulls me into a pirouette and pushes me to the floor.

"Ow!" I cry out. "I twisted my ankle! I hurt this one as a child! Oh, you selfish, brute-headed rhino!"

"Oh!" he cries loudly. "Patient two-oh-three has sprained her ankle! Here, let's get ye back to ye room, here's a love." He crouches over me, pulling his hat discreetly lower over his face. I note he has his back to the band.

"All of the long-term orderlies are on the stage," he says, whispering, "except for the new ones, who can't play a tune. Those are dotted around the place, and seeing as they only joined last week, they shan't know I am a patient from behind. Now stay quiet." He picks me up and hoists me over his shoulder.

He carries me out of the ballroom, "Ride of the Valkyries" playing endlessly in the background.

IN A PICKLE

Edgar
October 17th, 1885
Mr. Cropper's office

"I received your letter, Mr. Stanbury, and I'm sorry to be the bearer of bad news, but I'm afraid that you're not entitled to anything."

"How can that possibly be?"

"The law, my friend. The law. You can get your hands on as many loans as you can possibly gather, but you can't access any of the Damsbridges' money or property. And bear in mind that if you can't pay these people back, you'll end up in the debtors' jail."

How does he know I have taken loans, or is this just a very astute guess? I can only stare at the lawyer as he ignites another old-fashioned candlestick, his liver-spotted hands shaking as he does so. Noticing my gaze, he blows out the match and says, "It's terrible getting old, isn't it? I shouldn't be surprised if I set fire to this whole darn building one day, my hands tremble so terribly. I hope the landlord installs this electricity thing before that happens." He grins at me and though his watery blue eyes appear filtered, they sparkle with a sharpness as bright as any man's. "You're in a very difficult position, my friend."

I twirl the ring on my finger, caressing the emblem. "Yes, I gather that. Is there anything I can do? Anything at all?"

The old man coughs into his hand and looks at the contents for a moment before wiping it on his sleeve. "No."

"No?"

"Indeed not."

I wonder if he's playing with a full deck of cards. I must be entitled to something!

I should have gone to another lawyer. "Mr. . . ."

"Cropper. Mr. Cropper. Had that name for several decades, young man, and it's not likely to change anytime soon."

Frustrated, I reach into my pocket and reluctantly hand him a piece of paper. "Mr. Cropper, this is my marriage certificate. Now, as Lady Stanbury's husband, I am entitled to the real estate and all income of my wife's. I want access to it while she is incarcerated."

He holds it under the candlelight for a moment, and I almost snatch it back. He's surely going to set it alight, and then the evidence would be gone in an instant. He wheezes as he reads it through, and just as I am about to give in to my desire, he hands it to me.

"Still, my friend, you're not entitled to a bean."

"How so?" I'm desperate.

"What year did you marry Lady Anne?"

"As it says on the certificate," I say, frustration rising within me. "Eighteen eighty-four."

He laughs out loud. "What month?"

I suppress the urge to ask him whether he can read, and say tightly, "July."

"My friend, aren't *you* in a pickle? There's a little something called the Married Women's Property Act. Came into force, would you believe, in eighteen eighty-four. That means you aren't entitled to anything, as I already said. And to be honest, even if you had married her in *seventeen* eighty-four, you still wouldn't get anything." His eyes gleam like a snake's.

A very old snake.

Why did he bother asking me what year I was married if it didn't change the answer?

"Please explain this to me," I say wearily, resting my head atop my arms on the desk.

"Well, your wife is the only daughter of an earl whose property just so happens to be male entailed: happens all the time with these 'peers' and rich people. An old tradition, a way of keeping it in the family. But I'm sure you know all about that, don't you?" He pauses and my breath hitches in my throat. How can he possibly . . .

"But anyway, it's simple. The property, the real estate—the land, the house, all that expensive stuff, doesn't belong to her and never will. Therefore, my friend, it doesn't belong to *you* either. And even if there were no restraints of an entail and the property hypothetically did go to her, you still wouldn't be entitled to it because of the aforementioned law. If she doesn't birth a male child, it will go to some far-off cousin or obsolete uncle, I expect. It can pass through her, but not to her. Do you understand? And so, with the loss of your son"—he shrugs again—"I'm afraid you lost your only handle on the situation. Notwithstanding the fact that she's in a madhouse, of course, and will most likely never get out. Which is why you came to see me—I understand. But I'm sorry to say, my friend, that your presence in the manor is at the liberty and kindness of her father. At this moment in time it belongs to him. The fact that she's in a lunatic asylum doesn't strengthen your case: It weakens it."

Nausea rises in my throat, and I swallow. "Mr. Cropper, surely, there is something you can do to help me. There must be some sort of, *something*, for this situation?"

"Divorce her."

"But I—"

"What's the alternative? I am aware of your wife's case, Mr. Stanbury. Unfortunately, everyone is. I s'pect they even know about it over in France." He sighs. "Listen, in all likelihood, even if she gets better—and that's a very big 'if'—she will most likely be taken to trial and incarcerated at the jail for the next twenty years. What do you suppose happens to you then? Lord Damsbridge and I are friends, and I don't imagine for one second he'll let you live the rest of your days at the manor. Taking in mistresses under his roof while his daughter rots away in some cell? Ha! You have no rights to be in that house. None."

"But—"

"You want the money, yes. I understand. But, Mr. Stanbury, a bit of hindsight wouldn't go amiss here. I suggest—as a professional in these matters—that you commence divorce proceedings against your wife. There's many a loophole for this sort of thing for a man, and would be easy for you to do. In fact, if you say she was insane at the time of your marriage, or shortly thereafter, you are entitled to a straight-out annulment. Would you like me to arrange that for you?"

"No, absolutely not. I might hate what she's done, but I love my—"

"It would be much better for you, as you would be free to remarry. Find another rich woman, one who's not mad."

"No!"

The lawyer snorts. "Fine. Has her doctor advised you to divorce her?"

"No, he has not. He—"

He interrupts me. "Most unusual. Common advice is to do so." He sighs. "Right, okay. Mr. Stanbury, are you aware that she probably *was* mad when you met her, and you just didn't notice? It's perfectly all right for you to decide—"

"No. I do not want a divorce. What I want is my wife back, at home with me, and until then, access to a little money. I don't think that is a lot—or too much—to ask for."

He remains silent for a moment, tapping his nose with a long, dirty fingernail. "Have you ever been unfaithful to your wife, Mr. Stanbury?"

"What?"

"Tinkled the maid, coddled the cook, fluttered with the ladies down in the city—"

"No!" I'm offended.

"Ever slept with a relative? Your mother, for example?"

He's mad. He is as insane as my wife.

"Mr. Cropper, I'm sorry for having wasted your time—I see that now." I have started to rise from my seat when he moves surprisingly fast, darting out a hand to grab me.

"Sit down, Mr. Stanbury. I'm aware that gentlemen such as yourself don't like to be asked these questions, but we haven't finished. I was merely demonstrating what your wife would have to prove if she wanted to divorce you."

"What, that I had relations with my own mother?"

"Or brother. It doesn't matter, though if it were the latter she could sue you for buggery too." His eyes gleam, and all of a sudden I feel incredibly uneasy. "Plus intolerable cruelty, if you've ever knocked her around a few times, given her a black eye, that sort of thing."

Well, I never!

"I don't like your tone, Mr. Cropper. I've never hit a woman in my life, I've never had intercourse with anyone or anything other than a woman, and—"

He interrupts me, shaking his head. "I thought as much." He glances at my hand. "Nice ring you have there. Where did you get it?"

"Oh, erm . . ." I move it away, out of sight. How stupid of me to have worn it here. What if he recognizes it?

"Never mind—just trying to lighten the mood. Look, I was merely demonstrating the fact that she cannot divorce you. She can't let you go, even if she wanted to. But you can let her go. Your child is dead; that can't possibly be conductive to any sort of future relationship, can it? Learn from your mistakes, Mr. Stanbury, and move on. But next time, meet a woman who owns her own property and issue a child with her. Divorce her, accuse her of adultery. Then the child will go to you. As the father you have the right to keep it. The woman will most likely trade you the property for the baby. Women are like that. They'll do mostly anything for their own flesh and blood, sentimental fools."

"But that's—"

"Horrible? Awful? Treacherous?" The old lawyer leans forward and blows out the candle. The darkness makes his words ominous, fearful. "Do your morals really go against such a thing, Mr. Stanbury? I think not. Please don't try to fool an old hand. The law shall do as it pleases. It's there to protect—but it can also destroy. Remember that, my friend, and also remember I advised you to divorce her. Now, pass me my cane, will you? It's over there by that hat stand." Just like the candle, our conversation is blown out. He has dismissed me as easily as I would crush a roach.

Loath as I am to do as he asks, I oblige him, suddenly eager to be away from here, to be home.

Home?

I don't know whether to laugh, cry, or throw something.

He looks at me. "Do I amuse you, Mr. Stanbury?"

"Not at all," I say, still contemplating his last words. He rises slowly to his feet and takes the cane from me. "I simply had a bit of twitch in my nose, that's all. I recently broke it." A cracking sound comes from somewhere within him when he stands, and I wonder how he moves at all—yet he manages to hobble over to the door unattended.

"Blasted thing. Never broke a bone in my life: I'm careful about the people with whom I associate. Well, I can only imagine how hard it must be living in a house with no woman to look after you." He shrugs on his coat, eyeing me.

"I have servants, Mr. Cropper."

He looks perplexed for a moment. We stare at each other until suddenly he laughs.

"Of course you do, of course. Now. How could that possibly have escaped me? My friend—I do believe my mind is going. Used to be as sharp as a pin, I was. Now . . ." He puffs out his cheeks and looks around him sadly. "Now . . . I'm just a used-up bag o' bones, as they say. Can't see straight, and now I can't think straight. But mind me, my friend—I know all about the leprous arm of the law. And I'm telling you, you're done for if you stay in that house and don't divorce that woman. Do you know, when they changed the law and introduced divorce, the number of murders in this country declined in exact proportion to rising separations?" He turns and opens the door, a blast of icy wind whipping into the office. "If you think things are looking bad for you now, trust me and heed this warning: They will get a whole lot worse for you."

Is that a threat?

"Mr. Cropper—"

"Come, my friend, please. I don't want a snowdrift in my office in the morning. Look, I suppose there is a very slight, unlikely chance that your wife will get well, be released from the asylum, you'll have another child together—a son, who *won't* die—Lord Damsbridge will drop dead before your child, and you'll be happy as a king. Access to more money than you can imagine. But I don't expect it, and neither should you. You really should take the advice of an old man who has seen everything and heard even more. Truly. At this point, you have everything to lose and nothing to gain."

We make our way down the stone steps, silent, save for the snow crunching underfoot. I pull my thin overcoat tighter around me. He looks at me.

"I see you are set in your ways. I'm sorry I couldn't help you." He lifts his hat. "Good evening to you, my friend." He starts walking away from me, whistling a familiar tune, yet one I am unable to place. I grit my teeth when he suddenly stops and calls to me.

"By the way, my friend, our little conversation is free." His laugh echoes through the empty street as the blizzard swallows him whole, the dim glow of muffled gaslights hanging abstractly, dejectedly, in the air.

DAMN WITCH

Anne
October 17th, 1885
Bethlem Royal Hospital

What was I thinking?

That uneducated oaf of a man didn't have a clue what we would do once we were outside the building's entrance. Standing there, grinning at each other on the stone steps, the cold air refreshing in its recent rarity, we descended together, arm in arm. Our grins expanded ever wider once our feet touched upon the wet grass. However, mine faded as I quickly realized that neither he nor I had known what to expect. We must have looked like fools just standing there, immobile. What did we anticipate: an open door that would lead us straight onto a road? A carriage waiting for us perhaps? I looked at the gate, a large, imposing, locked gate that would be impossible to climb, and high walls surrounding a square courtyard.

Not even a glimmer of freedom.

Yet free people walk on the other side of those walls.

Irritated by this notion, I look at him.

"Well?"

"No need t' look at me so expectantly, girl. I haven't a clue either."

A whistle blew from behind us and I knew we had been found. I didn't fancy being put in the sack again, so I simply turned around, sat on the stone steps, and waited. He, however, had the brilliant idea of leaping into the nearest bush, which just so happened to be a rose-bush. There also happened to be another man hiding inside it. Both their startled squeals gave his location away.

That man will never get out of here.

But I will. I am sure of it.

"You fiends didn't let me wear a pretty dress!" I shouted as they dragged me to my cell, which they unceremoniously threw me into without so much as a single comment.

Left alone with my own company, I mentally attempt to burn the image of the gardens into my brain for future reference. Were there any trees next to the wall, or the gate? Was there a jailer outside with a bunch of keys? Was the soil soft or hard? Would it be possible to dig my way out if I should get into the garden again?

"Anne."

I push myself up as my cell door opens, revealing Fat Ruth.

"Go away," I say.

"That's not a very nice way to talk, Anne."

I blink at her.

"But I suspect you know that, don't you?" She moves farther into the room and closes the door behind her. She is holding something in her hands. "I mean, you are a lady and all. Aren't you?"

I keep my gaze on her. "Yes, I am. And you have no right to treat me this way."

She laughs. "'This way'? What way, Anne? What have I ever done to you, except bring you your food and make sure you don't harm yourself?"

"I—"

"I'm part of the reason you're not hanging by your neck, swinging side to side at the end of a rope, Anne. Everyone here: the doctor, the other attendants. Me. And you know what? Normally, I like my job.

Normally, I'd be more than happy to keep a poor woman such as your-self from the gallows. I'd feel sorry for any other person in your place. But you . . ." She comes closer and brings her face close to mine. Her eyes flick, searching. "You? Look at you. Your skin is perfect. Your cheeks are rosy." She takes one of my hands, roughly pulling it. "Your nails are straight, unbitten."

"Get off me."

She continues. "You don't smell. You don't have lice crawling through your hair." She lifts my foot and I squeal.

"You don't have any bites around the ankle—no fleas. How is it, Anne?" She drops my foot in distaste. "How is it that even insects and vermin won't deign to walk upon you?"

"I—"

"It's because you are *evil*. Even the rats know it, and stay away."

"I—"

Suddenly, she grabs me by the throat and shoves me against the wall. I can't breathe. I want to tell her to get off me, to leave me alone, that I haven't done anything to her, that if she'll just leave me alone I will—

The pressure around my throat eases. I open my mouth to speak—

"I—"

—and suddenly it fills with liquid, a thick, glutinous, foul-tasting liq-uid, and I try to spit it out, but she grabs hold of my jaw, pinning it closed, and I can't breathe again, oh, dear God, what is it? It's poison, it's—

I swallow.

"Dear God!" I spring up and slap her across the face. "Help, help! I've been poisoned!" I lift my hands to my face, intent on shoving my fingers down my neck, but she grabs hold of them and twists my arms behind my back.

"That, my precious lady, is croton oil. Doctor's orders."

And at her words, my bowels begin to cramp.

I bend over, clutching my stomach, but the biggest question re-mains unanswered.

Why am I here?

BOTTLE OF WHISKEY

Edgar
October 19th, 1885
Asquith Manor

I am nearing the end of writing a letter and reading through my papers when I am disturbed by Betty, a small servant girl of perhaps twelve years. She has yet to learn respect for her employer and does not understand the meaning of making herself invisible—barging into the library with a bang and demonstrating my point perfectly. I put aside the newspaper, printed over fifty years ago. Poor Mrs. Jordan.

My grandmother.

A tragedy.

"Oh, sir! Sir! There be a man t' see ye. 'Ee says 'ee is part o' ye family, like! I daenne know ye 'ad more family! I 'eard ye father was dead, like!"

"Child, don't you have any respect? I'm your master!"

"I—"

"Hasn't anyone ever told you children should be seen and not heard?" I can't decide if I'm angrier over the intrusion itself, the fact that she almost caught me crying, or her flippancy about someone's dead relative.

My grandmother would not be proud of me right now. I have dug myself into a very deep hole, and I don't know how to get myself out of it. The creditors loaned me money on the strength of my son, but now he's gone, and Anne is locked up. . . .

I haven't slept in a week.

My child is dead, my wife is mad, and all my servants disrespect me. . . .

The servant girl frowns and fidgets, hopping manically from one foot to the other as if she were standing on a pile of hot coals. She clutches a filthy cloth in her hands. "I ne'er did 'ear t'at one, sir! But—sir, 'ee said 'ee wants t' see ye right away! T' man, I mean! That's why I came runnin' in, but oh, please forgive me! I was in t' middle o' polishin' the silver, an' he knocked on t' glass! T' window, I mean! He din't even knock o' the front door, like!"

"Betty!" My morning is further disturbed by the arrival of Beatrix, who despite Anne's incarceration still manages to creep around the manor. Her relationship with Anne is unhealthy, bordering on obsession, and for the sake of my wife I tried to dismiss her, but discussions with Lord Damsbridge on the matter proved fruitless. He pronounced that it was up to Anne and Anne alone to choose her lady's maid, and neither he nor I could send her away.

We'll see about that. Time changes everything. She hates me and I've had enough of being treated this way.

I'm starting to hate right back.

In her hurry to stop the young servant, Beatrix doesn't knock either and my temperature rises. I rub my eyes. "Look, what is the meaning of this intrusion? This is absolutely unacceptable behavior from the servants of my manor." I stand up abruptly and—to my surprise—throw my pen at the wall. It bounces off onto the floor, splashing ink everywhere.

I gasp. I didn't mean to do that.

Betty twitches as if to run forward, but Beatrix restrains her by a hand on her shoulder. She whispers something to her, and the girl nods.

They are even talking about me, right in front of my face!

The older servant curtseys and nudges Betty to copy her.

"Apologies, sir. Betty is young and eager to please her *master*." Even my title—my well-earned *title*—is spoken in a tone of sarcasm. "She thought she did right by coming to you immediately, such was the urgency of the gentleman who requested you. I shall personally make sure it doesn't happen again." Her eyes meet mine for the briefest of moments, filled with the familiar hint of defiance and dislike. "And that rug, sir, belonged to Anne's mother. Her *dead* mother. I shall scrub it immediately—some things are simply irreplaceable, wouldn't you agree?" Before I can answer she turns away, pushing Betty out of the library. The door slams shut with a bang that reverberates throughout the house.

I drop to my knees, brush my hands through the cream fur. I don't need her help. I can clean it. It's all right—it will come off. . . .

I've rubbed it farther into the fibers.

I lean back and howl with frustration.

Perhaps this is the reason I was not born into the aristocracy. I can't look after nice things. I've spent my whole life believing that I was entitled to all this—a fancy house, shiny shoes, a tall hat on my head . . . worked for years to finally be here, and . . .

"Sir?"

I turn, slowly. Newman, the butler, is stood in the doorway.

"Sir, are you all right? What are you doing on the"—he hobbles over, leans over my shoulder—"oh."

"I've ruined it, Newman, absolutely ruined it."

He shakes his head, points with his stick. "No, sir. Miss Fortier will get that right out for you. You need to wash your hands, though."

I turn my palms over.

They are purple.

"For that, sir, all's you need is a weak solution of sulfuric acid. I'll have one of the footmen bring you a bowl and a cloth."

"Thank you, thank you so much." I want to weep. It is too much.

Everything is too much. My emotions are scattered. I don't know what is happening to me. I am quick to anger, and even quicker to tears.

And I have nobody to talk to.

"You're more than welcome, sir." He bows minutely, speaks softly. "It's all right to be upset, you know. I don't believe for a second you're crying about a damn carpet."

"I'm not crying, Newman," I say, rising to my feet. "I think some of the ink splashed in my eye."

He squints at me. "All right, sir. My mistake."

I nod, walk over to an expansive mahogany cabinet, pull out a bottle.

"Sir, there's a man waiting for you in the drawing room."

I gesture dismissively with the whiskey and fill up a glass. I swallow the contents in a single gulp.

The butler waits, hands folded neatly across his chest.

I pour another.

Relief. Just for a moment. Fire, and comfort.

"Well," I say, eventually. "Who is it?"

"A gentleman, sir, but I must profess I've never seen him before. He's rather . . . ahem . . . old, if I might say so? He was lurking around outside, peering through the windows. I don't think the poor fellow quite knew where the doorbell was." He looks at me doubtfully, as if not quite believing his own explanation.

I raise the glass to my lips. It's a creditor—it must be. Looking for me. I take a swig. "Did you ask him his name?"

"I did, sir. He said to tell you his name is Mr. Jordan."

I splutter, the whiskey flying out of my mouth.

"Are you all right, sir?"

It's him.

It really is him.

"I'm"—I can't breathe, cough—"I'm fine." The glass tinkles as I deposit it, shakily, inside the cabinet.

"Shall I send him away, sir?" asks the butler, perceptive as always. The man has outlived so many people, it's no wonder his acute observations are as well honed as a hawk circling its prey. He knows instantly I am afraid of meeting Mr. Jordan.

"No, it's quite all right. It's the whiskey, you know. Went down the wrong way."

Mr. Jordan's arrival is worse than that of a lender, but I must speak to him.

My wife's future happiness depends upon it.

The old man places a hand on my arm. "If you don't mind me saying, sir, he was a beautiful child. I know the other servants haven't been, well, as decent to you as they should have—especially after all this—and I'm sorry about that. They seem to forget that you are grieving. I know. I *know*."

I lean heavily against the cabinet and close my eyes, cover my face. My son. My beautiful, blue-eyed baby that will never get the chance to become a boy.

Newman clears his throat. "Sir, shall I inform Mr. Jordan you will be with him momentarily?"

"Yes," I say, without lifting my head. "Please."

He murmurs an assent, and the door closes with a quiet thud.

Shock. I think I'm in shock. I can only stand, and stare.

I couldn't save my son.

But I must save my wife.

Suddenly determined, I march across the room and retrieve my half-finished confession from the desk, the pen from the floor. I put them in my pocket. I was mad to write to him anyway. I've sent half a dozen letters in the last six months and not received a single reply. No, I will tell him myself. In person.

But not today.

No.

I will do as I have been taught. I am good at waiting. When Anne is released, I will tell her everything and together, we will be strong.

We will stand on his rotting doorstep, united in our finery, and we will laugh in his face.

This time, I will be a better man, a better husband.

This time, I will never let her go.

By the time I arrive at the drawing room, the butler is waiting outside the door.

"Can I get the two of you anything? Tea? Coffee?"

"Yes. Whiskey, please." I'm drinking far too much these days, but can't seem to stop. "Mr. Jordan is an old friend of my father's—may his soul rest in peace."

"Indeed, sir." He makes his way to the kitchen, and I know he will be returning within minutes. I quickly enter the room to face Mr. Christopher Jordan.

The man looks up as I enter, interrupted as he was in the midst of shaking ice from his boots onto the floor. He scrapes the rest of it off on the edge of a chair, where it falls onto the floor. I wince in disgust as he removes the dirty leather and flexes his dirty toes, the stench of his thick yellowed nails already permeating the room. Barefoot, he hobbles to the chair closest to the fireplace and sits down in a manner suggestive of ownership and familiarity, stretching his crooked legs out before him.

"Well, well, well. If it isn't Mr. Stanbury, lord of t' manor. I'd tip my hat at ye, except the butler put it on a hat stand," he says, laughing meanly. "Doing well for yerself, I see? There are so many things to amuse such a fine gentleman as yourself in here, isn't there? Books, a grand piano . . ." He arcs his arm and gestures to the wall. "A lovely painting. Who is she, Anne's mother? The poor thing's dead, in't she?" He looks at me and points to the chair next to him, as if it is he who should be inviting *me* to sit, and suddenly frowns. "What's wrong with your eyes?"

"Nothing's wrong with my eyes. What are you talking about?" *You old fool,* I think.

"Your eyes, Stanbury." He circles a forefinger around each of his own. "They're black. You look like a chimney sweep."

I reach up, remember. "Oh, that. I broke my nose."

"Hmm. You always were clumsy, a bit of an idiot. Well, I did the best with what your mother gave me. Come, sit, *Lord* Stanbury. Tell me about your life. Tell me what has gone on during the past six months, and how the hell you managed to misplace your wife. . . ." He trails off, a sly glint in his eye. "Pretty little thing, if she's got anything of her mother about her. I bet you enjoyed it, didn't you?" He cackles, raises his hips suggestively. "Though I should imagine it's like waving a candle in a cave now. Rather unenlightening, and pointless. The wind snuffs you right out before you get going."

"Father!"

"Your mother was just as useless after she had you."

"Shut up!"

"Look, take my advice. Women are useless after childbirth. That's what mistresses are for—or in your case, servants. You've got to put it somewhere."

"Will you be quiet?" I say fearfully. "They'll hear you."

"I'll speak as loudly as I like, son." He nestles back in the chair. "My, I've never sat on such opulent."

"Opu*lence.*"

"As you like. I see you're learning."

My chest tightens. "Father, what are you doing here? I wrote to you last week!"

"Well, my son, I have received no letter from ye—*you*—in over three months. 'Twas as recent as a fortnight ago I read of this horror . . . on the front page of the *Gazette*, no less! You've gotten us into a right mess, so you have." He digs deep inside his ripped pockets, pulls out a neatly rolled newspaper. "This is how I found out. Can you imagine?" He slaps the newspaper twice against my chest before I snatch it away from him.

"What do you mean you haven't received any letters—" The butler picks this moment to intrude upon us, but thankfully knocks hard twice on the door before entering. I quickly unroll the newspaper and sit on it. I adopt an air of relaxation and smile innocently at Newman as he hobbles into the room.

"Mr. Jordan? Can I offer you a glass of our premium whiskey?"

My father looks at me, the edges of his mouth curling upward. "Aye, 'twould warm me up, that would. Much appreciated. Thank you," he says to the butler, watching me over the top of the servant's head. The old man pours a small measure of the orange liquid into a crystal glass.

"Wud like more of that, young man," my father says, looking disdainfully into the glass. Somehow my father manages to insult people under a thin veil of politeness. He rarely gets away with it, though, and the butler is no fool. The blush that rises to his cheeks betrays the fact that he knows he has been insulted, but in his position, he can hardly address it. He merely pours more whiskey into the glass until it almost overfills.

"Sir, I do beg your pardon. It seems I've poured a little too much there. I'd hate for you to spill it upon such a fine suit. Here." He gestures to my father as if to take it away from him. "Let me pour a little out. Nothing but the largest of measures for such a fine gentleman— isn't that right, sir?" He looks at me: a picture of innocence.

My father, too idiotic to realize that the butler has gotten the best of him, waves him away and raises the glass to his lips. "No matter. More is better than less," he says in his ignorance, his bastardized English grating like teeth upon a stone. Taking a swig, he sighs with the happiness of a man who has sought solace in a bottle for many, many decades.

And I am following in his footsteps.

My own whiskey poured, a perfectly perfect measure, the butler leaves us in peace, placing the decanter and fresh glasses on the small table in between my father and me.

"There was no need to insult the man," I say through my teeth, raising my behind and pulling out the newspaper.

"'Insult the man,' you say? And how did I do that?"

Same as always. Looking for an argument. I sigh and let the matter pass, opening the paper. "Forget it. Why are you here? What possible reason could you have for taking such a risk?"

My father lifts his shoulders back and, raising his head, finishes his drink and pours himself another vastly generous measure. I hope he doesn't intoxicate himself before he leaves.

"I told you already. You never listen—that's your problem. I spent eighteen years of my goddamn life dragging your skinny arse up, and look at you. An idiot. I should've thrown you in the river and been done with it. Just read the news, will ye?"

I open it up, to find a page circled in black ink.

EVENING HERALD
OCTOBER 12TH, 1885

OLD COURT. October 6th, 1885.

Before Mr. Grantham.

241. ANNE STANBURY (28). For the willful murder of her recently born male child.

MR. CAMPBELL. Prosecuted.

Upon the evidence of Dr. Scott, the medical officer at Holloway Gaol, the Jury found the prisoner of unsound mind and unable to plead. To be detained during Her Majesty's Pleasure.

STANBURY, Anne Rose (28), was indicted for and charged on Coroner's inquisition with the willful murder of her male child.

Mr. Bowkin and Mr. David Campbell prosecuted; Mr. Hutchinson defended, at the request of the Court.

ELEANOR JAMES, nurse. I first attended to the prisoner during her first confinement one year ago. She was again confined on May 4th, and I then attended to her until August 1st. She got over this confinement well; she appeared happy and cheerful, and was a fond and loving mother. I next saw her on August 8th; she complained of feeling weak and suffering sleeplessness, and complained of loss of milk, not being able to feed her baby. At 11:30 that night I saw her for the last time. She was in bed with the baby. From my experience as a nurse, if a woman loses her milk after confinement, it often has an effect on the mind.

WILLIAM STRONG, 183, New Queens Road, Clapham. I was a neighbor to the prisoner and her husband, and they were thoroughly respectable people. Prisoner was a kind and affectionate mother to her little boy. Around 1:30 on the morning of October 5th, I heard the cry of a baby, and I saw light in the kitchen, which was most unusual. The baby seemed to be crying with great distress, and I thought it neighborly of me to knock and see if all was well, or if I could be of any assistance. I was concerned the baby may have taken sick. Through the window I saw the prisoner in her dressing gown; there was blood on her hands, and her arms were outstretched. The baby had gone silent, and at this point Mr. Stanbury entered the kitchen. I called out, "What has she done?" Mr. Stanbury came around and opened the door. He was pale and said, "Come and look." I went into the kitchen and saw the baby on the floor; near it there was lying a knife (Exhibit 1).

Dr. JOHN STANFORD, 4, Wandsworth Bridge Road. I attended to the prisoner in her confinement on May 7th and until August 1st. On October 5th, which was about 8 weeks after I had last seen her, I was sent for to Asquith Manor. I found her then suffering from puerperal insanity; that is a form frequently accompanying the stoppage of milk, and infanticide is one of the characteristics. The child had its throat cut, and was dead.

Cross-examined. I think she would not know what she was doing when she committed this act.

Dr. SCOTT, medical officer, Holloway Prison. I have had the prisoner under observation since August 5th. My conclusion is that at the time of committing this act she was not responsible for her actions.

Verdict, Guilty, but insane at the time of commission of the offense.
Unable to stand trial.
To be detained during Her Majesty's Pleasure at Bethlem Royal
Hospital, until such time she is deemed sane.

Seeing it on paper brings back that terrible night and I close my eyes, all of a sudden in physical pain.

"Ye see? How awful for a grandfather to read such a thing about his own bairn's bairn. So I'm sure you can now understand why I'm here, to see how me own flesh and blood—what I have left—is bearing up under such terrible circumstances. Of course, if you had written to me, as promised, I wouldn't be here." He sits up taller in his chair, fiddling with the glass—stalling. I know he wants to say something that I don't want to hear. He won't look me in the eye. Instead, he looks about him and fixes upon the painting of Anne's mother. "Oh, and I could use some more money. Me new wife fancies a little red dress that I can't possibly deny her."

I splutter.

"A 'new wife'? Father—you're, you're . . . you're practically eighty!"

"I am not dead yet, son."

"But how . . . how . . ."

"How can I get it up?" He cackles, lifts a bony finger to his nose. "You'll learn, son. And me wife, well—she's practically young enough t' be *your* daughter!"

I feel sick.

"No, I was about to ask how on earth you managed to find a woman who'll put up with you."

"'Tis none of your business 'ow we met. I just want a bit 'o money t' treat her, *Lord* Stanbury."

Money. All my father has ever cared about is money.

"I'm not a lord, Father, and never will be. And I suggest that you buy it for her, as I don't have anything to give you." Suddenly, all I can see is John's blood-splattered, mutilated body lying on the concrete floor: a physical throbbing imprinted behind my left eye. The fact that my father has a new wife barely dims—until it is merely a small speck of red anger on the horizon.

"Don't have any money? Pray tell, son, how that is possible? I see meself sittin' in a chair which costs more than my humble little house. . . ." He lifts his bottom and pats the seat pointedly. "And that decanter there could mortgage half of London for a decade too."

How *did* he find a new wife? What woman—in her right mind—would go within six feet of my father? God knows they should be forewarned about his temper.

I've never believed for a second that my mother fell out of that window when I was ten.

"Father, I sent you a postal order for fifty pounds last month. What happened to it?"

"I spent it, didn't I? That's what money is for—spending! I put food in your stomach and a roof over your head for decades, son. Don't you think I deserve more than fifty measly pounds for all that I've done? I got you where you are now! Surely, there's much more than that. Why, I thought that was nothin' but a wee advance." He pours another glass of whiskey; I follow suit.

"Father, I can't take out any more loans. John's dead and Anne's locked up, and . . . they only gave me the money because they thought I could pay them back. I fear the creditors will soon be after me."

He ignores me.

"Father, do you understand what I am saying? They won't loan me any more money while I am without a wife, without a son. They have no guarantee of getting it back."

He watches me, silent for some moments. Finally, he speaks.

"Well, I ain't waitin' sixteen years, son—I'll tell you that for nothing. Seventeen, by the time she grows the brat." He pours another drink, his eyes already beginning to glaze. "Then I really *will* be dead. Times a-tickin', son. You seem to have forgotten that while you're 'ere, living the life o' luxury, I'm forced to live in a cloud of smog, woken up at all hours by the rumble of horses' hooves across the broken cobbles and hawkers shoutin' out their goods at the crack of dawn before I've 'ardly had a chance t' open my eyes. . . ."

Does he think I don't remember? Does he forget I grew up in the very house to which he refers?

"Can ye guess how many times the crumpet man rings his bell before the clock tolls seven in the morning? Two hundred and thirty-seven times. That's a lot of ringing just outside ye front door, and I hardly get any sleep nowadays. I tried throwing a shoe at him once, but he called me a foul name and threatened t' hit me. Poor Vicky can't sleep either, bless 'er 'eart."

Vicky, is it?

"Where did you find her? A whore, is she?"

I expect him to be ashamed, but he merely grins. Blackened gums and stumps of teeth. "Aye, she is. And all the better for it—if you know what I mean."

My father is a coward, as are most bullies, and though his tongue can be sharp, his arms are thin and puny. The one time he had a fight, the woman knocked him clean unconscious and he lost his front teeth. Not that it made much impact upon his vanity: He never smiled much before anyway.

"But since she married me, she's not plying her trade anymore, so there's no money comin' in."

"I can't say I feel too badly about that, Father. I really can't." The truth is that right now I hate him more than ever. "I'm disgusted that you would marry a whore. But in any case, there's not much I can do. You can take the decanter if you want—I'll tell the butler we accidentally broke it, and one of the servant girls cleaned away the mess. I don't expect him to go checking on it. But I can't give you any money, for I tell the truth when I tell you I have none. "

He looks at the decanter. "Aye, I'll take it . . . but I'm taking it full with the whiskey, mind." Drunk now, he sways in the chair.

"Just don't drink it all in the carriage on the way home, will you?"

"You think I came in a carriage?"

"I don't care how you came, but you'll be going back in one. I don't want the servants or, God forbid, Lord Damsbridge to see you staggering down the driveway. I'll summon the coachman."

"You know there's only one way to get those creditors off your back, don't you?" he says.

"How's that?"

"Get your slag of a wife out of the madhouse. And soon. Remember who you are, remember your roots. You have work to do. We've waited our whole lives for this." He picks up his boots, struggles with the laces.

"I grew to love her—"

"Ye—you're not the first man in this family to be turned by beauty. But who are you trying to deceive? Me, or yourself? I want that money, son. It is mine. You know what will happen if you don't."

I do. I'll be put out on the streets, begging for my next meal. Arrested for vagrancy. All I ever wanted to do was make him proud, and now . . . I don't. He is a nasty, filthy, dirty, sad little man.

Tell him the truth, coaxes a scratchy little voice inside my head, a mouse nibbling at my brain. *Tell him.*

No, I have to wait.

Wait for what? The rodent starts to bite. My head pounds. *Just tell him.*

It hits me then that I am nothing but a coward. I have the perfect opportunity to explain that this is all over, that his plan is obsolete, but I can't.

I can't.

Not without Anne beside me.

But what if she can't forgive you? The rodent is chewing now, my vision blurred. *What if you tell her the truth, and she doesn't forgive you?*

No. She will. She'll understand.

She loves me.

Reaching into my pocket, I clench the letter tight.

My confession.

My absolution.

Do it. Just hand it to him. Explain the rest.

My father stands up, one boot laced, wobbles.

"What's t' matter wiv' ye, son? Ye look like you've swallowed a wasp." He laughs, croaks, coughs.

"I've done my duty. I've done as you asked. I need to tell you something, though. I—"

"No, you haven't. Not yet."

Tears sting my eyes.

"Father, will you listen? I've visited a lawyer. We aren't entitled to as much as we thought, and—"

"Son, we're entitled to everything. I know what I'm talking about—lawyers don't. Go find another creditor, will you?"

"I . . ." I falter. The moment has passed and in any case, he's too drunk to understand anything more I could say and I too am feeling the effects of the alcohol. "I'll write to you, Father." Wait; didn't he mention something about not receiving my letters—something important? I fill another glass and knock it back. Whatever it is can wait for another day. Hopefully, he'll go back to his little hovel, drink himself to death, and I'll be free. I fill another dram, but he snatches the glass out of my hands.

"No more for you, son. This won't last me the night if you keep swigging at it like that." He leans his head back and literally *pours* the ale inside. I was impressed with this trick once—when I was all of ten years old, and in awe of everything and everyone around me.

Not anymore.

No.

I feel nothing but disgust and resentment as his eyes widen in delight. He puffs out his cheeks, swirls the liquid around his mouth. "Ah. There you go." He smacks his lips together, frowns. He gestures to my hand. "Do ye still 'ave the ring?"

"Of course I do."

"Where?"

"It's locked away, safely. But why don't you take it with you?" *I don't want it. It's not who I am anymore.* "I don't think it's wise keeping it here. What if they find out—"

"You'll keep it on ye, son, t' remind you of yer roots. Don't get carried away like some idiot in love. Ye just look at tha' ring and remember that both I and ye should've been wearing that thing with pride, a long, long time ago." He makes his way toward the door, clinging on to the wall. He looks back and tries to wink. "Don't worry, son. As soon as ye get another child in 'er, and out of 'er, everythin' will be fixed. Just make sure ye keep the next one alive, 'ey?"

He slams the door on his way out.

A FINE FRAUDSTER

Dr. Savage
October 20th, 1885
Bethlem Royal Hospital

After prescribing a draught for a young man with boils that he insists upon popping and thus infecting, I wash my hands and wait for the next patient to come in. Enter she does, slowly, warily, looking to the floor, her face pale, her cheeks sallow. Nurse Agnus says something to her and gently pushes her farther into my office, before closing the door and leaving us alone to assess each other. Defiance flashes in her eyes and I stand up as leisurely as she comes over the threshold: matching and mirroring her movements.

"Good morning, Anne," I say, sitting in my chair so she is left standing.

She frowns at me as if unsure of my actions and looks at the seat in front of her, twiddling her fingers.

Her nails are rough, jagged.

"Would you like to sit, Anne?"

"I would. Thank you," she says, and does.

Thank you?

She is calmer this morning than the last time I saw her. Good old croton oil, works wonders. As my gaze meets hers, I inwardly marvel at the fact that I can look into the face of a murderess and still see an attractive woman. There is nothing more than the observation of a solid fact in my thoughts, though—nothing untoward. In a lunatic asylum, it is merely seldom that one meets with physical beauty. Degeneracy in nature is naturally in opposition to attractiveness and well-being; for good reason. Every parent wants a beautiful child, but not all parents are pleasant to look at, and unfortunately, unattractive parents equal hideous children.

When a woman is pregnant she should not look at, nor even *think* of, ugly people.

"How was your breakfast?" I say.

"Awful. Do I have to eat porridge every damn day?"

She has a point.

"Well, what would you like to eat for breakfast, Anne?"

"I should like some warm, golden, very buttery toast, if that's not too much trouble."

"Not at all," I say, scribbling it onto a piece of paper. "Now, Anne. I have done something for you and I would like you to do something for me. Can you tell me why you tried to escape last week?"

She frowns at me. "That's an idiotic question. I tried to escape because I'm not supposed to be here." She shakes her head as if bewildered at my stupidity. "Do you know what she did to me, afterward?"

"Who?"

"Fat Ruth. She made me drink poison, and it made me very ill. Is she trying to kill me?"

I consult my notes.

October 18th, 1885
  Croton oil administered with success. Patient became calm and compliant upon evacuating bowels.

"Ah yes. That wasn't poison, Anne. It was a treatment to help you feel better. Nobody is trying to kill you."

"Well, it was simply *awful*. I had cramps in my stomach for the rest of the day, and it was most humiliating."

It doesn't escape my notice that she doesn't question the word *treatment*.

"All right, I'm sorry it made you feel that way. You might not have to have it again. . . ." I close her file. "But, Anne, what I really want to talk about today is the escape itself, the gentleman you were with."

"What about him?"

"Did you notice anything odd about him? Do you think he is supposed to be here?"

"Well, I . . ." She stops, twiddling with the strings on her gown. "If I knew where 'here' was, perhaps I would be able to answer that question. Is it a workhouse? A home for wayward women?"

"If it was, would you expect to find men in here?"

She bites her lip. "Well, no—I suppose, then, it cannot be a home for women. It's not a workhouse, as nobody is making me do any work; and why would I be in a workhouse anyway? My family has a lot of money. Nothing makes sense. I wish you would just tell me."

"Anne, that man is a lunatic."

Her eyes widen and she grips the arms of the chair.

"Dear Lord, what on earth was he doing in here? Did you find him? Did you have him arrested?"

"He's already been arrested, Anne. That's why he is *here*."

"Where," she says quietly, "is 'here'?"

I don't answer.

Come on, Anne. Think—remember!

"He said something about his family putting him in here, which I simply do not understand. If you are kidnapping people for ransom, it simply doesn't make sense." She closes her eyes, breathing for a moment before opening them. "Also, he didn't appear to be the sort that would have much money. I'm very confused."

"Anne, let's forget the gentleman for a moment. I want to focus back on you. When the attendants took you back to your room, they said you were shouting, something about a song. Do you remember what that was?"

" 'Ride of the Valkyries.' " Her face lights up.

I try to push her memory back further. "Do you know where you heard it before?"

"I remember . . . I remember being at home. It was a special occasion, a family get-together. It was . . ." She trails off, her eyes glazed, her brow furrowed. "There were a lot of people. A special occasion. There were a lot of cards: beautiful blue cards. Everyone was of good cheer. People were dancing, singing. And a man . . . a man, he stayed by my side; I knew him well, somehow, and something else . . ."

"Yes?" I lean over, my beard brushing the desk.

"Something . . . small. I don't. I'm not . . ." She shakes her head. "I don't know, Doctor. It's like there is something there, in my mind, but every time I try to reach it—it disappears. It floats away, like a cloud. I remember feeling happy, and loved, and having a sense of . . . responsibility. There was someone, or something, that I was supposed to be looking after. I know that, but—I've never had a pet, sir. My father never let me have one. Said that they get too much fur everywhere."

The baby is there. Right on the edge of her memory. But I can't push her, not yet.

"Would you like a glass of water, Anne? Perhaps a dram of ale?"

"Water would be fine, thank you."

I pour her a glass.

"Can you tell me what month of the year is it?"

She looks at the clock—which shows five in the afternoon—and leans forward in her chair. Her eyes flick toward the window. "It is October—or thereabouts."

Disappointment hits me like a brick.

Patient is unaware of the month when asked. However, she is able to deduce from the time on the clock, the fire burning in the hearth, and on looking outdoors; to find it is dark, the leaves withered with still a few hanging on the branches; that it must be "about October." It is, in fact, mid-October. Her answer is formed not from memory, but deduced from reason.

"Can you tell me the last thing you remember, before being here?" I have asked her this before, and will continue to do so, until such a time as she recollects her life. And this is when she switches. Her eyes blaze, and anger bubbles up through her skin. It's almost as if I can see the fire blazing within her mind.

"I went to sleep. How many times must I tell you?" Her chest rises up and down quickly; her cheeks flush. I know her pulse and temperature are rising. She is indignant: in denial. Her mind won't let her access the memory.

"I don't understand what you want from me, but I do wish that you would tell me. I would like to go home."

I stand up, put a hand on her forehead. She flinches angrily.

Cool.

I pause for a moment. I've never met a patient suffering from puerperal mania who doesn't have a temperature.

"Anne, did you have a cold wash today? In the last half hour or so?"

"No. I'm filthy. Can I have a bath?"

"Perhaps," I say, studying her. Anne is unusual in that she doesn't *quite* seem to fill a singular diagnosis: doesn't wholly "fit" into any particular box. She has all the outward symptoms of "acute delirious mania"—memory loss, definite cause (puerperal psychosis), sudden onset—yet she does not have the fever, refusal of food, flushed cheeks, or incoherence of speech that normally accompanies it. In my assessment of the insane, the symptoms form the point of division between curable and incurable cases. Based on appearances alone, I would consider Anne an "incurable" case; however, puerperal insanity *is* curable. The danger lies in the possibility she may have other, underlying disorders—such as hysteria or melancholy.

I shall proceed slowly.

"Tell me more about going to bed that night, Anne. The night before you woke up here. Did you eat dinner? Did you—"

She looks to her lap and mumbles something under her breath.

"Pardon, Anne?"

She stands quickly, pushing her chair behind and away from her. It clatters to the floor. "I said you are perverted! Why do you imagine it appropriate to ask a lady the particulars of her going to bed? Would you like me to tell you that I sleep naked at times, in the summer when the heat feels like a blanket over my skin? That at these times I have no need of clothes? Is that what you wish to know? Why oh why am I here?" She starts to cry, and sways back and forth. She is upset, but so far she is not being violent and I have seen far worse than this.

The memory of a person suffering from mania is sometimes akin to listening to someone with a double consciousness. When talking of recent events Anne is calm and collected, yet when confronted with her memory of before the asylum, her angry, confused feelings resurface. Though interesting to witness, a mind protecting itself in such a way is frustrating to me as a professional—to be unable to reach her mind.

"No, Anne, you misunderstand me. I simply wish to know of your last memories of being at home, before you came to be here. Whether you believe me at present or not, you will, given time. You will understand and recognize me for that which I am: a doctor, trying to help you."

She peers around her, as if looking for something. An inspiration occurs to me.

"Look, Anne, behind me, on the wall. In fact," I say, standing and unhooking one of my certificates from it. "Here. Read it—please—and tell me what you see." I pass it to her.

DR. GEORGE SAVAGE
M.D., M.R.C.P.
PHYSICIAN AND SUPERINTENDENT
OF BETHLEM ROYAL HOSPITAL

"Well? Does this not offer proof that I am who I say I am?" I smile at her, and wait.

She is silent for a moment. She studies the frame, turning it over and running her fingers across the back of the glass. She frowns. This is it; this is the turning point. . . .

"It would appear that you are a fine fraudster, Mr. Savage, and that you wish to woo me with fancy letters. You forget that anyone could write these after their name—even me."

My smile disappears.

Working with the insane can be frustrating, for previously indisputable facts of life become negligible, and fantasies abound. They will not believe the sky is blue, or worse: that there even is a sky.

"What about the stamp, Anne? That cannot be faked; it proves this is a genuine certificate."

She glares at me. "What do you want with me, you fish-eyed fiend? Can I go home now?" she asks as if the previous five minutes had not occurred.

"May I have that back, please?" I say, gesturing to the frame. I should not have given her a pane of glass. I remember what she did the last time she called me a fish-eyed fiend—with a shard.

Yet once again, she surprises me.

"Certainly." She passes it over gently and smooths her gown. "What is my chair doing on the floor?" She blushes, picks it up, and sits down again. I release a breath. "I'm sorry. I seem to have lost myself there for a second or two." She shakes her head, as if to clear it. "You wanted to speak with me about the ransom?"

I find it difficult to keep track with her thought processes and moods. Her temperament flips as quickly as a blink, yet her delusion is fixed.

Patient's sickness is causing her ideas to flow along certain lines more rapidly than in health. At times, they are somewhat hard to follow in their rapidity of formation. No continuous thought process. Attention may be garnered momentarily. Long-term memory remains partially lost, past is left with an irregular outline—although she seems to be on the verge of a breakthrough. Remembers looking after something small, something important.
The baby.
For hypnotherapy.

"Anne, I believe that's enough for today." I press my bell and summon Agnus. Her young head peers around the doorframe.

"Yes, sir?"

"Can you escort Anne back to her room, please? And please ask Nurse Ruth to contact Dr. Tuke."

"Dr. Tuke. Of course." She moves into the office and takes hold of Anne's hand. Surprisingly, Anne doesn't fight her. Instead, she rises willingly, looking behind her as the attendant leads the way.

"You confuse me," she says, looking lost. "Why don't you tell me how much you want for me? You are a perfectly cruel, awful man."

AN ASS

Beatrix
October 21st, 1885
Asquith Manor

"Shush!" I whisper in a hiss, pulling Betty down from the window. "They'll hear us!"

"They won't, miss, they won't! But ye have t' look outside. I can see tha' Mr. Jordan, an' I think 'ee's stolen somethin'!" she whispers back defiantly.

"Why should you think he has stolen something, Betty?"

"'Cause 'ee has somethin' under 'is arm, an 'ee dinnae come wit' anythin'!"

Putting my hand on her shoulder, I creep my head slowly over the window ledge. Lord, when did I start indulging youngsters in their childish fantasies again? It seems only yesterday that Anne was a child of Betty's age, telling me stories about the comings and goings of our visitors.

Mr. Jordan is indeed standing outside.

"De ye see 'im? De ye?" She yanks at my arm, tugging like a monkey.

"Shush!" I say more forcefully this time, swatting her hand away.

"But, *miiiiiiss,*" she says, the title coming out as a whine. "He may be stealin' Lady Anne's things! P'rhaps Mr. Stanbury is sellin' 'er stuff. 'Ee's a commoner and got ne money, miss! An' look how *old* 'ee is!"

I ignore her, unwilling to enter into a debate either about Mr. Stanbury or about Anne. Watching Mr. Jordan, I almost laugh out loud when the man's hat is blown off by a gust of wind and he scrabbles for it uselessly. The hat lands in a wet patch of mud as a carriage enters the main gate.

"Betty, Mr. Jordan is outside because he is waiting for the carriage to take him home." I sit back down beside her and take her chin in my hands. "He's just an old friend of Mr. Stanbury's, and there's nothing else to it." I push her away playfully and lift myself up from the floor.

She crosses her arms and stamps her foot. "Miss, ye're nae listenin'! I'm tellin' ye 'ee has somethin' in his hands!"

"No, he doesn't. Now, come on, I'm not getting anything done today with all this talk of thievery and such." I give her my stern face and she relents, letting me pull her to her feet.

Thinking about Anne, I wonder if Mrs. Harding received the letter I sent. "Betty, you did post that letter to Mrs. Harding, didn't you?"

"Of course I did, miss," she says indignantly, opening the door and gesturing for me to pass through before her. "Ye said 'twas important. I wan' t' help. I wan' Anne back 'ere just as much as ye do. I am missing her somethin' awful. I dannae like Mr. Stanbury. 'Ee wants t' have us all fired, ye know." She looks at my face and notices that I still appear unconvinced. "It's not all stories, miss! It's nay!"

That I do know. We all know. Newman told us the discussion Mr. Stanbury had with Lord Damsbridge, not a week after Anne was taken away. I was the one he professed to be the worst, "lounging around" and "idly chatting with Anne, as if it is her job simply to be my wife's companion." Well, after she miscarried, his wife needed a companion more than ever. I offered her the love and support that he was unable to provide.

Anne deserves better than some lying, cheating, common piece of filth. Oh, of course he charmed her with his scrawny frame and destitute background. Anne always was susceptible to anything with sad eyes and an injured soul: motherless kittens, flightless birds, beetles stuck on their back.

Men without money.

But as soon as she lost that first baby, I saw right through his act. He didn't care about Anne. No. He *preyed* on her for her money, took advantage of her good nature, her impressionable, emotionally vulnerable youth.

And now look what's happened. The kitten turned into a lion.

No matter. I have it on Lord Damsbridge's authority he will be gone from the manor. Soon.

"You have nothing to worry about, Betty. It doesn't matter what Mr. Stanbury wants, or doesn't want."

"Is tha' 'cause of t' men who've been 'anging around, lookin' fer 'im?"

"Who?"

"The men, miss. I've seen 'em and 'eard 'em—they've been sayin' tha' now the baby is dead, like, Mr. Stanbury has gotta give them their money back."

"I . . . Did you ever hear the story about the ass and the grasshopper?"

"Nay, I ne'er did 'ear tha' one."

"An ass, having heard some grasshoppers chirping, was highly enchanted and, desiring to possess the same charm of melody, demanded what sort of food they lived on to give them such beautiful voices. They replied, 'The dew.' The ass resolved that he would live only upon dew, and in a short time died of hunger."

"What—so, are ye sayin' that Mr. Stanbury is goin' t' starve, like? Is he only eatin' dew? That's really stupid."

I laugh. "Not exactly, Betty. But he coveted something he wasn't entitled to, and it just might kill him."

She looks confused.

"Don't worry about anything, Betty. Everything's going to be just fine, just the way it was."

We stop at the door to the kitchen and I pat her on the head. She's a lovely child: incredibly loyal and loving toward everyone around her. She considers Anne to be a sort of older sister, in an admiring way. I know she wants to be just like her mistress. Anne always took the time to speak with Betty and inquire about her own and her family's health. A couple of times I caught Anne putting a shilling in Betty's grubby little hands.

"So . . . should we make Mr. Stanbury a proper breakfast? Is he angry with us because he's hungry? He does a look a bit—small."

"No, Betty. He has plenty of food. Stop worrying."

She frowns, and fiddles with her dress. "But that man did 'ave somethin' under 'is arm. I'm not lying."

"I know you're not lying, Betty. You're as honest as a puppy."

She smiles.

"Well, then, I'll be seein' ye!" With that she dives into the kitchen, amid warm shouts of greetings and endearments.

I climb the stairs to Mr. Stanbury's chamber. Anne's clothes need to be aired at least once a day. Thankfully, the moths haven't gotten to them yet, though I worry about it constantly. Her dresses must be perfect for when she comes home. I am making my way across the room, heading for the wardrobe, when I notice an errant sock on the floor. I bend down to pick it up and as I do so, I spy something underneath the bed.

An envelope.

I reach underneath and pick it up.

It is addressed to Mr. Stanbury.

I hold it for a moment. Do I chance to read it now? Where is he? I rush to the window and look outside. The carriage has gone; he could be anywhere. I run across the room and close the door. If he does come up, at least the turning of the handle will give me time to throw it back under the bed.

I sit on the bed and read it.

It's not what I thought it was, nor addressed to whom I thought. Tears dance in my eyes and for a moment I stay, confused.

This could change everything.

His father. He has written a letter to his *dead* father.

A droplet of water lands upon the crumpled letter, and I stare at it for some moments before realizing that I am crying.

What do I want?

I want whatever makes Anne happy.

She needs to know the truth.

She needs to see this.

INSTEAD OF PORRIDGE

Anne
October 22nd, 1885
Royal Bethlem Hospital

Fat Ruth has never given me her keys instead of porridge, and I have never had anything other for breakfast in this stinking hole of a place since the day I arrived here despite what the "doctor" promised. Liar. I feel almost destitute at times. Though they have started letting me out of my cell for longer periods each day and sometimes they even take their eyes off me, it's hardly enough time to make another attempt at escape. So I don't even try anymore.

I sit on the floor next to Grace under the watchful eye of Agnus. Grace has become my mute friend; I like the fact that she doesn't say much, and Agnus's presence is preferable to Fat Ruth's. Agnus treats Grace with nothing less than compassion. I see true sympathy in her eyes regarding our plight, but still, she is employed by these people, so she can't be that pleasant. I treat her with wariness, though she always tries her best to engage me in conversation.

This day, Agnus tells me Grace has been here for eight years.

"Eight years!" I exclaim. "Why in heavens did her family not pay the ransom?"

"Anne, how many times do I have to tell you?"

"Yes, yes, I have not been kidnapped," I repeat back to her, a sentence she repeats to me daily when I start becoming slightly hysterical about my current predicament. "Can you believe that the 'doctor' has a fake certificate hanging on his wall?"

"Anne, you are in a *hospital*. He really is a doctor."

I grumble. "Yes, yes . . . I must try to remember this."

"Yes, Anne, you must—if you ever want to get well and get out of here," Agnus says, softly brushing Grace's hair. She is forever brushing her hair. "And not through escaping. We are responsible for your safety, and we have force at hand if necessary. Do not make Ruth use it."

"She already did. She pinned me down and poisoned me."

Agnus sighs. "You got that man into a world of trouble, you know."

"What man?"

"The one you tried to escape with."

I make a noise in my throat.

At this point, I hardly care.

"How old is she, then?" I say, pointing at Grace. I do not wish to discuss escape attempt number one. Eleven, for the man. Nor do I want to be reminded of the fact that I was restricted to my cell for three days as punishment and emptied my bowels on the floor.

"Seventeen."

"Seventeen! She looks more like fifty!" I am incredulous.

"She is deaf and mute," says Agnus.

"Pardon?"

"Anne, open your ears. It is Grace who is deaf, not you."

I adopt a look of appropriate remorsefulness.

"She was suddenly afflicted by scarlet fever at only nine years old. Since then she has been unable to communicate. She gradually became insane."

"That's terrible," I say. I mean it. "But I spoke to her, that time I asked her to move, and she looked right at me!" I try to contradict what she has told me. It cannot be true that a young girl has had her life stolen away from her at such a precious age.

"She sensed your presence. Anyway, I didn't say she was blind, Anne."

"Hmm."

I ponder my situation.

"If I was deaf, I should kill myself," I say.

Agnus shakes her head, but I swear I can see the curve of a smile at the edges of her mouth.

"So, Agnus, is that your real name?" I move on the floor and sit next to Grace, where I take over Agnus's stroking of her hair. I give Agnus the brush, as I prefer to do it with my hands. It relaxes me, reminds me of stroking a horse. My horse. Ophelia.

"Yes, Anne, why wouldn't it be?"

I raise my eyebrows.

"Of course, yes, we are all conspirators in your grand kidnapping fantasy. Sorry. I managed to forget for a minute there."

"It doesn't do a lady to be sarcastic," I say.

"Who said I was a 'lady,' Anne? And anyway, I am not sorry."

Silence.

"Anne, could we drop the subject of your having been kidnapped for ten minutes?"

"I don't have a stick. How am I to tell how long ten minutes is?" I say. "Though I suppose we may chat awhile, if you tell me a bit about yourself and why you are here." I pluck a hair from Grace's head, and she winces. "Convince me, will you?"

Agnus doesn't notice what I did, and I feel momentarily guilty.

"I just want to help people, Anne."

"Ah, so you *are* in cahoots with my kidnappers!"

"No, Anne, oh no, you've misunderstood me." She holds her arms out to me and slowly rises to her feet. I move backward toward the wall. My breathing comes fast and heavy, and I consider running away.

"Anne . . . I'm a nurse, and I love my job. Every day, I feel like I am contributing—albeit in a very small way—to the world. God knows there's enough misery in it. We could all do with a bit of kindness, don't you think?"

I'm mystified.

"I'm making a difference to women, Anne. Women like Grace . . . and you. Especially you."

I fiddle with the strings on my gown and look at the floor, thinking. Why me? Does she mean "you" in the general sense of "you" or "you" as in, specifically, me? Is she trying to make it better for us poor, lost, kidnapped women?

I suppose it might make some ridiculous sort of sense.

"Listen," Agnus says, whispering. "Where do you suppose Ruth is right now?"

"Fat Ruth?" I say loudly.

"Shush, Anne! Just Ruth, plain and simple Ruth. Don't be so rude."

My good cheer returns.

"Well, Fat Ruth is busy chasing a suicidal hostage down from the roof." I smirk. "I heard her shouting as she wobbled down the corridor earlier. You know, she can't even run, she's that fat. The hostage is probably dead on the ground by now because she's so slow."

"Stop it, Anne."

"Sorry."

"I can see you're not. Well, listen, Ruth certainly doesn't appear to be within our vicinity right now, does she? In all likelihood she will be engaged for some time. . . ." She turns her head, left and right, right and left. "How about you and I retire for a cup of tea? It's past Grace's nap time anyway."

Perhaps I can steal her keys while she boils the water.

"That would be nice," I say, silently plotting.

When Grace is settled we venture to a small room that nobody uses. Agnus tells me it used to be the restraint room, but now that the hospital has lots of mobile restraints, it isn't needed anymore. She makes us a pot of tea while I sit down and pick at the table.

I don't try to steal her keys. I can't. She keeps them in her pocket, damn her.

"Thief," I say.

"Listen, Anne."

"Yes?"

"Be careful of Ruth. She is the leader here: of the nurses, that is. . . . Just last week there was a nasty incident involving a patient playing a game of backgammon with her," Agnus says, over her shoulder, as she stretches to retrieve two cups from the top cupboard.

They are not teacups: they are horrible, cheap, oversize *containers*. I shiver.

"Pardon?" I say.

"Don't irritate her, don't needle her, and for heaven's sake, never, *ever* call her 'Fat Ruth' to her face. She likes to act as if she has seniority here, above other employees, patients, and even the good doctor at times. Though the doctor doesn't stand for her when she does. She doesn't understand, like many of them here, I fear, the operations of the mind. And what she doesn't understand, she cannot tolerate, but she is not to blame for that. Entirely, anyway. Recently, she seems to almost be becoming a little crazy herself." She puts a dainty hand over her mouth and gasps. "Oh, I am sorry, Anne; I never meant to imply you were crazy, of course."

"Hmfph," I reply. She's crazy; they're all crazy. I'm the only non-crazy one here by all accounts. Crazy, crazy, crazy. "You speak French, right?"

"Yes, Anne, I do. Why is that so important to you?"

Oh, if only she knew. The only person who knows me in the whole world spoke French.

"I can tell all of my secrets in French," I say, mumbling. I am so desperate to tell someone—anyone.

Having stirred the tea, Agnus brings the cups over to the table, placing one in front of me and raising her own to her mouth. All five of her unadorned fingers squeeze the cup tightly. She blows on it as I make a show of peering at my dirty, dish-colored drink. She lowers her cup without tasting it.

"It's not poisoned, Anne. It may not be the best-sourced tea in the world, but it's all they supply us with here. Budgeting, or some such. Though I highly suspect drinking too much of it might be bad for our health, one cup won't kill you. Here—" She lifts my cup away from me and places her own in front of me. "Better?"

Marginally. I grunt. I can see her five uneducated fingers. "Where are the sandwiches?"

"No sandwiches, Anne."

"Well . . ." I take a small sip, and almost heave. "What about a sugar cube?"

"No sugar either, Anne."

I put my cup down and look at her. "Not even one, small cube?"

"Anne, why do you ask me this every single time you have tea? I must have told you this—oh, a dozen times or more. There. Is. Nothing. No sugar . . ." Her voice remains steady: She has the patience of a saint. She puts her cup beside mine and looks at me. "Anne, I brought you in here to ask you something. Or rather, to tell you something. Anne . . ." Her eyes dart around the room, and she quickly reaches across the table and takes hold of both my hands in hers. I struggle to maintain eye contact. I don't want to. "Anne, I am bound by confidentiality not to repeat anything you choose to tell me. I know I keep saying this to you, but, well, surely, you must want to speak to someone? Why not me?" She squeezes my hands. "God's truth, Anne."

Her hands are rough, working hands and I extract myself, picking up the poor excuse for my "tea." I stare into its depths, and wonder if I can see a face or two looking back. Agnus's voice cuts through the air. I have an idea.

"Do you want to hear something interesting?" I say, still not looking at her.

"Yes, I would love to, Anne."

I quickly reach over the table and grab the cups. Standing, I turn both of them upside down, my chair crashing to the floor, the horrible, poisoned tea splattering all over it and in between my bare toes. Ignoring her gasp, I lean my head back and perch both of the cups over my eyes. I stretch my arms out and twirl.

"Anne—"

I shout.

"You should really hold your teacup correctly, Agnus! It drives me crazy!"

"Anne, stop being ridiculous. Pick up your chair and sit back down." She says it in such a quiet, reasonable tone, that I can't help complying. Warmth surrounds my eyes, and I wonder if I've burned one of them. Oh well. I feel almost chastened. I do as she says and sit back in the chair, defeated.

"How much do they want for me? That's the only thing I want to tell *you*," I say. "I want to go home." I can't tell her the thing I really want to tell. I can't. Nobody in this world would understand, save two people, and neither of them is here.

MY HEART IS DEAD

Edgar
November 1st, 1885
Asquith Manor

There is blood on the walls. Anne is standing in front of me, holding a knife in her left hand. Anne, what have you done? I killed your mother, she replies.

She glides toward me slowly, her movements erratic and fast.

I killed your mother and I killed your son. I will kill myself soon and it will all be such fun. I'll slit my throat and I'll slit yours too. Then we can join John in hell and all shout Boo!

I wake with a jolt, the haunting taunt ringing in my ears. Sweat drips in rivulets, sticking my shirt to my back, and the sheets are soaked. The smell of copper hangs in the air, hijacked through my subconscious into the reality of the morning. A malevolent presence surrounds me and for a minute or two I bury myself deep under the covers.

One breath, two breaths . . . I count to ten slowly, filling my lungs with air that my dead son will never inhale ever again. In through my nose, blowing out gently through my mouth. A friend of mine forced this upon me once, minutes after I found John. Brandishing a brown paper bag, William had grabbed my head, pinned me with his hands, and suffocated me with it. The buzzing in my ears had quickly reduced in fever and pitch and I had rapidly begun to breathe normally: albeit with a bag attached to my face. I remember looking at William over my nose, over the bag, and wondering where on earth he produced a bag from when my wife had just murdered my only son. It seemed out of place, ridiculous somehow.

The day that Anne killed our child was the day I stopped breathing. I haven't been able to take a clear breath since. How can I, when half of me is dead?

John was my lifeline, my savior, my world, my heart, my soul. My very essence of life. How can the blood continue to run through my veins, when it ran out of his onto our kitchen floor? If my heart is dead, how am I alive?

A LIE BY OMISSION

Dr. Savage
November 1st, 1885
Bethlem Royal Hospital

Dear Dr. Savage,

It is with regret that I write to you rather than speaking with you face-to-face, but at present I am engaged in a rather tedious yet necessary business matter and will be away from London for a few weeks. Doctor, it has come to my attention that you have adopted a regime of mechanical restraint since the retirement of your eminent predecessor, Dr. William Rhys Williams. I shan't go so far as to echo the opinions of your contemporaries in labeling such methods as primeval; nor do I believe that in the future, you shall look back upon your defense of restraint with the same wonderment of those who encouraged domestic slavery. However, being aware of this issue arouses in me some sense of anxiety, as only a father whose own daughter is locked in such a place could appreciate. So, while I believe that your personal character is sufficient to serve your profession

*and henceforth my daughter well, I hereby request
that you do not put Anne under any restraints of this
manner, nor of any other, including that which is
termed "'chemical restraint."*

*I kindly beg you not to forget who I am, or the
contributions I make to the hospital.*

*Kindest Regards
Lord Damsbridge*

Folding the letter into eight, I bite my tongue and remind myself that
anger is poison.

It is one thing for a Lunacy Commissioner to attempt demands
and restrictions upon me, but for an amateur to instruct me in my
treatments—and with a rather clear sense of blackmail, at that! Lord
Damsbridge has the good fortune of birth and riches but the ignorance
of a peasant when it comes to the field of psychiatry. No doubt he has
read one of Dr. Bucknill's numerous articles and letters published in
the *Lancet*: that man has been doggedly pursuing his mission over the
past two decades to abolish the use of mechanical restraint throughout
the entirety of England. Damn journalists and their sensationalist
cosh! Their indulgence of one half-mad alienist could risk the very
future of psychiatry.

I pen a letter back:

Dear Lord Damsbridge,

*While I understand your concerns on the matter,
and agree to indulge you upon your request, I would
like to make my point known. First of all, I can only
assume, and, forgive me if my assumption has no
basis in fact, but I am fairly certain that you must
have read an article by the "eminent" Dr. Bucknill.*

While it would be improper of me to voice a negative opinion against a fellow doctor, I feel I have to say, quite forcefully, that he is wrong in his impressions. Mechanical restraint has been abused in the past, and regretfully, with that comes a sense of fear and public outrage against the practice. I am aware of this, and indeed aim to change such negative perceptions. Used sparingly, this method offers a substantial amount of freedom to those patients who would otherwise be controlled with the use of drugs: that is to say, medicated to the point of semiconsciousness by the chemical restraint to which you allude. I should be wanting in courage indeed, my lord, if I refrained from the use of those means simply based on their neglectful use and improper history. My profession has not yet reached the point of having fixed principles and so we are chiefly guided by experience. I am sure it will be of great comfort to you that I do not use these chemical methods on any of my patients. I must also impress upon you that Royal Bethlem Hospital prides itself on being an epicenter of excellence, providing a wide variety of methods of psychiatric investigation in the fields of both neurological and psychological research, and I value your very kind contributions. If you do not wish Lady Stanbury to take part in such, I will, of course, abide by your wishes.

Kindest Regards
Dr. George Savage

I omit mentioning the other research we perform, and the fact that Anne will be taking part in it.

Is a lie a lie by omission?

If so, I have just lied to a man who contributes thousands of pounds per year to this hospital.

And yet . . .

I consider myself to be a moral man and I abhor liars, but I cannot stand back and watch a young woman potentially be destroyed. Her father's ignorant and dogmatic incredulity with regard to a field he does not understand is dangerous.

After all, how long will it be before he blackmails me again, insisting his insane daughter is discharged while she is still mad? What if he does withdraw his funding? It is essential I work upon her quickly, for if he asserts his authority before she is cured, I fear for those around her. Lord Damsbridge himself would be in danger, though he does not recognize this fact. He is blinkered by his understandable, yet incredibly biased, feelings toward his own flesh and blood. He knows that she killed her child; he knows that she was insane. He wants her treated, and yet he deems to place rules and restrictions on my head! If I must apply treatments to Lady Stanbury away from the eyes and ears of her father, then so be it. There is nothing of more importance than the well-being of my patients.

I have no doubt that one day, this hospital will become the scientific and social center of the English lunacy world. I will prove to everyone that by adopting a wide variety of methods within psychiatry, we can cure almost every type of madness.

And one of my successes will be Anne.

I pen a second letter, this time to my close friend and eminent colleague, Dr. Daniel Hack Tuke, just in case he did not receive notification from Nurse Ruth. This trustee of Bethlem is a scientific sponge of a man who specializes in experimental psychology.

"Doctor?" Nurse Ruth peeks around my semiopen door. "Miss Fortier is here. Anne's maid—the lady she refers to as 'Beatrix.'"

"Wonderful," I say. What perfect timing. "Please show her in." Lady Stanbury's obsession with finding someone who speaks French implies to me something of importance between her and the maid.

Fortier is a name of French origin. It seems unlikely that this would be a mere coincidence, and mad as Anne is, most lunatics still retain some sort of grasp on reality. In this manner, there may be something I can use from their shared history that will allow me to establish a rapport with my patient. I have been looking forward to meeting the woman who now enters my office with a proud and dignified air.

"Miss Fortier, how wonderful to meet you. Thank you for making the journey to talk with me. Was it terribly long?"

"Not at all, sir. It's a good day for it."

The rain pounds against the window, and I thereby assume she is not referring to the weather.

"Miss Fortier, do you know why I asked you to come here today?"

She places her gloved hands delicately on her lap. "I do. You want to speak with me about my lady. How can I help you?"

"Tell me what sort of child she was."

"What do you mean, exactly?"

"Any trait in her character, any accomplishment she might possess, will play an important part in helping her trace her missing history, Miss Fortier. I want to know about her interests, her habits. Start when she was very young. Was she a playful child? An insolent child?"

Her eyes adopt a faraway glaze as she remembers, staring at a point slightly above and to the right of my head. With a deep intake of breath, she reverts her gaze to me and says, "She was a normal child, Doctor. Running amok around the fields, climbing trees, quite cheerful, considering her motherlessness. I tried to be some sort of substitute for that sad fact, though, of course, she considered her only friend in the world to be one of the servants, a girl her own age. I forget the child's name now. She did not view me as a friend then; she was more interested in exploring the woods and trees around her than she was in mathematics, French, music, art, or any other academic subject. Her interests lay in being a young girl, and playing with those around her."

"So you wouldn't say that she was a particularly gifted child?"

"No. I would say, with clarity, that she was a perfectly normal child, Doctor."

I open Anne's medical file and start writing.

No precocious traits as a child.

"Was she a nervous child?"

"No."

No nervousness in childhood.

Attacks of nervous disorder affecting the unstable developing nervous tissues of children can cause rapid and permanent degeneration. Had Anne suffered from this, it would most certainly have been a contributing factor to her current insanity. However, she appears to have been confident and happy.

Next is to focus on her education. Overeducation, or bad education, consists in the development of one side of the person at the expense or neglect of the rest.

"When she had her lessons, did you oblige her in that which she wanted to do with detriment to the rest?"

"No, Doctor. I taught her all manners of things, and she had lessons in each of them in equal amounts, whether she liked it or not. Despite what I said, when she wasn't off running around the grounds, she was an attentive and mediocre pupil."

"Did she excel or fail in any subjects?"

"No. She passed them adequately, and to the standard expected of a young woman."

"Any particular musical talent?"

"No."

"Artistic talent?"

"No."

"What of her accomplishments? Did she play the piano, the

zither?" Almost every well-educated lady can play at least a little of these. She shakes her head. "What about sketching, archery?"

"No. Well, she *can* play a tune on the piano . . . and by that, I mean one song. She used to play it over and over."

A surge of hope rises in my throat. "Was it 'Ride of the Valkyries'?"

She startles, blinks. "Yes. How on earth do you—"

I write a note.

Lady's maid has confirmed that that patient has recovered at least one memory. Patient mentioned that she remembered sitting around a piano, playing a song entitled "Ride of the Valkyries." This, according to her maid, is the only song she has ever been able to play.

Progress.

"Doctor?"

I wave an arm. "Continue, Miss Fortier, please. Was there anything else she enjoyed, any talent?"

"She excelled in reading, Doctor, and both she and I perceive this to be her accomplishment. She was an avid reader since a relatively early age. Naturally, Asquith Manor boasts a rather large library."

I don't like the sound of this. "Did she read alone?"

"Often."

"Did she continue reading into adulthood?"

"Yes, she did. Even now, she can almost always be found with a book in her hand." A look crosses her face and I'm not sure what to make of it. Is it smugness, or the hint of knowing something I do not? This woman gives me an uneasy feeling, and yet I cannot say how, or why.

Patient embraced useless book reading from an early age, allowed to educate herself through this means solitarily; most likely at the expense of social interaction. A certain element of defective education from a member of the weaker sex.

I frown at Miss Fortier. "You do recognize that a woman reading all sorts of . . ." I search for the word. " . . . sorts of . . . *rubbish* and stuffing her mind with useless nonsense is dangerous, don't you? Why, as her governess, would you allow this to happen?"

"She was, and remains, an intelligent person, sir. If she wanted to read, I let her do so. She didn't lose herself in fantasy or indulge in romance books. You never asked me what type of books she read. She learned astrology, politics, history, and nature through her books. They have served to improve her as a woman and I must say, I disagree with your rather old-fashioned sentiment indeed. Reading has helped her more than you will ever know."

Women. Most of them are bordering on the limits of insanity at the best of times.

I sigh. "Moving on, Miss Fortier. How was she during her pregnancy? I'm sure as the woman closest to her you would be aware of the most intimate details."

"Which pregnancy?"

I mentally deride myself. Of course, the miscarriage. I have seen these occur with frequency in the insane. Mother Nature steps in and procures the natural destruction of a child who runs a very great risk of being an idiot. As I said earlier, man is naturally choosy about finding a partner with whom to procreate. If he were to have intercourse with, say, a cripple, the outcome for the child would be very poor. Nature isolates, and kills that which she doesn't want repeated. Though I don't believe this to be the case with Lady Stanbury. No doubt, she merely overexerted herself.

"The second one, Miss Fortier. The pregnancy that led to her being here."

"Oh—well, she was anxious, of course. After all, if a woman knows ten or fifteen women, she probably knows someone who had died giving birth, or would later die. Isn't it true? Add into this equation that her own mother died in childbirth, and the loss of her first baby and, well . . ." She raises her arms, palms to the sky. "How would you expect her to feel?"

"I'd expect her to be naturally anxious. But did she do anything to console herself of these worries?"

She drops her hands back to her lap. "She read, Doctor. About everything."

"I don't really understand what reading would have done to comfort her—"

"Oh, it was more of a comfort than you'll ever realize, sir. She read all about pregnancy. She really is a talented reader. She even read some articles from the *Lancet.*"

My God. That's it. I start writing, quickly.

Anne was clearly distressed following the miscarriage she suffered. This grievance left Anne extremely susceptible to future mental problems. I do not believe that she fully mourned the loss of her first child, and when faced with her second pregnancy, she thereupon read any and all literature she could lay her hands on with regards to midwifery and childbirth in a misguided attempt to keep the second baby safe. This in turn filled her mind with apprehensions as to the horrors that might be in store for her, and she thus developed a cerebral disturbance.

 It is noteworthy here that Anne gained access to advice books, medical literature, and periodicals, and, having an intellect great enough to both understand and digest this information, Anne was open to terror and anxiousness regarding the impending birth of her second child.

 It is for this reason women should not educate themselves beyond affairs of the home.

I put down my pen; Miss Fortier has confirmed my suspicions. I know exactly what caused Anne's insanity.

Books. Women and their books.

"I think I have enough information, Miss Fortier. Thank you." I rise from my chair and call out to Nurse Ruth. Miss Fortier surprises me by being astute enough to catch my mood, for she instantly justifies her actions.

"I didn't mean to do her any harm, Doctor—"

"I'm sure you didn't. Yet you should have known enough as a governess to never let her read so much. You should never have encouraged her to become a *reader*. But the damage has already been done now, hasn't it? Unfortunately, Miss Fortier . . . women don't often think of the consequences of their actions until afterward. It is the nature of the beast."

The door opens. It is not Nurse Ruth, but Nurse Agnus. She smiles at me disarmingly. "I'm sorry, Doctor—Nurse Ruth had to chase a patient down from—oh!" She physically staggers backward when she sees Miss Fortier. "I didn't realize you had company. . . . Oh, Beatrix!" She moves forward as if to greet the older woman, but stops short. Her eyes flick to mine and she blushes. "I mean, Miss Fortier. I have heard much about you. How nice to finally meet you!"

I frown. "You know each other?"

"No," Miss Fortier says coolly, quickly. "I met her outside, just now." She turns to the young attendant, shakes her hand. "It was a pleasure to meet you, Nurse Agnus."

Women. Overly familiar, far too quickly. Left to gossip, by the end of the day they would be exchanging hair tips and putting lead on their faces. I interrupt. "Thank you, Miss Fortier. I bid you good day."

I want her out of my office. Yet she lingers.

"Sir," she says, rummaging in her purse, dropping it. She casts aside handkerchiefs and coins until she finds an envelope. "Could you give this to my lady? It's a very important letter, sir. She really needs to read it—"

I shake my head. "Nothing is more important, Miss Fortier, than the health and well-being of my patients. I don't think she needs any sort of outside stimulation or communication at this time."

Suddenly, Miss Fortier pales. Her lower lip wobbles and she

blinks, waves the letter up and down uselessly. "Sir, you have to give this to her. Please. It—"

"Is very important, yes." I snatch it out of her hand and throw it onto the desk. Women. Silly little women, who think that idle gossip and gushy letters are of any importance whatsoever.

"Tell her it's from me. Tell her that I needed to give it to her—"

"Fine. Once again, I bid you good day, Miss Fortier." I turn my back to her as she leaves the room, weeping.

I purposefully neglect to inform her that we don't, as a rule, pass communication on to patients.

FALLING APART

Edgar
November 1st, 1885
Asquith Manor

"Some people should be contented with their lot."

Splashing.

"Aye, I know—bastard pauper, lording it over us like, like . . ."

"Like a lord?"

Giggles, the spatter of water on tin.

"No, like a *bastard pauper.* I'll say it again. I'll say it ten times. He has no right to be here! At least we earn our bloody keep. And his face—Lord. Have you seen his eyes?"

"They're a bit . . . small."

"Shifty. Bloody shifty is what they are. His eyeballs roll around in his face. I'm never quite sure whether he's looking at me, for me, or away from me. It's creepy. Look at him, snoring, without a care in the world. Mouth open, catching flies, while our lady rots in some mad-house. It's not right, it's not. It's not bloody right. What I wouldn't give to pour a bit of this soap in—"

"*I* heard that he's in debt."

"Aye. Well, I'm not surprised. He's only interested in—careful, that water's bloody hot—the money. Beatrix said he had a visitor the other day too . . . and he *stole* something."

A low squeal of delight.

"Really?"

"Aye. She said the man was old and dirty, looked like a vagrant."

More splashing.

"How scandalous! Who do you think he was? We should tell Vicky."

"Vicky? The bloody scullery maid? We don't need to; little Betty can't keep a word in her head. Everyone knows now." A pause. "How can you *not* know?"

"Oh, I'm not one for gossip."

Low laughter.

I open an eye and look at the maids' backs.

"Oh, aye—you're a bloody liar, is what you are. You're the worst gossip of us all." The maid on the right playfully splashes her companion.

"Ouch! Mildred, that's hot!"

"Shush, be quiet! You'll wake him up!"

The wet maid points to her cheek. "Do you see a spot?"

"Aye."

"You've burnt me, you idiot. It better not leave a mark—"

"It won't. It's only bloody water. When have you ever known anyone to mark from water?"

"It's called a *scald*, Mildred. Jesus, you can be stupid sometimes."

Carefully, slowly, I ease the covers toward the end of the bed.

"Aye, well, at least we know it's hot enough."

I stand up. "Hot enough for what, ladies?"

Mildred shrieks and raises a hand to her chest while the other covers her mouth. They scramble to their feet.

"Oh! You frightened us for a minute there, sir." Mildred flusters with her dress, her collar. "I hope we didn't wake you. Here." She nudges the other maid, gestures toward the door. "We'll be on our way."

I raise myself to my full height, stretch. I've had enough of being treated like this, of being spoken about as if I were the devil. It ends today.

"No. Stay for a moment." They stare at me, and I realize I am naked from the waist up. "I have a bit of a problem. See, while I was quite entertained listening to your idle, inane chatter, I must admit that I didn't *quite* understand all of it. Help me out, ladies; tell me more. I'd love to hear your opinions about me and my *wife*."

They blush, look to the floor.

"No? You don't wish to help me with my problem?"

Silence.

"Would you like to know what my problem *is*? Let me tell you. My child is dead, and the woman I love is locked away in a madhouse."

Mildred sniffs, turns away.

"Despite this, you seem to have nothing better to do than gossip idly—and slanderously, I might add—about a grieving man. You don't know anything about me. You live and serve in this house to receive a roof over your head, food in your belly, and a salary, not to make assumptions about a man you have never spoken to, never acknowledged. You have never made me feel at home here, and I don't know what I did to make you hate me, but let me be honest. I despise you for it. You are the finishing touch upon my misery.

"It is not my fault that An—my wife—went mad. It is true that I may not be the best husband in the world, but I am learning. I just want my family back."

The maid with a mark on her face bursts into tears. "Oh, sir! We never meant . . . we never meant you any harm. I'm sorry. I mean, *we're* sorry. Aren't we, Mildred?"

Mildred fusses with her apron, straightens her hair. "I accept that you're grieving, sir, but I will never accept an equal as my master. You—"

"Mildred!"

"—are no better than the servants in this house, and I stand by that. I don't care if you despise me: The feeling is mutual. You insulted all of us by marrying above your station, and you deeply wronged the lady. I know all about inheritance, see, *sir*, and I firmly believe that she went mad because of you. If she had married a gentleman—a true gentleman—then she would have felt protected. Instead, she was the one looking after you, always making sure you had enough money in your pocket, ensuring that you had nice clothes." She looks me up and down, purses her lips. "You're weak. A true 'master' would never, ever explain himself to the help!"

"I—"

"It was too much for her, and because of it she became insane and killed the child. His death is on your head, and if you truly love Lady Anne, you should leave her alone. Go from this house. We all hate you for what you've done and I, for one, will never, ever forgive you. That poor little bairn . . ."

I've never done anything to make you hate me, I want to say. *I've never raised my voice or my hand. Why can't you see my suffering? Why won't you help me?*

Mildred makes a sound underneath her breath, and I see myself reflected in the twist of her sneer.

A man. A small, pathetic, sad little man who cannot inspire the least respect from those beneath him.

No more.

No longer will I beg for understanding and kindness.

"Whether you like me or not, I *am* the master of this house while Lord Damsbridge is not here," I say, marveling at my tone. Calm, assertive, without even a hint of the trembling in my heart. "Your opinion of me and the current situation is not important. What *is* important is my morning bath." I take a step toward them, gesture toward the washtub. "That looks too hot. I hope you were planning to fill it with some cold water too."

Mildred opens her mouth.

"Don't speak. From now on, I don't want to hear you. I don't want to see you. You will all blend into the shadows from now on, is that understood?"

The burned maid turns to Mildred. "Look at what you've gone and done now! That bloody trap of yours—"

"What did I just say?"

She blinks.

Good.

"Now that I've explained your role as my servants, I will tell you about my duties as your master. It's up to me to keep you safe, make sure you get your food, your medicine, visits, et cetera. I certainly don't want my maids having any accidents. They happen all the time. The servants' stairs are especially treacherous."

They stare at me, openmouthed.

"Those steps are ridiculously narrow. I've seen the way you have to turn your feet to the side just to take a step. I also know how carrying something heavy—let's say, a bucket of water—can tip one's body forward, throwing it off balance."

I smile at them.

"And to think, if such a thing were to happen, there's no banister to catch you if you fall. Now, take this water away and remember: It would greatly reduce your risk of death if you got the temperature right the first time."

At that, I turn my back upon the maids, leaving them with the trouble of removing a washtub full of boiling water. I walk across to the window and trace my fingers along the leaden squares.

No longer will I listen to whispers in the dark, walk among nudges and glances and gossip.

If they refuse to respect me, they shall fear me.

THUNDERCLOUD

Anne
November 1st, 1885
Bethlem Royal Hospital

"I hear you like to play the piano." The voice shocks me and I turn around quickly, ready to flee. Agnus grins at me and I almost smile back, before remembering that I have nothing to smile about.

Got to cover it up, got to bury the alum. I need to bleed now.

It is time.

"I don't know where you heard that," I say, continuing to dig my hole. "Don't you know that everyone in here is a liar?"

Agnus nudges me in the side and lies next to me on the grass. She kicks her feet back and forth, and I find myself worrying about grass stains. She points to the sky. "A storm is coming—look at the size of those clouds! How dark and depressing they are!" She plucks a piece of grass from the lawn, a sly smile on her face. Raising herself onto her elbows, she thrusts it at my face. "Just"—she jabs the blade into my nose—"like"—and again—"you." I swipe at her arm and she laughs, rolling onto her back. "Oh, Anne. You're nothing but a grumbly little thundercloud."

"I am not," I say petulantly.

"Oh, you most certainly are!" She rolls onto her side and squints at the growing pile of dirt. "Anne . . . are you trying to *dig* your way out?"

"No. Don't be ridiculous."

"Well, then, what *are* you doing?"

I flick at a piece of soil and it bounces off her hat.

"What does it *look* like I'm doing?" I say, matching her tone.

"Well, now . . ." She peers at the foot-deep hole. "I'd say you're digging a grave. And I know just who you'd like to put in it."

"Really?"

"Really. Her name begins with *R* and ends with *H*."

I shake my head. "No, her name starts with *F* and ends with *T*."

To my surprise, she bursts into happy peals of laughter.

"Ooo, you really don't like her, do you?" She sighs. "Here, shall I help? She drank the last of the milk this morning, so, for the moment at least, we have a common enemy."

I look at her perfectly pale hands, her beautifully cut nails. "But you . . . you're going to get filthy."

"Oh, Anne, I'm not afraid of a bit of dirt." She plunges a fist into the soil. "Though it's nice to hear you're concerned about my welfare."

I'm not, but I don't say so.

We sit and dig in companionable silence for an hour, and after a while it starts to rain. I expect Agnus to run inside at the first droplet, but she merely reaches up to pull my shawl tighter around me and smiles, oblivious, it seems, of her own discomfort. The water seeps through her hat, through her dress, and a river of rain runs down the side of her cheek, but she keeps going—thrusting her hands again and again into the hole that steadily fills with water. Another woman screeches past us, holding an iron bar up to the sky, and for a moment, I almost laugh. This tweak of my cheeks, the involuntary tugging of my mouth makes me realize that the tension has dropped out of my shoulders; my back feels a little straighter, my head a little lighter, my thoughts a little clearer.

I realize that I am sitting in a puddle of mud.

"Agnus . . ."

"Yes?"

"I'm really not very well, am I?"

She stops digging, and I throw the alum crystal in while she's distracted. Now it just looks like any other piece of dirt.

Oblivious, she raises her palms to me. The fingers are all crinkly and brown. "No, Anne, you're not. Why ever else do you suppose you're sitting outside, digging holes in a thunderstorm?"

GRAB A BUCKET

Edgar
November 1st, 1885
Asquith Manor

It takes the maids over an hour to fill the tub to my apparent satisfaction. I keep making them go back and forth to the kitchen—the water is still too hot, now it is too cold, now it is too hot again. Hatred burns in their tired joints, their aching limbs, their swollen feet.

It should make me feel worse, but it doesn't.

I feel much, much better.

I finally have control of the situation.

When at last I have had enough, I tell them to leave.

I go to my washbowl—satisfied—and splash water on my face. Blindly, I reach out for the towel, but instead, my hands settle around something hard and lumpy.

I open my eyes.

A wooden giraffe.

My dead son's only toy.

Oh-ho, the spiteful little bitches.

I turn the animal over in my hands, run a finger along its gently pointed ears, the depressions of its spots.

I was so happy when I bought this.

And now . . .

. . . I'm not.

I'm bloody fucking miserable, and most of all, I'm angry.

At the world. At these fucking circumstances I've found myself in. I never asked for this; I never wanted any of it. All I wanted was to be happy, but I didn't know how. How can anyone be happy if they've never been taught? All I learned from my father was how to become an alcoholic, a failure.

It was Anne who taught me about being happy. It meant a tickle in my stomach, a pleasurable feeling at seeing her face, walking around with a smile all the time for no apparent reason.

And it is Anne who has taken it all away.

My son.

My dead, poor, murdered little son.

Anne.

Anne, Anne, Anne, Anne.

You fucking murderous whore.

Furious, I launch the giraffe at the window. It bounces off the lead and lands safely upon the rug.

Not enough, not enough. I need to find something, hurt someone, *do* something.

I'm going out of my fucking mind.

I grab the half-finished bottle of whiskey from my bedside table and run out of the room, into the next. As I take a swig of ale, my eyes settle upon the crib. How have I slept in the room next to this every night? No wonder I have nightmares! I rush over to it and start kicking it repeatedly—alcohol sloshing everywhere—not stopping until the wooden slats crack and fall apart, not caring if I alarm the servants with the noise. Eventually, a pile of broken wood lies on the floor, which I scoop into my arms. Before I know what I am doing I am running along the hallways, lined with paintings of ancestors long deceased from this world, and then I am outside in the garden wearing nothing but my night wear, making a fire, upon which I make a pyre of the cot. The heat and smoke sting my eyes. I stare, and I drink.

"Oh my God!" The shout barely rouses my attention from the flames, the fire I am currently imagining Anne burning within. *Burn, whore, burn.* "Sir, oh dear!" Miss Fortier nearly runs straight into me, in such a hurry to get to my side. Why? What the fuck does she care? I bet she's in on the gossip too. I bet she's the one who started it. "Goodness heavens above! Fire! Sir, sir!—let me get some water, immediately! I'll fetch a bucket!"

I grab her arm as she turns.

"Don't bother, *Miss* Fortier," I say, stabbing the flames with a stick. "It's a good fire. A right bonny bonfire indeed. Poke it; look at the sparks it sends up."

Wide eyed, she glances down at my hand—my hand that still holds her. I release her with a jolt and turn back to the pyre. I throw the stick upon it as she rubs her arm.

"They used to burn women at the stake, you know," I say, watching the flames lick at the sky. "I think they still should."

"Sir, what *is* it you are burning? What if the land catches fire? Oh, sir . . ."

"It's my wood. I can do whatever I want with it."

"Sir—"

"Enough," I say, raising my voice.

Anne, you whore.

She dithers.

You fucking murderous whore.

"Return to your duties, Miss Fortier, and leave me be," I say.

Burn, burn, burn.

She looks to the bottle, and then to my face. "Sir . . ."

I wonder what she's thinking. I wonder how many people she's going to tell. I wonder why I don't feel ashamed. I look her in the eye as I take another gulp.

My silence unnerves her.

"Sir, I—"

I click my jaw.

The unspoken threat gives her pause, and she turns from me and runs back toward the house, lifting her long skirts high above the mud.

Maybe I can control myself; maybe I can't.

Maybe I can forgive myself; maybe I can't.

But I will *never* forgive that bitch for murdering my son.

Right now I could easily throw her into this fire and laugh while she burns.

Burn, burn, burn, burn.

Anne has ruined everything, *everything*.

My whole life is falling apart.

I finish the rest of the alcohol, let the smoke wash over my skin.

I will get my wife back.

I must.

The mother of my child, the murderer of my baby.

The love and the hate of my life.

SUPPING AT BELLADONNA

Anne
November 15th, 1885
Bethlem Royal Hospital

Mealtimes in the parlor are the worst.

"I keep telling them I'm not on drugs," says the woman opposite me, blinking slowly. "There's nothing wrong with my eyes. They are big and pretty, just as they should be."

I put down my spoon and study her. She has the largest pupils I have ever seen.

"You look like an owl, Mildred!" cries the woman sat next to her, giggling uncontrollably.

"You *do* have very large eyes," I say. "She's right. It's not very attractive. But at least you don't have a hooked nose, or crinkly skin."

"But what fault is it of mine? My mother has big eyes; so does my father."

"Some things are just inherited, I suppose," I say, returning to my soup. "It's not your fault. Blame your mother. She should have been more careful about who she lay with."

"Did you . . ." Her eyes protrude a little bit further. "Did you just insult my mother?" A crust of bread bounces off my forehead.

"Pardon?"

"I said"—she raises herself slowly from the table—"did you insult my mother?"

"Are you mad?"

"I—" She blusters with her skirt, her eyes growing larger. "How dare you!"

"Oh, it wasn't meant as an insult, Owl—what's your name?"

She squints, slowly tearing at another slice of loaf. "Florence. My name is Florence."

It is your name you should be concerned about, Anne.

Why?

"Florence, has anyone ever suggested that you are mad?"

"Of course she's mad. Her whole family has been supping at belladonna!" screams another inmate, poking Florence with a spoon. "Why do you suppose her eyes are so large?"

Florence rips the spoon out of her neighbor's hands and launches it across the room. "I don't *drink* belladonna, you idiot; I put it in my *eyes*. That's what I keep telling them. There's nothing wrong with wanting to be beautiful." She looks at me. "However, in answer to your question, it has been suggested, yes."

I notice how skinny she is, how she peels the bread to pieces but never actually eats any of it. I look at her knuckles, her wrists. The bones poke against the skin.

She has an eating disorder, a . . . oh no, it cannot be true . . .

"Florence," I say shakily. "Can you tell me where I am?"

She smooths her gown, sits back in her chair.

"Obviously, you are in a madhouse." She smiles at me. "Hasn't anyone told you that, dear?"

I feel very strange all of a sudden. I drop my spoon into the bowl and look around.

It is not my name you should be concerned about, Anne, but your own.

Why am I sat in a dining hall full of commoners? No, it's not even that. There is something very, very wrong with these women. They remind me of an underdeveloped cabinet card: their faces visible but unfocused, blurry around the edges. A fault in the development of life. And the other woman I met, weeks ago—the bald one with blisters on her scalp.

I jump to my feet and run out of the room. I turn into the corridor.

Look, Anne.

I run to the windows. Bars on all of them.

Look, Anne.

I grasp and pull every door handle I can find. Every one is locked.

Look, look, look. . . .

And suddenly I see, really see. I see everything I've seen a dozen, two dozen times, but it is as if I have been viewing them through water, or a heat haze. The women. The women. Dozens of them—just as I thought—but they are all wrong. Their smiling faces are missing teeth. Their flawless bodies have gained bruises. Their friendly expressions are blank, scratched, manic, uneven. They cry, shout, throw themselves against the walls—but they are not screaming for their freedom. The jailers are not hurting anyone—nurses, Anne, nurses—no, they are helping the women: caressing arms, wiping brows, soothing tempers, carrying linen, baskets, keys. There is not a man in sight. Everything is just as it was but wrong; details—*look, Anne, look*—gas lamps surrounded by metal bars, table edges wrapped in batting.

I bang my fists against my head.

What is happening to me? What have I done . . . ?

I fall to my knees with a sob.

Oh, dear, sweet, merciful Lord—what have I done?

"Anne!"

It is impossible that I have been kidnapped. I should have realized; how could I not have known? How could my mind conjure up such, such . . . madness?

"Anne!" Agnus catches me as I am about to crash forward.

"I feel ill, Agnus—oh my, I feel so sick. My stomach hurts and I think I'm going to vomit—"

"Anne—"

I grab hold of her hands and pull her arms around me.

"Please hold me, Agnus. Please. I don't know what's happened to me." I bury my head in her bosom and she pauses for a moment, before pulling me into a tight embrace.

"I don't know what I've done, but it hurts, Agnus—it hurts in my breast and I think I've done something awful. I feel as if I've jumped from a high building, or pushed someone off." I don't know how to describe the feeling that threatens to overwhelm me and I clutch her closer, tighter. I can't breathe.

"It's all right, Anne. You're safe. You're okay. I've got you, I've got you." She repeats the words over and over again as I let myself be held and rocked, rocked to sleep like a . . .

Baby.

"So you still don't remember anything before waking up here."

Baby. Somebody had a baby. Who?

"No, sir."

Not me. I'd know.

"Can you tell me where you are?"

The man—*doctor*—gestures with a hand, leans across the desk, and takes hold of my arm. I let it hang, limply.

"I'm in an asylum. I had some sort of . . . episode? Hysteria, I suppose."

His fingers search the edge of my wrist. "How do you feel about that?"

He presses, hard.

The doctor.

"Frightened, sir. Frightened and ashamed."

"Well," he says, frowning, letting my hand drop, "pulse is good, full. Slightly raised . . . There's absolutely nothing to be frightened about, Anne. And as for feeling ashamed, there is no need." He starts writing about me in a file; I know it's about me because I can see my own face, caught forever in a forgotten moment. When was that taken? Who took it? "However, Anne, you did *not* have an attack of hysteria." He rises from the desk and lights a cigar, blowing the smoke toward the ceiling.

"Put out your tongue, please," he says.

I do, the taste of smoke settling in my mouth.

"Hmm." He stubs the cigar out on his desk, next to a blotch. It looks like an ink stain, or blood.

He places his hands on my face. Squeezes. "Any pain about the face or head?"

I think, remember.

"Yes, I often have a pain." I pat my hair. "Just here. On the top."

"Hmm . . . are you menstruating?"

"No, sir."

His lips press together tightly. "Not completely unexpected. As soon as you recover your memory, I imagine your courses shall return to normal. Open your eyes for me. Wider. That's it." He pulls upon my lower eyelid, makes clucking sounds that remind me of a chicken. "No sign of anemia. Good, good . . . this is all very good."

"I—am I all right, then? Can I go home?"

He sighs. "You've made wonderful progress, Anne, but until you remember your cri—uh . . ." He swallows. " . . . the *incident*, I'm afraid I cannot, in good faith, discharge you. There's also the small matter of your physical health. It is imperative that you start menstruating, for one."

"Oh, I'm sure I will," I say, fiddling with the strings on my gown. "But how . . . I don't know what it is that I have supposedly forgotten, so how on earth am I supposed to remember?"

He stares at me, smiles.

"Very astute, Anne. A most reasonable question. I've already contacted a colleague of mine, a Dr. Tuke. He specializes in this sort of thing and arrives in the morning."

Morning.

"Well, then, I suppose I shall just have to wait a bit longer, shan't I?" I give him a wobbly, brave little smile. "But, Doctor—do you suppose I can have toast for my breakfast, please? I'm ever so bored of porridge."

He chuckles. "Thinking of your stomach, as always. Of course you can." He is back to the folder, scribbling furiously. Scratch, scratch, scratch.

"Thank you."

He dips a chin. "You can leave now, Anne. I'm finished here."

Of course you are.

And so am I.

MARRIAGES ARE UNHAPPY

Dr. Savage
November 22nd, 1885
Asquith Manor

"Thank you for coming to see me, Doctor. I fear I am not in a fit state to make the journey to the hospital today."

His hands shake as he lifts a glass of water to dry, cracked lips. His eyes are bloodshot, his face pale, his voice weak.

"Mr. Stanbury, you don't look at all well," I say, looking around. Having never stepped foot inside a house so grand before, I'm rather taken aback by the size of it. The furnishings appear to be influenced by some obscure European country, and splattered with Middle Eastern, possibly Arabic, figurines.

"Anne's mother, I believe," he says, noticing my gaze. "From what little I can gather, she liked to travel a lot before she became pregnant with Anne. Lord Damsbridge keeps her souvenirs around, I guess as some sort of shrine to his lost wife. She loved France, apparently." He shrugs. "I suppose it shan't be long till I shall be making a shrine to Anne, smelling her nightgowns, and going to sleep caressing them."

I frown. "Why would you think that, Mr. Stanbury?"

"I—oh, no reason." His face crumples. "I've been thinking some awful things, Doctor—things I'm too ashamed to tell you about. When I finally realized that she, she . . . killed our baby, and it was no mistake, I . . . I had some really dark ideas." He shakes his head. "I don't know. I'm confused. I miss her, Doctor—terribly, but at the same time . . . well. It's something we'll work through together, I suppose." He sinks a little lower into the chair, his shoulders slumped. "I am not a bad person, Doctor, despite rumors to the contrary. I may have made some bad decisions in the past, but one thing is the God's honest truth: I loved her. I really did at the end."

"Rumors? What about?"

"Oh, me. The servants, you know. They hate me." He sighs. "I was happier before, when I didn't have to pose. When I didn't have to constantly watch my q's and mind my t's. When I didn't have to put myself above the servants, but sit among them. I'm a fake, Doctor, and they know it. They've got nothing better to do with their time than gossip. You'd never think they had actual jobs to do. No, they prefer to spend their time taunting me, provoking me. Whispering behind my back. That sort of thing. I swear they've been coming into my room too while I've been asleep. I put a layer of bran along the floor last night, to check, and this morning it was disturbed."

"Mr. Stanbury, you . . ." I trail off, stunned. *Bran* on the floor? "Why do you think they're coming into your room?"

He shakes his head. "I don't know. I don't know anything anymore. I suspect they're searching for something. Sometimes I find my drawers have been rifled through: papers moved, letters missing . . ."

I smile, minutely, worried that he may be suffering from acute delirious mania. "Mr. Stanbury, grief can cause depression and melancholy—which is all very normal—but occasionally it can put some very strange thoughts in your mind, making you see and feel things that may not be real. Have you seen anything that shouldn't be there, hearing voices, anything like that?"

He surprises me then.

He laughs.

"Oh, Doctor. I don't envy you. I can't imagine what it must be like, wondering if everyone you meet is mad. No. Although I almost wish I did have a voice in my head, it's been so long since anyone spoke to me. It's just . . ." He lowers his head. "I miss my wife, but I don't know if I can love her anymore. Do you understand that? I can't . . . I can't solve the absurdity of someone I love killing someone I love. I just—" The great clock on the wall strikes the hour, and he flinches. "You see? God, I'm a mess."

"Mr. Stanbury, most men don't *ever* love their wives. Not at the altar, not even on their deathbed. They go through a life together built out of convenience and nothing more. Marriage is rarely for a joining of minds and hearts; most marriages are unhappy, and half the reason my profession exists. You two had something that most people are never lucky enough to experience, and I truly believe you can get it back."

He looks up at me, sharply. "What's the other half?"

" 'The other half'?"

"Of your profession, why it exists."

I look at the picture of Anne's mother. "Women, Mr. Stanbury. They accomplish fifty percent of the world's madness simply by being born female."

For the first time since my arrival, his eyes flash with a light akin to interest.

"That doesn't surprise me one bit, Doctor."

"Nor me. I do have some good news for you, though."

He squints.

"Anne is progressing. She no longer suffers from delusions, and accepts that she is in an asylum. She still can't remember you or your son, but that's perfectly normal at this point. A colleague of mine will be visiting Bethlem in the coming days and together, we are going to attempt to bring out these lost memories of hers. Isn't that wonderful?"

He stares at me, silent, his eyes filling with tears.

"Mr. Stanbury?"

"I—I don't know what to say. What does this mean, exactly?"

"It means that she is no longer in isolation. She's doing wonderfully. She's made friends with one of the nurses—Agnus—and some of the other patients. She—"

"Agnus?"

"Yes, sorry, one of our newer nurses. She is recovering, Stanbury. I'm fairly sure she will be home within months, if not weeks."

The expected reaction doesn't come. He doesn't laugh, doesn't cheer. He doesn't even smile. Instead, he sighs heavily and I detect a faint whiff of sour ale.

"Stanbury, are you drinking a lot?"

He mumbles something under his breath.

"Stanbury?"

"No." He answers the question angrily, defiantly. "Well, a little. Yes, I suppose so. But what do you expect? I've lost my child, Doctor. You tell me my wife is progressing, but as of now, I don't know if I even care. I don't know if I want her back or not. I don't know if I love her or hate her. I don't know how I'm going to react to seeing her. But then, she's put me in quite a position. One in which I need her." He stretches out an arm, points. "See the desk over there? That's not mine. Nor is the floor, the windows, the door, the figurines; hell, I'm only here from the kindness of Lord Damsbridge, and how long do you suppose that will last?" He wipes a hand across his brow. "How did I imagine I could merely step into a gentleman's shoes, and expect to walk as one?"

"What do you mean—"

"Do you realize, Doctor, that I have no claim over anything here? I could quite literally be thrown out, rightly or not depending on your point of view, at any time. I told you that the servants hate me. Every time I walk into a room, they all become silent. I *know* they are talking about me, making fun of me. I *know* that they've been going through my things. Two of the maids filled my washtub with boiling water the other day—they tried to *hurt m*e, Doctor! I've gotten myself into a bloody situation here that I can't control. I—fuck it. . . ."

He leans over the chair and pulls a bell rope.

"Yes, sir?" An old man enters, dressed immaculately in a uniform that clearly denotes him as the butler of the household.

"A bottle of whiskey, please."

"Yes, sir."

While this brief exchange between master and servant occurs, I ponder whether to further mention his drinking. The man is in a difficult position. His grief and confusion have led him to drink, and yet I have had many a person admitted to the asylum for this reason. Grief, anxiety, and depression, topped with acute alcoholism: He worries me. He is already displaying delusions of persecution—the servants filling a tub with scalding water? I doubt it. A man who drinks is liable to suspect people and plots of all kind. There is no man more dangerous than a drunkard with suspicions. Such a person is likely to carry about a weapon and use it, out of a misaligned need for revenge, jealousy, or just plain old hallucinations.

"She hid the pregnancy from me for five months, Doctor."

"Pardon?"

"For five whole, long months. I should have known something was wrong when she wouldn't lie with me anymore."

"Hid the pregnancy? You'd notice, surely. She isn't some peasant without a husband. How could she possibly have thought she would get away with it?"

He laughs, bitterly. "She's rich, Doctor. Haven't you noticed? We have the luxury of separate rooms. She didn't even have to change her normal clothes to hide it—she always wore fully boned corsets during the day anyway, and at night she undressed in private and then donned her normal nightgown, which was very loose. We only occupied the same bed when we were . . . you know. And even *that* became very irregular since the miscarriage."

Concealment of pregnancy is against the law, for good reason.

"Why? Why would she hide her pregnancy?"

He takes a long, slow sip of his ale. "I don't *know*, Doctor, and that's the point. She said it was because she wanted to make sure the baby was viable, didn't want *me* to go through the misery of losing another child before it was born. But now . . ." He trails off, runs a finger around the edge of his glass. "Now I just don't know. I didn't support her after the miscarriage. I found it—and this is going to sound terrible—underwhelming. She was only a couple of months along; they're not even a real child at that point, are they? I mean, they haven't grown enough. The baby is not really a *baby* until it's born, is it? So I wasn't upset like she was. It didn't feel like a big loss to me. So when she said she was protecting me . . . she was lying. She had to have been; it doesn't make sense. Could that have been a sign of her impending insanity? Did I miss the warning signs? I'm just so confused." He sighs. "I just wish that I had been able to prevent John's death."

"I—" I am momentarily lost for words. There are other reasons that she may have hidden the pregnancy, reasons that I don't want to consider. Reasons that surely do not apply to a woman of such standing. I wave my misapprehension away.

"Mr. Stanbury, I don't think there's anything you could have done to prevent what happened; I think you're looking for signs when there weren't any. You feel responsible, and I understand that. But in all likelihood, she spoke the truth. Women are strange creatures, and the sooner you accept that, the happier you will be."

"Perhaps." He looks at his empty glass sadly.

"Look," I say with a joviality I don't feel. "I would like you to try something." I pick up the bag that I carry everywhere and pull out an item.

"How are you sleeping?" I ask him as I hold the item in my hands.

"In fits and bouts. I have nightmares."

As I thought.

"About your child?"

"Yes. And Anne." He fills another measure, and I notice how wrinkled his clothes are. I suspect he slept in them. "Do you have any friends you could call upon?"

"None."

"What about hobbies, interests? Do you enjoy entertainment, the theater, for example?"

He laughs and says, bitterly, "It was the damn theater that started all this. Damn William the Fourth and Dorothea Bland to merry hell." He raises his glass. "God bless you, Grandmother."

I realize he is drunk already, and what I supposed was his first glass of the day is probably his fifth, or sixth.

"Why did you call me here today, Stanbury?"

He looks at me with a forgotten expression. "Well, because I wanted an update on my wife, of course."

"Nothing else?"

He frowns at me. "Such as what, Doctor?"

"Help, perhaps?"

"'Help'? For what?"

I shake my head, and offer him the object from my bag.

"What is that?"

"Chloral." A temporary prop to the drunken. Though there is danger from chloral, there is aid to be gotten from it too. "I don't normally like to prescribe it, but . . . you need to start getting some rest. You need to be strong for your wife. It's a sedative and a hypnotic and will help you sleep. Mr. Stanbury . . . I'm worried about you."

He takes the bottle from me, eyeing it suspiciously. "Don't worry about me, Doctor. I'll be fine. It's just a phase, I'm sure. I'll get through it with the help of good old ale."

"There is one thing, though, Mr. Stanbury."

"What?"

"It is incredibly dangerous to take this with alcohol. You must stop drinking at once."

He laughs and puts the bottle of chloral in his pocket.

"Doctor, drinking is the only thing keeping me from *joining* my wife in the madhouse right now."

"I assure you, Mr. Stanbury, alcohol is not a coping mechanism.

Are you aware of how many alcoholics I have in my asylum? Too many to count. Nay, alcohol is not stopping you from going mad, but it *will* drive you mad. You must listen to me." I reach out to him and he flinches, withdrawing from me. Tears dance in his eyes.

"Stanbury," I say gently, dropping the prefix. "Take some drops tomorrow evening: not tonight, as if you take them on top of alcohol the side effects, as I mentioned already, can be quite unpleasant. Take them tomorrow on a clear head, and get a couple of good nights' rest. I'm sure that afterward, you will be feeling more like yourself." I pick up my bag and walk to him, placing my hand on his shoulder. Sometimes simple human warmth can do wonders for a lost person. Within seconds, his shoulders start to shake underneath my fingers, and I give the man his dignity by pretending not to notice.

At last I give him a firm squeeze and wish him good-bye, leaving quickly to the muffled sounds of his sobs echoing in the empty room behind me.

He is a man whose tastes and temperament keep him apart from the rest of the world, and I don't know how best to help him.

THEATRIC SOMNAMBULIST

Anne
December 1st, 1885
Bethlem Royal Hospital

"Anne, wake up."

I open an eye and peer into the darkness.

"No." I pull the blanket over my head. "It's the middle of the bloody night. Later. Go away."

The covers are whipped from my body, and a lantern shines in my face.

"Agnus!" I hit out at the light and scramble up the bed. "Give those back!"

She throws them into the shadows.

"It's not the 'middle of the night,' Anne. It's already five."

"And what sort of hour is *that* for starting the day?" I cross my arms and try to control my temper. "Seriously, Agnus—please. It's cold, and I'm tired. Give me another ten minutes."

"Anne, if everybody in the world was ten minutes late for work, what do you think would happen?"

My eyes are stinging. I try to keep them open, but I'm so, so tired.

"Agnus, if everyone woke up to find themselves in a madhouse, what do *you* think would happen?"

"I would be queen, of course."

"What?"

"I'm not mad. So, think about it. The one-eyed man rules, in the kingdom of the blind."

"What?"

"It's 'pardon,' Anne, not 'what.'"

Oh, it's too early for such nonsense.

I get out of bed and scrabble around on the floor.

"I'm tired, Agnus, because last night was the first night I truly realized that I'm surrounded by lunatics. My very life is in danger here." Where is the blanket? "I couldn't sleep a beat because I kept expecting one of those crazy women to come in and eat my liver. I don't want to get up unless it is to go home."

"Anne." The sound of fabric scraping across the floor. "You're not having the blanket. Seriously. Come on, Dr. Tuke has traveled all this way especially for you. Afterward, I'll make you a cup of tea."

I want to stamp my foot. Throw something.

"With a sugar cube. The doctor gave me some, especially for you."

I'll bet he did.

Grumbling, I follow her out of the room.

"Aha, there you are! Good morning to you both!" Dr. Savage opens his door with a flourish and a smile, one arm wrapped loosely around the shoulder of an older gentleman. "Come in, come in!" He pats the man on the shoulder, detaches himself, and opens the door wider. Agnus and I dip a curtsey. "What a fantastic morning this is, ladies! My old friend, here at last!" Happiness and excitement permeate the air, fighting for room with the smoke. "This, ladies, is Dr. Tuke. He is both a trustee of Bethlem and a world-renowned specialist in psychic analysis. That is to say, artificial somnambulism."

I scrutinize him. He is taller than Dr. Savage, but very, very slight.

His skin is almost gray, and he wears a jacket with some strange sort of red and black star on it.

I ask him what it means.

"It's a symbol, Anne. It means I am a friend, both in the literal and symbolic sense. A friend to the world, and to you."

Well . . .

"And what is 'artificial somnambulism'?"

"A fancy name for hypnotism, Anne. Now come, sit." He points to a newly appointed chaise longue. "Sit—excuse me—I mean, lie. Lie down, dear. That's it."

Suddenly, I feel very exposed and vulnerable. "This won't hurt, will it?"

He engages me with a wide grin. "No, not a dot. Have you ever been hypnotized before, Anne?"

"Hyp—what?"

"Hypnotism, dear. Mesmerism, if you prefer."

"Uh—no. At least, I don't believe so. I'm not entirely sure what it entails."

He snorts.

"Not surprising." He looks over his shoulder. "It's rather hated in England—now, isn't it, Savage?"

Dr. Savage groans. "Only because they invented ether."

Dr. Tuke chuckles. He puts a hand on my forehead. "Don't worry, dear. It's ever so popular over in France, and I use it with great success at the Retreat. Now, I am going to try to put you to sleep. This is normally successful in around fifty percent of people and, would you believe, one hundred percent of frogs and fowl. Remember: I am a doctor of medicine, and have sworn by the Hippocratic oath."

Agnus lifts up her lamp, illuminating the doctor. I don't believe in hypnotism, so I have absolutely no fear of it. I am slightly scared, however, to be faced with my memories.

Dr. Tuke kneels on the floor beside my head. "That's it, Anne. Lie back, flat if you can. That's right. Are you comfortable? Good." He rummages through a pocket and pulls out a watch.

I laugh out loud.

"Is something amusing, Anne?"

"I'm sorry, Doctor . . . Yes, it's just . . . when I was mad, I believe I had a fixation with wanting to know the time." I gesture toward the timepiece. "I could have done with one of those a week or two ago."

"She did," says Agnus, and I am pleasantly reminded that she is still in the room. "She was always asking for a stick, and—"

Dr. Tuke swivels. "Quite, madam. However, I need absolute silence for this to work. Please mind your manners or leave the room."

Agnus opens her mouth, but I quickly answer for her.

"Nurse Agnus didn't mean to be rude, Doctor. She's just trying to help. She has been very kind to me over the months, and I would like her to stay."

Agnus blushes.

I smile.

"Please."

"Well," Dr. Tuke says, "all right. Now silence, everyone. Thank you. Anne." He leans over and dangles the watch about eighteen inches above my face. "Can you see the numbers and the hands clearly?"

"I can," I say, not sure if I'm supposed to speak or nod.

"Excellent. Now, I want you to maintain your gaze upon it. Do not look at me, do not look at Dr. Savage, and do not look at Nurse Agnus. Do not deviate from the watch—do you understand?"

"Yes," I say again quietly. This is ridiculous. What a bunch of quacks.

"Savage, with the means of this watch, I am going to attempt to induce a cataleptic state. Please write down everything you observe."

"I will."

"Anne, carefully follow the second hand with your eyes—not your head, just your eyes. I want you to keep watching until it has swept its way around an entire circle of one minute. Can you do that?"

I can. I watch closely, curious. Will it suddenly burst into a magical ray of light? Will rainbows dance above my head, with flying pigs and unicorns? It is five and thirty exactly. The hands are a beautiful ornate and tarnished gold, the face a rather unsettling and curious blue.

"Has it moved all the way around?"

"Yes," I say, blinking, still staring at the blue, feeling slightly ridiculous.

"Grab hold of the watch for me, please."

I lean forward and lift my head, intent on snatching it out of his hands, but surprisingly, my fingers brush nothing but air.

"Face expressionless, eyes fixed. Savage, we have induced the first state."

"Marvelous."

"Anne, you are now unable to speak."

Why not? The words form inside my head, but stick inside my gums. My tongue is full, invading my mouth—it is too large to move, too wide to create words. *What did you do?* Something is wrong. What has he done? Dear Lord, they've given me a stroke. A torrent of fear shudders up my spine and I spring upright, panicked, yet as quickly as the fear came it is gone, replaced by a feeling of sleepiness, haziness. I lie back, comfortable, relaxed. The clock is in front of me again and all I can do is stare at its face: its beautiful, ornate face. The face is blue; the hands are gold. The face is blue; the hands are gold. Blue, gold, blue, gold—the colors whirl, faster and faster until they join together in a blur and suddenly it is taken away.

"Tell me your name."

I can't, I can't open my mouth. . . .

"Muscles of articulation suspended, Savage. You are writing all this down, aren't you?"

"I am, Tuke."

"Good. Everything she does and says too, please. Anne, I want you to sit up."

I do. I want the watch. I need the watch.

He holds it in his hand.

"Place your right hand, palm down, on top of the watch."

I should be surprised to feel my arm move of its own accord, but I am not; it all feels so wonderfully . . . normal. The watch, the watch, the watch, the watch.

"Now, Anne, you are unable to take your hand from the watch. You shall follow wherever it may lead, even if you do not wish to do so." He stands up and my legs follow, our hands forming two sides of a perfect oyster, the watch a pearl, and in this curious position we walk across the room. I am dimly aware of other people—somebody moving out of our way—but I can't think who they are, nor do I care. I cannot resist; I do not want to resist. But suddenly he pulls away from me—he takes the watch and I am left standing with my arm outstretched, confused. . . . He pockets the piece and pulls out a pencil.

"Anne, this pencil is red hot."

And before I can move, he places it on my arm.

A burning, horribly intense pain overwhelms me and I pull away, horrified.

"Did that burn you? You may answer the question."

"Yes!" Tears well in my eyes and I want to cry, I want to tell him that he tricked me, he promised he wouldn't *hurt* me and yet he did, he *burned* me and it really, really hurts and I cradle my arm underneath the other. Water, I need water. That's what you do for burns, you put them under water, but it has to be cold, not too cold—otherwise it makes the burn worse—and he is looking at me and I don't hear my voice, oh no, the words are not coming out—they are bouncing off my teeth and my tongue is too large again; there is no room in my mouth for them; they—

"Good. Very good. Anne, put your arm back in the outstretched position."

No, no! It hurts, no, please don't make me, why are you doing this to me? I never hurt you, I never hurt anyone, ever. My arm is moving, no, no, no, why—

"This time, Anne, when I place the pencil on your arm you are quite unable to move away. Here it is and again, it is hot."

Oh, dear Lord, the pain, the pain, my skin is sizzling like a pig on a stick, a stick—how funny—and the words, they are not words; they are a scream and I am silently screaming and everything is red, red, and red.

"Did that burn you? You may speak. You may move."

"Yes!" I'm crying and I sit on the floor. Oh God, I can't bear it. Mucus bubbles in my nostrils; saliva drips from the side of my mouth. I'm drooling now, dripping spit like an idiot, and oh God, this is what they do. This is how they make you really mad. I'm going to become insane and it's all my own fault for being here. I should never have—

"This is brilliant, Tuke!" a voice says from somewhere inside the haze, deep within the red—why isn't somebody fetching me some water? Why aren't they taking me to a hospital? It hurts, it burns . . .

"I know. Wonderful, isn't it? She's very suggestible."

"I would never have thought—she really believes she has been burnt! Induced hyperalgesia. Remarkable! This is one for the books."

"It is. I will be sure to acknowledge you, my friend."

"How are her vitals?"

My arm is burning; everything is red—suddenly, a flash of white light. I'm blind; they burned my eyes!

"Pupils are slightly dilated."

"Marvelous."

"Reflexes?"

Somebody hits me in the knee.

"Knee jerk unaltered; no ankle clonus."

"Sensation?"

"Hold on, I'll prick her."

A light pressure upon my foot.

"Analgesia complete, no reaction to the pin. She can only feel what we tell her she feels. They should never have stopped using hypnosis for surgery, the ignorant louts."

"I agree, my friend, I agree. What's next?"

"We should probably stop her arm burning, poor thing." The red voice takes hold of my arm and I can smell somebody's breath—sour, riddled with cigars. "Here, Anne, there is no more pain," the voice says, and it is true—the burn is gone, the blister has popped, the fire has been doused.

"Breathing is becoming slower."

"That's because she's not in pain anymore."

"Shall we put her under now?"

"Yes. Anne, listen to me. Close your eyes. Close your mouth."

I must be underwater now because everything is cool and calm, the redness has turned to blue, the voice is muffled.

"How long now?"

"Not long. Less than a minute. Anne, you can no longer breathe."

And the water is deep; it's over my head. I struggle for the surface, but there is none, the blue is becoming darker and darker, and oh, I can't breathe, my lungs are bursting, bright lights sparkle behind my eyelids, and—

"Anne, you are dead."

—and I fall backward; my back hits something solid—it feels like a floor, but how can it be? I am underwater and my eyes are closed, my mouth is closed, my lungs are closed, dark bubbles burst in front of me, and the blue fades to black.

The voice is right.

I am dead.

ONLY WAY I KNEW HOW

Dr. Savage
December 1st, 1885
Bethlem Royal Hospital

"I see Geoffrey has not found himself yet," Tuke muses, gesturing to a long-haired man who is crouched by the side of a rosebush, digging a hole with his bare hands. "He might be a good candidate for our work, Savage." Seeing us, Geoffrey waves enthusiastically for a moment before resuming a compulsion of twenty years.

"He's already been hypnotised on numerous occasions; unsuccessfully, I might add, by Mr. Smith."

"Mr. Smith from the Royal Psychical Society, I presume?"

"The one and only," I say, glancing around the garden with some frustration. "I wonder if we should ask him for a third opinion regarding Lady Stanbury's revelation." Under a deep somnambulistic state, Lady Stanbury told us about the night of the murder, and her disclosure was most disturbing. "Is it possible she was telling the truth?"

Tuke tuts. "No, Savage. You and I both know that a deep hypnotic state is capable—indeed *likely* in some subjects—of producing delusions. The lady seemed to be an excellent fit for hypnosis—loss of memory, suggestible, especially in the first ten minutes—but once again the experiment failed. She's just not ready to face up to what she has done. Though she can't continue to believe that she has been kidnapped anymore—there is too much evidence around her to the contrary—she simply cannot, *will* not, accept the fact that she killed her child. You said she was intelligent, educated, that she read a lot, right?"

"Right."

"There you have it. That sort of thing is in the newspapers every single day. Undoubtedly, she read something in the *Daily Telegraph,* and her subconscious has thrown it up as a delusion during hypnosis. A delusion that is slightly more believable and rational than the rest, I agree, but still a delusion and nothing more. Delusions come from the person's experiences, Savage. Take the man who believes his brothers are swindling him, plotting to kill him to take over his business. This is quite rational. But in context, it's probably a delusion. Anne can't accept that her baby is dead. That's all, Savage. Sometimes you worry over nothing." He frowns. "She had all the physical symptoms of puerperal mania, did she not?"

"She did," I say, and then I remember. "But she didn't have a fever, as I would normally expect."

"Pah." Tuke laughs, claps me on the back. "I've had many an insane patient without a raised temperature, Savage. What is it about this woman that worries you so much?"

"I—" I don't know. I can't put my finger on it.

"My friend, when you hear hooves, don't waste your time looking for zebras. Order a good bout of hydrotherapy for her, and be done with it." Tuke gestures to Geoffrey. "Geoffrey, young man, how are you on this fine and pleasant morning? Eating soil again?"

The man is filthy, his face and fingernails blackened with soil and all manners of dirt.

"Aye, sir. I think I've finally found meself, though. I'm under that there bush, right over there. I found some sort of crystal too, but I ate it. It's given me a bit of stomachache."

"That's a pity. It may have been worth some money."

Geoffrey's face sags. "Do you think so? Oh, p'raps I shouldn't have eaten it. It was white and clear but a bit dirty, ye know, and it smelt like a woman."

"Stones smelling of women now, 'ey? Whatever next?"

"It did, sir," he says, indignant. "I know what a woman's scent is, and I'm tellin' you, it smelt like a goddamn *woman*."

Tuke smiles. "What did it taste of, then?"

Geoffrey grimaces. "A bit salty, sour, coppery, like. It made me mouth pucker, like eating a lemon. Hey, do you think you can you 'elp me dig meself up?"

Tuke looks to me. I shrug. "I'm an old man, Geoffrey. I shan't be doing any digging at all. If I did, I fully expect it would be my own grave I should fall into once I was finished!"

Geoffrey frowns. "Do ye suppose *I'm* dead, then, sir? Could that be me very own body buried under there?" He looks around him. "P'raps I should leave meself there, then, like. I don't fancy seein' me own body if it's dead."

"How about going inside and having a nice pot of tea, instead?"

Geoffrey licks his lips, a white circle appearing around his mouth. "I'll do that, sir. What a good idea! Have a good day, gentlemen." He walks away, making an odd sort of snorting, hitching sound.

Tuke's beard flutters in the breeze, and as I watch him watching the patient leave, I suddenly feel . . . bereft. It's been a long time since I saw my old friend, and even longer since he treated patients—twenty years. Already. In that time, tuberculosis has worn away at his frame, eaten his skin. How fast time falls from underneath our feet.

The difference a day can make; an hour, a minute.

Thirty seconds.

How long does it take to smother a baby?

"How are you, these days? How's your chest?"

"Me?" He rubs his hands together, blows, stamps his feet. "My lungs are just fine, Savage. I've never felt better. Right now, though,

I'm bloody cold. Oh, Savage—get that sad look off your face. It's insulting, and it doesn't suit you. I'm fine, perfectly fine. Now, shall we go and finish our notes on the young lady? The sooner we finish, the quicker we can retire ourselves."

"Sounds like a marvelous idea, my friend," I say. He puts a bony arm around my shoulder and I think of his skeleton; I think of death.

The gravel crunches underneath my feet as Lady Stanbury's words echo inside my mind.

"I couldn't let him take my baby; I wouldn't let him take him away.

"I took him away first."

"Remember, Savage, even the insane are made in the image of God. We might not understand His plan, but He has one."

Does his plan include mothers killing their own children? I want to ask, but I don't.

I already know the answer.

It happens every day.

"I did it because I love my child. Wouldn't any mother care to do the same? I didn't feel guilty when the blood ran over my hands, yet neither did I feel vindicated. I just felt I had protected my child in the only way I knew how."

Yet there is a world of difference between killing a child accidentally, in a fit of insanity, and murdering an innocent baby in cold blood.

"I knew exactly what I was doing, and I'd do it again."

BACKSIDE OF A HORSE

Anne
December 20th, 1885
Bethlem Royal Hospital

"Argh!" I yell loudly at Fat Ruth. "Why don't you put your own filthy, stinking backside of a horse in here instead? Argh!" My head is dunked again and the coldness of the water numbs both my skin and senses. Her fat hands release my head, and I splutter at the surface, enraged. How dare she instigate such cruel treatment, against anyone, for any reason? "What exactly are you trying to do, kill me?"

I scream.

"How I would love to, Anne, but no, I'm not. This is a treatment for crazy people and will restore you to sanity. Plus, I remember well you pouring your filth over me, and I think a girl such as you needs to learn some cleanliness." I am dunked again. Underneath the frigid water all sound disappears, apart from the heartbeat pounding in my ears. Dear Lord, how is this supposed to make anyone well? The coldness turns into a thousand hot pins, pricking my skin all over.

"This is enough to make a sane person insane!" I shout when the pressure on my head is relieved for mere seconds. "You fat, fiendish elephant!" Back under I go. I don't know how many times this happens, nor do I have any sense of how long I am kept in the ice-cold water. Long enough for me to start daydreaming. I can feel my grasp on consciousness ebbing. I'm drowning. The white-glazed tiles covering the walls start to turn gray and fuzzy.

Hands grab me, lift me, and start roughly rubbing me with a towel. "This towel stinks!" I manage to shout, but my voice is muffled by another towel promptly wrapped around my head and face.

Oh, what a sight I must appear. She makes me so angry, I can't stand her. Even though I am sane, when I am around her I still need to swear and shout and act hysterical. She is cruel, and inhumane, and I have never done anything other than call her fat. Why shouldn't I? She *is* fat! Oh, it's all right to call someone beautiful, if they are; or ginger, if they are, but it's not all right to call someone fat . . . when they *are*? Look at what she is doing to me! I am wet, bedraggled, naked, and covered head to toe in towels that have never been washed, while two women manhandle me. Thank God there is nobody here to witness this indignity!

"Ruth!" a female voice calls from the doorway. "What are you doing to Anne?"

"Doctor's orders," comes Fat Ruth's reply, muffled. "Treatment. Restores blood flow to the brain, don't you know?"

"I didn't see any orders to this effect," says the voice. The towel around my head is removed, and I am face-to-face with Agnus.

"Well, he made them!" replies Fat Ruth defensively. "Perhaps you were too busy fawning over your little woman here."

"Hello!" I say, with genuine pleasure. Agnus—my protector, my savior. I know with her, at least, I am safe.

"Hello, Anne," Agnus says. Her face looks sad, and a little concerned. "You'll be coming with me now."

"She stays with me," says Fat Ruth, jerking at my shoulders.

"No, she's coming with me, unless you would prefer me to report what I just witnessed to Dr. Savage this afternoon?"

Fat Ruth smirks, pushes me away. The towel falls to the floor and everyone can see my nakedness. I cover myself up as best I can.

"As you like. I don't know why I bother. Honestly, it's like working in a leper colony in here. Except *she's* worse." She spits on the floor. "Take her. She's nothing but a dirty baby killer, and I never wanted to look after her right from the start."

Her words crystallize in the air and shatter, hitting me with a million shards of glass, cutting into my skin and freezing my thoughts.

My soul turns to ice.

"Look, Agnus, she doesn't even have the decency to apologize for what she's done! Daddy's little princess—*murderous* little princess—born with a golden spoon up her arse."

"It is her misfortune, Ruth, not her crime."

"What, to be a spoiled little bitch?"

"No, you ignorant fool." She sighs, takes me gently by my hands. "Come on, Anne, let's go, quickly." She bustles me across the cold tiled floor, along the corridor, and into my room. "On the bed, Anne, quickly—get under the blanket. I'll be back." She momentarily disappears, only to swiftly reappear with a bundle of cleanly folded linen.

"Quickly, before you catch your death," she says softly, and my teeth are knocking together—I can't stop them; I'm so cold, so cold—and she starts to dress me, hurriedly, gently. I sit still and meek while she twists and turns my limbs into the clothes. When she is finished, a semblance of warmth creeps upon my skin and the shaking stops, but I can't feel my fingers or toes.

"I want to die. Send me back in there, let her kill me—"

"Anne, Anne, Anne—shush now, shush." She pulls me to her and envelops me into a tight embrace. *Let me die. Let her crush the air out of my lungs.* I don't deserve to breathe; I never want to breathe again. I bury my head into her bosom, farther, farther . . . Could I suffocate myself? If only Fat Ruth had really drowned me, I would have died in peace. I would never have known what I did. . . .

"Your extremities will be the last to warm up, I'm afraid." A muffled voice, a vibration in my head. Agnus, she's talking to me, why? "At the moment, your body is trying to preserve and divert heat to your internal organs. You're in a slight state of hypothermia. I cannot warm you up too quickly, I'm sorry. It's dangerous if I do."

Don't warm me up.

Let me die.

I push her off me, and start to take off the clothes.

"Anne, no!"

"I want to die, I want to die," I mutter, my teeth chattering. I can't undo the string on the dress; my fingers won't work, they won't bend, and I howl in pain and anger.

"Anne—" She tries to grab at me and I hit out.

"Let me die!" I scream into the air. I don't want to hurt her, but I will, I will, if she tries to stop me from hurting myself. What can I do? How can I do it?

The window.

They put bars on those.

The wall.

Yes.

The wall.

My head.

I run at it as fast as I can. *My baby, my baby, oh my God, I'm so, so sorry, I—* The door suddenly opens upon its hinges and large arms grab me from behind; thick hairs brush against my naked body.

I kick and scream and cry. I want to wake up. Why won't anyone wake me up? I'm here and I'm drowning, I'm dying, I'm . . .

"There, now, there." A slight pinch to my arm, a man's voice. I'm lying on the floor and the light is too bright, too real, too . . .

Life.

The baby that will never see the sun ever again.

I want my breath to stick inside my mouth. I want to suffocate on it.

DEEP SHADE OF RED

Dr. Savage
December 22nd, 1885
Bethlem Royal Hospital

Today I found Anne possessed of a most positive disposition. During our meeting, she answered questions thoughtfully with an evident insight into her past insanity while displaying an accurate awareness of her present orientation. She is logical in her thinking, and has clearly reestablished in her memory the chain of events that brought her to Bethlem. She is able to face and accept what happened that night in Asquith Manor, and recollect what happened before. What became clear to me during our discussion is that which conspired against Anne to predispose her to puerperal mania both before and during her pregnancy.

Anne was clearly distressed following the miscarriage she suffered before her son was born, and it is in my professional opinion that this grievance left Anne extremely susceptible to future mental problems. I do not believe that she fully mourned the loss of her first child, and when faced with her second pregnancy, she thereupon read any and all literature she could lay her hands on with regards to midwifery and childbirth in a misguided attempt to keep the second baby safe; naturally, given her history of reading since she was but a child. This in turn filled her mind with apprehensions as to the horrors that might be in store for her, and she thus developed a cerebral disturbance. She tells me that she has always read since she was a child: growing up in an environment that secluded her from peers of her own age made her seek to find comfort inside books instead of with people. This constant and voracious reading is a contributing factor. It is for this reason women should not educate themselves beyond affairs of the home.

As the pregnancy progressed she developed nervous disturbances ranging from mild irritability and crossness, to upsets and fretfulness. These conditions she displayed were unfortunately dismissed by her midwife and doctor at the time, being wrongly interpreted as a natural response to the excitement, discomfort, and trepidation associated with pregnancy and childbirth, rather than an indication of the onset of a severe mental illness.

Anne confesses to me that on more than one occasion, she voiced her concerns with the midwife, and was simply told to acquire an air of serenity, cheerfulness and good humor "essential to her own health and that of her offspring." While this was in no way bad advice, this demonstrates to me that Anne's declining mental state was certainly overlooked in its initial stages of decline. The abrupt loss of her milk was noted by the midwife, but no real concern was raised over this.

In the present day, I find her mania symptoms much receded: her flesh is no longer loose, her complexion no longer sallow, her tongue no longer tremulous. Her appetite is great and is satisfied. Her menstruation has recommenced, she sleeps well at night, and no longer harbors delusions of persecution or experiences hallucinations. Her memory has returned in full. She now accepts that she has suffered an attack of the senses.

Though she is clearly distraught, I do not feel she is a true danger to herself. I find Anne both respectable and redeemable after her period of rest and rehabilitation here at Royal Bethlem Hospital.

Recommendation: discharge to Witley at earliest convenience to grieve and adjust.

A letter stating such to be sent to the Home Office regarding a possible release date.

Satisfied, I lean back on my chair and throw my pen on the desk. This is what I have been waiting for, this moment. But it always seems that when one patient takes a turn for the better, one takes a fall for the worse. Geoffrey, poor man, seems to have come down with some sort of poisoning—it seems to be alum. But how, and where he got it from, I don't know. I need to read through some files, find out if anyone—

A knock on my door disturbs me.

"Please enter," I call.

The door opens and standing in the doorway are Ruth and Agnus: my two best nurses. Ruth looks rather angry, and Agnus appears defiant. My, what is it now?

"Dr. Savage, this is utterly disgusting!" Ruth shakes her head and marches up to my desk. Her bosom heaving, she points a finger in my face and opens her mouth like a fish, only to close it when she apparently loses her train of thought. Her face is red with suppressed rage. Agnus flicks a look at Ruth and nods at me in indulgent understanding.

"Ruth is somewhat agitated, sir," Agnus says, the hint of a smile hiding underneath her serious facade.

I take it from her. "Thank you. Now, Nurse Ruth, whatever ails you? Come, sit, before you pop a vein in that head of yours."

Agnus sits while Ruth turns a deeper shade of red and glares at me.

"I shall sit, sir, in a moment."

"As you please."

Agnus looks to the floor, and I swear her shoulders are twitching.

"Again, I ask you, Nurse Ruth, what ails you this morning?"

"That Anne!"

"Lady Stanbury, you mean?" I stand up. "And I believe she is a person, not an object to be referred to as 'that.' Nurse Ruth, do not get ahead of yourself; I believe it is both prudent and necessary for you to address a lady by her given title, is it not?"

"No *lady* would kill her own baby! And anyway, we call her Anne to her face, so why not behind her back?"

I sigh. Ruth has been a fixture at Bethlem as long as the rafters that hold the building together, but she is fast losing her objectivity.

"And no nurse would speak such ill of a patient in her charge. Plus, I believe you understand why we called Lady Stanbury by her first name for a period of time: in order not to further confuse her mind by being associated with a name that held no identity for her. Now, Nurse Ruth, I strongly suggest you gather your senses and speak plain to me."

"I am simply furious, Dr. Savage, sir. Absolutely speechless, in fact."

"And why is that?"

"Because Lady Stanbury seems to believe she is soon to be going home! And all because of this one!" Ruth points at Agnus angrily.

"Actually, Ruth, it was your treatment that cured her," Agnus says, smiling.

"What treatment?" I ask.

"The hydrotherapy. Like you told me," Ruth says, crossing her arms over her chest.

"Yes, I did authorize that. What exactly is the problem here?"

"Ruth called Lady Stanbury a 'baby killer,' Doctor."

"Oh, you little snitch!" cries Ruth, raising her arms in frustration and clenching her fists together.

"Well, you are the one that insisted you speak to Dr. Savage, Ruth! What do you expect me to do? Keep quiet about it with you acting so crazy?"

"How dare you call me crazy! I work with the crazy! I am certainly not crazy!"

"I think you must be, a little bit, to work with them," says Agnus quietly.

"Nurse Agnus . . . ," I gently reproach her. The last thing I either want or need is a battle of women in my office.

"That day when Lady Stanbury came to see you, sir? That morning, Ruth had given her the cold bath treatment and called her a murderer," Agnus says quickly. "Specifically, a 'baby killer.' Anne was really distressed when I arrived—I think Ruth had her in there for much longer than three minutes, sir. I took her out—she was practically hypothermic—and it was then that Anne told me she remembered. She *explicitly* said that it was *Ruth's words* that made her remember. That's really cruel, sir. What an awful way to find out that not only is your baby dead, but you killed it. She went crazy for a while afterward." She claps a hand over her mouth, blushes. "Sorry. She became . . extremely upset, but luckily Mr. Davis was passing by—you know, the attendant from M1A—and he came in and gave her a sedative."

"Is this true, Nurse Ruth?" I am livid. "Did you keep Lady Stanbury in the water for more than three minutes?"

"No!"

"Did you call her a 'baby killer,' Ruth?"

She notes that I have dropped her title, and becomes even redder. "Yes, sir."

"Pardon? I can't quite hear you."

"Yes, sir!" Ruth shouts the words. "It is true! Of course it is true! She's a liar, and she's no madder than either you or I! She's faking it!"

"I think, Ruth, that it is you who is slightly 'mad' at the moment. First, and listen well, *I* am the chief medical officer here at Bethlem. Anything and everything you do and say to any patient has my authorization before you do, say, think, or feel it. You have been here long enough: You know well that shocking patients with words about their deeds is not indicated in the management of puerperal psychosis, and could have pushed Anne further and deeper into her madness. Lady Stanbury is here only for rest and recuperation, her insanity being only temporary. You are also aware that these women, *such as Lady Stanbury*, should be treated as if they will recover completely, as being aware of temporary conditions in a lunatic asylum can make these women insane permanently. Calling her a 'baby killer' could have resulted in utterly disastrous consequences for Anne, and unhinged her mind completely. You took it upon yourself to issue forth derogatory and unfeeling comments that were not of your authority, and for this I issue you with a verbal warning. If I hear any more complaints of you treating any of your patients, *especially* Lady Stanbury, in such a manner, or indeed, doing anything without my prior and explicit say-so, you will be out of employment quicker than a rabbit on fire. Do you understand me?"

"But, but . . . but it was after the treatment she returned to sanity!" Ruth splutters.

"That is as may be, Nurse Ruth. But I see that you have missed somewhat the point I was trying to make here. You are not in control. Whether it was the plunge bath that returned Lady Stanbury's senses or not is *not* the issue at stake here. What is clear is *your* inability to respect rules and authority. This is your first, and last, warning."

I turn to Agnus. "Nurse Agnus, great thanks to you for seeing Lady Stanbury to back to warmth and health after her cold 'treatment' here with Nurse Ruth. I greatly suspect it was your humane and kind treatment of Anne that led her back to her senses, considering how abruptly she was somewhat rudely jerked into the present reality, courtesy of Ruth here. I have never known a single word or a cold bath to cure any inmate of any manner of insanity, ever, in just one admin-istration."

Agnus nods solemnly.

"While I consider removing Anne from your charge, Nurse Ruth, you do well to mind me and what we have discussed here today. Now go. I have much work to attend to. And may I suggest you give the Red Book a read, for I have never seen you pick it up. There are things you could learn in there, including respect."

With a disgruntled look in Agnus's direction, Ruth rises from her chair, curtseys slightly to me, and exits the office in an angry flurry of aprons and skirts. Agnus rises to follow.

"Nurse Agnus, dear." I stop her.

"Yes, Doctor?"

"Watch over Anne carefully while she is with Nurse Ruth, and report to me immediately any instance of which I need to be informed. I trust you to do your duty as well as always."

"Yes, Doctor. I will. Good day to you."

"Good day, Nurse Agnus. Now please close the door behind you."

The door shuts quietly, and I am left alone with my notes and a headache.

Sometimes I feel as if I am in charge of two sets of patients, the nurses on one side and the "real" patients on the other.

Why did women decide to enter the workplace? If they want money and respect and equal rights and opportunities, well, I say let them have it.

But dear Lord, let them be quiet!

YOU'VE SEEN A GHOST

Anne
January 25th, 1886
Bethlem Royal Hospital

"That be a fine pattern you sew there, my lady." A withered hand rests gently on my shoulder, and squeezes.

"Why, thank you, Dolores," I say, looking over my shoulder and smiling. It feels unnatural, tight. Dolores must be ninety if she's a day, and I'm surprised she can even see my sewing. Most likely she cannot, but still—the kindness of this woman has astounded me during my recent days here, on the new floor. She takes it upon herself to walk around the dayroom, for many hours in the mornings, aided with two walking sticks in her hands and a heavy shawl on her back. She offers pleasantries to everyone she meets, always quick with a kind word. Yesterday, I found her talking to Grace, telling her what beautiful eyes she had, and "a bonny lass indeed you be indeed, my dear." I swear Grace smiled at her too. Another woman, Esther Base, killed her baby in a fit of insanity, but now she thinks it's a ball of paper. She strokes it, kisses it, sings to it . . . but sometimes another patient will rush by and rip it up. Then she becomes hysterical. I can't imagine how she would cope without Dolores, as the nurses seem to ignore her. She comforts

Esther, finds her a new piece of paper. I feel awful for this woman. Imagine seeing your baby ripped to pieces once or twice a week by a raving lunatic, and never understanding that you are the one who is insane. . . .

I've realized that there are a few women here, like me. I've also noticed that we are the lepers of this world; worse, it seems, than the rest. The nurses give us a wide berth and treat us with an extra helping of cruelty—less food, an unsuspecting pinch to the armpit, an unkind word here and there.

I suppose everyone has to have someone to look down upon.

Every day is a struggle for me now. Part of me misses my "insanity"—I was happier when I didn't know what I had done. Every time I close my eyes I dream of John. I dream of him being taken away from me and I run. I try to catch him, but the man has him and he's taking him far, far away and I know I will never see him again, never hold his hand in mine, never smell his skin and kiss his hair. I dream of him growing up without me, becoming a man, hating me for letting him go. Then I wake up and realize that he really is gone, gone from me, and the nightmare seems better than the reality.

If it weren't for Agnus, I would have fallen apart, or taken this needle to my throat and gouged it out.

I push the needle harder through the fabric, jabbing at the material. It doesn't matter anymore—life, I mean. Some days, I don't know why I hold on to it. What have I to stay alive for? Sure, they've given me even more freedom, but what does that really mean? The truth is that I am not free at all. Moving up a level within the hospital and being given a dressing table, an extra chair, and a looking glass in my room is merely part of an illusion. And perhaps I do not deserve any of it. Perhaps I should never walk out of those gates. The doctor assures me that I won't be here for much longer: I started my courses while at Witley, and as soon as he receives the received necessary signatures, I will be on my way.

But I do wonder whether I should beg with him, plead with him to please let me stay here. I deserve to have a sentence as terrible as Esther's— to see my baby murdered in front of me day after day after day. The nurses are right. John is gone and I have blood on my hands. A spot, a spot!

The dayroom in which I sit and sew is "large and airy"—so they say—but I don't care. Sunlight shines through the windows and I can see the green grass, the blue sky, but I think it should be gray to match my mood. Gray, gray, gray. It upsets me to see such a beautiful day and not be able to enjoy it. I wish it would rain.

Rain. The hole, the alum. Did I bury it well enough? Perhaps I should dig it back up, wash it. Perhaps I should stay here forever.

Unwanted tears prick my eyes, and I lower my gaze to the table. The nurses on this level are cruel when I cry. Agnus comes up when she can, but I believe she has a new patient now, someone else to look after. I'm sane now. There's nothing more for her to do. But I can't stop thinking about what she told me, about her mother. I want to know more. If I'm branded such a monster—not knowing what I did—then I want to know more about those women who cruelly, coldly, and *consciously* hand their children over to be murdered.

"Lady Stanbury."

I look up and Fat Ruth is beside me. "Yes, Nurse Ruth?"

"Ah, I see you respond to your name now. Funny, that. And what a surprise to see you! I thought you'd never leave F1A, never mind go to Witley. Enjoy it, did you?"

"It's none of your business. What's F1A?"

"The lower level, you imbecile. Are you . . . are you *crying*?" She smiles: My pain gives her pleasure. "Why are you crying, Anne? Surely, it can't be because . . ." She lowers her voice. " . . . you killed your baby, can it?"

"No. I pricked my finger on the needle," I say shortly.

"Hmm. Well, then, let me see."

"No."

"Give me your finger!" Fat Ruth raises her voice and pulls my hands from my lap. Her eyes widen. "There are no marks!"

I remain silent. I consider putting the needle through her face.

"Leave me alone, Fat Ruth," I say quietly, so low that only she can hear me.

"What is that, Baby Killer?"

I grab her hand and pull it underneath the table, twisting her fingers back before she has a chance to cry out. "I repeat, leave me *alone*, Fat Ruth." I spit in her eye. The saliva trickles down her cheek as she stares at me.

"That's right. You will damn well leave me alone from now on, or I swear it so, I'll have your job. You'll be out on your ear before you can say my name. Yes, my name. I know my name now. My father is the Earl of Damsbridge. . . . Do you know what that means? Let me make it clear for you: He knows people in high places. Why do you suppose I am here instead of the criminal asylum, Broadmoor?" I laugh. I want her to leave me alone. I want to scare her. "And yes, I killed my baby and I'll damn well not pause at killing you either, if you don't leave me the hell alone."

Fat Ruth gapes. I grab the needle and plunge it into my thumb, once, twice, three times. Blood swells like teardrops. I squeeze it, and the blood starts running out, down my hand, down my wrist, all over my needlework.

"Sometimes, Fat Ruth," I say quietly, "you have to be strong enough to hurt yourself."

"My lady! You're bleeding all over the quilt!" Dolores has finished her round of the dayroom and is once again behind me. Ruth is still next to me, staring.

"Oh, Dolores! I've ruined it!" I start to cry again, this time openly: for nothing, for everything; everything except the stupid quilt.

"Dear, dear, that's nothing a bit of cold water won't fix! Don't worry. I can clean it right up. Cold water's the key, plenty of it, and fast. Here . . ." Dolores grabs the patchwork from me and bundles it around her neck. "I'll wash it for you, my lady. You'll never know a thing." She hobbles off, humming a song.

"Did you just threaten me?"

"Pardon?" I wipe the tears from my face and turn to gaze at Ruth. She hardly seems so big anymore. "You look like a scared hippopotamus. Should you really be working with crazy people if they frighten you so easily?"

She pales and turns away. Her face has a tint of green.

"Faint, will you?" I ask, taunting, really digging it in, getting my own back for all the horrible things she ever said to me, the way she treated me, the way she treats others. Poor Esther is stuck in this place for the rest of her life, and this bitch is going out of her way to make her miserable. I hate it; I hate her; I could kill her. "If I really wanted to hurt you, Ruth, do you think the other nurses would come to your aid?" I lift the needle menacingly. "I don't think you have many friends here, *Fat* Ruth." I inch the pin toward her.

She pushes her chair back from the table, practically toppling in her haste to get away from me.

I smile with satisfaction.

A CHICKEN BONE

Edgar
February 5th, 1886
Bethlem Royal Hospital

"Doctor, good morning."

"And a good day it is, Mr. Stanbury. A good day indeed. Indeed." The excitement radiates from the doctor, yet it fails to bring a smile to my face. It took all the effort I possess to make it to the hospital today, and I almost told the coachman to turn back twice. The rain battering against the windows matched the hammering of my heart; the rocking motion of the carriage made me nauseated. The mere thought of seeing my wife again made my head pound. I was utterly alone in my misery.

"Stanbury?"

I still am.

"Stanbury?"

I always will be.

"Stanbury!" The doctor calls my name and bangs his hand on the desk.

"Yes, Doctor?"

"I had to call you three times. You seem a bit pale. Are you all right?"

No. I'm not all right. Nothing will ever be all right ever, ever again. I can't believe I'm here—why am I here?

Do I really want that bitch to come home?

Home?

What a joke.

"I'm fine," I say, forcing myself to meet his gaze. I turn my lips upward in a parody of a smile and it hurts my face: the muscles used to express happiness left long unused.

The doctor gazes at me, twiddling a pen in his hands. He's studying me. I know he is. Soon, he will ask me if I took the chloral.

A file is open on the desk in front of him.

"I asked you here today because I have good news, Stanbury. Very good news. But tell me, how are you? Did the chloral help at all? How's your drinking?"

And there it is. But why the fixation with the ale? There is nothing wrong with a man having a few whiskeys. I'm not like my father. I don't drink to excess.

You're lying to yourself.

Well, maybe. I don't care. I'm lonely, and whiskey is my friend. He and I travel to a place where the world is both brighter and duller, a perfect place where no memories, thoughts, or emotions exist.

"Oh, it worked," I say, neglecting to tell him that I took a small amount of the chloral with alcohol against his advice, and it *didn't* work. And then I lost the bottle, so I don't even know if taking more would help. Oh well. Who needs chloral when my friend, Mr. Jacks, sends me to sleep at night?

I do my best to appear cheerful and contrite, but the effort pains me. "It worked wonderfully, Doctor. And I have nipped my drinking in the bud, as they say. It was the grief, Doctor—I fear I let it get a grip of me for a small while. But I am feeling much better now. Thank you." I try not to breathe in his direction, in case he smells the whiskey I drank not half an hour ago.

There is more than one way to cure travel sickness.

His smile makes my stomach flip.

"Well, that's wonderful news! Brilliant!" He looks as if he is about to clap, but thankfully doesn't. "Mr. Stanbury, I am *very* relieved. I must say, I was worried about you. You still look a bit . . . peaky, but I suppose that's to be expected given the circumstances." He puts a pair of glasses on his nose, fiddles with the arms. "This hospital, this superb building and so many others alike it, right across the country, promotes the aid and recovery of poor souls who have lost their senses, their minds, and in several cases, their families, dignity . . . even souls, if you believe in that sort of stuff. Through the wonder of modern medicine and the application of moral therapy, Bethlem has a most esteemed record of patient recovery. Your wife is one of its successes." He pauses, waits for a response.

"Is she cured, then?"

He smiles. "Yes, yes, she is."

I don't know whether to thank or punch him. Vomit rises in my throat and I choke it back.

Does that mean . . .

"Through a routine of work, exercise, and rest and an emphasis on community life designed to recondition the brain, she is restored to her senses. She remembers you. She knows what she has done, but all danger is passed. I don't think she is likely to kill herself. She seems rather—accepting of the situation, so don't worry about anything, but keep an eye, all the same."

Yes, it does. It means she is coming home. My eye twitches as I think of Anne, of John, of happiness, of misery.

"Her father has been informed. I sent a letter. It's very unfortunate he's not able to welcome his daughter home. Does he always work away so much? It's imperative that someone watches over her, and monitors her behavior in the coming weeks and months."

"I don't know . . ."

" 'Don't know' what?"

If I want her back.

How can I say it? How can I tell him that I'm scared—not of what she might do, but of what *I* might do?

I can't.

"I don't know whether he always works this much," I say. "I've never noticed. He lives in the dower house, so Anne and I barely see him."

He scratches his beard. "No matter. I'm sure she can trust you." He picks up the file, stands. "I love this part of my job, Mr. Stanbury. As we teeter on the brink of medical salvation, patients like Lady Stanbury reinforce our achievements to those that doubt us, fear us, call us 'mad doctors,' alienists, what they will. There are several classes of people out there, other doctors, lawyers, political figures, that do not share my opinion as to the efficiency of restful, pleasant surroundings in the treatment of mental disorder. Do they forget that we 'head doctors' are distinguished members of the M.R.C.P.? Those ignorant fools forget or oversee this extremely valid point! They condemn us as crazy as those we treat, and insist upon choosing to believe in the virtues of 'medicine out of a bottle'!" He shakes the file angrily. "Chemical cosh! Bromide, paraldehyde, and chloral hydrate, unfortunately—ever-present concoctions to be found in every asylum in existence! Tremendously addictive, not altogether as innocuous as those prescribing them would have you believe. Sulphonal! Yes, they have their uses, but not for the primary cure of lunatics!"

Evidently, he has forgotten that he prescribed me one of the very things he now refers to as "cosh."

"Times are changing, Mr. Stanbury. Soon, we will be in a new century. But enlightenment will occur throughout the medical profession. I am sure of it. I hope for it, at the very least." He purses his lips together, sighs. "The sad truth is, we are steadily becoming overcrowded: not just here at Bethlem, but in every asylum. Before long, they are bound to become understaffed, underfunded, and grossly undervalued. Any idiot can see that this outcome would not be the most propitious climate in which to engender bright new ideas, or ideals. An increased inmate population . . . but enough of my deliberations. Sometimes I get carried away." He tucks the file underneath an arm, smiles. "Any questions?"

"What happens now? Do we just go home and . . . act like nothing ever happened?"

"No. But you try to move on. If she wants to talk about it, be there for her. If *you* want to talk about it, contact me; don't overload the poor woman's mind. Aside from that—try to find peace, Mr. Stanbury. Support each other. Try to reignite the love you had. But don't go too far . . . be careful. There is a chance she might relapse if she was to birth another child."

"We—" Wait. "Are you telling me we can't try for a baby?"

"I would try to avoid it as best you can. I'm not saying that she would definitely have another attack, but in my clinical experience I have certainly seen patterns of repetition affixed to puerperal mania. Take precautions as far as possible."

And just like that, the decision is taken out of my hands.

I decided months ago that I wouldn't harm her, that I wouldn't go through with my father's plan, but the thought was still there—the security that another child would bring.

Selfish.

You are selfish.

The rat bites inside my head.

Pregnancy has caused us nothing but pain and misery.

I don't need a child anymore.

All I need is my wife.

Do I?

"A combination of baking soda and vinegar, or a premade solution of carbolic acid, tannin, and salicylic acid, usually does the trick, Mr. Stanbury. There are a few ways to prevent unwanted pregnancies."

"I understand," I say, thinking of dead babies and children that would never be born, never created.

"You fidget, Mr. Stanbury. Are you anxious to see your wife?"

I nod.

Rising from our chairs, we leave the office and start the journey to Anne's room. The asylum seems lighter, brighter, and somehow altogether more cheerful than I remember on my last visit. A large fireplace fills the dayroom through which we walk with heat and light, and a woman sits next to the fire, sewing. It is a cozy atmosphere, and a sense of hate floods through my veins. Anne would have liked it here. She did not suffer. A finch hops around inside a gilded birdcage and I think of me, of the manor. The stories I hear of neglect and abuse in lunatic asylums quite clearly don't apply to Bethlem.

"It's lovely in here," I say, taking in my surroundings. Dr. Savage stops in his tracks, beams. "Thank you, Mr. Stanbury! To have our efforts appreciated by those closest to our patients is no mean feat." We continue walking, and as we pass a door a loud thump comes from within, startling me.

"Oh, that." The doctor turns and shakes his head sadly. "That is the incurables room, containing the very few patients we have been unable to bring about any sort of recovery. It is for everyone's happiness, sanity, and safety that they are segregated from the rest. Generally, after a period of one year we discharge all patients whether they are cured or not, but for these few there is no alternative. They don't have any family. There's simply nowhere for them to go. Transferring them out to another asylum is not an option I favor." Stopping outside the door, I look through the glass panel. Inside are six or seven patients and four nurses, or at least that I can see: The small transparent square makes for a limited viewpoint. It is chaos. Numerous women, some shouting, some screaming, some singing, some banging: all of them making the most god-awful din. The doctor leans over my shoulder and peers through the glass. "Gives them a place to be themselves without disturbing others who do not appreciate the volume." A nurse rushes past and stops a woman from banging her head, in what appears to be a deliberate move against that of another patient. "Are they violent?" I ask, enthralled.

"No, they're not violent, despite appearances to the contrary. Just loud, more than anything. But sometimes disagreements happen between individuals, much the same as in the outside world."

An elderly woman approaches us in the corridor, politely nodding. "Good day to you, kind sirs," she says, stopping and reaching into a wicker basket.

"Good day," I say, watching her, warily. I raise my eyebrows at Dr. Savage.

Slowly, she pulls something out of the basket.

I step back.

Brandishing something gaily aloft, she cries, "A bone! A human bone!" She starts to laugh: Alarmingly, her gums are blue. "Can you see, kind sirs? A bone! Oh, how can I walk? They have taken the bones from my legs. Look! Doctor, can you put it back in for me? Oh, I beg you! With that, she falls to her knees and holds the "bone" aloft.

I squint, lean closer. It is a chicken bone, quite possibly a wing.

"Gertrude. A patient here. Lead poisoning. Thinks we are stealing her skeleton piece by piece," Dr. Savage says, by way of explanation. He shouts, "Nurse Ruth! Please come and fetch Gertrude, and kindly stop letting her eat chicken!" An attendant pops her head around a side door and looks at me darkly.

What did I do?

"Yes, sir," Ruth says, grabbing Gertrude by the arm and leading the mad, cackling woman away from us.

We pass down the rest of the corridor without incident, finally stopping outside a strangely familiar door.

Yet this one has a handle.

Behind it hides my wife.

My love.

The murderer of my baby.

TAINTED BY HATE

Edgar
February 5th, 1886
Bethlem Royal Hospital

Anne flings herself upon me as soon as we enter the room. "My love!" she says, clinging to my waistcoat, sobbing. "I'm sorry. I'm so, so sorry." Oh God, I'm not ready for this. I don't know what I'm supposed to do. My emotions are scattered to the wind. There are too many things to think about this woman, about me, about life and death and . . . She buries her head against my chest. My instinct is to offer comfort and tell her that I love her, but I can't, I can't. I don't know if I do.

"You two should sit down." The doctor's hand is suddenly on my arm. Thankful for the interruption, I gently disengage myself from my wife and let him steer us across the room. She sits on the edge of the bed and I look down at her oily hair, her pale cheeks. I think of the blood that still rushes to her skin, her beating heart. Why? Why does she have the right to breathe when she stole the breath from my son?

Am I so full of hate that I may never be able to forgive her?

"Anne." I say her name, and nothing more. There is a disconnection between my thoughts and my words.

The bed crackles as I sit.

"I'm so happy to see you," she says, and reaches out for my hand. I flinch, move away. I imagine what I would do if we were alone, if the doctor wasn't here. Would I kiss her?

Or kill her?

"Edgar, I . . . I'm sorry." She starts to cry and it reminds me of John, of his catlike mewling in the middle of the night. I watch the tears drip down her face and wonder whether he cried when she hurt him. "I never meant to do it, Edgar, please." She bends over and places her hands on her stomach—her empty, barren womb. "Please, please forgive me. I need you to understand, I need you to console me, I need you . . ."

I need you.

And there it is. The reminder.

". . . I need you to forgive me, Edgar—because I will never forgive myself."

I look at her then—truly *look* at her—and I find the saddest thing of all.

My wife is gone.

The ever-present smile has vanished from her lips, the sparkling vivacity lost from her face. Her newly reddened eyes twitch with grief as she grabs nervously at her gown, the nails bent, brittle, bitten almost entirely away, and slightly yellow. The bones of her wrist press painfully against the skin, and bruises bloom across her legs. I barely recognize her, and instantly feel guilty for swallowing a mouth of disgust.

I did this to her.

She is a living reflection of my lies, and I don't know how to fix her. I don't know how to fix myself.

I close my eyes for a moment.

I'm sick of the words we tell each other, the mistruths we tell to ourselves.

At my next words, I set my future as the sort of man I want to be.

An honest one.

I open my eyes.

Take her cool, sweaty hand in mine.

I don't flinch.

I don't move.

I look her right in the eye and tell her what she wants to hear. What I need to say.

Need.

Greed.

Life.

Death.

"I love you," I say, calm, quiet. "I love you." Twice. And I cry then too, for a past that brought nothing but bloody murder.

I will find my wife once again.

But before I do that, I need a drink.

MADNESS OF A MAN

Anne
February 5th, 1886
Outside

Edgar offers me his hand, and duly assisted I lift my skirts and climb
up into the carriage. Although convention calls for the coachman to
hand me in and out of the cab, Edgar prefers to assume this role when
we are together, and I let him. He seems different, though; his hand is
weak and I almost topple off the steps.

The coachman nods respectfully in my direction, tips his hat. I
want to wave him away, to tell him not to nod at me, that I am not worthy of his respect. It feels strange to be in the outside world, and I
never thought it would. I thought that going home would be easy. But
in this moment, when I bend my back and duck into the cab, I realize
how insulated I have been for the last three months. I haven't been able
to wear my own clothes, to choose my own breakfast, to touch and buy
leather and silk and fabrics. I haven't breathed in the scent of a horse
or the sea. I haven't looked at the stars. I haven't felt sand between my
toes or a man between my legs. And that was all right. That was safe; I
don't want any of those things anyway.

All I want is my son.

I remove my hat and sink back into the maroon leather seat. I sigh with pleasure and instantly experience a shock of guilt. How dare I feel comfort beneath my derriere! How dare I appreciate the colored glass on the windows! I take a breath, breathe.

Just breathe.

I realize that I don't want to go home. Edgar looks ill and he won't stop staring at me, as if I am about to go mad again, or do something stupid. I get the feeling that he doesn't want to be near me, but is fulfilling his husbandly duty with gritted teeth and a false smile.

I know him too well.

I'm scared.

The carriage door slams and I jolt out of my seat.

"Careful, Anne," says Edgar as he takes his place beside me. The smell of sour ale dances on his breath and as he reaches into his pocket, I see why. While I spent an hour preparing myself to leave, he spent an hour . . . drinking. Pulling out a rather large flask, he unscrews the top and takes a gulp, staring at me with bloodshot eyes, challenging, daring me to say something. I don't. How can I? After all, I took his son away from him. I can't imagine *ever* being in his position. He *hasn't* forgiven me, though; I *know* he lied in the asylum, in front of the doctor. Why? If he doesn't love me anymore, doesn't want to touch me, then why didn't he say so?

Why won't he just let me go?

"I'm sorry," I say, and he shifts, laughs.

The tone sounds eerily familiar.

It sounds like those I heard at night, carried on the wind over from the male section.

The laughs of a lunatic.

I curl my body away from him.

He is broken, a different man.

I avert my gaze, look to my lap. I can't bear to see the drunken grief in his face; I can't. I fiddle with my gloves, taking them off the fingers one by one, a centimeter or so each time, then pushing them back.

I try to smile.

"Well, I'm glad that's over with," he says, and takes another swig of ale. He offers me the bottle. "Want some?"

I shake my head.

"Fine. More for me." He shifts himself across the seat and turns away, leaning his cheek against the window. A lone tear trickles down his face as he cradles the flask beneath his breast, rubbing a thumb up and down the silver.

The distance between us is impenetrable.

"Edgar, do you hate me?"

He makes a sound from deep within his throat, takes another swig.

"Edgar—"

"You know, Anne, I didn't always love you." His words are aimed toward the passing woodland, their sound almost lost beneath the thumping of the carriage. "But I never hated you. Not then." He takes a deep breath and exhales, misting the pane.

"And now?"

"Now?" He wipes a sodden sleeve across his face, hawks a ball of mucus upon the floor. "I would say that I do, sometimes, yes. Mostly when I'm drinking this stuff." He shakes the flask. "But then, feelings and words never can be trusted when one is under the influence of alcohol, can they?"

I swallow. "Edgar, darling, I know this is hard for you. And I'm sorry. I'm so, so sorry. I never meant to hurt him. I never—"

And suddenly his face is in front of mine, his hands inches from my throat.

"Anne . . ." His face shudders with repressed rage. "Don't ever mention what you did, ever again. I love you, but I'm afraid there's a deep hate flowing inside me, and if you talk about John, I swear, the dam will break. I don't want to hurt you: Don't make me. I want to fix this." His hands shake as he eases them back to his sides, and a part of me longs to reach out and touch him, to take ahold of his trembling fingers. But I don't.

I can't.

"I'm scared," I say, a whisper underneath my breath.

"So am I, Anne." He closes his eyes, his head swaying to the left and right as if listening to music only he can hear. "So am I."

BLUE-BLOOD WHORE

Beatrix
February 5th, 1886
Asquith Manor

Dinner is stifled and awkward as Mr. Stanbury steadily drinks himself toward a state of drunkenness and debauchery. Having dismissed both the footman and the butler earlier in the evening in a bid for privacy, he talks to Anne but gains little in return. Anne sits still and mute throughout, merely picking at her food and barely engaging in his conversation. From the clandestine position I have taken in the kitchen, I am able to observe their interactions through a high-up window, balancing somewhat precariously on a wooden worktop, and offer Anne a modicum of support. She knows I am here, minding her, though it cost me a hairpin. The cook is rather ruthless in her negotiations when it comes to anyone other than herself entering her personal domain, but I don't mind. We all take what we can get in life.

I stretch up on the tips of my toes. Mr. Stanbury's glass is now emptying with increasing rapidity, and short, sharp bursts of utter nonsense spill from his mouth. "Filth, blue-blood whore, murderer." To her credit, Anne is bearing up tolerably well, though her hands shake in her lap.

"You hid the pregnancy from me until I found out, when you were five months gone! What were you planning to do, conceal him until he was born? Was your purpose to do away with John all along?"

"How can you say that? I was frightened to tell you, Edgar. I saw how heartbroken you were after the miscarriage. I wanted to keep our baby safe, until it was the right time. I *loved* you, Edgar, loved you with all my heart. I didn't care that you were poor; you were unlike any man I had ever met and I just wanted to be with you! I was willing to share everything I was, everything I had, with *you*, my mind, body, soul . . . *money*! I loved your kindness, your sense of humor, and what did you do?"

"I didn't do anything, Anne. I loved you."

"You're a liar."

"I—" He splutters. "Yes, I suppose I might be, but then I didn't kill our son, did I?"

"Not directly perhaps. . . ."

"And didn't I specifically ask you not to mention it?"

"I didn't. You did—"

"I told you what would happen if you mentioned John, didn't I? The dam is very close to breaking, Anne, and I won't be responsible for my actions. I'm warning you. . . ."

"No!" Anne finally loses her temper, stands up, and throws a glass of water in his face. She screams through her tears, "How dare you 'warn me'? You selfish bastard! You *stupid*, selfish bastard—you don't even realize what you have done, do you? If you hadn't been a sneaky little *liar* right from the start, then none of this would ever have happened! You've made me the way I am: This is your doing, Edgar, not mine!"

"You killed him, Anne, and by God, I'm going to have my way with you and kill you!"

It is time to intervene.

I jump down from the worktop, my foot knocking off a copper

pot. The sound it makes is terrifyingly loud in the empty kitchen, and I freeze. If he hears it, he might just kill the both of us. I need to calm him down.

I backtrack quickly through the kitchen, running down the series of corridors that take me back and around to the formal entrance of the dining area. The large manor house was constructed in such a manner as to have means for the servants to go about their daily work without being "seen or heard" by the family of the residence, and though this structure offensively equates the help to rats, it serves a purpose when needed.

This evening, the eighth of a mile that normally provides a service is now an inconvenience. By the time I come to the entrance, out of breath, I fear I am too late. But the gathering of servants outside the door reassures me that they haven't killed each other . . . yet.

"Miss, miss!" Betty runs toward me, clings to my leg. "Oh, miss, he's bein' horrible t' her. He's—"

"Shush, child. Lower your voice. He'll sack all of us. I've told you this before." I look pointedly at the rest of the staff: the garden boy, both of the footmen, a couple of maids, the butler. Newman looks embarrassed, acknowledges me with a small bow. The others appear concerned.

"Madam. We heard banging and shouting and, well, we're worried about the lady. We didn't know whether to enter or not."

"Let me handle it, please."

"Is there anything we can do?"

I look at the maids, whispering to one another. "Yes, Newman, can you make sure everyone goes back to their proper places? I'm going to try and remove the lady; I think Mr. Stanbury is drunk. He should let her go without too much of a fuss, so long as it's just me. If he sees you lot—well, you know what he's like."

"Aye, we do at that," says the garden boy. "I hate him. I wish she'd never met him. Since he arrived, this house has been a bloody miserable place to work in. And I'm outside most of the time."

I nod. "I know, I know. Please leave now. All of you."

"I loved you."

"And I loved you!"

"Then how the bloody, fucking shit did we end up in this mess?"

I continue to listen at the door for a few minutes, curious.

Silence.

Then:

"Why did you do it, Anne? Please just tell me why. I can't stand it, I miss him so much. Please."

A pause.

"I can't tell you, Edgar. Literally, I can't. Please don't make this any harder for me. I was ill. I don't know why I did it. I'm sorry. I can't stand to see you so unhappy, but . . ." Another pause. "I can't do this anymore. I can't."

"What do you mean, you 'can't do this anymore'?"

"I just . . . can't. I can't be here with you, not after everything."

"What do you mean, 'can't be here with me'? What do you intend to—"

I enter unbidden.

"My lady, sir," I say loudly. They both pause: Mr. Stanbury with a glass inches from his mouth, water dripping down his face, and Anne—darling Anne—clutching a napkin, crying. I walk briskly to the table and drop a low curtsey.

The smell of whiskey permeates the air.

Mr. Stanbury blinks, finishes his drink, and stares blearily at me. Anne says, "Beatrix, what are you—"

"You!" Mr. Stanbury throws his glass across the room. Anne covers her ears and shrieks as the glass shatters across the wall. "How dare you barge in here—"

"Edgar, she hasn't done anything. Leave her alone—"

"No!" He stands up and flings the table over, china, crystal, candles, and gravy flying everywhere. "No! She sneaks around this manor like creeping fucking Jesus. She's always spying on me!" He fixes his gaze upon mine, and a chill runs down my neck. "I hate you. I fucking *hate* you—do you fucking understand?" His words are blurry around the edges and slur into one another. He wobbles, takes a few steps toward me. "I hate what you've done to me, what you've made me become."

"I haven't made you 'become' anything, sir," I say quietly. "You've achieved all this quite by yourself—"

"Edgar—" Anne reaches for her husband and places a hand on his arm, but he pushes her away.

Gently.

"She has, Anne. She's made me into this person—a replica of my father. You left me alone, and *she* left me alone, and everyone laughed at me and I drank, Anne; I *drank*, and now I'm drunk. And you—you gave me everything, and I loved you for it. But everything's gone now, isn't it? Love, hope . . ." He laughs bitterly. "Do you know, I had this strange belief that rich people would be happy. *Happy.* But you're not happy now, are you? Who the fuck is happy in this fucking room?" He points a finger at me. "Are you happy?"

"Uh—I—"

"No, you're not happy either. But then, you never were. You have the most miserable face I've ever seen. Even your cheeks sag toward the floor. You *hated* it when I walked into this house and married your precious protégée. You hated *me* for it" He sinks down to the floor and sits among the mess, places a hand on his forehead. "I'm sick of you, all of you. You've treated me like filth since day one. You all seem to think I've done something wrong, something awful, but I haven't. I haven't done a thing. I'm not the one who killed a child. I never meant to harm any of you and look at what you've done. Look at what you're doing. You've broken me." He starts to sob. "I'm the most unhappy man in the world."

• • •

"What a mess!" I say, spluttering over my words. "And his language! I've never heard the *F* word so many times in one sentence. And you—what you did, well . . . of all the malicious, spiteful, wicked things to say to you!"

"Shush, Beatrix. Please." Anne looks around the corridor fearfully, as if lunatics hide in the shadows. "I don't want everyone knowing our business."

"Anne, everybody already knows—"

"I don't *care*," she hisses, whirling. She takes a deep breath, swallows. "I don't care. He's grieving and I didn't want to see it. I never want to see it again. Oh, I hate him—of course I do. I'll never forget what he did, what he was going to do, but . . ." She pauses at the foot of the stairs, turns. "But I can't help remembering the good times too."

"What did you think of the letter? For a while there, I almost changed my mind, but after seeing this and hearing him talk to you . . ." I glance at the clock. It shows two and thirty, but it can't be: The hands have been stuck on that time since the night the baby died.

"What letter, Beatrix?"

"The letter, the one I gave to the doctor. I told him to give it to you. I told him it was from me." Realization hits me like a bolt. "He never gave it to you, did he?" The statement comes out of my mouth dull, flat.

"Beatrix, I have no idea what you're talking about, but if you tried to send me letters in the asylum, that was a really stupid thing to do."

"I know, I know, but . . ." *But it was important. I was trying to do the right thing.* Was it, though? I mean, after everything he has done, how he is treating her now . . . no. Any doubt I may have had is gone. Instead, for the first time in my life, I lie to the woman whom I consider to be my very own daughter. "Oh, I was just being silly. I missed you and . . . Anne, your marriage is over. You know that, don't you?"

"I do." She clutches the banister tightly. "Don't misinterpret my grief, Beatrix, for forgiveness. When did he start this drinking?"

"He's always been a dirty drinker." I fish around in my skirts, looking for my timepiece. I find it, flick it open.

One and twenty.

Plenty of time.

"No." She takes slow steps up the stairs, as if the burden of being alive is too heavy to bear. "Not like this, he wasn't. I mean, when did he start becoming a foulmouthed, violent, verbally abusive pig?"

"After you were sent to the asylum."

"Hmm." She stops outside her bedroom door. "I suppose that's understandable." She turns the handle, enters. "Do you have any idea, Beatrix, how wonderful it is to open a door freely?"

I nod.

"No, you don't. You don't know what it is to be locked in a cell for an entire day and night, to have the fear of not knowing when someone is coming, or even *if.* You don't know how it feels to stare at four bare walls, a patch of sky. You don't know what it is to be hungry, abused, at the mercy of people who carry around keys in their pockets and hatred in their hearts."

"I—"

"No, Beatrix. I hate the way everyone thinks they can put themselves in someone else's shoes. They imagine a little scene in their head that is far from the reality of experiencing it for real. Why, I can imagine how wonderful it must be to bounce upon the moon, but I'm sure if I were to go there for real, it would kill me." She stares at me— hard. Her tears are gone. "I can also imagine a world, one in which Edgar and I live happily and peacefully. I can imagine us together, in love. But the reality, I fear, will be far, far different."

I close the heavy curtains, light the lamp next to her bed. She sits on the edge of the bed as I undo her laces.

As her corset unravels, my hands reel back in shock. She has ribs where there were none before. Lumps along the length of her spine. Her shoulder blades press sharply against her skin, as if they wish to sprout into wings. Bruises flower on her upper arms, bloom across her wrists. And beneath all this, an unhealthy shade of grayish—yellow. Everywhere.

She has been badly treated, underfed.

My God, how much she has suffered.

And all in the name of love.

I tuck her carefully into the bed, deep among the plump cushions and warm fabrics. I pat the quilt along the length of her body, cocooning her from the outside world, from everyone who ever has, and ever would, try to hurt her more than she has hurt herself.

"I deserved it, Beatrix," she murmurs. "I deserved it."

"Hush, now," I say, stroking her forehead. "Hush."

She closes her eyes, yawns. He tongue is pink; her teeth are small. She reminds me of a kitten.

"I love you, Anne."

She smiles, turns away, faces the wall.

I stay beside her for some time until her breathing slows, her chest rising and falling in the manner of sleep. And even then I stay. I sit and I watch over the woman who used to be a girl, used to be a baby. A baby in my arms, the most beautiful, precious thing in the world.

Vulnerable.

Innocent.

I sit and I watch and I weep, for all of us. I don't want anything else in this world, except for her happiness. She is everything to me.

I lean over, kiss her cheek.

She moans, rubs the kiss off.

"It's all right, Anne. It's only me," I whisper, hoping the words seep through into her dreams. I reach into my pocket, check the time. One and fifty. My fingers brush against the cold smoothness of Mr. Stanbury's ring, the cool edge of a glass bottle.

I pull it out, hold it to the light. CHLORAL. DO NOT MIX WITH ALCOHOL.

What a surprise I had, finding this beside his bed. And full too!

I didn't know what to make of all the bran on the floor, though. No doubt I trampled all over it, but . . .

Well.

The light shines through the glass.

Empty.

I hope it is enough.

I hope that whiskey makes him sick.

As I blow out the lamp and pick my way through the darkness, a clap of thunder vibrates through the house.

A storm is coming.

And I don't refer to the weather.

MISSING IN HER HEAD

Edgar
February 6th, 1886
Asquith Manor

Tap, tap, tap, tap! The water rains down the side of the church, droplets casting off and landing on my head. Tap, tap, tap, tap! A large black raven dives, landing beside me, and starts pecking the gravestone in front of me. Tap, tap, tap, tap! The Epitaph reads LADY ANNE STAN-BURY—*03/08/1857–10/04/1888. Darling daughter, wife, and murderer of your child, how we miss you, none but God alone can tell, but in heaven we will meet you, until then, farewell.*

The raven pecks harder and faster and louder, with mounting aggression, fixing me with red eyes ablaze with fire.

Tap, tap, tap, TAP!

"Sir!" An urgent voice cuts through my dream. The tapping increases in sound, and I realize I am in my bed, the tapping of the raven's beak a knocking at my chamber door.

"Mr. Stanbury, sir!" the male voice calls again, practically beating the door down.

I sit up and my head reels. I think I'm going to vomit.

Jumping out of bed, I realize in hindsight what a bad idea this was. My stomach rolls, bursting to give up its contents, and I am sick where I stand. The liquid stench gushes over the silk linen in a great, heaving, copious steam of bile.

I think I can see a few carrots.

Sweet Jesus.

My nose hurts too. Why? Did I walk into a door?

"Sir!" The hammering on the door is unrelenting, matching the throbbing in my head.

I am quite embarrassed to have any servant view me in such a state . . . but how am I to clean up the mess? The smell alone makes me gag.

"Who is it?" I shout, my throat burning.

"James, sir."

I quickly throw a blanket over the mess, swallowing bile. "Come in."

He practically bolts through the door, pausing when he sees the bran all over the floor, the blanket, and the splashes of vomit. He raises his eyebrows questioningly and immediately I resent his sparkling boots, his perfectly pressed livery.

I begrudge his *normalcy*.

Standing before me, he bows slightly and waits. I stare at his outfit. "Sir?"

The brass buttons twinkle in the early-morning light.

They mock me.

Why couldn't I have settled for such a menial role? Perhaps the servants were right. I should never have married above my station. Instead—"Sir?"

I could be wearing a uniform that merely defines my salary, instead of my whole life.

James no doubt has a woman who loves him—perhaps he even has children. The fact that I've never thought to ask, never taken an active interest in anything concerned with the servants—not even the friendly little butler, Newman . . .

"Where is Newman?" I say.

"Newman, sir?"

"Yes, Newman." My knees are trembling and I sit back on the bed.

A groan whooshes out of me as I put my head in my hands. I have never, ever, *ever* felt so sick in all my life. How much did I drink last night? I remember arguing with Anne, shouting at Miss Fortier. Then lots of crying, of hating myself, of hating my wife, of wanting to—

"Sir, Newman is out looking for . . . Oh, I have grave news!"

—kill her.

"Sir . . . Lady Stanbury is missing."

"What?" The words are sludge, thick and cold, yet a laugh splutters out of me before I can halt it. "Missing? James, she has been missing in her head for some time. What do you mean, 'missing'?"

"As in . . . gone, sir. We cannot find her, though we tried our best to do so prior to alerting you, in case it was a false concern."

A vague sense of unease creeps over my skin.

"Gone?" I repeat. "Gone to where?"

"Well . . . ," James stutters, his cheeks turning red. "Excuse me for saying so, sir, but that is the point. We don't know where. If we did, she wouldn't be missing, would she?"

And, despite everything, the servants are still rude to me. They can't help themselves. Since that day with the maids, and the bath, they became a little more respectful, a little more fearful, but still. . . .

Here we are.

I have to—I *must* make them respect me.

"She's probably just parading the grounds, you idiot boy," I say, the flippancy in my voice hiding a very real, deep, ugly concern. I shake my head, indicating his stupidity. "Did you look in the rose garden?"

"We checked there already, sir."

I sigh. "James, you're panicking about nothing. My wife has been locked up for, let's see . . . three months, or thereabouts? She's no doubt taking her time to readjust and revisit all that she has missed. She is probably enjoying the grass and the sky"—life, I think, enjoying life—"and wishes to spend time alone. Now, surely, this makes more sense than her being 'missing'? What, do you think she ran away? Where would she go?"

"No, sir, I . . ."

"Vanished, like a puff of smoke?"

"No, sir. . . "

"Killed herself?"

James looks to the floor.

Perhaps that was in poor taste.

"Sir?" James's leg shakes up and down, his foot stamping a staccato upon the floor. "Sir, what should I do? We're all really worried, sir. Maybe we should contact the police—"

"No." I hold up a hand. I need him to go; I need to think. "Not yet. In all probability, knowing Anne—which incidentally I do—she has taken it upon her pretty little head to go for an early-morning wander, and neglected to tell anyone."

"Sir?"

"James?" I reply stupidly.

"Sir—what do you want me to do? She's *gone!*"

"She hasn't 'gone,' boy." *She has,* I think. *I will never see her again.* A black terror squeezes my heart, but I can't let him see it, can't let him feel it. "Don't you think it's understandable, given the circumstance of recent months, that she might be a little forgetful?"

"Yes, sir. No, sir, I . . ." He wrings his hands. "Sir, we found blood."

"Where?"

"On her bedsheets, sir."

Blood.

Babies.

Miscarriages.

Courses.

Of course!

I laugh again at my thought process, at the pun that leads me to a relieving realization. Suddenly disgusted by what has occurred, I say, "I think that is for the womenfolk to discuss, James, not men, and certainly not such an underling as yourself." Satisfied now, I turned my back on him, move toward the window. "Kindly see to my toilet: As you can see, I am filthy. I wish to clean myself up before I follow this ridiculous notion of Anne being 'missing' any further. Do I make myself clear?"

"But, sir, I was supposed—"

My temper flares, and I shout, "Do you understand your role, boy? Or do I need to make myself clearer, shout a little louder? Why do you all make me treat you like this to gain any sort of respect?"

"I—"

"Just fill my bath."

"Yes, sir." Meekly.

"And be quick about it. Fetch one of the maids too, see that she attends to this messy business of my bed."

"Yes, sir."

"At once."

"Yes, sir."

SOMETHING DREADFUL

Beatrix
February 6th, 1886
Asquith Manor

Lifting the heavy iron from the black silk, I replace it on the oven top and take off the grease paper, holding it to the light. Darn grease stains. Discarding it, I put a fresh piece of blotting in its place and start again with the second iron that has been heating while I used the first.

I may have to use a little benzoyl. This dress took me an age to sew, and I'll be darned if I'm giving up on it.

Just as I am angrily throwing aside the second paper, a voice beside me says, "I think ye ought t' try a little beer on that, miss."

Startled, I almost drop the iron. Standing beside me is Betty, poor child.

"Betty, you gave me the fright of my life!"

"Sorry t' intrude, miss," she says, curtseying. "But I brought ye breakfast. James is nowhere t' be found, and I couldn't have ye starve, now, could I?"

"Oh, thank you, Betty," I say. The toast is beautifully done, golden and buttery. Just how both Anne and I prefer it.

"Ye most welcome, miss," she says, turning to leave.

"Betty?"

"Yes, miss?"

"What did you say about the beer?"

"Beer, miss. Ye mix it wit' a bit o' water and ammonia, put ye sponge in it, dry it, and put it on ye silk. Good as new it will be, good as new." Betty beams as if she has just informed me of the meaning of life.

"How do you know that?" I ask gently. She is a scullery maid; how can she possibly know about the treatment of expensive silks?

"Me ma, miss. Before she got sick she was a lady's maid, just like ye. She ne'er forgot what she learned, and she passed it on to me when I was but a bairn."

I smile at her. She is still a bairn, but doesn't realize it. Oh, for the days when we were both young and innocent!

"Well, Betty," I say, pausing. I know better than to ask her how her mother fares—if her daughter is in service as a scullery maid, I have no need to inquire. Betty's position speaks for itself—her mother must be awfully poor to send so young a child out to work. "Thank you. After all my years as a lady's maid, I never did hear that one."

Betty beams so hard she looks about to burst. "Well, miss, I'm glad t' have shared somethin' wit' ye. I hate scrubbin' the pans an' pots an' gettin' all sweaty." She hops a little on the spot. "Ye know, miss, I hope one day to be like me ma, a real lady's maid, but I hope I can service one as kind as Lady Anne—oh, I mean, Lady Stanbury . . . I still get confused sometimes." She blushes a pretty pink. "But I'm so glad she's back!"

"As am I, Betty. Don't worry about titles too much; you are not the only one to get confused. All of these titles are frightfully complicated. I once addressed a duke as 'sir.' Imagine!"

Betty giggles. "Miss, ye didn't!"

"Indeed I did. And it was mortifying, but I am still alive, and I am still employed, so a mix-up of titles is far from the worst thing in the world you can do, little Betty. But never mind. You will learn in time, whether you like it or not."

"Miss, ye toast will be cold. Please, I best be on me way," she says.

It is most unlike Betty to be leaving me voluntarily; normally, she flutters about my skirts as much as she possibly can. Probably she is eager to see Anne.

"Of course." I pick up a piece and take a bite in front of her. Swallowing, I declare it to be the best toast ever made, and Betty looks as if she will explode. She still hops, obviously torn between me and her idol.

"Go, child. I know how many chores you have. By the way, though, could you kindly tell James to come and see me when you find him?"

"I will, miss. I most def'in'ly will." With that, she skips out of the room.

What an utterly delightful and most charming child. Could enchant the birds right out of their nests.

I must ask Dorris, the housekeeper, about getting me some beer.

Turning the oven off, I put the dress aside. I wash and dress and take the stairs to Anne's chamber. Stepping onto the landing, I am greeted by the most unusual sight of Newman and James huddled together. Evidently hearing my footsteps, they turn in unison toward me.

"What is happening?" I say, stopping in my tracks. I have never seen them loitering like this outside Anne's chamber, and I am unsure how to react. "Is the lady unwell? Why did she not call for me? Is the call system broken? Newman, I did mention it to you before!" I am indignant.

"Miss Fortier, the bell structure is perfectly fine. However, whether Lady Stanbury is fine or not is yet to be determined," Newman says.

"She is missing!" splutters James. "I told Mr. Stanbury, but the man wouldn't hear of it. He is in a bad state—not emotional, though, if you grab my meaning. The man vomited all over his bed, his nose is the size of a pancake, and I swear I saw flecks of blood on his hands too." He grimaces.

"Let me into her chamber," I say.

"Certainly, madam, but please take heed to look about you carefully. You are surely the person best placed to see if anything is missing."

Why would I need to see if anything is missing?

Have we been robbed?

Standing aside, the gentlemen let me pass. The room is dark, the curtains still drawn closed from last night. The oil lamp is lit, casting an eerie orange glow over the bed. I look underneath it: The chamber pot is empty. Either unused or already cleaned, which tells me at least one thing. But I keep this knowledge to myself.

The covers have been flung to the floor as if in great haste, and the sheet underneath is marred with brownish red streaks. Dried blood. Perhaps my lady had her courses, but then again . . .

"Did you see the blood?" I call out to James and Newman.

"We did, madam, though we wish we hadn't. Most disrespectful to have seen a thing like that—from our lady, no less," Newman calls back, and I hear him mumble something to James.

I suspect they both wish they could burn out their eyes at this moment, and it wouldn't surprise me if Mr. Stanbury commanded them to. Once he had sobered up enough to realize the potential severity of this situation.

Sobering up . . .

Wait.

Mr. Stanbury was drunk last night. He was aggressive and verbally abusive toward Anne. According to James, he was sick this morning, and wearing a swollen nose. This most surely indicates an abundance of alcohol consumed, by a man ill with grief, consumed with anger, and out of his mind at dinner.

And now, this morning, Anne is missing.

I can't say for definite whether her courses are due, as with her having been away I have not been able to monitor them. If they are, it is most unlike Anne to have allowed this embarrassment to have occurred, unless it caught her by surprise, which happens to all women occasionally.

But if not . . . where has this blood come from?

Why is Anne nowhere to be seen?

Is there a perfectly innocent explanation hidden in all this?

Or is it something much more sinister—and obvious?

"James," I say, coming out of the room. "Find Betty. She can ride a horse faster than anyone in this house. Tell her to go to the nearest police station immediately. Newman, bring Lord Damsbridge. I think something dreadful has happened."

BRANDISHING A RAKE

Beatrix
February 6th, 1886
Asquith Manor

From the moment Betty took off on the horse, word spread fast: through the kitchen, down the corridors, across the gardens, into the stables, and into the ears of everyone employed at Asquith Manor.

The only person who as yet remains uninformed was Lord Damsbridge, who is nowhere to be found—not in the dower house—but this does not surprise me. He often takes off on business matters without informing the servants.

Newman, James, and I told everyone that the police were shortly on their way, and all errands were dropped. All of the house's staff is therefore gathered in the hallway an hour later when the policemen arrive, picking their way through the grand entrance slowly, purposefully, looking left, right, up, down, and everywhere all around them as if they expect to find Anne hiding in a rafter, or perhaps behind the door. Betty stands a ways behind them, peering around their legs and looking worriedly at me. I give her a quick smile.

"Now, what's all this fuss about a murder?" The taller of the three gentleman steps forward, takes off his hat, and casts a suspicious

glance over everyone. Mrs. Cook wipes her face on her apron, her snif-
fles the only answer to his question. I hesitate as to whether I should
speak first or wait to be directly spoken to. I decide on the latter.

"My name is Superintendent Blake, and these are my two senior
officers, Inspector Drum, and Inspector Jones." The other two nod,
standing behind their boss, as the man in charge walks farther into the
house, coming to a stop a few feet away from me, but not looking at me.
"Who is in charge of this manor?"

Nobody speaks.

He tuts and shakes his head.

"You, madam," he says, pointing to Mrs. Cook. "Why are you
crying?"

Mrs. Cook wipes her eyes daintily and curtseys, nearly toppling
backward in her grief. "Why, sir, because by all accounts, our lady has
been butchered!"

"Really? 'By all accounts'? That's the story I've just been told by
this little lass behind me too. Girl, come in here." Betty creeps in and,
looking up at him, stands as still as I've ever seen her.

She's stopped hopping.

"Little one, what was your name again?"

"Betty, sir."

"Go and stand over there next to your contemporaries, please."

She scuttles over to me and half hides herself in my skirts. I brush
my hand over the top of her head, soothing her. She trembles under
my touch, and I wonder what happened to make her so scared.

"You." The Inspector directly addresses me, coming over and
standing so close to me that I can see my reflection in his badge.

"Yes, sir." I curtsey just perfectly, never taking my eyes from his.

"What is your name?"

"Miss Fortier."

"Can you tell me what is going on here? Because I must say, I'm
rather puzzled."

"Puzzled by what, sir?"

"A young girl comes running into my station, crying loudly about a murder, and her mistress being missing, and blood on a bed. Now, to me, this rather flimsy evidence does not a 'murder' make. Yet I indulge the child, and bring two of my best officers all the way out here to investigate, and yet on my arrival, I find only servants. Where is the master of the house?"

"I don't know, sir."

"You don't know?" He stands back from me and addresses the rest of the house. "Does anyone know where your master is?"

Silence.

Sniffing.

"Well?"

Betty scuffles her feet along the floor.

I decide to take the lead. "Sir, Lord Damsbridge often has business needs to attend to, so it's not unusual for him to be absent."

"Really? And what about"—he pulls a notebook out of his pocket and squints at it—"a 'Mr. Stanbury'? He is the husband of the missing woman, yes?"

"Yes, he is, and he's in his room, sir."

"Why is he not down here with you lot?"

A cough.

A mumbled obscenity.

"Miss Fortier, why is the master of the house not here?"

I don't know how to tell him it's because half of the household wishes to kill him, and the man is probably scared for his life.

He sighs. "Right, seeing as nobody wants to answer that question, here's the most important one. How long has Lady Stanbury been missing?"

"Since this morning, sir."

"'This morning'?"

"Well, since last night, I suppose."

"Well, which is it?"

"I don't know, sir. She was here last night, but then she wasn't this morning."

"I'll kill 'im!" a voice comes from outside, and all of us turn to the sound. Within mere seconds, Daniel comes bounding up the steps, leaping two of them at a time, shouting at the top of his lungs, "I tell you, I'll kill 'im! Where is he, the bastard?" He comes to a dead halt when he sees the three policemen, the garden rake hovering above his head. Yet the superintendent doesn't let his surprise show at all, not moving a muscle. Even his face remains still.

"I suggest you lower that weapon, son."

Daniel does so.

The superintendent sighs again. "Put him in the drawing room, lads, and make sure he stays there." The two inspectors drag Daniel away with quite unnecessary force.

The superintendent turns back to us. "Can anyone explain to me what just happened?"

The only response he receives is the ticking of a clock, until it is interrupted by a very young, very shrill voice.

"'Cause Mr. Stanbury kilt Lady Anne, an' 'cause we all want t' kill 'im! I mean, Lady Stanbury!"

"Betty!" I hiss at her, and she hides farther among my skirts as the superintendent approaches us.

"Forgive the lass, sir. She doesn't know what she says."

His impassive face meets mine. "I think this she does, Miss Fortier. Out of the mouths of babes, and all that. Little one, come out of there at once."

She peeks out of the fabric, her hand clasped firmly around my leg.

"Is it true? Does everyone believe that Mr. Stanbury has killed Lady Stanbury?"

"Yes, sir." Quietly.

Something flashes across his features, before he turns away from us and moves his arm in a sweeping gesture. "Does anyone else have a weapon about their person?"

Shakes of the head all round, but Mrs. Cook turns a deep shade of red, and one of the laundry maids turns a peculiar shade of white.

I'm not the only one to notice.

"Ladies?"

Mrs. Cook reaches under her skirts and pulls out a large pan while the maid drops a poker from behind her back onto the floor.

"Hmm." Superintendent Blake walks over to them, shaking his head. "And what were you doing with these?"

"I was drying the pan, sir."

"I'm sure you were . . . Mrs.?"

"Cook. Mrs. Cook."

"Well, kindly make your way to the drawing room also, thank you. There's a good woman," he says as she guiltily follows his order. "And you, child?"

The maid who dropped the poker looks at him and promptly faints, her head crashing heavily against the floor.

"And I'm sure she was poking the fire. All of you, outside, immediately. I will speak with you again shortly." The two inspectors come back into the hallway, one of them carrying the rake, and they startle as they notice the maid on the floor.

"What happened to her?" one of them says.

"She fainted, lad. Who is guarding the boy?"

"Smithson, sir. A fat woman just ran in there too. What did she do?"

The superintendent shakes his head. "Come on, lads, the rest of the men are where they should be, correct?"

"Yes, sir. Sir, isn't this the house where that woman killed her baby last year?"

"Yes. Now, everyone, like I told you, outside. Now. Before I arrest the lot of you."

Betty refuses to let go of my skirts as we make our way outside, and I ask her if she is all right.

"I'm all right, miss, thank ye. But they scare me, those police. Are they gonna arrest us all, like 'ee said?"

"No, Betty. It's just a threat. He has no reason to arrest us. You've done well today, my child." I kiss her on the forehead and hold her tight while the police go about their business of finding Mr. Stanbury.

In the bedroom.

Drunk.

Scared.

Just where we want him.

WASH IN YOUR OWN PISS

Edgar
February 13th, 1886
Local jail

My hands are shaking and I don't know if it's because of the lack of whiskey in this place, or out of fear. I wish that I was still drunk, and that this week had been nothing but a figment of my imagination, but these walls seem very real, as do the steel bars that prevent me from leaving this cell. The bruises on my arms are very real too.

"Mr. Stanbury?" A policeman approaches my cell, coming to a standstill mere inches from the bars.

"Sir! Please can I have some water?" I jump up from the bed, and hold out a long-since-empty cup.

He tuts and takes it. I follow his footsteps down the corridor until he disappears from sight. My throat hitches, but thankfully after a few seconds, he reappears.

"Here." He pushes the cup toward me with such force that half of it sloshes onto the floor. It's all I can do to not fall to my knees and lick up the precious, wasted liquid. It is tepid, but I don't care.

I gulp it, and wipe my mouth. "Thank you, I—"

He interrupts me with a low, aggressive utterance. "Murderer."

A laugh explodes out of me, just as it did when James, the footman, suggested that my wife was missing. Just as it did during the indictment, when the charges were read against me. "You are all mad. She's no doubt taken off for a walk."

"And a week later, there's still no sign of her? That's a long bloody walk, mate."

"Well, perhaps she went to visit some friends and neglected to inform anyone. She is, after all, a lunatic." I correct myself quickly. "Was a lunatic. *Was*."

"I don't think so, Mr. Stanbury, and neither does anyone else. Is that why you killed her? Because she is a 'lunatic,' as you say?"

"No, I—"

"Because she murdered your baby, right? You decided to get your revenge. You waited for her to be discharged, all the while plotting, and then as soon as she was released, you—"

"No!" I throw myself upon the bars. "No, no, no! You have it all wrong. You have everything wrong! I didn't kill her. How could I? She's my wife, for God's sake!"

He looks down at me and sneers. "*Was* your wife, you mean? She's dead."

How, what? Did they find her body? Can it really be true?

"Did you . . . Is she . . . I mean . . ." I stumble backward, dropping the cup on the floor. "Is she—"

"Dead?" The policeman crosses his arms. "Is that what you were going to ask me? Is that what you are trying to verbalize, you drunken fool?"

"I . . . I—"

"You left enough blood of hers on the ground for any jury in the land to convict you. There's no way she 'walked' anywhere. Corpses don't generally move. This means you put her somewhere afterward. So, where did you put her, huh?"

"I . . ." I fall to the floor. Where is that smelly, stinking blanket? I want to cover myself in it. I never want to move, ever again. My life is over.

"Get off your hands and knees, you piece of scum."

No, no. I shall not. Nobody listens to me. Nobody knows me. I just want to be away from here, anywhere but in this cell. I don't deserve to be here. I haven't done anything wrong. . . .

"Here." He throws something into the cell, something that makes a tinkling sound as it lands, glinting, in the corner. "Lord Damsbridge sends his regards." I pick up the object and open my hand.

My ring. I lost it a while ago; sure I'd put it in my desk drawer. My *locked* desk drawer—the safest place I could think of. Confused, I turn it over and over in my palm, searching for an answer in the gold.

How has the policeman gotten my ring, and why?

What does he mean by "Lord Damsbridge sends his regards"?

"I don't understand," I say, shivering. "I simply don't understand. How did you get this? Where did you find it?"

"Yours, is it?" he says. "Funny. I could've *sworn* that was your wife's family crest. Sorry. Your *dead wife's* family crest. Strangest thing, eh? As I said, your father-in-law sends you his regards."

And just like that, all I have done, and all that I am, has been discovered.

They took it.

I *told* Dr. Savage that someone had been going through my things, and now I know it was the truth.

They really were.

I have lost everything.

"I have been set up," I say, picking up the ring. I cross over to the bars and hold it out to him. "This is proof, irrefutable *proof*, that whatever they tell you is a lie. I no more murdered my wife than I murdered my son." I sit on the floor, my arm held aloft. "It wasn't me, it wasn't me. He can't punish me like this. You have to believe me."

The ring is whipped out of my hand and pocketed, before he squats and brings his face close to mine. An inch of air is all that separates us, yet it is as insurmountable as walking through the metal bars.

"Have you looked in the mirror, Mr. Stanbury? A fine shiner you've got there. Fought you, did she? You know, I'm actually wondering now, given the value of hindsight and all, whether you had something to do with your son's death too. But no matter. If we can't get you on that, we can certainly get you for the murder of your wife. There's more than enough proof you killed her, and many a man has been hanged on circumstantial evidence." His nose wrinkles as he sniffs. "In the meantime, I suggest you try to get some sleep or, at the very least, a wash."

He knows.

His stance, his sneer, his cold dismissal of my very valid argument is wrong. Very wrong. Unless, of course, Lord Damsbridge is . . .

I've been so stupid.

"How much is he paying you?" I wipe my face, so weary now, so tired. Tired of living a lie. Something happens inside me, a snapping of something essential to life. I'm tired of the plotting and planning and living on the edge of a knife. Tired of life and death and love and insanity and drink and everything. Tired of constantly trying to demand respect, and failing at even that. But mostly I am tired of being me, the son of my father, the one who started this whole thing. I was never anything to him but an instrument: one he sent out into the world to do his own dirty work.

"I don't know what you're talking about," he says, unperturbed, brushing invisible dirt from his trousers as he stands up. He is so close to me that I hear his knees crack.

"You do," I say, forcing sound into my throat, unwilling to give up, not just yet . . . not yet. "Your eyes betray you! Lord Damsbridge! How much is he paying you to set me up?"

His face twists into something approaching a sneer, part disdain, and part disgust, as if I were nothing but something rotten on the bottom of his perfectly shined shoes.

I realize that he will never admit it, and try a different approach. "Look. I know that you know what I'm talking about. I *know* it. But if you won't admit that to me, then I understand that too; no doubt he is paying you far more than you could ever earn on your salary, and I, more than anyone, understand the pull and the attraction of money." He continues to stare at me. "But can you at least take me somewhere so I can have a wash, sir? You even said yourself that I smell offensive."

His jaw works, and for a moment, I imagine with relief that my words have registered with him. Until he says, "Wash in your own piss, murderer."

"Jones! Inspector Jones!" A new voice echoes down the long gray corridor. "Jones!"

"Ah, that's my signal to leave. I want to leave you with just one thing, Mr. Stanbury." He throws the ring into the air, catches it, and smiles. "Crime just doesn't pay in the end, does it?"

DETECTED CONCLUSION

Dr. Savage
February 13th, 1886
Local jail

The police regard me with suspicion as I enter their domain. They manifest their collective impatience with the insult of an alienist's intrusion by twitching awkwardly or outrightly ignoring my presence. Some officers move away while the more curious among them remain, gossiping quietly. Hostility crackles in the air, amplified by the usual shouts and howls echoing from the cells beyond. One particular officer leans against a wall, idly tapping his truncheon against his upper thigh, eyeing me from underneath his hat as if I were the criminal. No doubt he is new and restless—eager to arrest someone.

"Gentlemen," I say politely, dropping my bag onto a small chair in the entrance hall. My purposefully deferential tone hits the right nerve. A few chests puff out; truncheons withdraw. For the moment at least, they feel their rightful authority over me has been exerted. I am reminded of birds twisting in the wind as the flock's prejudicial enmity flies away.

"All right, boys, quiet down." A dissenting murmur ascends through the group as an incredibly tall gentleman steps to the forefront and nods at me. He is almost military in his manner, and I wonder if he was in the force.

"Good evening, Doctor. I'm Superintendent Blake from the Criminal Investigation Department, in charge of this lot for my sins. I'm afraid that the more immature among us are rather morbidly excited by this most unusual case. However, these two gentlemen behind me, Inspector Drum and Inspector Jones, are slightly more professional in their approach and that's why the rest of this raggle are still sergeants." A collective snigger rises through the crowd, and the superintendent apparently notices for the first time that one of the alluded-to "professionals" appears to absent. "Where is Inspector Jones?" He turns to the other inspector, a prematurely white-haired man. "Inspector Drum?"

"I think he went to take a piss, guv," calls someone from the crowd.

Inspector Drum shrugs.

Superintendent Blake puffs out his cheeks. "Are we all assembled here for a reason, you bunch of conkers? Stop your gawking, and attend to your duties! We're up to our ears in criminals as it is! Go, all of you, now!" The men start to disperse. "Blight!" The superintendent yanks the collar of a man walking innocently behind him, practically decapitating the poor fellow. "Go and find Inspector Jones. Tell him to meet us in the kitchen." He pushes him away and Blight quickly disappears through a side door.

"You've caused quite a hubbub among my men, Doctor. Now, let's have a nice pot of tea while we wait for Inspector Jones. I think he has a bladder problem; he's forever disappearing of late. Inspector Drum, run ahead, will you, and put the water on. There's a good fellow." I pick up my bag, and together the two of us start walking through the station.

"Now, Doctor, I can't say I'm happy to be seeing you again so soon. Doesn't reflect well upon us as a force, I'm afraid, when people go around killing each other and going missing, and here we are supposed to be *preventing* crime. Half our station is out already. I won't lie to you—the whole damn town is inhabited by lawless buffoons. But most of the crimes are relatively petty and victimless: larceny, prostitution, drunkenness, vagrancy, and of course, the occasional domestic dispute. None of which ever end up in court, even if someone dies." We come to a door, and he rummages in his pockets, eventually pulling out a set of keys. He struggles with the lock for a moment, before noticing my silence. Turning to me, he raises his eyebrows. "Ah, you're probably thinking I'm a heartless bastard, aren't you? Sorry, Doctor. But the truth is that most murder victims don't get much attention. I mean, who cares if another prostitute is found dead?" He tries the door again and resorts to kicking it until it pops open. We descend a long, gloomy staircase. "But an infamous, aristocratic woman—well, that's different."

"It should not matter what part of society one comes from, Superintendent," I say, trying not to look too closely at the inhabitants of the cells on either side of me. "Every victim deserves justice. After all, ranking is merely an accident of birth."

"Is it? Can't say I've ever thought of it like that. Look, no matter. Fifty of my men are out now, continuing the search for Lady Stanbury." He scratches his chin. "I must say, though, I'm rather shocked by this turn of events within such an eminent family. I mean, what are the chances of a husband and wife both committing separate murders? There's got to be more to this than meets the eye, Doctor." Entering the kitchen, Inspector Drum and four steaming mugs of tea await us, the former wobbling precariously on the back two legs of a chair. We settle down. The drink is bitter, but comforting on such a cold night.

Inspector Drum tells us that Inspector Jones is on his way.

"Where was he?"

"Blight came running in, red as a prawn, boss. Told me he was on the pot."

The superintendent raises his eyebrows at me. "I don't suppose you'd look at the man's waterworks for him, would you?"

"No damn alienist is coming near my private parts," says the errant inspector, entering the room and looking at the drinks. "No offense, Doc, but I'd rather see a proper *doctor*." He pushes his tea away from him as he sits down. "No tea for me, thanks," he adds, an expression of dislike on his face. I can't decide whether his countenance is born of the conversation, or if he is just naturally predisposed to rudeness.

Inspector Drum starts laughing. "He can't even have a drink without running for a piss!"

"I can recommend a different doctor for you, Inspector Jones," I say.

"Are we here to discuss my cock, or are we here to solve a missing person's case?"

Anger. Negativity. Presumptuous.

"I think it's a murder case, actually," Inspector Drum says, slurping his tea.

The superintendent leans over and swats him on his ear. "Doctor, you're here because Lord Damsbridge specifically requested that you join us on this case. We're not likely to refuse him much: not when he contributes so generously to our funding. Anything he asks, we'll try our very best to accommodate, you understand?" He pauses and takes a long sip of his tea. "Anyway, what kind of men would we be if we didn't do it out of the goodness of our hearts? The man's only grandson is dead, and now his only daughter is missing. The bugger might be rich, but he's lost everything that matters."

I nod.

"I'd say thousands of pounds in the bank matters," says Inspector Drum. "We should be paid more in all. Working seven days a week just ain't natural, sir."

The superintendent pulls a face and ignores him. "Anyway, Doctor, he says that you know Mr. Stanbury reasonably well from your contact with him while looking after his wife." He turns to Inspector

Drum. "The one who is missing, lad." He drains the rest of his tea slowly, before adding thoughtfully, "So far, there's no body."

"I reckon we'll find one soon enough, though, boss. Probably she's been dumped in the river, and it'll take a week for her body to bloat and rise. All that blood in the garden?" He shudders. "Nobody can bleed that much and survive. Hey, maybe this mad doctor would like to have a guess where the body is." He leans over the table toward me, his eyes shining. "I'll bet you a shilling to a shit it's in the river."

I cross my arms and lean away from him. Superintendent Blake looks uncomfortable. "Inspector Drum, kindly desist with your un-warranted, unfounded allegations and imaginings. Why did I ever make you an inspector?"

"'Cause I'm good, boss." Inspector Drum sits back in his chair. "I see you're not a gambling man, Doctor."

"No, I'm not. Leads to degeneration of the mind."

"Really? Bloody hell. Perhaps I should stop, then. Anyway, I'll find the woman, bet or no bet. Got a nose like a hound, I have."

"You have in all, always sticking it into other people's businesses," says Inspector Jones. "Sir, if I were you I'd let me do the investigating on this one." He looks pointedly at Inspector Drum. *"Alone."*

"Need two of you, lad."

"Well, what about teaming me up with someone else, then?"

"Oi, what's wrong with me?" Inspector Drum says.

"You're presumptuous, careless, idiotic, stupid, and your tea tastes like piss," Inspector Jones replies, his face stony.

"How would you know? You haven't even tasted it! And if it does, then it tastes like your piss, most probably, seeing as you have a prob-lem with your—"

"That's enough, lads. Why, you are quite an embarrassment! Look, Doctor, the broad and the short of it is that it's not just Lord Damsbridge who wants you here. I also have a duty to inquire as to whether the prisoner is of sound mind. We can't send him to trial if he's not, and again, that's something you can help us with. I know there needs to be two reports, so I've already contacted another doctor. He should be arriving in the next few days to give an impartial assessment of Mr. Stanbury."

Inspector Jones mumbles something about getting Inspector Drum's head tested too.

"So, Doctor, there you have it. A few of my lads are already convinced that he's gone ahead and murdered this poor lass, as you can see." He frowns at Inspector Drum. "I'm sure I taught you to *detect*, Inspector, not to jump to conclusions."

"Aye, you did, boss, and that is my detected conclusion."

"Idiot," says Inspector Jones.

"Where is Mr. Stanbury now?" I ask, keeping my opinions and thoughts of this whole situation to myself.

"In a cell, of course," says the superintendent, draining the last of his tea. "He's not too happy about it, but then, none of them ever are. It's not exactly the Langham Hotel here."

"I'd like to speak with him."

"Yes, obviously, but first let me tell you what we've found. One of the young maids in the employ of Lord Damsbridge took it upon herself to get on a horse and come down to the station. It took a while to garner that her mistress had gone missing under suspicious circumstances during the night, but when we eventually learned of the lady in question's name, we moved quickly. We all knew we were potentially looking at a revenge killing right from the off. Some of my officers said that they wouldn't blame the man for doing what he did to the woman who killed his child, but they were the ones who found the disfigured baby in the family's kitchen last year. I immediately took these men off the case, as their emotions would stop their ability to be objective and contribute effectively to the investigation.

"We arrived at the house, and I sent some of my men to conduct a search of the area surrounding the manor.

"I decided to examine the boudoir first. On entering Lady Stanbury's chamber, I immediately found what appeared to be a small amount of blood in the middle of the bed. On checking her windows, which incidentally were free of any obstruction, I found them locked and indeed bolted from the inside. I tried to unlock them and though it took me quite some time, I managed to do so. Looking out, I saw the room was high and on the second level of the house, with a good thirty- or forty-foot drop to the ground. So whoever entered her room, if indeed anybody did, must have come through the inside of the house.

"Nothing seemed overtly amiss in the room, no obvious signs of a struggle. The lady's entire toilet was lined up neatly atop a vanity table. The mirror was intact and covered with a black sheet.

"I wondered if any of the furniture had been moved from its original position, though a struggle could have ensued without anything being displaced. Or the perpetrator could simply have tidied up after himself. But we needed to check. We summoned one of the housemaids from the garden. She tearfully clarified that everything was in its proper place.

"Underneath the bed was a chamber pot, which was empty of any bodily fluids. This indicated that whatever happened to Lady Stanbury did so before the light of the morning, when she most likely would have made use of it. Of course, if a crime had indeed been committed, the cover of night is a tool of even the most idiotic. It doesn't take a genius to work out that you're less likely to be seen under a blanket of darkness while everyone is sleeping.

"It wasn't until I found a long trestle of hair, hidden at the edge of a rug with its roots still attached, that I realized a crime had indeed been committed. This wasn't something as simple as an unhappy woman running away. One of my men bagged it. It takes considerable force to remove one's hair by the very roots on that which they grow, Doctor.

"I didn't find anything else in the room, or in any of the others. My men and I went over them, three, four times: ever careful to pay attention to even the smallest of details. We almost expected at any moment to come across a body stuffed inside a wardrobe, or perhaps bundled in a fireplace. But we didn't. That was it. All we found was the blood and the hair. Yet the garden gave us some more information— much more. A patch of blood-soaked ground, roughly five feet in diameter, a man's bloody footprint, and a lady's garter.

"Mr. Stanbury refused to come out, and it took two of my men to break the door down. They found him weeping in the corner next to a vomit-ridden bed. He was clutching a candlestick. They told me the smell of stale alcohol hung heavily in the air and around his person, though a cold bucket of water indicated that at some point he had tried to wash himself. And the weirdest thing is that the floor was full of bran." He shakes his head.

"So there you have it, Doctor, a whole wealth of circumstantial evidence that points to a murder. But we've got no body. And without one, it's going to be difficult to do a damn thing. You've got to speak with him and find out what on earth happened."

WHAT RING?

Dr. Savage
February 13th, 1886
The cell

As the warden draws back the bolt on the cell door, a mess of stinking rags huddled in the corner jerks at the sound.

"Stanbury?"

Silence.

"What happened, Stanbury? Did you drink alcohol with the chloral I gave you? Did you take it the night Anne disappeared?"

He shifts slightly.

"Stanbury?" I reach out to him, recoiling as a terribly strong, fecal stench assails me. Embarrassed at my own reaction, I take a deep breath through my mouth and ask him as gently as I can what happened.

He still doesn't move.

"Stanbury!"

A voice comes from underneath the blanket.

"He's got the ring, Doctor. The ring. They know everything."

"What are you talking about? What 'ring'?" I suppress my frustration. "Focus, will you? Did you take the chloral together with the alcohol? This is important, Stanbury. You could end up in prison—or worse. I need you to tell me."

"No, no, no. I didn't." He shrugs the blanket off him and moves toward the light, his whole body shaking. As he draws closer, I gasp. His eyes are almost completely red, riddled with burst blood vessels. "Remember, you told me not to mix them. I couldn't give up the drink, so I never took it. At least, not that time."

I breathe a silent sigh of relief. Thank God. If he admitted taking chloral and drinking, then my reputation would be in tatters. Never mind the fact that I told him not to combine the two: Alcoholics are notorious for not abiding to instructions. I would therefore be deemed negligent for putting the chloral in his hands. If the governors found out I prescribed the drug to him, and he had killed his wife while under its influence . . . I would lose my job and be shamed. I could even be deemed an accessory to the murder. Mr. Stanbury would go free, of course: The medico-legal world knows that chloral plus alcohol equals temporary insanity.

I mentally shake off my concerns.

There is nothing to worry about.

He said so himself—he didn't combine the two.

Then what happened?

I look at him more closely. The last time I shook hands with this man, he met my gaze and told me he had stopped drinking, yet the sour smell of recently ingested whiskey had danced on his breath. I had chosen to ignore it, too excited was I in my want to return him to his wife. I was selfish and overeager to discharge Lady Stanbury into his care. How could I have been so blind? I was a fool to think he could ever have forgiven her.

He lied then and he is lying now.

I am a doctor specializing in psychiatry. My gift lies in detecting personalities and secrets, digging up the truth and seeing people for who and what they truly are. Why did I not see in him the need for revenge, rooted in blood, anger, and ale?

That day in Asquith Manor.

"When I finally realized that she, she . . . killed our baby, and it was no mistake, I . . . I had some really dark ideas.

"I miss my wife, but I don't know if I can love her anymore.

"The servants all hate me. None of this belongs to me. Our marriage was a sham."

The potential for harm was always there.

Oh God.

"I put bran on the floor. They've been sneaking into my bedroom at night, going through my things."

Alcoholic delusions.

Mr. Stanbury clears his throat, a deep, phlegmy sort of grunt. "I need a drink, Doctor. My hands won't stop shaking." He stretches them out toward me. The grime and dirt do little to conceal the giveaway symptom of delirium tremens. I fondle the paper in my pocket. The certificate I am about to fill.

"I'm worried I'm getting really sick, Doctor."

"You're feeling ill because you're withdrawing from the alcohol."

"Well, can you get me some?"

"I can't, Stanbury. I can't give you anything. I'm sorry."

"I . . . Okay, but I didn't hurt her, Doctor. . . . It's all a conspiracy. They took the ring, for God's sake! The only reason they would have taken that is to show me what they've done, to tell me that they know, to make sure that *I* know what they've done. They—"

You're a liar, I think. You hid your drinking from me, from your wife. You lied; you told me you had nipped it in the bud. And now you've driven yourself to delusions. You've drunk so much that you've killed your wife, a poor woman who never meant to do anyone any harm. Alcoholism is not an excuse for murder. I told you it was harmful. I told you that I was worried about you, and you didn't listen.

"Stanbury . . . who are 'they'?"

He uncoils himself and screams, then punches the wall. "My damn father-in-law! The policemen! My wife! The maid! All of them, they're all 'they'!"

It's worse than I thought.

"Do you remember being brought here, Stanbury?"

"Yes, of course I do!" He paces with renewed life. "It was my wife who had memory loss, not me!"

Reaching into my pocket, I take out my notebook and pen, ready to write, when he crosses over to the bars and shakes them.

"I am not your goddamn patient! Don't be writing anything—listen to me! You have to get me out of here! I'll tell you the whole story as long as you promise to save me, Doctor; you have to save me from this mess I find myself in. I didn't kill anyone—I didn't! Is it not enough that my own flesh and blood has been torn from me? Is it not enough that I am sober?" He throws himself onto the floor, begging me with his eyes and with his hands. The anger flows out of him as quickly as it came, and his body starts to shake with great, heaving sobs.

I drag a chair over to the bars and instruct him to tell me everything, right from the beginning.

He raises his head, looks at me imploringly. "I'll tell you everything Doctor, everything. I didn't kill my wife. You must believe me."

By the time Edgar finishes telling me his story, my head hurts.

His tale is wild and utterly unbelievable. To consider it would imply that Lady Stanbury is alive.

But it would also mean that she was never mad—just very, very clever. That she deceived me. But how? She had all the signs and symptoms of puerperal mania. She killed her baby. That much is an absolute fact. I've seen the pictures. There was a dead baby on her kitchen floor. I diagnosed her. She had amnesia, hysteria, mania. Therefore, it cannot be true.

It is a physical impossibility. I have never met a woman intelligent enough to do such a thing, and don't expect I ever will. Mother nature simply did not equip them with such foresight nor acumen.

"You purposefully set out to seduce Lady Anne?"

He nods. "Yes, and it was easy. Laughably so. I'm ashamed, Doctor, but at that time I truly didn't have a sense of moral honor. When my father came up with the plan, I never . . . I never questioned him. The thought of living in such a grand house washed away any fears or concerns I might have had about playing a role, lying to an innocent woman. Well, I always meant to deceive her, but I never expected to fall in love.

"I'd been working there for months—my father made me get a job as a ticket taker. We knew she loved the theater. I hoped against hope that one day, just once, she would walk in during my shift, and just about when I had lost all expectation that she would ever come in at all, she did. She came right up to me and her hand brushed against mine." He laughs, bitterly. "I nearly dropped the ticket, Doctor, and now I wish I had. I wish I had torn up that ticket and spat in her face and chased her away. I wish I had told her the truth." He starts to cry. "But, Doctor, she captivated me. I had never before seen her up close and . . . oh, she was so well dressed! Her skin had never seen the sun; her hair had never been knotted. She literally shone with vitality, life, and *money*, and then she smiled at me and called me 'sir'—sir! I'd never been called that before. This woman, *the* woman my father set me out to deceive, was the woman I had been searching for all my life. I didn't fall in love with her instantly—I admit that. But soon enough, my enemy became my love. She bought me a suit once; well, I don't know if she bought it or *where* it came from, but as soon as I put it on I was . . . transformed. It felt like a cloak, a covering for not only my skin but who I was, and everything my father represented. Suddenly, I was a man people would nod to, bow to, and *everyone* called me 'sir.' It felt like a dream. I was proud. It was a metamorphosis. She cocooned me in a suit and turned me into a butterfly.

"And then I moved into the house, and everything changed. The servants would whisper behind my back. I told you about the two maids, didn't I? They hated me for marrying Anne, and they let their feelings show. They were disrespectful, rude . . . They were awful to me, Doctor. And when Anne, when she . . . went away, they became worse, because there was nobody there to shelter me from them. I realized that without her, I was nothing, and had nothing. I started to resent the fact that circumstances had landed me in this position, where I had no money anymore and was looked at with disgust. I had thought myself raised to the position of a lord, but I was never anything except what they told me I was. A beggar in a gentleman's suit."

"So you hated her for raising you up?"

"No, I merely resented her for leaving me alone as I crashed back down. I *never* hated her—not even now. Oh, I might've thought I did when I was drunk—and I'm ashamed for how I acted when I was—but I never, ever hated her for killing our child. I hated how she made me feel. I hated her condition and the fact that my child was dead, but I *never hated her*. Not unless I was drunk, but . . . well, I've explained all that." He pauses, traces a circle in the dirt at his feet.

"Did you kill her?"

He looks at me, tears in his eyes. "No. Everyone thinks I did, because she made me angry at myself, and I turned that anger on her, but I didn't. I didn't. I love her."

There are more murders committed through love than hate, I think. "And what about the money? You seduced her for her fortune, right?"

He shakes his head and laughs mirthlessly. "Yes, I suppose that's how it started out. For my father, it was most definitely about the money. He believed he was entitled to it, that it was his birthright, my birthright, my future children's birthright. For a while I was convinced too. I really thought that I was taking back that which was denied to my grandmother, a woman who fell in love with a king and died alone, in poverty, in France."

"King?"

"King William the Fourth. He seduced my grandmother—Dorothea Bland—or 'Mrs. Jordan' as she was more popularly known."

"William the Fourth? But he was married to Princess Adelaide of Saxe-Meiningen."

"Yes, but this was *before* he was married, when he was merely the Duke of Clarence. He lived with Dorothea for twenty years, had ten illegitimate children with her, and threw her away for the sake of politics." He spits the word into the dirt.

"I don't understand," I say. "Are you telling me William the Fourth was your grandfather?"

"No."

"Then what has all this got to do with Lord Damsbridge?"

Stanbury shuffles, impatient. "It has everything to do with Lord Damsbridge! That bastard king left her destitute, yes—but there's not much she could have done—a woman, going against royalty—no, it's not him that we were trying to claim from. My grandmother was the greatest showgirl of her time, Doctor. She attracted the attention of wealthy men from all over the world. After she was shunned by King William, she finally found the love and security she had craved for many years—in the arms of the sixth Earl of Damsbridge. Unfortunately, he impregnated her and refused to honor his commitment.

"Don't you see? Two men, both wealthy beyond anything you could ever imagine. One woman, desperately seeking security for her children's future. William the Fourth provided for his illegitimate children, but the sixth Earl of Damsbridge refused to acknowledge that my father was even his son. Ultimately, it was Dorothea who suffered—never having known true love—and my father . . . forced to grow up in poverty because he was a bastard child that the earl denied all knowledge of. Dorothea hated the earl for that—she hated knowing that when she died, her young son would grow up penniless and alone."

"My God," I say.

He nods. "My father asked the earl for help, Doctor. And it never came. He never lifted a single finger. He *never* acknowledged his bastard child. Do you understand now?"

"Your grandfather and Anne's great-grandfather are one and the same?"

"Yes."

"But, Stanbury, don't you see the irony here? What this . . . William, king, earl, whoever . . . did to your grandmother . . . how they made her feel . . . Can't you see that your actions would have been just as bad? Worse, in fact? Can't you see—"

"But I wasn't going to do it!" He wipes his nose on a dirty, snot-ridden sleeve. "Well, I was . . . but I didn't! I told you—from the moment I fell in love with her, I couldn't go through with it. And that was after she lost our first child, Doctor. I saw her then—truly saw her. She was nothing like her father, or his father before him—she was just like Dorothea. A woman. A woman who would love her child, and who would love a husband if given the chance to have one. My grandmother never had that chance, Doctor, and I fell in love with Anne because she was everything Dorothea should have been. Not just a mother, but a wife." He takes a breath, pauses. "The hatred, the resentment . . . it had gone on long enough, Doctor. My father has lived his entire life feeling nothing but pain, jealousy, and resentment, yet I . . . *I* had the privilege of falling in love. I didn't want to contribute to any more hate. I didn't marry her because I loved her. I *stayed* with her because that love grew.

"But then my father, I knew he would never believe that, and even if he did he would still want the money—would still want me to go through with the original plan—so I did what I could. I took out loans, and I gave him all the money. I tried to make him quiet, satisfied. I tried to make him leave us alone. To let me live with Anne as her true husband, a gentleman, just like he always wanted me to be, but without hurting anyone."

He sighs, starts to cry. "I wish I had just refused. I wish I had told him to rob a bank, if he wanted money so badly. I wish I'd never met her—all she has done is bring me pain. It's not worth it, Doctor. Love is just not worth it. When you lose it . . . it hurts too much. I can't bear it."

Guilt. He's feeling guilty and all this . . . rubbish is just a delusional fantasy caused by his excessive intake of alcohol.

I sigh, ready to leave and give my opinion to the superintendent. I've had enough of this family. I just want to get back to my hospital. My home. A niggle itches at my memory—his mentioning of the king—as intangible as a dream, fleeting, untouchable, and I let it go. "Did you follow Anne for long?"

"I didn't have to. My father has been telling me all about her family my whole life. I was born to be her husband, Doctor. He gave me no choice. He showed me Asquith Manor when I was ten years old. I knew everything about her: where she went, who she visited, her hobbies—"

"You said your father was dead," I say flatly.

"Yes, well, I had to. That's what he wanted me to say. The man is alive and unfortunately reasonably healthy. I can give you his address, if you like."

"So you lied."

"Yes, I lied. But I shouldn't be hanged for a mistruth! You must find my father; he will confirm everything I've told you. Please, you have to help me. This is a damn bloody setup! They want me dead! They blame me for Anne killing our child, and this is their revenge!"

At the risk of pandering to a desperate man, I write the address and he calms slightly. I don't question him any further. I can't possibly ask him where he put the body. Not now. At least this will prove—one way or another—whether his story has even a small measure of truth to it. Perhaps then I can follow it further, though I don't expect anything to come of it. I tell him I must leave, and he nods.

"I loved her!" he calls as I walk away. "I loved her, I loved her! I would never have hurt her, ever!" I ignore him, fill out a certificate, and hand it to Inspector Jones along with the address of his father.

"Sane, eh?" He smiles and folds the paper in four before slipping it into a pocket. "Bloody shame, isn't it? Poor woman."

I nod, eager to leave. Yes. He is sane. He is responsible. Drink often gets blamed for producing insanity, but not in this case. He couldn't cope with what she did, killed her, and is now trying to justify his actions with a ludicrous story.

Crime itself is not proof of a defective mind.

I turn away, but the inspector stops me with a hand on my arm.

"Hold up, Doc. Our boy in there is suffering from alcohol withdrawal, isn't he? Is there anything I can do to make him feel better? It must be bloody awful if not havin' a beer can do that to you. Do you reckon he feels as bad as he looks?"

"Just some hearty food and plenty of water. Thank you. Very kind of you." I give him a halfhearted smile and take another step toward the door.

"Wait a sec! If I drink too much beer, will I get like that too?" He looks worried. "Especially with my, erm," he whispers, "water problem. Bit embarrassing. Don't want to discuss it around the lads."

I pat him on the back. "No. Mr. Stanbury has been drinking spirits very heavily, for a period of some months. I shouldn't worry. You're quite all right to have a beer or two, though I would advise you to have a doctor look at your"—I flick my eyes across his crotch—"you know."

His face brightens, and yet the smile doesn't quite reach his eyes. "Thanks so much, Doctor. You've just made my day. I'm off to the pub."

As I leave the building, a very strong sense of unease cloaks me under its shadows, a sense of something being very, very wrong.

I mentally rebuff myself and shrug it off.

My work here is done.

A DUCK WITHOUT WATER

Beatrix
February 17th, 1886
Asquith Manor

Forcing the last of my clothes in to my suitcase, I add a purse of lavender for the finishing touch. The contents threaten to burst at the seams, and in an effort to flatten them even further, I sit on the suitcase. My eyes start stinging again and I wipe my handkerchief over my face, sniffing.

"Miss? Oh, miss!" Betty comes running in and jumps on me, crushing me in her embrace. "Miss, ye don't 'ave t' leave, do ye? Oh, miss, I couldn' bear it 'ere without ye!" A tear trickles down a red and flushed cheek. Her bottom lip wobbles, and she holds something in her hands. It scrunches as she moves against me.

"What do you have there, Betty?" I gently push her away from me.

"What?" She stares down at her hand and opens it. A ball of paper falls to the floor. "It's nothin', miss. Stupid idea anyway." She draws back a tiny foot to kick it, but I am quicker than she. I snatch it up and open it.

It is a child's drawing, but one that could have been drawn by a girl or boy much younger than Betty.

"Oh, you darling thing . . ."

She starts to cry. "I thought if I cud just draw 'er well enough, then I cud make lots of them an' put 'em on trees, and give 'em t' people and stuff and maybe someone wud find 'er, but I'm not good enough. It doesn't look anythin' like 'er! And I don't know 'ow t' write, so 'ow cud I put 'missing' at t' top anyway?" She takes it from me and crumples it back into a tight ball. "And now it doesn't matter, 'cause you're leavin' me too!"

I don't have the heart to tell her that a poster, no matter how well depicted, would be useless. Instead, I focus on the second issue. "I have to go, Betty. What's a lady's maid without a lady?"

Her lip sticks out even farther, and she embraces me again, harder.

"It's like a sock without a shoe, Betty," I say, into her hair.

She stops crying for a moment and looks at me, her arms entwined behind my neck, her sweet breath blowing gently upon my nose.

"Or like, like . . ." She leans back, blowing out her cheeks and rubbing her eyes with the backs of her grubby little hands. The poster is all but forgotten. She tentatively joins in the game. "Like, miss . . . the grass without the sun?"

I smile. "A duck without water."

"A man without a hat."

"A man without a hat, Betty?"

She giggles. "Well, miss, they don't 'alf look funny when they take 'em off."

"Don't be saying that to Lord Damsbridge, now—he's quite paranoid about that bald spot of his!"

She bursts into happy squeals of laughter. Oh, the beautiful, innocent fickleness of youth! "Miss, ye know what else?"

"I know that you've helped flatten my suitcase, you fat lump."

She laughs even harder, because she knows she's anything but. "But, miss, they're even stranger without their clothes on! Men, I mean."

"Betty!" I swipe her gently across the ear. "How would you know that?"

"Well, ye remember tha' mornin' when none of us cud find Lady Anne? I mean, Lady Stanbury?"

"Yes?"

"I crept into Mr. Stanbury's room, like, 'cause I could 'ear 'im shoutin' at Mr. James an' I was, erm . . . I was—"

"Poking your little nose into other people's business?"

She blushes. "Well, p'raps a little . . . aye, I was—but I saw 'im naked, miss!"

"Who, Mr. Stanbury?"

She nods furiously and starts talking even faster: unsure whether she is in trouble or not. "Only from behind, though, miss, and I thought I might o' seen a bit of blood on 'im, now I think about it." She hops off me and looks to the floor. "On 'is hands, like."

How could she have seen that?

"'Ee 'ad 'is back t' me, and he was bent over, like, takin' off 'is clothes. I didn't see that much o' 'im, miss, not really, only his back and his, erm . . . behind bits—his bottom—and well, when 'ee threw t' dirty clothes' out o' 'is way, I noticed 'ee 'ad dried blood on 'is fingers."

"Did you tell the police?"

"No, miss. Nobody asked me. I mean, even them inspectors what came round askin' everyone, like, they dinnae ask anythin' of me, not afta I spoke wiv' them in t' police station."

"Would you be willing to tell them?"

"Oh yes, miss, o' course. I'd kill Mr. Stanbury wit' me own 'ands, so I would, if I got t' chance. I never liked 'im, but nobody ever listens t' children, do they? Especially just a maid, like me."

"They'll listen now, Betty. I promise."

I sweep her into another hug, and the both of us hold tight, neither wanting to let the other go.

"Betty?"

"Yes, miss?"

"Can you keep a secret? A really, really big one?"

Her lip threatens to wobble again, but she smiles and makes the sign of an X in front of her chest. "Cross me 'eart, miss."

I whisper into her ear, *"I'll be back someday to look after you, I promise."*

WRONG SIDE OF THE ROAD

Dr. Savage
February 18th, 1886
Old Bailey

No matter how many times I enter this building, the assizes never ceases to impress upon me a feeling of inadequateness. Built though it was to accommodate perhaps three or four hundred men, on this day at least twice that many have squeezed their way in. I can only guess at how many extra benches have been crammed inside—the gallery is practically bursting past its capacity. Everyone is jostling for a good view and leg space.

When the clerk finally orders the prisoner brought up, I breathe a sigh of relief. I'm not sure what morbid sense of curiosity made me attend today. I didn't want to come and I don't wish to stay, but again, that feeling of uneasiness clutches my soul and glues my feet to the floor as surely as if someone had shackled them to it. Perhaps I need to atone for my mistake and see justice delivered.

The murmuring around me ceases as the room falls silent save for one fellow's screech. Curious, I follow the sound. A man clutches precariously to a pillar, his friends jeering from behind him.

Mr. Stanbury moves slowly into the room, dressed in the black uniform of a prisoner. It hangs loosely on his thinner-than-usual frame. They've cleaned him up a bit, though, which pleases me. Yet when the odd flash of photography temporarily lights up his face, I see a haunted, terrified man.

I pull out my writing pad. If I write everything down, I can reflect upon it and grow as a physician.

Dullness of perception. Introverted. Slowness of reaction. Aversion to light.

Classic symptoms of an alcoholic.

I sigh. My heart goes out to him, but he murdered his wife. I discharged an innocent, fragile woman into the hands of a man who planned to murder her, and I never saw it coming.

It is partly my fault she is dead.

I must atone.

I must understand why my judgment was so lacking.

It cannot happen again.

I turn my attention back to the courtroom and study the man walking alongside Mr. Stanbury. His publicly appointed defense lawyer, no doubt. Once seated, the lawyer idly begins to pick his nails, barely noticing the weeping man beside him. The buzz in the courtroom commences once more, amid much finger pointing.

"I'm going to have them all arrested for rioting, or at the very least, routing . . . the bloody ruffians." A hand lands upon my shoulder and I flinch. Inspector Jones stands above me, grinning at my surprise. He has something green stuck in his teeth. "There must be another two hundred of the buggers outside, all pushing and shouting to get in." He squeezes my neck firmly before diverting his attention to the young stranger sitting next to me. "Sir, can you move out of that seat? Official police business."

The young man looks up at him, then at me, and yawns, apparently unimpressed with Jones's rank and much more interested in getting a decent glimpse of the proceedings. Slowly, he says, "Listen, mate . . . I've been sat 'ere fer a bleeding age waitin' to see this. Ye can bloody well stand." With that, he turns away from us both, yawns again, crosses his arms and legs, and settles in for the long haul.

"Do you want to be arrested for obstruction of justice?"

The man doesn't even blink. "Bull's cock. I ain't obstructin' nuffink. You bleedin' bobbies, all a bunch o' tarts, ye are."

"Right. We'll do this the hard way, then, shall we?" Inspector Jones winks at me, then raises his voice above the crowd. "Arrest this man at once!"

Suddenly, we are the center of attention, and a few lightbulbs flash in our direction. Mortified, I turn away and my eyes meet those of my dead patient's father. Lord Damsbridge is watching us, observing the spectacle with a hint of disgust.

Inspector Jones is now holding the man by his collar.

I wonder if Superintendent Blake taught him how to do that.

"Hey, lemme go, ye bleedin filth bag!"

Another two officers swiftly descend upon him, and the crowd parts a clear alley to the doors as the sergeants drag him out, the man kicking and contesting his innocence loudly. Cheers and whistles follow his departure, a surprising bout of entertainment for the excited spectators.

Inspector Jones dabs at his brow, grinning, before bending over and wiping the seat of the vacated chair with his sleeve. Satisfied, he wiggles himself down into a comfortable position.

"As I was saying, Doc . . . ruffians, the lot of them. You can tell a lot by a man's disposition, such as that idiot I just had arrested. I guarantee you he's a criminal, and we'll find something he's done. One more piece of scum off the streets. You mark my words, Doc: Men like your hitherto friend over there have an innate desire to walk on the wrong side of the road."

I look at him, incredulous that an enforcer of the law could be so judgmental. Surely, a man is innocent until proven otherwise? It is a well-known fact that certain people are uncooperative with the police, for no other reason than that they simply abhor authority. It doesn't necessarily mean they have committed a crime. Mr. Stanbury may be an alcoholic, and he may be guilty, but I shudder to think that everyone, innocent and guilty alike, could be treated like this until final judgement is passed.

He sees the expression in my features and smiles. "You think it's only alienists such as yourself that can see the badness and the madness in men? You should try doing my job for a week, or even a day. Human beings are a sorrowful lot, and the more of them we clear from the streets, the better. I can tell just by looking at Mr. Stanbury that he's guilty of a crime. Nineteen out of twenty men who go on trial for murder are guilty of it, you know. I don't need to know about phreny—what's it—"

"Phrenology."

"Whatever. I only went through the bloody motions of going through the house because it's my job, and because I'm not superintendent. Yet." He puts his feet up on the chair in front of him, much to the annoyance of an elderly lady. She starts and glares at him but remains silent, turning back to watch Mr. Stanbury.

"Nineteen out of twenty?" I say, incredulous. "What about the innocent one, then?"

"Doc, you've got a lot to learn. I reckon spending all that time inside the madhouse has made you lose a bit of your capacity for reality. Do you think the judge up there cares about the 'innocent one'?" He gestures to the galley around us. "'*One*'? Come off it. Capital punishment is necessary so society can be protected. And if one or two men and women slip through the net?" He shrugs again. "Who cares, Doc? Humans make mistakes. The few innocent are a justifiable sacrifice for the greater good."

He continues, warming to his theme.

"Anyway, he's not innocent, Doc. Take a good look at his past, his character. His reputation is as important as what he's done, and from all I've heard and seen, he's a bad one. You watch, Doc. He's going to be found rightly guilty, and he's going to hang for it."

He throws something metal up into the air—a ring—catches it, and smiles.

A ring.

I WAS WARNED

Edgar
February 18th, 1886
Old Bailey

Everyone in here wishes me an agonizing death. "Those who enter, leave hope behind ye," I say, quietly, my sobbing starting anew at the thought.

My lawyer rouses himself and frowns.

"Be quiet, lad," he says gruffly, before resuming his sleeping position.

I wonder if he is embarrassed by my tears, or just annoyed at being out of bed.

"It's Dante," I tell him in a whisper, but he either doesn't hear or chooses not to respond. I want to punch him, but I don't have the energy. At least I can be grateful that the shaking in my body seems to have subsided somewhat; it is only when I lift my hands now that a slight tremor affects me. I'm never, ever touching alcohol again. Ever. Rather than wanting a drink, I find the thought of one makes me feel physically ill.

I hide my hands in my lap, lest the trembling be wrongly interpreted as a sign of nervousness, of guilt.

"What's going to happen to me?" I press the man, whispering. Someone somewhere is paying him to do a job, and the least he can do is tell me what's going on.

He blinks rapidly at me, his bleary eyes watering. "I said, be quiet! Please! This court business is the most laborious form of legal business. Do you know how many good lawyers have given it up to make their own fortunes in private practices? I would go straight into my own office too, lad, if I had the money, but I don't. So please. Let me mentally prepare. I've had no sleep at all this week, and if you want me to defend you, I suggest you let me get a few minutes' rest before the circus begins!" He moves away from me as far as the cramped space between us allows, and puts his head back on the table. I know that the pattern in the wood, the grain of it underneath his elbows, will be imprinted into my mind forever.

Within minutes my lawyer starts to snore gently, and I wonder at him. This man probably holds my very life in his hands, yet he prefers to sleep instead of asking me questions. Doesn't he want to know my side of the story? Doesn't he want to know whether he is defending an innocent or a guilty man? Doesn't that make a difference to how he is going to defend me? I want to stand up and scream and demand a different lawyer, but something tells me that would serve only to work against me.

I scan the crowd quickly, anxiously, looking for a friendly face. There is none to be found; the jury offers me nothing but twelve solemn faces, and it dawns upon me how alone I am and have always been.

Except for those brief months in which I had a son.

Tears threaten again, as I am hit anew with grief. Will it ever leave me?

I close my eyes. The trial. Focus on the present.

What was I doing?

I was looking for a face in the crowd.

I open my eyes.

Is my father here, then? Has he come to watch the downfall that he created?

He is not.

Bugger him, the bloody alcoholic. I hope he takes his stupid wife in her stupid red dress and throws himself off a cliff. I hope he rots in hell.

I thought I'd lost everything, but now I may well lose my very life. The fear of death makes me realize how very badly I wish to live, even without my son.

My father and I were playing a game that we were never going to win and we have been deviously outwitted, with the worst consequences.

I wonder what part, if any, Anne had to play in all this.

I wonder where she is.

I wonder what happened to her.

Is it even slightly possible that I did have a role to play in her death, without realizing it? Is it possible that I killed her, just as she wanted?

I'm so confused.

I'm still wondering when the counsel for the prosecution walks in.

It's Mr. Cropper. Lord Damsbridge's lawyer—the man I approached shortly after Anne's incarceration. He winks, and suddenly his words come back to me.

"If you think things are looking bad for you now, trust me and heed this warning: They will get a whole lot worse for you.

"When they changed the law and introduced divorce, the number of murders in this country declined in exact proportion to rising separations."

The hairs along my arms and legs stand on end, a crawling up my spine.

It was there all along.

I was warned, and I didn't listen.

A BITTER TASTE

Dr. Savage
February 18th, 1886
Old Bailey

I recognize that man. For a moment or two I am unable to place him, his face half-hidden underneath the generic lawyer's wig. Yet as his eyes rise to meet my own in a brief meeting of acknowledgment, it dawns on me. Of course, he is Lord Damsbridge's own personal lawyer, and I met with him once or twice, albeit briefly, when dealing with Anne's case and subsequent incarceration. He is renowned to be a genius with the law: spinning tiny, seemingly unrelated threads into a detailed, beautiful conclusion of impenetrable evidence into which his victims are seamlessly bound and caught.

I glance over at Mr. Stanbury. By the horrified expression on his face, he too just realized who he's up against in this trial.

Will the lawyer be lenient, considering the extenuating circumstances of Mr. Stanbury's grief and subsequent drinking problem? Will the prosecution consider that despite all evidence to the contrary, no body has been found?

What if Lord Damsbridge eventually blames me?

Will I be sitting at that defense table next month, next year?

No, it wasn't my fault. How was I to know he was planning to murder her? But the fact that she disappeared the day after her release from my charge no doubt casts some doubt in people's minds as to my skill, and this bothers me almost as much as the next thought that enters my mind: the last thing she told Tuke and me under hypnosis.

"I did it because I love my child. Wouldn't any mother care to do the same? I didn't feel guilty when the blood ran over my hands, yet neither did I feel vindicated. I just felt I had protected my child in the only way I knew how."

Suddenly worried, I turn my head, searching for Lord Damsbridge. He is sitting at the prosecutor's table, a small smile on his face. His expression is not that of a man whose daughter has just been murdered. But then, what do I expect? Every man deals with grief in his own way. Perhaps he smiles at the notion of justice.

My friend would despair of me—poor old Tuke. He always did tell me I got far too involved with my patients.

"All rise!" the clerk's voice thunders across the room, and hundreds of people stand as the judge himself enters the court, his white wig a little larger than those adorning the lawyers.

"Here he comes, the good old hand of justice," Inspector Jones says, digging me in the side. "He's a toughie, this one. Couldn't have gotten a better man for the case. He never lets them get away with murder." He laughs. "Get it? Get away with murder?"

A bitter taste presents itself in my mouth, as it dawns on me rather rapidly that I dislike this man sitting next to me.

Immensely.

I can't help myself. Something isn't right. "Did you check the address I gave you?"

"A what, who?"

"The address, Inspector. When I left Mr. Stanbury the last time I visited him in the jail, I asked you to check out his father's address for me."

"Oh, that. Yes, I did."

His eyes shift to the right and in that instant I know instinctively he is lying. Before I can say more, the judge takes his place in the high wooden dock and the clerk's voice booms around the court.

"Be seated!" A universal rustle of clothing and plummeting of heads indicates everyone's acquiescence.

I continue in a whisper. "And? What did you find?"

He hisses under his breath, "His father was alive and well, contrary to what I believe he told Lord Damsbridge and his daughter. Why do you suppose a man would lie about his own father being dead? Disgusting, that is, and merely proves what a despicable character he is."

Wait.

Mr. Stanbury told the truth about something.

"Anyway, none of it matters. All that matters is justice is served here, today."

"What did his father tell you?"

"That any son of his that laid hands upon a woman was dead to him. He said that he would help the investigation in any way possible, and in fact, gave us some very important information." He grins at me, an excited, morbid sneer.

"What did he give you?"

He sucks air through his teeth and waves a hand dismissively. The court is now silent; we should not be talking.

"Look, can we discuss this later? All will be revealed, as they say. Watch and learn, Doc. Watch and learn."

NOT A GENTLEMAN BY BIRTH

Edgar
February 18th, 1886
Defense table

When the judge enters the court, my stomach rebels. I grab hold of my lawyer's shoulder and squeeze. The room tilts as if I were on a ship.

"Ow! What was that for? I told you to let me sleep—" He rubs his eyes and blinks, seeing the man for himself. "Oh, right." His freshly rested eyes glint behind a sheen of excitement, or possibly anticipation.

"The judge, he's here—"

"I know. I can bloody well see him. Look, lad, don't speak now! The prosecution are about to present their case." A man with long hair takes to the stand and reads out the indictment, and my plea of not guilty.

The "clerk" continues on, presenting two medical certificates, both of which declare me sane.

The clerk stands down and Mr. Cropper takes his place, adjusting his wig and coughing loudly.

"May it please you, gentlemen of the jury and Your Lordships, that I am counsel for this case brought against the prisoner, to bring him to justice for a desperately heinous transgression." He speaks softly, quietly, so much so that I struggle to hear him as do most of the members of the jury; several are leaning forward in their seats. "I am overwhelmed with gratitude that so many of you feel personally affronted by what has occurred, and I thank you all for your support in attending today." He turns around and points a twisted finger in my direction. I lower myself down farther into my chair, but not before I return the gesture with a look of absolute hatred. I hope he knows I know, the bloody bastard. Oh, wait. Everyone is looking at me. Damn. What if they saw that? They are going to think I really am a murderer. What should I do now? Cry? Adopt a serious expression? Should I meet their gazes, or stare at the floor? I chew on my nails and inspect them instead. The old man continues.

"The prisoner at the bar stands indicted for that awful level of crime, gentlemen. That of murder. And not just any old murder—oh no—but one born of the utmost calculation and intention. A murder of the woman this man promised to cherish, love, and value for life. A woman who gave him everything, and from whom he *took* everything. His wife."

He winks at me and turns back to the jury box.

I start to stand but think the better of it. Killing an old man in front of several hundred people would certainly ensure that I go to the gallows. Perhaps if I'm quiet, I still have a chance. After all, I'm not guilty of that which he accuses me. I know that now, without any doubt.

"The prisoner I just pointed to is Mr. Edgar Stanbury, not a gentleman by birth, but referred to as such by virtue of the marriage to his victim: Lady Stanbury, formerly known as Lady Anne, the only child born of the eighth Earl of Damsbridge. She was a woman who inherited her father's morals, a woman of the noblest heritage, a staple within our community, a pillar of strength, a model of virtue. Though society was initially outraged regarding her involvement with the death of her baby, I'm equally sure that that very same society now feels only pity and sympathy for a woman who didn't understand what she did—who had a *disease*—and was thus certified insane. Yet her own husband was unable to garner those compassionate feelings that even a perfect stranger would find hard to suppress.

"The crime Mr. Stanbury committed is so shocking, so *repellent*, that many of you in this room will find it difficult to believe that such a scheming, evil man exists in our world today. Believe it, gentlemen. He has been proven to be sane, unlike his wife was. She was merely a victim of his inherent deceitfulness. He knew exactly what he was doing. We will prove motive and opportunity. And you, members of the jury, have a very important job to do here today: that is to fairly, swiftly, and justly find him guilty of his crime.

"On the night of February fifth, 1886, Lady Stanbury was discharged recovered, sane, after a three-month stay at Royal Bethlem Hospital, where she had undergone treatment for puerperal mania. Her husband, Mr. Stanbury, escorted her back to the house, where they both indulged in supper, and he *over*indulged in alcohol. He is a known alcoholic, gentlemen. During the evening, he became more and more verbally abusive toward his wife, and at one point threatened to kill her. This was clearly heard by several witnesses, and directly observed by the lady's maid—Miss Fortier. Upon hearing her mistress's distress, Miss Fortier intervened and took Lady Stanbury to her bed, whereupon she settled her to sleep. Lady Stanbury was afraid of her husband at this point, but believed she had been taken to safety. Sadly, she had not, gentlemen . . . as by the next morning, Lady Stanbury had vanished. One of the footmen, a Mr. James, ventured to inform Mr. Stanbury of his wife's disappearance, whereupon he found his master in a very disheveled state, reeking of alcohol and acting strangely. The police were contacted, Mr. Stanbury was arrested, and evidence was found that Lady Stanbury had been murdered."

He moves his gaze away from the jury and pauses, looking to the ceiling, before sighing and saying, quietly, clearly, and slowly:

"To this day, Lady Stanbury's body has not been found. Tragedy, an absolute tragedy."

One member of the jury dabs a handkerchief under an eye.

"I'm sure the question on many of your minds is this: How can one possibly suggest that a murder has been carried out in the absence of any body? Indeed how can we find it prudent to try a man on such a charge? Well, not least of these reasons are that she was well-known, gentlemen, for being both an earl's daughter, and having her face across the front of every newspaper in the land but a year ago! If she were still alive, she would have been seen, and found, by now! Authorities up to *three hundred miles away* from the scene of the crime were notified, and she hasn't been found!" The jury nods thoughtfully.

"Experience has taught us, gentlemen, that a train of circumstances above that of human contrivance—coupled with a wealth of circumstantial evidence—*does* a fact make. I don't wish to take up too much of your time regarding the rather more salient points at such an early moment in the trial, but I want you to hear, learn, and remember these words throughout this trial: corpus delicti. Body of evidence. We have more than enough of this for you to find this man guilty. You will all have the chance to learn and review the case as you see fit, but remember these words!" He smacks his hands down hard on the bench, causing a juror in the front to flinch. "It is most important! I will establish clear evidence of a murder—without any reasonable doubt—and once you have heard the information and witness attestations for yourselves, you will find that absence of a body cannot stop you from finding this man guilty. As a well-known passage in Genesis says, 'Whoso sheddeth man's blood, by man shall his blood be shed.' It is your duty, gentlemen, to dole out the swift hand of rightful justice." He bows slightly, coughs up another part of a lung, and rasps, "Your witness, Mr. Smithingson."

"Blood be shed"? Oh God, they really are going to push for the death penalty. I grasp my lawyer's leg. "Blood," I whisper weakly. "They want my blood."

My lawyer pushes my hand away and sniffs. "I know they do, lad, but never fear. I shan't let them take a drop of it."

He pats me on the back, stands, and takes the floor. Mr. Cropper flashes him a predatory smile.

"Gentlemen of the jury, there's nothing quite like a bloodthirsty lawyer, is there?" He chuckles to himself, and a few members of the jury nervously titter politely back.

"But it is not your duty to be so, gentlemen. I actually find it . . . what's the word . . . ?" He waggles a finger in the air. "Reprehensible that my colleague here would even suggest it." He flashes a smile at Mr. Cropper, who glares back at him stonily. "Quite. Look, we're all human here, and we all make mistakes. I'm sure some of you—no, *most* of you have done the odd little crime or two? Perhaps pinched a sweet from a shop as a boy, or lied about your taxes?"

"Absolutely not!" calls one of them, in a disgusted and offended tone of voice.

"Oh, come on, course you have. Anyway, no matter. There's no crime in lying. Only if you get caught, as they say." He laughs again, and starts to pace up and down, before adopting a look of seriousness. "Which is why it is so . . . unfair that my innocent client is even here! It is almost blasphemous! Do any of you want to be a modern-day Pontius Pilate? Because you will, if you hang my client—"

Mr. Cropper jumps up. "My lord, that is slanderous in the extreme, and I resent the implication, to which my colleague has just referred, that I am some sort of . . . bloodthirsty murderer!"

The judge bangs his gavel, frowning. "I agree. Mr. Smithingson, kindly keep references to the Son of God out of this, will you?"

A small titter comes from the back of the galley while the jurors regard my lawyer with disgust.

"I didn't say anything about Jesus; I was talking about the man who crucified a man he shouldn't have—"

"Enough!"

"Apologies, my lord."

"Just get on with it. And be professional. This isn't a bloody fairground."

A reporter starts scribbling on his pad and I can only imagine what the newspapers will be headlining tomorrow. What in hell is my lawyer doing? I want another one. He's useless; he's going to send me to my death. The jury stares at my public defender in collective disgust.

"It was merely a comparison—no need to get so angry about it. Anyway, you will learn, gentlemen, during this trial that there has been no murder. This is all a big bloody farce. Why, if there had been, why is the prosecution not showing us a body? Because they don't have one! Did you know, in 1660, two men were hanged for a murder, and shortly afterward the dead victim turned up? *Alive!* Walked right into his house, he did! He'd been taken as a slave to Turkey. Do you want a repeat of that—now? What will Lady Stanbury say if she turns up and you've gone and killed her bloody husband? This ridiculous, archaic notion of an eye for an eye, a tooth for a tooth . . . Christ—anyone would think we were living in the seventeenth century! This is the *nineteenth* century! There is no such thing as a perfect murder, gentlemen. Evidence *always* remains. Yes, we have the blood . . . but whose blood? It could be anyone's—why, it could even be animal blood! There is no link between this blood and Lady Stanbury having been 'murdered'!

"I repeat: There is *no evidence of murder*, not even of a crime! The only thing my client is guilty of is that of a sin which is innocent in the eyes of the law and judged as a transgression only in the eyes of his fellow man: that he, a commoner, should have fallen in love with an aristocratic woman. My, it's almost *Romeo and Juliet* all over again. My earnest colleague here gave you a legal term to remember, and now I shall give you one. Corpus delicti. The very *same* phrase. It also means that a crime must have been proven to have occurred before any man or woman can be convicted of such crime. And that, gentlemen, is why you have no choice but to find my client innocent. That is all. Thank you." He walks back toward our table, a childlike grin on his face.

"Did all right up there, didn't I, lad? Say, did I tell you this is my first trial?"

AT THE EXPENSE OF YOUR OWN

Beatrix
February 18th, 1886
On the road

"Stop! Stop that carriage at once!"

My lord, that child cannot keep her words in her head. Although my heart aches to give her another, long-lasting cuddle, prolonging my departure will only serve to increase her childish grief. The carriage moves steadily onward, each bump and knock of the cab taking me farther away from my home and closer toward my fate.

"Madam," says the coachman. "There's a strange-lookin' woman running after us. What should I do?"

Another inhuman screech: a wrenching of a soul torn apart. Can she really be so unhappy?

"Give me my baby!"

That is not the voice of Betty.

I sink down into the seat, closing my eyes as if to drown out the sound, as if to hide.

"Madam, whoever she is, she just fell over into a puddle of mud. Should we not stop for her?" His tone wavers uneasily as he shouts over the wind, and the carriage starts to slow down.

I run a hand over the window and press my face against it. There is indeed a woman lying prone on the ground, covered in wet dirt, screaming.

"No, carry on, Mr. Davies."

The carriage issues forth with a jolt as the coachman obeys my order, whipping the horses harder.

How is she here? She shouldn't be here.

"Tell me where he is!" A thud hits the back of the carriage.

Uncharacteristic anger rises within me. "Stop the carriage, Mr. Davies."

"But, madam, I thought ye said t'—"

"Stop the carriage at once!"

I nearly smack into the screen as he pulls back on the reins with force. Instead of waiting for him to lower the steps and assist me, I jump down into the road, my boots crunching and squelching in the sludgy mix of gravel and rain. I ignore the splatter kicking up onto my dress as I rapidly approach the woman, her face paling in color as she sees the expression of anger on mine.

"Why are you throwing rocks at our carriage?"

"You've got my baby!" She picks up another rock and stands, wobbling, squinting through the rain in anguish toward the cab. "I know you have!" She tries to rush past me, and I take the stone from her before grabbing her, noticing absently that my hands encircle her upper arms with ease.

"Let go of me!"

I pull her toward me, so close that the individual veins in the whites of her eyes resemble a wildfire.

"We don't know anything of you, nor of a baby. Do you want to be arrested for vandalizing our coach?" I shake her. "Well, do you?"

She starts to speak before being taken over by a heave and vomits a stream of weak, watery green bile onto my shoes. Letting go of her in disgust, I take a step back as she falls onto the ground.

"Madam?" Mr. Davies pokes his head around the side of his box, shielding his face from the rain. "Is everything all right?"

I don't expect he can hear anything from there, nor see much either.

I wave at him as I call out, "Everything's fine! Merely a woman who has lost her way!"

"Well, she shouldn't be out in these parts, all alone!" he shouts back. "Here, I'm sure we can give 'er a lift t' the next town?"

"No, we absolutely cannot! We can't go around picking up every vagrant we see, Mr. Davies! And I fear she is sick! Get back into your place—please! I will deal with her!" He continues to peer through the rain for a moment longer, before deciding that this is a matter he has no say about. His head pops back where it should be, and the girl and I stand alone.

She looks up at me, her eyes fixed on the rock I still hold in my hand. Rain runs down her face and mixes with snot, tears, mud, and pain.

"Miss, I just want my baby. Please. I don't mean ye any trouble, I wouldn't 'ave 'armed ye." She shudders once, twice, ten times, before I realize she is ill dressed for the weather and shaking uncontrollably; the skin of her bare arms is a dusky shade of blue, her lips two slabs of ice. "I walked all t' way 'ere, miss. I been walkin' fer three days. I 'aven't eaten, and I feel terrible. But I just want my baby. Please."

Any pity I might otherwise have felt for this woman—though on closer inspection she is a mere girl—is overshadowed by my love and loyalty to another woman who means everything to me, and whom I will do anything to protect.

I kneel in front of her. "You gave your baby away. In fact, you paid someone to take him—isn't that correct?" The girl moans, and rocks back and forth in the mud. "How much was his life worth to you?"

She doesn't answer me.

"How much?" I scream in her face, and she blinks, confused by my fierce onslaught.

"Two pounds, but she wanted five—"

"'Two pounds'? Two measly pounds?"

She starts to cry harder, floundering in the wet dirt. "I didn't do anything t' 'im, miss. I got a job as a wet nurse, and I needed someone t' look after 'im. She said she would, tha'—"

I poke her in the chest.

"Ow! Listen, I—"

"You paid someone to take your own child, and in doing so sentenced him to death. Giving all of your milk to some rich woman's child at the expense of your own?" I spit into her face. "How could you? How could any mother kill her own child? Did you enroll him into a burial society too? I suppose you did. You disgust me! Do you have any idea what he would have survived upon? Do you? The dregs of bottles left around from others, and that's if he was lucky. How about a bit of dirty water, piss-ridden from the sewers? You can throw a bit of laudanum into the mix, because that's the only thing that keeps a hungry child's appetite suppressed and stops his crying. These babies die, you evil wench . . . slowly and painfully, through starvation, dehydration, and loss of their own mother's love!"

Mr. Davies chooses this moment to interfere again, this time poking his head above the carriage roof. "Everything okay, madam?"

"Everything's quite all right! I won't be a minute more!" I call, before lowering my voice once again and trying a different tack. "Listen, whatever you did in the past I'm sure you did it for the right reasons at the right time. I—"

"I didn' give 'im away t' 'ave 'im die, miss! I gave 'im t' Mrs. Harding so's she could raise 'im fer a while! I was forced out of t' workhouse an' nobody else wud 'ave me! Wet-nursing was t' only thing I could do; what was I supposed to do? I needed t' earn a living, or we'd both be dead! When I went back to get 'im, Mrs. Harding tried t' pass off another baby t' me—she tried t' tell me tha' another child was mine! She sneered at me an' laughed: She said tha' babies change a lot in a month, but it wasn't 'im, it wasn't—I know my own son. . . ."

She doesn't realize that her child is already dead and that the same death is almost upon her now. In a day or so she will be found frozen solid to the ground, and buried by a stranger in an unmarked grave. Just another victim of the brutal British weather. Yet she continues talking, teeth chattering, without even a shawl to pull around her, oblivious of her fate.

"Mrs. Harding eventually said tha' she was mistaken, tha' a rich lady paid one hundred pounds fer 'im, that 'ee was adopted out. She said 't'as better I didn't know t' name o' t' woman, like, in case I changed me mind. She said I was lucky, like, as most babies that get wiv' 'er end up dyin' o' stuff, but Mrs. Harding didn't know that I never meant Caleb t' be adopted out. She kept sayin' somethin' about how's I wanted me baby dead or I wouldn't 'ave contacted 'er. I didn't know what she meant . . . I kept on at 'er, miss; I only wanted 'er t' keep hold of him fer a while etill I saved up enough to be able to look after 'im myself. But then she said she didn't know t' name o' t' lady anyway, an' she laughed in me face when I told 'er she should ne'er 'ave given 'im away , an' she called me naive and stupid. But I ain't stupid, miss. She went t' the outhouse an' I snatched a load of papers from t' side, an' I ran 'ome, an' one o' the letters mentioned t' 'ouse up there." She points behind her, weakly, in the general direction of the manor. "I know tha' Mrs. Harding spoke t' someone in tha' house, madam— she'd written a receipt. Someone there gave 'er a lot o' money. They must've paid her fer somethin'!" She wrings her hands, desperate now. "So's I went back t' confront 'er, like, but she was gone. I can't find 'er. I've been t' the police, but they don't care. So's I been tryin' t' find my baby ever since. He ain't dead, no matter what ye say. I'd know. A mother would know! I just got t' tell them, t' rich people up there, that if they've got my baby, they've got t' give 'im back. He's not theirs, he's mine. . . . I'm sure they'll understand. They've got to. . . ." She stops and breathes heavily, almost unable to fill her lungs. I imagine each inhalation filling them with crystals of ice. Perhaps she will freeze from the inside out.

I stare at her awhile longer, practically frozen myself in sheer amazement. I wouldn't believe it unless she was cowered in front of me, right here, right now. Sheer blind luck and a mother's determination have led her to our very doorstep.

Though I can understand the power of the latter more than anyone.

A mother will never let her child go, and will literally walk to the ends of the earth for him; to hell and back if need be, into death itself. It is a sad ending for this woman, though, who failed to protect her son.

I stand up. "We don't know of any baby being adopted in these parts. The only people who live in this house now are an elderly man and a bunch of servants. The lady who lived here is dead, and so is her child. And it was her own child—I saw her swollen stomach. I'm sorry, but you've come to the wrong place. You must be mistaken."

She makes to join me but falls back into the mud with a small frown on her face.

"Are ye sure? But . . ." She looks about the field, gazes at the emptiness. "But . . . this was t' last place I cud think of. . . ."

I realize that I need not have bothered stopping the carriage. This woman is no threat to us. Her blue lips tell me all. She will be dead within the day.

"I'm sure. Now, I'm sorry, but I really have to leave now." I brush my skirts, dismissing her.

"Miss, miss . . ." A pale hand—a hand of a child—reaches out and clings limply to my dress. "Cud ye take me t' the nearest inn? Or village? I'm so cooooooold. . . ."

I flick her hand off me. "I'm sorry, but no. We don't pick up vagrants." And with that I run back to the carriage.

I force myself not to look back.

AN EVOLUTIONARY THROWBACK

Dr. Savage
February 18th, 1886
Old Bailey

"His head, sir. His basilar-metrical angle is thirty-eight degrees."

Mr. Cropper nods thoughtfully as I yawn and attempt to stretch my legs. I can't imagine where the prosecution found a phrenologist, never mind their reasons for bringing one in. It is a field much outdated, and almost everyone disregards their opinions. I don't ever consult them.

"Can you explain to the members of the jury the significance of this finding?"

The phrenologist sits straighter in the witness box. "Of course I can, yes. You and I, sir, have an angle of around twenty-eight degrees, or thereabouts."

"You can tell that by looking at me, can you?"

"Well, not exactly, but I can make an educated guess, sir. You only have to look at Mr. Stanbury to see he's an evolutionary throwback."

Someone in the gallery snorts with suppressed laughter.

" 'An evolutionary throwback,' Mr. Chime? Is that an insult?"

Mr. Chime shakes his bushy eyebrows. "Not at all, sir. It's a medical term."

It most certainly is not. This is exactly the reason these idiots have no place in, or near, my asylum.

"Look at his sloping forehead. His ears are unequal, by one millimeter."

"Right. What is the significance of these angles, please?"

"Oh. Based on my reading, he's a murderer all right."

"Mr. Chime! The client is innocent until proven guilty!" Mr. Cropper softly rebukes him, but he doesn't mean it. After all, it's his witness—and his words bleed with sarcasm.

"Oh, I'm sorry, sir. I just meant that—"

The prosecutor waves his words away with a flick of his hand. "It's quite all right. But please refrain from such comments before the defense objects to them."

"Okay. I—"

"Instead, kindly rephrase. Do you mean to say that the defendant likely has murderous tendencies owing to the shape and size of his head?"

"Yes, that's exactly what I mean. Meant. Mean." The witness blushes and pulls on his eyebrows.

"Why is that, Mr. Chime?"

"Oh. Right. Because, well, studies have been done for decades now, comparing the skulls of animals and humans, murderers and innocents, and the findings are conclusive. Animals and humans who kill have a larger basilar phreno-metrical angle."

"Kindly explain to the jury what a basilar-phreno angle is."

"It's the measurement taken from the opening of the ear to the eyebrow, and along the horizontal plane—that's sort of an invisible line. I guarantee you he's got killer tendencies. I never met a single case of a murderer with a basilar phreno-metrical angle less than thirty-five degrees, just like I never knew a man with an angle of twenty-five degrees or less to have the disposition or inclination to kill. His is thirty-eight, so . . ." He shrugs. "This type of head is that of a low and vicious person, sir. He's more like an animal, sir, than you or I. His skull is like that of a carnivorous animal."

"'A carnivorous animal.'" Mr. Cropper turns to the jury. "Did you hear that? *The defendant has the skull of a bloodthirsty, wild animal.* And we all know what wild animals like to do, don't we?" He walks up and down, waggling a finger.

"I object!" Mr. Smithingson jumps to his feet.

"What is it now?" asks the lawyer curtly.

"You can't compare my client to a carnivorous animal. I have never heard of anything so ridiculous!"

Mr. Chime interrupts. "I can, actually, sir. It's a medically proven science."

The lawyer glares at the defense.

"Sit back down, Mr. Smithingson. Only object when you have an actual reason to, please. Thank you. Continue, Mr. Chime."

"As I was saying, my lord, carnivorous animals like to kill. They like to *kill*, gentlemen." He pauses, passes his eyes across the room. "Just like the defendant."

That was unnecessary, and has absolutely no basis in scientific fact. I wait for the defense to cross-examine.

"Your witness," says Mr. Cropper as he makes his way back to the prosecution table.

Mr. Smithingson stands. "I have no questions for this witness."

The judge looks shocked, as am I.

"Are you sure, Mr. Smithingson?"

"I'm sure. Thank you."

WANTS TO KILL ME

Edgar
February 18th, 1886
Defense table

My lawyer sits back down and I kick him angrily under the table. "Why didn't you defend me?"

"What am I supposed to say? I objected, didn't I? I haven't a clue about phrenology. I'm sorry! If he says you've got a basilar-something head of thirty-eight degrees, who am I to argue with scientific fact? How can I say, 'No, he hasn't, sir. He's got an angle of twenty-three,' and then what? He measures your head in front of everyone and we get made to look like fools?" He squints at me. "And you do have a rather sloping forehead, lad. . . ."

"You do realize Mr. Cropper wants to kill me, don't you?"

I'm desperate. I want to claw at him, shout out loud, throw a rock at someone.

"Of course he does, lad. That's his job. Shush, will you? I need to listen."

I sit back, exhausted. The bastard lawyer is now questioning one of the policemen.

"You arrived at the house in the morning, arrested a couple of servants. Then what happened?" Mr. Cropper says, pacing the floor.

"We found Mr. Stanbury crouching in a corner of his bedroom, half-naked and holding a candlestick."

"What happened thereafter?"

"My men took a plaster cast of the footprint found in the garden and some photographs of the scene while I escorted Mr. Stanbury back to the station, whereupon he was in too much a distressed and drunken state for anyone to take any statements from him."

Mr. Cropper walks over to the prosecution table, rustling about underneath it for a minute before pulling out something white. He holds it up in the air and approaches the witness box. "Is this the cast you made of the footprint?"

"Yes."

Mr. Cropper goes back to the table once again, coughing as he reaches for another piece of evidence. He holds it up. "And these are the photographs?"

The policeman looks at them. "Yes."

"These, gentlemen of the jury, were taken from the crime scene. Excuse the gruesomeness—there's a lot of blood in some of them." He happily passes the photos around the jury, and turn by turn each member scrutinizes the small pictures. One man pales. The lawyer waits a few minutes before collecting them back, and I wonder at a justice system that will show "evidence" to perfect strangers whom the accused has never seen. I don't know what those photographs show.

"What did you do when you arrived at the station with the defendant?"

"We carried out normal procedure. Booked him in, took his particulars."

"How was he acting, at this point?"

"He tried to fight us off and he was rather incoherent."

"'Incoherent'? In what way?"

"He kept rambling about plots and kings and an actress called Dorothea. He didn't make any clear verbalization of anything that made sense. He was clearly intoxicated, so we put him in a cell."

"Would it be normal practice for you to seek the advice of a doctor, in these cases?"

"No, if they are obviously drunk, then we let them sleep it off."

"If they are mad, would you then call a doctor?"

"Yes, of course."

"So in your opinion, he was not mad."

"No, I clarify: He was drunk."

"Do you think he murdered his wife while he was drunk, in that case?"

"I—"

"My lord!" My glass of water almost tips as my lawyer jumps to his feet, bumping into my own arm with his. He doesn't apologize. "I must object to this line of questioning. My learned *friend* is using a loaded question. How is the witness supposed to answer? If he says yes, he is agreeing that in his opinion, my client killed his wife while drunk, yet if he says no, it equally suggests to the members of the jury that my client killed his wife, but while he was sober!"

"I agree, Mr. Smithingson," the judge says, rubbing his eyes. "Be seated. And you, Mr. Cropper: I suspect you know better by now than to use such underhand techniques during an interrogation of a witness. Rephrase the question, or move on to the next."

Astounded, I lean back into the chair, finally allowing a small flicker of hope to rest on my lips. Mr. Cropper's own mouth moves into a downward curve.

"You may continue, Mr. Cropper."

"Yes, my lord." His wrinkled old hand gestures minutely toward me from beside his waist, a tiny, almost imperceptible pointing gesture, as his thumb points toward his neck and moves in a sideways motion. The smile dies on my face. He just gestured the death penalty at me!

"Apologies for the interruption, Superintendent Blake. Now, where were we? Yes, I was asking you what part you believe Mr. Stanbury had in the murder of his wife."

The policeman is silent for some time, before raising his head and saying, "You might want to rephrase that question too, Mr. Cropper, for I cannot even say for sure, upon oath, that a murder has even been committed."

Gasps rise through the court like a flock of birds taking to the air. The policeman ignores the fuss he has created and continues.

"It is possible that one has, even probable. But I am a policeman, not a mathematician, sir. Has violence occurred within Asquith Manor? Yes, I would say so, definitely. Is Lady Stanbury missing? Evidently so, yes. Can I say for sure she has been murdered? No, I cannot. You must realize, we have not found a body. How can I say in absolute certainty that a murder has been done, less so who the perpetrator is? I suspect everyone and no one: I am merely a detective, sir. It is your job to find the truth."

The silence in the court is complete, less the sound of Mr. Cropper's heavy wheezing.

"Indeed it is, Superintendent Blake, which is the very reason you have been called to the stand to give your testimony. Let me ask you something: Are you aware of the legal term to which I earlier alluded, corpus delicti?"

"I cannot say that I am, no."

"This means, quite literally, body of evidence, Superintendent Blake. It has been taken by some laymen rather literally in recent years, hence the term 'no body, no murder.' This misinterpretation has led some people to go around killing at whim, as they believe that if they hide the body well enough, they cannot possibly be charged with a murder." From somewhere, the sound of someone nervously tapping their feet is the only accompaniment to the prosecutor's words, and seconds later a man from the galley runs out of the court.

"But they are desperately mistaken. Body of evidence, Superintendent, means that if there is sufficient evidence of any means, be it physical or circumstantial, the person accused *can* be charged with murder. So I now must expand upon your response. You believe there has been no murder, as there is no body?"

The policeman looks a little pale as he answers uneasily, "Yes...."

"Yes?"

"Erm—I'm not sure what you want me to say, sir."

"I don't want you to say anything, other than the truth. Superintendent, given the amount of blood at the scene, the hair, the signs of violence, Mr. Stanbury's behavior . . . do you believe that it is possible a murder may have been committed?"

"Well, I can't say for certain that one has, sir. I mean—"

"How much blood did you find at the scene?"

"A lot, sir."

"Can you quantify 'a lot'?"

"The patch on the ground would be indicative of at least four or five pints."

"I see. How is your medical knowledge, Superintendent?"

"Not as good as a medical man's, I expect."

Someone guffaws, and is swiftly escorted from the courtroom.

"If I was to make a patch of my own blood on the ground, right here, right now, by opening up my wrists or my throat, a patch the same size of that found upon the grass, what would happen to me?"

"You would die, unless medical attention was given to you most urgently."

"And were there any medical men on the scene?"

"No."

"Any evidence of any first aid being administered whatsoever by anyone at any point?"

"No."

"Let's get back to the footprints. Did you find any significance with them?"

"Yes, they were the same size as Mr. Stanbury's feet."

"So we have clear evidence of violence being committed, a patch of blood large enough to kill a man—who, by the way, gentlemen of the jury, holds more blood in his body than a woman—we have footprints next to the blood the exact same size as Mr. Stanbury's, and a missing woman. Is that about right, Superintendent Blake?"

"That is correct, yes."

"Then that will be all. Thank you for your cooperation." He turns and looks toward me but addresses the superintendent. "Please remain where you are, as I'm sure the defense has something to say to you."

Superintendent Blake's head drops onto his chest, and he puffs in and out with a long, slow breath. He visibly deflates on the stand as the judge calls for a brief recess. Does he believe me innocent, then?

Is at least one person in this large and unfriendly world finally on my side?

And if so, is it enough?

ACTIONS WITHOUT PROOF

Beatrix
February 18th, 1886
Old Bailey

I arrive at the courts during a recess, much out of breath and sweating despite the cold. I use my elbows to push my way through the crowd until I reach the prosecution table.

"Damn the man, Cropper! You brought in a bloody hostile, inadequate witness!"

"Don't worry yourself. He's only one man on the stand. I know what I'm doing. Focus on Mr. Chime. He was good, wasn't he?"

The two men speak in low voices, my ex-employer a deep shade of purple.

"I don't care about Mr. Chime. I care about the policeman who has just shone bloody doubt on the case. I'm not happy about this. At all."

"Well, you *should* care about Mr. Chime—as he has just verified for the jury that your son-in-law has the same characteristics of a murderous animal. They won't forget that, trust me. Fret not, my lord."

A squeak involuntarily passes my lips, and Lord Damsbridge whips his head around.

"And you. Where have you been? What took you so long? Why

are you all wet?" His voice raises an octave as he fires his questions at me. I am momentarily lost for words.

"I got caught on the road, sir. The mother of—"

"Look, I don't have time to listen to your excuses. It doesn't really matter now that you are here."

"But, sir, the mother of—"

Mr. Cropper sensibly moves away from us. My ex-employer follows him with his eyes for a moment, before returning his attention to me.

"Why are your hands shaking? I hope you're not about to have an episode of hysteria, Miss Fortier. Most insane asylums are quite unpleasant, or so I hear." He leans closer, putting his hand over mine, the warmth of his skin seeping through my gloves. The threat is implicit and, pretending to have an itch, I move my hand away. A small smile crosses his features: He knows.

"You better not be having doubts, Miss Fortier—"

"I'm not, my lord!" I interrupt him in my hysteria, struggling to keep my voice level. He needs to know about the girl, about what I've done. Perhaps he can save her. He can do anything; he can send a cab to pick her up. "It's just, if you'll listen to me, I had the most awful confrontation on the way here with—"

He misunderstands my despair.

"Remember what he has done—what he was going to do. Remember the letters, Miss Fortier. The letters from Stanbury's father, the plan. Think of Anne. He does *not* deserve your sympathy."

"He has not my sympathy, my lord," I say, tears now falling freely down my face. I feel no shame, merely exhaustion. "But you must listen to me. You don't know what I did—"

He turns away from me.

I am entreating a wall.

I'm relatively sure I'll one day be joining my ex-employer in hell, but what else was I to do?

Anne's mother saved me from death when she found me in the

street all those years ago: filthy, semiconscious, and covered in blood. Yet I have returned that favor covered in more blood. What would her dear voice say to me now, if she were here to witness all that has transpired? Would she be angry, disappointed?

I have no regrets over doing what we had to do. I would do it all again. But seeing that distraught mother on the road, leaving her there to die . . . it has pricked a conscience I never realized I had.

The judge returns too quickly and calls the court to order. Mr. Stanbury notices my appearance, and I imagine his gaze entreats me to help him. I look away, ashamed, at the tall police officer I met once before.

The defense lawyer rises and starts to speak. He looks fresh out of the university.

"Mr. Blake . . . a few things bother me about this case, and I'm hoping you can enlighten me. Are you willing to do that?"

"Of course."

"Good, thank you. What time did you say you arrived at Asquith Manor on twenty-fourth April, 1886?"

"Just after ten in the morning."

"Right. So at that time, people would be going about their work, wouldn't they?"

"Yes, I suppose."

"Yet when you arrived, the servants had been called away from their work to wait for your arrival. Is that true?"

"Yes."

"Is it suspicious that a cook would be holding a pan, and a maid a poker, in the middle of a working day, Mr. Blake? The tools of their trade, if you will?"

"I suppose not, no, but—"

"Yes . . . I know—you said, and I quote: 'presumably to make an attempt on Mr. Stanbury's life.' What confuses me is why you would jump to such a preposterous conclusion."

Silence.

"That was a question, Mr. Blake."

"Oh. Well, uh . . . I thought that because there were threats being made, and the boy with the rake. I've explained this already."

"But doesn't this frankly unjustified theory give the members of the jury an impression of the defendant's guilt? After all, most people don't go around the place killing others without a motive. So to imply that they were after Mr. Stanbury implies that they had some sort of revenge to wreak . . . which in turn suggests motive and guilt on his part in Lady Stanbury's disappearance." He turns to the jury, his smile met with a few approving nods.

Mr. Cropper and Lord Damsbridge speak lowly and rapidly to each other, but I am unable to hear what they are saying.

"Let me raise the issue of this 'boy with the rake.' Now, according to you, he harbored some rather untoward intentions toward Mr. Stanbury. Yet none of us can presume to know the motives behind others' actions without proof. Why, for all we know, the stable boy could have had amorous affection toward the lady, and decided to take it upon himself to do away with the competition! Just because one man threatened Mr. Stanbury does not mean that other members of the staff, holding perfectly innocuous objects at the time, had similar motives—"

Mr. Blake interrupts. "They looked guilty. Why, the younger maid fainted when confronted—"

"Mr. Blake, never, ever interrupt counsel. Wait a moment. Are you suggesting that 'looking' guilty is the same as being guilty?" He starts to laugh. "Is that what the police force does now? Arrest anyone who looks guilty?"

The superintendent flushes as the lawyer raises his hands to the sky.

"You don't need to answer that. Your hesitation is enough. It is all nothing but a load of supposition! Incredible, really. I'm almost lost for words. I am lost for words, in fact. Please give me a moment."

The lawyer strokes his chin for a few minutes, the only sound in the court that of anticipation and the odd, nervous whisper. I sneak a glance at Mr. Stanbury. Some of the color seems to have returned to his face and he is sitting up straighter in his chair. His gaze is fixed hopefully on his lawyer, who seems to be exceeding all of our expectations. Perhaps he does have a chance, after all. Where that will leave us, I have no idea. But I'm not sure I can have a third death on my head. Two by my own hand . . . Surely, even if he was found not guilty at trial, we could still figure something out. There is always a way . . . always. I look hopefully at Lord Damsbridge, meaning to say something to him, but he is lost in the muted conversation with Mr. Cropper, gesturing angrily toward the witness box. I don't need to see any more of this. I can't bear to watch. The girl's face flickers behind my eyes: already a ghost. Glancing once more at Mr. Stanbury; for what, I don't know—the possibility of redemption? To tell him with nothing more than a look and a grimace that I'm sorry? I rise from my seat. But he doesn't notice my leaving any more than anyone else does as I walk out of the courtroom.

I wipe an arm across my face, stemming tears I have no right to bear.

I promised my loyalty, my life, to a woman who was everything to me. Her heart, nestled safely within my bloodstained hands forevermore.

My heart weeps for all of the innocents that have ended up paying dearly for our sins.

ERRORS OF JUDGMENT

Dr. Savage
February 18th, 1886
Old Bailey

Miss Fortier brushes past me as she exits the courtroom, wiping at her eyes. It is only the second time I have seen her, and in doing so I remember the time she was in my office when Nurse Agnus referred to her as "Beatrix," and Miss Fortier's quick, curt reaction when I asked whether they knew each other.

"I met her outside, just now."

But Agnus couldn't have been outside. She was with a patient. So how . . .

"'Arrest anyone who looks guilty,'" mumbles Inspector Jones from beside me. "Like we do that."

I can't help myself. My words leave my mouth, pickled with uncharacteristic spite. "Well, yes, you do. You arrested that man who sat next to me not an hour ago, and he hadn't done anything."

The inspector looks mortally offended. "He insulted a police officer!"

The man is a pigheaded idiot.

Mr. Smithingson gathers himself and finally interrogates Superintendent Blake further, establishing that it is quite possible Mr. Stanbury was hiding not out of guilt, but out of fear, and that holding a candlestick to defend oneself against a rake-wielding man is hardly a crime. Everyone has a right to self-defense.

He throws doubt on the case, and into my mind.

A fearful man would be acting almost the same as a guilty man. Both would be defensive, scared, unable to meet people's eyes, shying away. Both would lie, but for different reasons. Both would be acting mad; both would be in fear for their lives.

He rather expertly clarifies and reinforces the fact that Superintendent Blake is not a medical man, and therefore could not accurately suggest that there were "four or five pints of blood" on the ground. He suggests that any man of the house could have left the footprints: even a woman, since it is not difficult for someone with a smaller foot to don a shoe of those larger than her own. He makes it clear that there is no evidence of Mr. Stanbury having been drunk: Someone, of course, could have planted alcohol upon his clothes. . . . Why, Mr. Stanbury himself may have spilled some upon himself! He discredits the suggestion that the defendant was acting drunk by suggesting he was in shock and fear—both of which are apt to make a man act differently, even vomit from sheer nervousness—and berates the superintendent for not consulting a doctor immediately upon Mr. Stanbury's arrest. He reinforces the point that though the river was searched, no body was found, and even suggested that Lady Stanbury disappeared of her own accord. "She was mad, after all.

"Is it possible that your police work wasn't up to a high enough standard to adequately, and unbiasedly, investigate the scene and the defendant properly?"

"I resent that."

"I'm sure you do, but answer the question. Would you consider the investigation you did on this crime scene to be of a substandard level?"

"No."

"I disagree with you on that, Superintendent, and even go so far as to suggest that you were negligent in your duties." He rubs a finger against the side of his nose, not so subtly implying that the policeman is a liar. "Of course you wouldn't admit fault, especially in a room full of reporters, and I'm sure everyone in this room can understand that. Pride in one's own work and all, even in a job half-done. But after pride comes a fall, Superintendent."

Pride in one's work.

Errors of judgment.

Anne. She didn't quite fit into the "puerperal mania" diagnosis. She didn't have a fever. She didn't have incoherence of speech. She didn't refuse her food.

Further witnesses for the prosecution are called up during the next two hours, the jury listening to Mr. Cropper with a sycophantic respect bordering on reverence. Two maids declare that Mr. Stanbury was angry, violent, had thrown objects around the house and threatened to push them down the stairs. The cook of the house, aptly named a somewhat ironic Mrs. Cook, testifies to overhearing Mr. Stanbury threatening his wife on the night of her subsequent disappearance. She had been hiding in the kitchen, she says, as the lady's maid, Miss Fortier, had bribed her with a hairpin to watch over her lady from the relative safety of the cook's domain. But Mrs. Cook feared as much for the food in her icebox as the maid did for her mistress, and henceforth assumed a position in the shadows in the back of the kitchen, thus overhearing everything that Mr. Stanbury said to Anne. "He all but threatened to rape her, he did, and then choke her to death afterward!" she declares to the jury, causing a silence to overcome the courtroom, broken only by a voice somewhere, saying, "I've never heard of anything so preposterous. A woman cannot be raped by her own husband; it is her duty to lie with him!" which is "Hear, hear'd!" by someone else.

Mrs. Cook's testimony has proven invaluable for the prosecution, as when Miss Fortier was called to the witness stand she was nowhere to be found. Five more servants are called in turn, whose combined testimonies strongly corroborate Mr. Stanbury to be of suspicious character, mean temperament, and a quick-to-anger disposition. All of them admit the fact that he was the cause of Anne's insanity and, in turn, the death of her baby. Mr. James tearfully describes the painful task of informing his master of his wife's disappearance, only to be dismissed as a fool. "He laughed," says the footman sadly. "He laughed when we told him we'd found some blood." Even the young girl, Betty, testifies to the fact that she saw Mr. Stanbury "washing blood from his hands." The butler testifies to the house having been locked up securely that night, so it was impossible that anyone entered from the outside. Surprisingly, none of them heard anything but the rain during the night: no sounds of violence. Lady Stanbury appeared to be her normal, sane self—a little sad, but that was to be expected. Inspector Jones testifies to his alcohol withdrawal symptoms in the jail, and my very own certificate is produced as evidence of his sanity on the night of the crime.

Eventually, the last witness is called.

Lord Damsbridge takes to the stand, and is asked on examination the reasons why he never looked for his daughter when he found out she was missing.

"You didn't search for your daughter?"

"No."

The galley gasps.

"My lord, kindly explain to the shocked members of this courtroom the reasons as to why you did not search for your daughter."

"Because I knew that she was dead, and I knew that Mr. Stanbury had killed her."

"Presumptuous!" shouts Mr. Smithingson.

"Agreed," says the judge. "Lord Damsbridge, please tell us facts, not feelings."

"Apologies."

"Accepted. We all know how hard this must be for you." The

judge glares at Mr. Stanbury before instructing the prosecution to continue.

Mr. Cropper coughs, and does so.

"Why would you think such an awful thing, my lord?"

Lord Damsbridge raises a hand to his brow, where it settles like a mask. He speaks downward, into the table. "Because it was always Mr. Stanbury's intention. Well, not to kill my daughter, at least, I hope not. . . . God knows I would have done something, anything to protect her from that. I would have sent her to France, or America . . ." His voice trails off as he is overcome by grief and chokes back a sob. His hand moves to wipe red-rimmed eyes.

Mr. Cropper patiently waits for his client to compose himself while dabbing away a few tears of his own. "My lord? Are you ready to continue?"

"I . . . I . . . I think so."

"We all sympathize with you, and yet only those who have a lost a child of their own could possibly declare to truly empathize with you. You have the whole of the courtroom's condolences, I'm sure." He pauses. "Now, tell us about this plan of Mr. Stanbury's to which you allude."

Lord Damsbridge sighs. "He wanted to inherit my estate. He came from a poor, working-class background and purposefully seduced my daughter to get her pregnant."

Somebody titters in the court. "If only it were that easy!"

"But, my lord . . ." Mr. Cropper shakes his head. "Isn't this a little . . . weak? How could he possibly know his plan would work?"

Lord Damsbridge's eyes flash. "It only takes one man, sir, to make a woman with child. She was young and naive. Here was a man, armed with flattery and mystery. Who knows whether she lay with him willingly or against her will? All he needed to do was put a child inside her, and the deed was done."

"But she could have walked away, my lord. She wasn't forced to marry him."

Lord Damsbridge mumbles something.

"I'm sorry. Can you repeat that? We didn't quite hear you."

"I said, I made her marry him! What—do you imagine I would allow her to have a bastard child? Imagine the shame! When I found out, I was embarrassed to call her my daughter. I was angry; she was selfish to get herself into such a position! She had no concept whatsoever of the damage she had done by getting pregnant outside of marriage. I thought I had raised her better than that, but . . ." He sighs, sadly, before his anger surfaces. "If she had given birth to a bastard child, Asquith Manor would have reverted to the Crown upon my death, and my own daughter would have been left destitute! The manor would go to some obsolete male relative, and Anne would be left with barely a penny. She wouldn't be able to marry anyone else— nobody will take on a woman with an illegitimate bastard—and what would she do then? Get a job as a governess? What would happen to the baby? Mr. Stanbury knew all this, as should you. That is the reason he did what he did. He knew about the entail! The moment she became pregnant, he had her! Anne would never have survived a divorce, or having her child taken away from her. The child was mere fodder to him, merely a means of extortion! I'm getting older, sir, and probably don't have many years left on this earth. Mr. Stanbury knew that too—though it hardly takes a genius to work it out." He starts to cry, and the judge looks distinctly uncomfortable. "I made her marry a murderer to secure her future! It is all my fault!"

Mr. Cropper proceeds gently. "How do you know that was his plan, my lord?"

Lord Damsbridge sniffs, and semicomposes himself. "Shortly after Anne's miscarriage, tradesmen started calling at the dower house, demanding money. Turns out, Mr. Stanbury had taken out loans, which he promised would be repaid with interest when he claimed his inheritance."

"'Inheritance'?"

"Yes. Of course, at the time, I assumed these people had made a mistake. Mr. Stanbury was poor. He came from a common background—there's no way he had any sort of inheritance coming to him. But then the creditors showed me a piece of paper, signed by Mr. Stanbury."

"What was it? What did it say?"

"It was a debenture. It outlined the fact that upon my death, Mr. Stanbury would become the sole guardian of John until he became of age—effectively becoming the possessor of the estate and all of its funds."

"But what if you didn't die? I mean, what if John was of age and then you died?"

Lord Damsbridge shrugs. "Well, the money and estate would go to him directly, but in reality, it wouldn't make any difference. Imagine a young boy, brought up alone by a loving father, torn from his true heritage—being told fairy tales every night of his wicked mother, evil grandfather, and magical mansion on the hill?" He laughs then. "Boys idolize their fathers, sir. You don't think he would fulfill his father's promise, and pay off his father's debt? Like I said, Mr. Stanbury would be sole guardian."

"'Sole' guardian?"

"Yes, well, obviously that caught my attention—the intent to divorce her, regardless. But I didn't mention anything to Anne, not then. I didn't want to barge in making wild accusations against the man she loved." He sighs. "Eventually, I discovered that he had managed to receive several hundred pounds from creditors over a three-month period. But I didn't know where the money had gone. I tried to find out if Anne knew anything about it. I dropped subtle hints, but she seemed oblivious of her husband's dealings. I couldn't find any stacks of money anywhere in the house. I was confused. I didn't understand why he would have done that—taken out so many loans. He had everything he needed, a roof over his head, food in his belly, access to Anne's monthly payments . . . unless, of course, the debenture was true.

"Shortly afterward, Anne came to me with a letter she found, hidden inside one of the books in our library. It was a letter of blackmail. She was shocked to find that someone had been threatening me, but the paper was yellowed with time. It wasn't written recently, and I had certainly never seen it before. On closer inspection, we saw it was dated 1834, and was actually addressed to my grandfather—the sixth Earl of Damsbridge. The most curious thing, however, was not its contents, but Anne's reaction to the wax seal."

"What was her reaction?"

"One of shock. She raised her hands to her mouth and just . . . She became very pale. She told me that the impression was familiar to her. I looked at it again and realized that it was my family crest."

"Why was this strange?"

"Well, we haven't used seals for decades. It was an old tradition that was naturally dropped when my grandfather evidently lost, or misplaced, the ring. We have a sixteenth-century tapestry with the crest on it—in the attic—but Anne had seen it somewhere else. And there was also the fact that this was my grandfather's seal. It was unique. Nobody else in the world had it. So think about it—if he received a letter of blackmail, how was it stamped with his seal, unless someone he knew had stolen it?"

The court becomes silent.

"I—right. Where did Anne say she had seen the seal before, then?"

"On a signet ring. In a desk."

"Whose desk?"

"Mr. Stanbury's."

The galley gasps.

"She said she was looking for something or other—and Mr. Stanbury had apparently left his desk open. . . ."

The ring! The ring Mr. Stanbury said went missing, the ring he said "they" had taken, to let him know they had set him up. . . .

A ring . . .

Slowly, I turn toward the policeman. "Inspector Jones?"

"Shush, be quiet."

I repeat his name more forcefully.

"What? What?"

"Whose was that ring you were playing with and throwing in the air earlier?"

"What? I don't know what you're talking about."

"The ring." I hiss the words. "Mr. Stanbury told me that 'they' had the ring; that 'they' used it to taunt him . . . to show him that he was being set up."

The policeman frowns. "Doc, I have absolutely no idea what the hell you're talking about." He squints, looks me up and down. "Does working in a madhouse mess with your mind? I mean, it's got to, right? Being around crazy people all the time, it's got to . . . oh, whatever. Be quiet now please. He's still talking."

I take a breath; I can wait. I'll wait until Lord Damsbridge stops talking, and then I'll force him to show me.

I feel ill.

The earl continues. "Of course, when she didn't find what she was looking for, Anne simply put the ring back inside the drawer. At the time, she was barely curious—I imagine she closed the desk with a frown on her face and a shake of her head. However, once we realized the significance of the ring . . . well, we didn't want to raise Mr. Stanbury's suspicions. We—"

"Why didn't you confront him?"

"Because we didn't know exactly what his motives were, or how he came to possess the ring. Remember, all of a sudden, the man we thought we knew turned out to be a stranger. We were confused.

"The ring meant that Mr. Stanbury had, at the very least, some sort of connection to an unknown person who sent a letter of blackmail to my grandfather, many years before. I don't believe in coincidences, sir, and at this point I put in further effort to find out exactly what was going on, who Mr. Stanbury really was, and where all his money had gone. I eventually managed to trace a postal order he had sent to an address in London. It didn't take me too long to find out that he had been sending money to his dead father. A father who was very old but very much alive."

Again, another truth.

Just as Mr. Stanbury said.

"Well, that confirmed it for me, but it wasn't enough for Anne. She wasn't willing to accept the fact that she had been seduced and impregnated just for access to her money. She loved Mr. Stanbury. She didn't want to think anything bad about him. I . . . I—"

I grab hold of the policeman's arm.

"Oi! What the bloody hell do you think—"

"Empty your pockets."

"What? You're crazy, Doc. Get off me. I'm bloody warning you, I'll have you arrested. I'll arrest you myself, right here, right now."

"I know you're lying to me. I knew it earlier, when you told me you visited Mr. Stanbury's father. You didn't, did you?" I shake my head, clench my arm tighter around his forearm. "Mr. Stanbury admitted everything to me in the jail. He also told me that he was being set up."

He narrows his eyes and roughly pries my fingers away. "Doc, if you can read people so well, how could you have been so wrong? I mean, you of all people should be able to judge people. If you honestly think that this is all a big conspiracy, and that I have Mr. Stanbury's ring, and that we all 'set him up,' what does that say about you? It means that you were wrong about Lady Stanbury, doesn't it?" He moves his face closer to mine, spit landing on my cheek. "What will it be, Doctor? Who were you wrong about? Were you wrong then, or are you wrong now?"

The speck of doubt in my mind ignites into a sizable flame.

"I did it because I love my child. Wouldn't any mother care to do the same? I didn't feel guilty when the blood ran over my hands, yet neither did I feel vindicated. I just felt I had protected my child in the only way I knew how."

"What will it be, Doc? Either way, you've fucked up."

The flame starts to burn everything in its path, memories entering my head in quick, startling flashes.

"She hid the pregnancy from me for five months."

"Hello, Beatrix."

"Why is she not at Broadmoor?"

Is it *possible* I have judged one with the sins of the other?

The hypnosis session.

I don't know. I just don't know.

I need to hear more.

Mr. Cropper interjects.

"My lord, at this point I would like to give this witness a break. I think, as the father of the recently deceased victim of this trial, he deserves as much assistance as we can give him. I kindly request a recess."

The judge looks to the defense. "Any objections?"

Mr. Smithingson sits with his arms crossed, looking most unhappy. His jaw tics, as if pulled by an invisible hand. "None, my lord. None whatsoever."

DEAD MAN'S WALK

Edgar
February 18th, 1886
Old Bailey

Dead Man's Walk.

That's what they call the stones underneath my feet, the walls on either side of me, the ceiling above my head. I look up, and almost trip. My lawyer grabs hold of my arm.

"Watch it, lad. You—"

I shake his hand off me. "Have you ever won?"

"What?" He turns his red-rimmed eyes toward my own, and for the first time I notice how disheveled he is.

"I said, 'have you ever won?'"

"This is my first trial—I told you. I've been awake for about a week preparing for it. I'm really angry with you right now, Mr. Stanbury. What were you expecting here? You talk down to me because I didn't 'defend' you with regards to the phrenologist's opinion about your head, yet you neglect to tell me that you took out loans—wrote a bloody, incriminating debenture, for Christ's sake—and then sent money to your father, who, by the way, you told everyone was dead!"

"I—"

"Do you have any idea of how hard it's going to be to prove your 'innocence'? You have totally, wholly, incriminated yourself beyond belief and I just don't know what to do with you."

"You never gave me a chance to tell you!" I shout at him, shocked by the strength of my own voice yet emboldened by the sound. "You preferred to sleep at the table rather than asking me any questions! What did you expect me to do?"

My lawyer's face turns grim as he opens a door at the end of the walk. "Well, miscommunication between a defendant and his lawyer is not a rarity, Mr. Stanbury. Let us call a truce, as they say. I suggest you and I clear this up once and for all. Tell me everything you can about these letters. Tell me your motives, everything—right down to what color socks you were wearing when you wrote them. I want to know if you have enemies, Mr. Stanbury, and whether one of them could have been your wife."

BLINDED BY MEDICAL TEXTS

Dr. Savage
February 18th, 1886
Old Bailey

"Please, my lord, continue."

"Right. So, after I found out that Mr. Stanbury had lied about his father and taken out loans, I started to monitor him. This is going to sound terrible, but please believe I only did this for the protection of my daughter. How could I stand by and take no action? When I didn't know exactly what his intentions were? I—"

"What did you do?"

He looks to the judge. "I'm sorry if I broke the law, here, my lord . . . but"—he turns back to Mr. Cropper—"I intercepted his mail. Most of it was nothing—a letter here and there from a creditor, which wasn't a problem as I just paid them off, but eventually I opened one from his father. In it was a gentle reminder to his son to stick to the plan."

"'Plan'?"

"To seduce, impregnate, and eventually divorce my daughter. He told Mr. Stanbury not to be turned by a pretty face, to make sure he hurried up and got a son out of her."

"That's disgusting!" shouts someone, from behind me.

"You see, he knew. He knew that I would make them marry. Anyone with half a brain in their head knows that bastard children cannot inherit. He was going to take Anne's child away from her. It implied as much in the debenture."

"Do you have these documents? The letter of blackmail, the debenture, the letter from his father?"

"I do."

"Please read them out to the court."

LETTER OF BLACKMAIL

Monday 2nd, December, 1834.

Dear Lord Damsbridge, Sixth Earl of Damsbridge,

> *Please pardon the poor paper on which this letter is written, unfortunately, with a scratchy pen and, I am sorry to say, produced in the poorest of light. Yet it is with much hope that I write to you, as I feel you will be naturally overwhelmed with joy to hear the good news I am about to impart.*

> *I fear I shall linger much if I do not make myself plain as quickly as possible, so I take a deep breath and advise you to do the same before you read any further.*

> *I am your son.*

> *My name is Christopher Bland. I was born on February 5th, 1814. My mother, Dorothea Bland, told me much about you growing up, yet it is only recently I learned of your true identity in the form of a letter that, much to my grief, I only recently stumbled upon, many years after her death—in Paris. My lord, I was much affected by the contents of this letter, and*

feel it is my honorable duty to uphold the memory of my mother who was a wonderful woman in many, many ways, yet died alone, in abject poverty, in France.

I have attached a copy of my mother's note. I have retained the original, for reasons that shall no doubt become very clear to you. I would gratefully suggest that you read it immediately before reading onward with this letter.

"Can I stop you there, my lord?"

"Yes, certainly."

"Do you have a copy of the mother's note?"

"No. This was the only letter I could find. But I can deduce from the next words that whoever wrote this letter believed himself to be the illegitimate, yet rightful heir to the Asquith estate. I can only assume that this missing letter, from the writer's mother, clarified as such."

"Right. Please continue."

The contents of this letter being what they are, I ask only that you have the decency to treat me like the son that I am to you, and I will thus keep your secret— lying with another man—as any good son would do to protect his father. I realize that this letter could not only cause great scandal, but may also incite you to lose your life. For a son having recently discovered the true identity of his father, it would be a shame if I was to lose him so soon to the noose.

I wish for instant recognition, dear Father, and to be fully written into your will, granting me full heir apparent to all that you have naturally bestowed upon your other, legally legitimate son, the seventh

Earl of Damsbridge. He is welcome to keep the title; I ask only for the property, land, and all personal possessions that would have been my due, if only you had possessed the decency to marry my mother.

I know that this may be rather a difficult task for you and your lawyer (if you don't have one, I suggest that you employ one as soon as possible). Of course, I am looking out for your interests, dear Father.

I realize this may be quite a shock to you, yet I believe if you look to the wax seal on the back of this letter, it will prove to you that I am who I say I am, and I have the power to love you as much as I have the inclination to ruin you. The relationship between a man and his mother is most precious, dear Father, and the only way I can bear your abhorrent treatment toward her is if you make amends with her son, your son, thus enabling her to sleep well among the dead. A relationship with my father is something I have never known, but wish to remedy at your earliest convenience.

Yours Affectionately,
Christopher Jordan.
Aka—Your Loving Son

"Dear Lord, they threatened your grandfather with buggery?"

"Yes, they did."

"A hangable offense."

"Indeed."

"Merely because he had relations with Dorothea Jordan—Mr. Stanbury's grandmother?"

"Yes. She stole the ring from my grandfather, in order to blackmail him in the future. It was proof of their relationship."

DEBENTURE:
ASQUITH MANOR ESTATE
£50 0s 0d

In consideration of the sum of Fifty Pounds advanced to me by. . . . . of. . . . ., I, the undersigned, Mr. Edgar Stanbury, at present residing at Asquith Manor, London, hereby covenant with the said. . . . ., his executors, administrators, and assigns (all of who are hereinafter constituted in the term "the said debenture holder") to pay or cause to be paid to the said debenture holder the said sum of fifty pounds on or before the first day of Lord Damsbridge's death, current holder of the estate and all of its assets, or upon the death of Mr. John Stanbury, as yet unborn—whichever should arise first—with a covenant that should the Lady Stanbury lose the current child, to extend this agreement for the birth of one more subsequent child. I covenant to pay interest on the same sum after the rate of £5 percent per annum, from the said last-mentioned day till payment. And for the purpose of securing the repayment of the said principle money and interest, this debenture is one of a like series of debentures numbered respectively 1 to 10 inclusive, constituting in the aggregate a sum of five hundred pounds.

Signed, sealed, and delivered by the above-named person, Mr. Edgar Stanbury, in the presence of. . . . .

I hereby declare that the above document was executed on 1st October, 1884.

LETTER FROM THE FATHER—
HITHERTO REFERRED TO AS
MR. STANBURY SENIOR

*Son what are you doing all this time is pasing
and I haven't heard anything from you in sum months
don't ignore me you know we are doing this for are
family and for are future you better go threw with it
son if you don't divorc her then she will influence you
and the law mite change she mite be able to take your
son away from you and if she does that you will not be
guardian, you will not be able to be guardian of your
son and if you are not guardian you will not have
acces to all of his funds befoor he becomes of age and he
mite not love you women are evil she will turn him
against you and you will lose everything and all of
this will be for nothing. You get a son Edgar you
divorce the stoopid woman and you gain control do
you understand me these loans are not enuf to live
forever.*

"Who was this woman, the grandmother?"

As the words are read out to the court, I start to panic. Everything matches up; everything that Mr. Stanbury told me has been the truth. Every single thing out of his mouth in the jail has been proven here, right in front of me. The crazy plot that I put down to the ramblings of a desperate man, of a delusional man, of an alcoholic. All of them, confirmed and true.

Though Mr. Smithingson attempts to twist the content of the letters, he cannot dispute the fact that Mr. Stanbury's signature glares brightly on them, for all the jury to see. When Mr. Smithingson rises for the cross-examination, he asks Lord Damsbridge only one question.

"How could Mr. Stanbury have possibly known the child would be a boy? It had to be a boy, didn't it? After all, the entail could not pass to a girl."

Lord Damsbridge looks at the lawyer scathingly.

"His job was completed, sir," he says, almost sneering, "when he put a child in my daughter's stomach. Because he knew I would make them marry. If it had been a girl, do you imagine for even one moment he would have stopped? He would have had my precious child popping them out every year until a boy came along, a little like Henry the Eighth. Surely, I shouldn't have to explain the obvious to such a learned man as yourself?"

The doubt in my mind clears. Both Mr. Stanbury and I have been set up.

By none less than the wonderful, eminent Lord Damsbridge.

Mr. Stanbury is innocent.

There is no way he could have been lying.

It is here, on paper. Written in ink, sealed with wax.

Mr. Stanbury was *telling the truth*.

And so was Anne. The hypnosis session didn't fail, as I thought it had.

It *worked*.

"Are you all right, Doc?" A voice in my ear. Inspector Jones. "You don't look so hot."

I ignore him, thinking. I look at Mr. Stanbury, try to get his attention. However, he doesn't notice me. I don't think he sees anything. He is staring into space, into his impending doom.

"There wasn't any allusion to murdering your daughter, though," Mr. Smithingson continues. "No mention at all, in any of those papers. How can you say, then, that this was his intention? To kill her? Because according to you, that was the plan."

"It was not the plan, sir, and I never said it was. If you were worth half your ilk as a lawyer, you would have realized something the jury did long ago. His plan was to get his hands on Asquith Manor, the house that his father and he both believed belonged to them by rights, by virtue, as ironic as that may sound, of his bloody grandmother—Dorothea Jordan, previous mistress of the Duke of Clarence—sleeping with my grandfather."

"Then why would he kill her?"

"He killed her, sir, afterward. Don't you understand? When my daughter went mad and killed their son, she destroyed any chance of him getting his hands on the estate. With the death of John, and being told by the doctor that she could not have any more children, his plan was ruined. He had nothing to show for all his hard work except for debt and failure. Now, I don't know whether he killed her because of this, or whether he killed her in revenge. And I don't think that the distinction is even relevant. He *murdered* my darling, beautiful daughter. Are you stupid?"

Nobody addresses the fact that, grieving father or not, a witness just insulted and verbally slandered a lawyer in front of the eyes of the world. Somebody in the galley starts a slow clap, which gathers pace and tone until the court is one slow, twisting, grinding beat of evil hearts and minds.

Mr. Smithingson looks around him, his eyes that of a wounded man. He opens his mouth and closes it. But, bravely, he continues—going on to portray the servants' attitudes, their jealousy that someone of their own ilk and station in life should lord it over them through merely impregnating an aristocratic woman. He intimates that the young scullery maid, Betty, was coerced and influenced in her testimony.

Though Mr. Smithingson does manage to poke a few holes into Mr. Cropper's well-spun web—reinforcing the fact that Lady Stanbury had only been discharged from a madhouse the day before and could have run away under another hallucination or drowned herself, that she may have simply been scared of her husband and fled—it's not enough to convince the twelve gentlemen on the bench.

Is it possible that she ran away? Could I have been wrong, and discharged a mentally unstable woman?

Could she have killed herself, as Mr. Stanbury said?

"The ring. They have the ring.

"This is a setup."

No, no. As awful a possibility that might be, I know, *know*, that she was sane on discharge.

The only question remains as to whether she was *insane* on admission.

If Mr. Stanbury has been telling the truth—which he now appears to be—then she could be alive.

And if she is, that means she did indeed set him up.

And if she did . . .

Dear God, if that is true, then . . .

It changes everything.

The defense lawyer continues his speech despite its ineffectualness.

"This man is as much a victim as the missing lady. A pawn of his father's. He never wished to lie and cheat his way into a life not his own, oh no . . . he was coerced into it by the man who was supposed to protect him! He was brought up, gentlemen, believing in a fantasy. His father would have thrown him out of the house had he not complied with his wishes, and there is, gentlemen, an element of . . . What is the word? Brainwashing. Mr. Stanbury never, ever meant to hurt Lady Stanbury. He was, and is, merely a victim of circumstance. . . ."

And so on. The courtroom quickly becomes a private theater: one lawyer's account of a good, but innocent man, and the other lawyer's of a vicious, vengeful killer. Mr. Smithingson makes various other salient points, yet he is unable to completely shatter the rather clear picture issued forth by the prosecution. He is hesitant, unsure. The members of the jury, sensing his weakness, tolerate him with barely disguised contempt and boredom, as if his valid hypotheses are merely a waste of their time.

Eventually, he mutters something about resting his case. He is outnumbered, and outwitted. He may be defending an innocent man, but the public doesn't care.

I look at Inspector Jones.

He is smiling.

I failed as a doctor.

As a man.

Someone once said that any ordinary man is able to detect any form of insanity as well as a physician.

Perhaps a physician can make mistakes just as any ordinary man.

"Made up your mind yet?" Inspector Jones's voice, hot inside my ear. "You know, I do hear that sometimes—just sometimes, mind you—innocent people are sent to their death."

I look at him, and he smiles.

He confirms my fears.

Lady Stanbury is alive.

A woman—a mere *woman,* has gotten the best of me, and she is going to send her husband to his death.

My head buzzes. What should I do? If I attempt to search Inspector Jones's pockets, he'll have me arrested. I don't doubt it for a second—he is provoking me; he wants me to. He knows that by the time I get anyone to listen to my story, the trial will be over and Mr. Stanbury . . .

I must help him.

The jury members rise and make their way into their chamber to make their decision, and the defense lawyer's eyes meet mine. I wave desperately, and he inclines his head.

Mr. Stanbury is innocent, yet my very own words have helped condemn him. I was wrong. I've been blinded by medical texts and a clinical eye. I didn't listen to Mr. Stanbury; I didn't heed my very own doubts.

I should have looked for zebras, not buried my mind when I found horses.

Because now I fear there is no jury in the land that would not convict.

RISK LOSING EVERYTHING

Beatrix
February 18th, 1886
On the road

The carriage shakes and jolts as I finally reach the last mile of the journey, the sun having long dipped beneath the horizon. However, the carriage lamp illuminates the cab, and though much wearied by my journey, I allow myself to peer through the darkness of the glass. I don't allow myself to dwell upon what I have done; instead, I think of Mr. Stanbury's father, a miserable alcoholic who grew up resenting the world but unable to do anything about it, other than push his own son to bear the burden. A man too stupid to realize that the prostitute he is living with is a spy, employed by Lord Damsbridge to immerse herself into his house as his mistress—her only job to lie with him and save any letters that he might receive from his son. My employer wasn't stupid enough to stop all mail getting through—of course, Mr. Stanbury's father still received a couple of letters from his son. Just enough to make him relax, to make him think that the plan was going ahead. But then Mr. Stanbury himself stopped writing . . . and his father turned up on our doorstep.

A man who went on to give his own flesh and blood over to a mob that will sentence him to death, for the price of a year's worth of whiskey.

A man who will surely now die alone, the prostitute having done her job, having earned enough to open her own boardinghouse.

Funny, how some people will sell their children, while others will risk losing everything just to keep them.

The carriage finally struggles up the long hill that takes me to my final destination, a place I never imagined I would be but somewhere I know I belong. With the woman who will always be my daughter, not of my body, but of my soul. My redemption.

I cannot keep the smile off my face as the cab stops outside a small house, hidden among a copse of orange trees and hibiscus shrubs.

I laugh when the coach driver opens the door and a tiny hand reaches out to grab mine.

THE ONE IN TWENTY

Edgar
February 18th, 1886
Court cell

"It is not enough that you cry out your innocence! There is nothing I can do! The jury hates you so much, you have condemned yourself as surely as if you put the noose around your own neck! They have proof of you being a liar, and when liars start to speak nobody believes them. How do they discern you're not lying now, when you were lying then? Or were you lying about lying then? When do you stop lying?"

"I don't know," I say, unable to answer any of his questions, watching my lawyer pace the six-by-eight-foot cell. "But I didn't do it. I swear on my dead son's memory."

He makes as if to kick my chamber pot, but thinks better of it when he notices it has not been emptied for days. He wrinkles his nose in disgust and turns back to me. "And to keep the bloody ring in the house—what were you thinking?"

"I kept it locked in the drawer. I never—"

"Well, it wasn't good enough, was it? Why did you even have it *near* you? Why didn't you—"

"My father made me. He said—"

"Your father's almost as deluded as you are! Where is that ring, by the way?"

"I don't know. The policeman had it—"

"'You don't know, you don't know'! Forget it! You should know! Lad, I don't think it even matters anymore!" His mood switches rapidly. "You have practically signed your own death warrant! Lord Damsbridge has sealed beyond doubt your motives for the crime! What kind of idiot are you, acting on your father's say-so? There is the issue of respecting your parents, Stanbury, and another of being idiotically naive and blind to their faults and eccentricities. As for opportunity . . . well, they've got you on that too, haven't they? I'm not even sure if I believe you're innocent at this point—" A knock on the cell door comes, and I flinch. Mr. Smithingson scowls at me. "Ah, here he is now. Hopefully, lad, our saving grace." The metal door opens and swings outward, revealing the somber face of Dr. Savage.

"Doctor."

"Smithingson." He enters quickly, shutting the door behind him. My lawyer speaks quickly.

"Right, lads. We must be quick about this. Doctor, this man is going to hang. Despite my antics in there, I don't see how I can possibly save him from the noose. Quite clearly, my client plotted with his father to take over the earl's title and estate by having a son, and murdered his wife when she became insane and took that away from him. Now—"

"I didn't kill her," I interrupt. "But she might've killed herself—"

"Shush, lad. Now, Doctor, what I want to know is this. What are the chances of having our boy here being unfit to plead?"

I leap from the table. "You're not putting me in some godforsaken lunatic asylum! I'm not mad!"

"Be quiet, lad! Before I walk out of this courtroom and leave you to hear the bell toll for you, alone!"

I close my mouth and sit back down. Dr. Savage comes over and rests a hand on my shoulder, answering Mr. Smithingson but looking directly at me. I see sadness in his face, and a trace of bewilderment.

"We can't. It's too late."

"We can say that he's insane. Then he'll walk free—"

Dr. Savage becomes angry. "Mr. Smithingson! Don't you realize that to put in a plea, you needed to pursue the unfit-to-stand-trial plea before the trial began?'"

"I . . ." He looks around him helplessly. "I know, but it wasn't appropriate before. I didn't think this would go as far as it has. They don't have any evidence—"

"Well, they obviously have enough to woo the jury. You can't put in an insane plea now, not anymore, not at this stage. I've testified in many cases where the defense have tried to pull an insanity stunt out of their pocket at the last minute when it seems that they are losing beyond all hope, and I have never once seen it stop any man or woman going to the noose! The judge and the jury are not stupid; do you not think they don't know it is the desperate move of a desperate man? He has already been declared sane at the time of the offense, and to attend trial. I myself signed one of those certificates!"

Both my lawyer and I gape at him. Mr. Smithingson sniffs, addresses Dr. Savage.

"If the jury do find him guilty of murder, Doctor, the judge's hands are tied. Do you realize that? He has no option but to deliver punishment based on precedent. Common law itself binds future decisions. We have to do something. . . ."

I barely hear the lawyer's words as he starts rambling, "stare decisis" this and "matter of first" that. I can only stare at Dr. Savage. The man whom I considered a friend: my only friend.

He has betrayed me.

The whole world has betrayed me.

"No, Mr. Smithingson, none of that would work at this stage. The only thing we can do is expose the truth. And I think I know what that is, but I need your help. First of all, I don't believe your client killed his wife."

"You don't?" He looks bewildered and peers around him. "Well, who did, then?"

"Nobody. I highly suspect she is still alive."

I almost weep in gratitude. A lone tear snakes its way down my cheek, settling upon my lip. I lick it off.

Salty.

"But why, how . . ." My lawyer trails off and sits down on the floor. "Is it too much to ask what the bleeding, bloody hell is going on here? Can you fit it into"—he looks at his watch—"three minutes and forty-two seconds?"

"I'll try my best," Dr. Savage says, before bending and sitting next to my lawyer. I'm not even tempted to offer him my chair, now that I finally have one.

"Let me tell you both what I'm thinking. Remember when your wife was admitted to Bethlem Hospital?" I move to answer, but he shakes his head. "Just let me speak. It was a strange enough request at the time, that a woman found unfit to stand trial should enter Bethlem. All criminal lunatics get sent to Broadmoor. Naturally, I put this down to the fact that her father contributes heavily to the hospital's fund. With enough money, you can do and request almost anything, unfortunately. Yet I accepted her as I saw her as a genuine case . . . Why would I not?" He laughs bitterly. "To tell you the truth, I'm still not sure. But here's the thing. I only realized, as time went by, that Lord Damsbridge had only started contributing six months before Lady Stanbury killed your child. *Six months.* That indicates to me that he was getting ready to be able to stick his nose in and watch over his daughter. Number one. Number two: She never quite fit into the diagnostic box of puerperal mania. Sure, she did on the surface, but there was something about her physical symptoms that never quite tallied with the psychological ones. She was both manic and melancholic. Usually, patients suffering from puerperal mania are one or the other, not both. She never had a fever. She never spoke incoherently. She never refused her food. She never had flushed cheeks—instead, she was always pale, sallow. But who was I to think otherwise? Everyone is different. If there's anything I've learned from science, it's that one man can have a pulse of fifty, and another a pulse of one hundred. And they can both be perfectly well. Next, she didn't remember you, which was unusual enough to pique my interest at the time but unfortunately not my curiosity. Again, I put it down to her individuality; assumed she had other psychological processes underlying the puerperal mania. Understand me, gentlemen—she was a woman who had been certified as insane by two other doctors, *both* of whom cited puerperal mania. She had already been put in a 'box' and I—well, I didn't question anything that seemed slightly out of the ordinary. It wasn't enough. There was the fact of the dead baby. Number three: Her periods began shortly after she 'reverted' to sanity—but a few days later, another patient of mine became ill with what I suspected was alum poisoning. I couldn't for the life of me figure out how, or where, he could have gotten it—but all his symptoms pointed to it. This man, he—well, he likes to dig in the garden. He eats anything he finds. You know what alum is used for, don't you?"

He waits, blinks. "As an astringent, gentlemen. It stops bleeding."

"What?" I interject. "What are you saying?"

"I'm saying that she went to a store, either the pharmacy or—Lord, you can buy it in the bakery, for heaven's sake. Don't you know what they put inside bread these days?—bought a piece of alum, and stuck it inside herself to prevent menstruation."

The lawyer pales. "That's . . . disgusting."

"Well, it isn't really. As I said, it's just an astringent."

"Why would she do that?" I ask.

"As I said, to prevent her courses. Insane women don't bleed. She knew that. Which naturally leads me on to:

"Number four: Her maid told me that she liked to read, that she could always be found with her nose in a book. She also told me that she read the *Lancet*. Do you know what that means? It means, gentlemen, that while I thought she was reading literature to keep her baby *safe*, she was actually researching how to prevent her courses and fake puerperal mania!"

"I . . . what?" I say, clutching the chair.

"Just wait a moment. I need you to hear this. Number five: Stanbury, you said the bran on your bedroom floor was disturbed. Frankly, I assumed you were suffering from delusions of persecution. But you weren't and I'm sorry—they must have been searching for the ring. How did Anne even find it in your desk? Were you drunk? Did you leave it open? It hardly matters now! Number six: The policeman told me that Lord Damsbridge specifically asked for me to assess you in the jail. He said that it was because I knew you, and that made sense. But now I see it was all a setup. He knew that I had seen you at your lowest, knew that you had confessed your conflicting emotions toward Anne, knew that I had seen you drinking. He therefore knew I would be more likely to accept that you murdered her, and that you had motive—in other words, also certify you as sane. Number seven: That ridiculous scene with the phrenologist out there? Hardly anybody takes them seriously anymore. They are just trying to make you look as bad as they possibly can. Number eight: That Detective Jones. He's in on it. I know he is."

"I told you!" I leap up and punch the air. "I told you!"

"Yes, shush, I'm nearly done. Number nine: You told me she hid the pregnancy from you for five months. I then believed it to be her anxiety, and her love for you as her husband, to not cause you any grief if she miscarried for a second time, but I now think she hid the pregnancy from you, as if she was planning on giving birth to the baby and never letting you know you had a son. I assume that her plan must have originally been to give birth quietly somewhere, perhaps to disappear herself. Perhaps she hoped you would leave, and she could return in secret, or perhaps she planned to live her life with the child in obscurity. Who knows? But I do guarantee you that if she had access to those documents of yours, then she came up with a plan. A plan you thwarted by noticing her pregnancy."

"How could I not have noticed?" I say desperately. "You must be wrong, Doctor. You must be. Surely, anyone would have noticed her pregnancy, especially her own husband. . . ."

"Did she stop lying with you?"

"Yes, but—"

"Well, there you go. There's many a servant girl who gives birth on a bed of straw and goes to work in the morning, with nobody being any the wiser. Women can hide these things, Stanbury, with a clever combination of trickery, deception, diversion, and unfortunately . . . good clothing."

No, no, this can't be right; this can't be real. She loved me. I know she did. She wouldn't have done this to me. . . .

"She knew you were going to divorce her, Stanbury. She knew you were going to prevent her from having access to the baby—"

"The Custody Act—"

Dr. Savage whirls upon my lawyer. "Damn the Custody Act! You and I both know it doesn't work, and so did she! She was more intelligent than any of us ever gave her credit for!" He turns to me, the desperation in my eyes reflected in his own. "You thwarted her plan, Edgar, to quietly give birth and take the child safely away, so she hatched a new one.

"She actually admitted killing the child to one of my attendants. Oh—I knew she killed the child: That came out wrong. What I meant to say is that she admitted doing so while she was sane. And now the letters, confirming the story you told me about William the Fourth and Dorothea Bland. Oh, drat, the hypnosis session! Of course!"

My mouth is hanging open. What is he telling me? I verbalize the question, but he ignores me, pulling anxiously at his beard. We already know she killed my son. What on earth is he trying to tell us?

"Who has been hypnotized?" asks my lawyer from the floor. Dr. Savage ignores him. "I should have known from the minute she admitted everything!" He looks to the ceiling and shouts. "Damn you, Tuke! Our research was far from finished, you old bat!" Who is Tuke? I don't have any time before he gazes at me and continues talking a mile to the dozen. "Why, those letters that have almost convinced the jury of your guilt only prove that she was telling the truth in the hypnosis session, and that you are an innocent man!"

"I am utterly confused," says the lawyer.

"It's quite simple! Those documents show the prosecution that you had motive to kill her. Either in revenge for her killing your son or in frustration that she had thwarted your plans. However—look at it the other way around. Lord Damsbridge has *admitted* that both he and Anne knew that you were planning on taking her child away, of using your son's claim on the estate to benefit financially yourself. If they knew that beforehand—which they did—then they had just as much motive to get rid of you as you did of her."

My heart is racing. "Are you saying that Anne . . . thought I was going to take the child from her? But . . . she never told me. Why didn't she ever ask me? I was waiting for the right time. I was going to tell her everything and then . . . then it was too late. She'd already killed John and was arrested. Is she alive? You need to find her. You have to—"

The doctor flinches, as if stung. "One in twenty . . . by God, you are to be the one in twenty!" He leaps up and runs to the door. "I repeat: Your wife saw those papers while she was pregnant! She believed you were going to take the child away from her, so she took the child away from you! She knew that if you divorced her, she would lose her child forever, but as she was unable to divorce you, she did the next best thing! My God! A woman will do anything to keep her child, and I mean anything!" He hammers at the door. "Guard! Let me out at once!" He turns to me, a manic look in his eyes. "The key to your freedom, Stanbury—I have it! I wrote down the transcript of her confession! Guard, let me out!" He kicks the door. "Guard!" The door opens, and he runs out.

My lawyer and I look at each other, each as confused as the other.

DID WE DO THE RIGHT THING?

Beatrix
February 18th, 1886
A small cottage . . . somewhere

"Of course we did the right thing, Beatrix. Really, I can't believe you're even questioning it. I'm so happy now," Anne says, lifting a cup of beef tea daintily and carefully, ever mindful of the babe in her arms. "My father was right."

"But, Anne, he's going to be hanged. The father of your child is going to *die*."

"Well"—she places the teacup down gently—"that's his fault. If he had been content with a two-parent family, none of this would have happened."

I blink back tears, wipe my face.

She continues, lost in her memory. "I could've helped him. I would have continued to love him for the rest of my life. I would have given him any amount of money he wanted. Do you know, when I first saw him, I felt sorry for him? I *pitied* him. Wearing that drab little uniform, punching holes in tickets for a play he couldn't afford to watch. I wanted to brighten him up, bring some color into his life. Can you believe that?"

I can. Anne has always felt for those who need more. She always felt she had too much. She wanted to give everything she was, everything she had, away to help others. And then she changed; she became this twisted person who sits before me.

"I wanted to show him what life could be like. And, oh, he was like a child! When I bought him his first suit—well, I have never seen a man so happy for such a simple pleasure. His amazement astounded me, and he made me appreciate my own life, my own luck. I loved how he made me see the world differently, how his eyes made me see the small things. How privileged I was to have toast every morning, to lie in a warm bed at night, to have servants who looked after me and kept me safe. He made me love who I was, and I never did that before. I loved his appreciation. He made me feel like a god—I had this power to make him happy and, in turn, myself." She continues to rock the baby, constantly stroking his face, running a finger along his ear. "But he betrayed me, Beatrix. He was lying the whole time. He never loved me. I was just a vessel for the thing he really wanted—a child. Specifically, mine. He was going to divorce me and take John away."

"Maybe we could have fought him in the courts. You—"

"No," she says quietly, resigned. "No. My father told me that would never work. I did my research, Beatrix, and he was right. Edgar, as the father, would have been granted immediate and full custody of my son. I would have had to petition for custody—for mere access!—through the courts of chancery!"

"Anne . . ." I look at her face: her happy, shining, bright face. All I ever wanted was for her to be happy. I take a breath. "Anne, there's something you should know."

"What's that?" She lifts her gaze from the baby.

"Edgar—he wrote you a letter. I mean, he wrote his father a letter, but it was about you. And him. I gave it to Dr. Savage, but when I asked you back in the house, that . . . the night of . . . *you know*, you told me you didn't receive any letter."

Her eyes darken. "You also told me that the letter was from you, Beatrix."

I look away, shamed. "I know, I know, but . . . he was so awful to you that night, and . . . I was trying to protect you, Anne. I really think he might have hurt you, in the end. He was so angry, and drinking so much ale, and—"

She shifts the babe, puts him gently in his cot. He squirms for a moment, lifts a hand as if reaching for his mother, and then slowly, slowly, drops it to his side.

"What did it say?"

"It . . . I made a copy, Anne. It was so important at the time, I—"

"Give it to me."

I reach into my skirts and pull out the crumpled piece of paper. I'm not sure why I kept it. I guess I never thought things would become as bad as they are. I didn't realize that so many innocent people would end up dead. I thought it was just a baby, a dead baby, and a man, put in a cell.

Anne snatches the letter from my hand.

> *Dearest Father,*
>
> *I'm sorry that I have not always been the son you wanted, and that I have not always been able to meet your expectations. I tried my whole life to be the boy— the man—you wanted me to be, but even now I'm sorry to say that I must fail you once again.*
>
> *Shortly after meeting her, I realized that I wasn't playing a part with regards to loving her. It was as easy as breathing, and it was real. I never realized she would be so beautiful. I know that you told me never to let myself be turned by a pretty face, but, oh, Father, she's so much more than that. She's intelligent; she reads so many books that she amazes me. Sometimes she tells me about the stories she reads and . . . I never*

had anyone read me a story before. I feel like a child. It's simply magical.

She's kind; she bought me a suit when she saw I had no nice clothes.

She took me into her home and her heart, and has opened me up to something I thought I could never experience.

Love.

Father, it is the most wonderful feeling in the world. It isn't lust. I don't see her as an object; I see her as this absolutely incredible, amazing person. She's my best friend, Father, and I never had one of those before. I don't want to be a liar and a cheat; I just want to be a husband and a father.

So I'm writing this letter to tell you I can't do it. I'm sorry. I've written this letter so many times, over and over and over, but now . . . [teardrop on page]

[scrawl]

she's made a mistake, Father—I think she must have accidentally dropped John in the kitchen. He's dead and she's been taken away and . . .

I must pause here, as a few months have passed. I now sit in the library of the manor, alone. I've always been alone, Father, but I've never felt so lonely before. They say she is mad. They say she didn't know what she [not readable]

I'm drunk. I'm becoming like you. I need to stop this hate in my heart.

[scribbles, crossed out words]

I can't do it. I can't be alone. I don't hate her, but I hate you for making me lie. For putting me in a position where my son is dead, my wife is mad, and I can't even tell her the truth [teardrop]

[smudge]
How can I betray her trust, before I've ever really
earned it?
[crosses, teardrops, ink stain, illegible]
I hate you, I hate all of you.
I only love her, and my son.
They are all that matters.

"Well," she sighs, handing it back to me. She gestures to John. "Am I supposed to believe that?"

"Anne . . . ," I stutter, speechless. "That man poured his heart out. Look at the writing. He's gone back to this letter, over and over and over again, turning it into something more like . . . a journal, because he was terrified of his father, terrified of what you would think . . ."

She frowns. "Yes, I suppose he was. And he *should* have been terrified of what I thought. But it doesn't change anything. I know it should, but . . . it doesn't. I've hated him too much, for too long, for this to make any sort of difference. You tell me to look at the paper—at the teardrops and the tragedy—but *you* have a look at it, Beatrix. *Read his words.* Remember what he was like the night I was discharged from the asylum—"

"That's why I didn't tell you. I—"

"Don't interrupt me. He always used to speak over me, and I hate it. I won't stand it from you. You know what it is like to want a child, Beatrix, and I know what it is to be without a mother. We provided that for each other, and for that I am ever grateful to you. This letter . . ." She shifts her gaze to John with a smile of love. "Doesn't change a thing. He could have changed his mind, Beatrix, on a whim. The simple fact that he was willing to do it in the first place—and, oh, he didn't because I had a pretty smile and bought him a suit?—come on. He was a mess. We would have had an argument, and he would have stormed off down to the local lawyer and demanded a divorce.

We brought out the worst in each other. By what right, by what law, can my child be taken away from me?" She gazes at John. John, John, John. All about John. "A child needs his mother—his real mother— above and beyond anyone else. Nothing can replace that, I'm afraid. Here, could you make me another?"

Silent, I take the cup from her. *John.* His tiny hands are curled up in front of his face, poking out of the blanket swaddling him, almost as if in his sleep he is already trying to hide from the world into which he was born. A horrid world where young women sell their babies for pennies and baby farmers murder them for a price.

I walk the five steps it takes to transport me into the kitchen, a tiny space. The entire home is tiny, not much larger than that I grew up in. But this house is indeed a home. The glow from the log fire sends a dusky orange light over everything. Anne has surprised me. I don't know what to think. I keep remembering the girl I left to freeze on the road, Mr. Stanbury's look of terror as he sat in the stand.

Years ago, I worked for a lady. A mistress who had me pinned me to a dirty mattress while three strangers ripped my baby from my womb. I was no use to her with child, and so of course that was the most logical solution.

Except it wasn't logical. She didn't have an ounce of intelligence in her head when she made the other servants stick a piece of wire into me. Nobody stopped to imagine for one moment that they might end up killing not only their maid's unwanted child, but me as well.

That's how Anne's mother found me. Bleeding to death by the side of a road in France.

"Beatrix? You've been in there an age!" Anne calls to me, still sure of herself, of her actions. I adopt the same tone as I pick up the two steaming cups and carry them back into . . . what? The drawing room? The parlor? This is the only room besides the kitchen on the ground level.

"I'm quite all right, Anne. Here." I put the tea on the small round table beside her.

"Thank you." She picks the baby back out of his crib, sits on the chair, and starts to rock him back and forth. "Sends him into a deeper sleep," she says, answering my unasked question. She stops after a few minutes.

"Would you like to hold him for a while?"

He's asleep, I think. *Why are you holding him all the time?* And no. No, I can't. Not now. I look at him, and . . . all I see is an innocent baby, disfigured beyond recognition, as battered and bruised as the one they scrambled inside my belly. Except it was on the outside, and this baby was fully grown, alive. I took part in an innocent child's murder, and then I murdered its mother as surely as if I had raised a knife against her when she came to claim him.

"Beatrix, I can see the worry etched into those ever-deepening frown lines of yours. Will you stop it? It's done. It's over."

"I'm thinking of a baby, Anne, killed, butchered, by us—by you." I've always been open and honest with Anne, but this time she flinches as if I have pinched her.

"My God, Beatrix. Do you have to? We didn't kill him. His mother did. As soon as she handed it over to Mrs. Harding, she signed that child's life away. She knew *exactly* what she was doing, but no doubt she acted as if she was a martyr—giving the baby over to a better life, not a shorter one. She would have heard the babies crying for want of food, and still, she pressed whatever sum she could afford into Mrs. Harding's hands." She laughs then. "In a way, we've done that woman a service. We've done what she herself was too frightened to do . . . too guilty."

"But, Anne, she didn't mean to. She wanted her baby back—"

"Oh, Beatrix—please! Spare me! She didn't have any right to call herself a *mother*. No doubt she had a pitiful little cry at the door, kissed her baby on the forehead, and promised to check in on him from time to time. She walked away, Beatrix."

"But she never realized—"

"Then she's an idiot. A poor, stupid idiot. What—do you mean to tell me she didn't realize that the one-off payment meant she would never see her child again? If it wasn't for us, that baby would've starved to death in a rotten, filthy room. Don't you think that giving him chloroform and sending him to sleep was kinder? At least he didn't suffer." She looks at me then, with a strange expression. "You *did* make sure it was dead before you . . . disfigured him, didn't you?"

I close my eyes.

"Well, you don't have to answer that. Look, Beatrix—that woman would never have gotten her child back, regardless of what we did. He was dead as soon as she handed him over with five pounds—"

"Two. She paid two."

"'Two'? Jesus, but that's cheap. I thought the going rate was five. Well, well, well." She sighs. "Beatrix, who *knows* what might have happened to that child? Mrs. Harding was obviously disreputable—you told me yourself about the room for the ones who had been sold for a lump sum. You said that they were half-dead. That poor child knew nothing but misery in his short life, and we put him out of it. That's all. I risked the *gallows* to keep my child, I faked *insanity*, I pulled my own hair out by its *roots*, so don't you *dare* start to come over all high and mighty on me now."

"Yet you will sit back and watch another innocent die."

"Yes."

"Edgar is going to hang, Anne."

She sighs. "That wasn't the plan, Beatrix, and you know it. If he had taken Mr. Cropper's advice, if he had just divorced me and gone away . . . At the very most, I expected him to go back to his hovel with his tail between his legs as soon as I was arrested, and forget all about this nasty episode of his life. Unfortunately, the man was more stubborn than I thought."

I listen to her as she tries to justify her actions, just as I justified mine. I thought I was looking after her, keeping her safe, just as she wanted to keep John safe, but . . . for the first time in her life, I no longer adore her. Love her, yes. Stand by her? Forever. Lie for her? As deep as hell runs black. But sit here and be unable to judge her? I cannot.

"If we hadn't done it, I would've lost John. I wouldn't have seen him until he was sixteen years old—by law, Edgar could have kept me away until then, until John was of age to make his own decisions—and who knows how much Stanbury might have poisoned his mind against me by then? It wasn't the money, Beatrix, as I already told you. I would've given him everything. If I could have, I would've given him the estate. I would have lived in poverty. But give him my son, my baby? Never. How could I miss my child's first words, his first step, his first haircut? The most precious thing I'll have around my neck are the arms of my child . . . while all he has now is a rope."

I can't look at her; I can't answer.

"Don't worry, Beatrix. We'll be home soon. A couple more months and I can turn up at the house claiming to have lost my mind again, and then we can 'adopt' this little one to cure the grief of losing my husband and son. We'll make a big show of wanting to adopt a child. We'll put it out to the local community, and then we'll say we chose this little one here."

"Anne . . ." I trail off. "I left that child's mother to die by the side of the road."

A small, sneaky look of slyness crosses her face.

"Well, in that case, who are you to judge?" She stands slowly, pulling John tighter into her breast. "You were fighting for your child—me. Don't think I don't know you see me as your daughter. You fought for me, Beatrix, just as I fought for John. Now," she says, crossing the room and leaning into my cheek, "you're just as bad as me."

Her kiss is ice.

"The only truth in this world is a mother's love for her child, and I don't regret a thing." She turns from me, taking her son to bed.

We all enter this world covered in blood. Some of us survive the brutal entry. Yet only a few of us exit it without any still on our hands.

A MOCKERY

Dr. Savage
February 18th, 1886
Bethlem Royal Hospital

"Wait for me here!"

I don't give the coachman time to reply and can only hope that he heeds my request as I run up the stairs into the hospital and sprint into my office.

Everything is just how I left it.

A mess.

I search the papers on my desk frantically, swiping one after another onto the floor. When I get to the wood, I'm ankle deep among notes and files and yet none of them are what I am looking for.

What did I do with the transcript?

I start emptying drawers.

"I did it because I love my child. Wouldn't any mother care to do the same? I didn't feel guilty when the blood ran over my hands, yet neither did I feel vindicated. I just felt I had protected my child in the only way I knew how."

There it is!

As I move to tear off the page, a previous entry catches my eye.

*Anne was clearly distressed following the miscarriage she suf-
fered. This grievance left Anne extremely susceptible to future
mental problems. I do not believe that she fully mourned the
loss of her first child, and when faced with her second pregnancy, she thereupon read any and all literature she could lay
her hands on with regards to midwifery and childbirth in a
misguided attempt to keep the second baby safe. This in turn
filled her mind with apprehensions as to the horrors that might
be in store for her, and she thus developed a cerebral disturbance.*

*It is noteworthy here that Anne gained access to advice
books, medical literature, and periodicals, and, having an intellect great enough to both understand and digest this information, Anne was open to terror and anxiousness regarding
the impending birth of her second child.*

My legs become weak, and my stomach drops even further. How
could I have missed this? How could I have missed everything? She
didn't read to keep the baby "safe" as I previously assumed; she read
to learn the symptoms of puerperal mania!

*"She always was an avid reader, Doctor. It helped more than
you know."*

Everything has been a lie, everything!
I sit and read.

*ANNE: Beatrix did it, and it was easy. She answered an ad-
vert in the newspaper, told the woman she had a healthy baby
that needed to be put out to nurse for a while.*
TUKE: Who was the woman?
*ANNE: She called herself Mrs. Harding. I doubt it was
her real name. Beatrix didn't use her real name either.*

TUKE: Then what happened?

ANNE: Well, Beatrix asked her a few questions first, how many children she had, etc. Mrs. Harding said she had none. That's why they were looking to adopt. That it was just her and her husband, but they had not been blessed with children. That she would give it a good home, for a small fee.

TUKE: Did they arrange to meet up?

ANNE: Oh yes. Beatrix took John and met Mrs. Harding at the railway station. Mrs. Harding wanted to take John there and then, but Beatrix told her that she wasn't getting John, or any money, unless she showed her her home. She wanted to make sure John would be well cared for. At this point, Mrs. Harding became agitated and rude, started to walk away. That's when Beatrix knew she had found the right one.

TUKE: And what happened when she arrived at the house, Anne?

Swiping the entire file, I make it to the office door in two strides, when I bump into someone coming in the other way.

"Oh, Doctor, sorry. I—"

"Agnus?"

Nurse Agnus, coming into my office.

An office that she knew was empty, until now.

"Doctor, I—"

I grab her by the arm and push her up against the wall.

"Doctor! What are you—"

"Tell me what you know! You knew Lady Stanbury wasn't insane, didn't you?"

She blinks at me, her face inches away from my own, but it is Miss Fortier's face and words I hear inside my head.

"She was gifted in the art of reading."

Gifted in the art of reading.

Reading.

TUKE: And what happened when she arrived at the house, Anne?

 ANNE: She found babies, of course. Dozens of them. Many of them half-dead already.

By Lord, Nurse Ruth was right!

"Well, did you? Child, if this be the case, an innocent man is about to be sentenced to death in"—I look at my watch—"half an hour, or thereabouts! Tell me!"

"Doctor, I . . . What do you mean she wasn't insane? Who's about to be sentenced to death . . . surely not that Mr. Stanbury? I remember him well—he was such a lovely-looking young man. I read about him in the newspaper recently, but I don't understand what you're asking me. . . ." Her blond hair loosens from its bonds and wisps around her face, making her look every inch the child that she is.

I resist the urge to shake her, and let go. I don't know if she knows anything or not, but I don't have the time to interrogate her. It's at least a ten-minute cab ride back to the courthouse, and I need to be there before the jury decides Mr. Stanbury's fate. . . .

"Sir?" A tugging at my arm, a gentle voice. I realize I am bent over on the floor. This burden is too much, too heavy upon me. All I ever wanted was to make people well, and my good intentions have been made a mockery of.

"Sir, all's I know is that Miss Fortier asked me to take a job here. I was told to look after Lady Stanbury—Anne. But that's all I know. I wasn't told anything about her not being crazy or anything like that. . . . She said—"

"And," I say, slowly, "was it also your job to report back to her?"

She hangs her head. "It was. I did. But there was no harm in it, Doctor; I just let her know that Anne was well. . . ."

Doctor, it has come to my attention that you have adopted a regime of mechanical restraint since the retirement of your eminent predecessor, Dr. William Rhys Williams.

I never questioned it. I never questioned how he knew such a thing. Oh, how could I have been so blind?

"Sir." She reaches out, touches my hair. "Sir. Please don't get me into trouble. There was no reason to question Beatrix's motives. I always quite fancied doing my nursing exam anyway, and it's nice to have a bit of extra money to buy some nice things for me and me mother. And I've really enjoyed working here, sir. I hope you don't think I've done anything wrong. . . ."

A clock starts to toll, and I realize we've been talking for five minutes.

"Good Lord, child! Move out of the way! I must get to the courthouse!" I sweep past her, bumping her accidentally on the way, and I hear her gasp, but I don't stop . . . I don't look back as I leap down the steps. I don't look up until I get to the gates and raise myself up to get into the coach.

TUKE: What happened then, Anne? When she found all these babies?

ANNE: What do you think? She took one.

It's gone.
The cab has left without me.

UNTIL YOU ARE DEAD

Edgar
February 18th, 1886
Defense table

It takes the jury twenty minutes to make its decision.

They bring in closing speeches, whereupon Mr. Cropper brings tears to the jury's eyes. Mr. Smithingson seems merely outraged and resorts to slander of the prosecution. He has lost his ability to speak objectively, and it is the driving nail in my coffin. "They speak words not as evidence, but as a barely concealed, narratively loaded pile of rubbish!" The jury members have already made up their minds. Listening to the obviously inexperienced defense lawyer is akin to a mosquito buzzing around their ears on a midsummer's evening.

The judge stands. "Mr. Foreman, have you agreed upon a verdict?"

"Yes, we have. We find Mr. Stanbury guilty of murdering his wife."

The world turns hazy.

The judge passes his sentence.

I don't hear or see anything after "hanged by your neck until you are dead."

POPPED RIGHT OFF

Edgar
February 25th, 1886
Newgate Prison
Condemned cell

"Hey, do ye 'ear tha' sound? They're out there testin' t' drop wi' bags o' cement. Do ye know ye're less than fifteen feet away from t' gallows right now?" The prison warden pokes me through the blanket, taunting me. When I refuse to answer, he continues. "I 'ope they tested ye weight properly, like; ye got t' same executioner who decapitated some poor fella' last year. Ye want t' know 'ow? T' rope was too long, like, and 'is 'ead popped right off his shoulders. I saw it meself, made a right mess, it did. 'Ee . . . but ye might just get lucky; the year befoor 'e failed 't 'ang a man, 'cause t' trapdoor wouldn' open. Again, and again, the funniest sight ye ever did see. In t' end, the lucky man's sentence was commuted. Think the angels were smilin' on 'im that day."

"Go away," I say, huddling farther into the mattress. They weighed and measured me yesterday. Now I know why. I wish the other warden would come back. Although I'm not interested in playing cards or dominoes right now, his gently pressing attitude for me to engage on some level is preferable to this evil idiot, who is perfectly nice while in the others' company but a demon by himself. He leans in close to me.

"But what I want t' know is, will t' angels be smilin' on ye today, Stanbury? Or d' ye reckon t' ropes gonna be t' long, like, and pop ye head off just like a conker?"

I ignore him, thinking of my son. His face, his tiny hands, his wisps of hair . . .

"Ye know, I 'ope they've got a good rope: strong, fine, an' soft. I 'ear Mr. Berry uses rope made out o' fine Italian hemp. Such a waste. It's a pity, though . . . tha' the woman's family can't come an' see ye hanged. Stupid law." He pokes me again. "Hey, I 'eard durin' your sentencin' ye wept like a baby and screamed for mercy. Did ye wife scream fer mercy, when ye killed 'er? Did ye think she knew she was goin' t' die? How does it feel now, like, t' know you're gonna die in . . ." He pauses. "Fifteen minutes? Eight in the mornin' . . . wha' a time t' 'ang a fellow. Think they'd let ye 'ave a lie-in, wouldn't ye?" A knock on the door resounds around the cell. "Aye, up, no doubt that's t' chaplain. Ready t' confess ye sins? Not tha' it'll do ye much good." The door unlocks with a click. "Bu' I suppose ye know you're goin t' 'ell, don't ye?"

"Brutus, find Grover please, would you?" asks the chaplain as he passes the warden. He is old, and I weep at the sight of the wrinkles and grooves I will never get the chance to wear. He comes and sits on the edge of the bed and lays a hand upon my cheek, turning my face toward his.

"Child, don't cry. . . ."

"Has the reprieve come?" I say the words quietly, barely daring to ask them for fear of the answer that has come many times before.

The chaplain remains silent and rummages around in his robes. "I have come to pray with you, my child, and ask once again for your confession and repentance. I have also brought you some wine." His hands shake, and a droplet of water appears on the back of one of them.

A tear.

I sit up and grasp his leathery hands in mine. "Father, the reprieve?"

He shakes his head sadly. He has two tear tracks down his face, and in that moment, I understand.

Nothing more can be done. "Child, the transcript was inadmissible. Your wife was classified as insane when she made that 'confession.' Anything said under hypnosis cannot be taken as fact. There is too much evidence against you, and nobody is willing to go up against an earl. Especially when a sentence has already been passed. I tried. I spoke with Dr. Savage; he went to the police about the ring, but they didn't believe him. Nobody has ever seen it. Inspector Jones said the doctor must've been mistaken, that he never had any sort of object about his person. The doctor wholeheartedly believes you to be innocent, so much so that in fact he resigned. He doesn't feel himself worthy of the title of 'doctor' anymore. I believe he is outside, protesting in your name."

I get out of bed, stand up shakily, and walk the ten steps toward the barred windows. The sky is clear, blue. How can they kill me on such a beautiful day? I turn to the chaplain and swallow. "Someone told me that one out of twenty men hanged are innocent. How many is that a year, Father?"

He stutters, "I don't know, child. I don't know. But perhaps it's better you atone—"

"What for? For the crowd? For you? In a few hours, I shall pay the penalty for a crime I did not commit with that of my life. I do not need or want to make a false confession to appease the conscience of those who will stand idly by and watch me executed."

The chaplain looks pale and brings a hand to his mouth. Just as he is about to say something, we are interrupted by another knock on the door.

"Good morning, sir." A large, blond-haired man approaches me and bows respectfully. He holds a long leather strap in his hands, and in that instant my legs fail me. Just as I am about to drop upon the floor, he reaches forward and grabs me under my arms, helping me over to the bed. "My name is Mr. James Berry, and I have been appointed as your executioner." Behind him stand a large group of men, Brutus, Grover and the prison governor the only people I recognize among the fourteen or so men.

"I am innocent," I whisper. "I am innocent. You must believe me. Oh God, oh God . . ."

This time, when he grabs hold of my arms it is not to help me, but to condemn me. He silently works the strap around my upper arms, securing them to the sides of my body.

Oh my God, it's happening. They're going to kill me. . . .

"I am innocent, I am innocent, I am innocent. Oh, God, please do not let them hang an innocent man. . . ."

The chaplain begins to recite some sort of sermon as hands gently lift me, and I recognize some words and phrases from the burial service yesterday. My mind shifts, and I am half carried, half dragged across the cell, surrounded by men whose names I do not know to a song of everlasting love, forgiveness, and repentance. Somewhere close by, a baby is crying. One of the warders pushes on the side of the wardrobe, and I barely have time to wonder at his action before the world goes white. There is something on my face, and now I am blind. I can't see where are they taking me. . . .

The sound underneath my feet becomes hollow, and I am stopped. Someone wraps something around my legs, and a coarse, itchy ring lowers itself around my neck.

"Make sure you pinion him tight, now, there's a good lad."

Hemp. The hangman's rope is made of hemp.

Anne. My love, my heart. I'm so sorry. I never set out to hurt you. I never meant to deceive you. I never meant to speak to you so badly, but I was drunk, and I felt sick, and everyone had treated me so badly for so long that I lost my mind. I think of her then, wrapping her arms around me, passing over our son. Tears of joy on an innocent's face, a finger the length of my fingernail curling itself around my heart. Two blue eyes blinking at the wonder of a new world, the smell of soft skin. *I will love you forever, my son, and I will always be there for you. Your mother and I together, we will watch you grow and fill your life with love until the day we die. For I have found peace and happiness in a place I never expected.* My wife, a woman whom I set out to deceive, and yet never would have: a woman who found all the wrong words in all the wrong places and believed that I would take her son away from her, never seeing the true letter that is still left, unsent, telling my father the truth of the situation. A woman married to a coward who has signed his own death warrant by never revealing the truth to her. A crunching noise, an agonizing pain shooting through my neck and I can't breathe. It hurts. My ears are ringing, and I can smell my child. I can breathe his essence.

And I see everything.

You bitch.

I go to heaven with the scent of my son's breath in my lungs and the curve of his smile wrapped around my heart.

I love you both.

AUTHOR'S NOTE

While this novel is a work of fiction, it is inspired by real events. Many of the events in the novel come directly from historical case studies, psychiatric textbooks, memoirs, and newspaper articles. The rest of the story is made up of fictional likelihoods, my own speculation, and interpretation drawn up over years of research. Some historical characters have been invented; however, most are real, historical people.

Dr. George Savage (1842–1921), though little remembered today, was a well-known alienist at the end of the nineteenth century, and medical superintendent of Bethlem Royal Hospital until his retirement in 1888, following a scandal concerning the number of patients who died in his care. I have taken a liberty with the date of his retirement for the purpose of this novel, and also the reason.

His lack of any major contribution to the theory of mental illness means that he is but a minor figure in the history of psychiatry. However, he was well-known for his case-based approach (as evidenced in this novel) and was the only psychiatrist to appear on the cover of *Vanity Fair*'s "Men of the Day" when he was awarded a knighthood in 1912. Today, he is probably best remembered for taking care of Virginia Woolf, who famously portrayed Savage as an unpleasant doctor in one of her novels, *Mrs. Dalloway*. The reason for this? Savage believed that Virginia's wisdom teeth were causing her depression. He removed them. It didn't work, and resentful of this pointless loss of her teeth, Virginia got her revenge.

I have tried to capture Dr. Savage's true personality in *The Medea Complex*, and much of the dialogue and notes utilized with the care of Anne in this novel are *real*, taken from real patients he treated. These can be found in his books, which I have referenced at the end of this book. The treatments I have described, attitudes, and experiments are all real, and all took place in the time period in which this novel is based. I have attempted to keep the "fiction" as close to "fact" as possible.

Esther Base (unknown) was a real patient who was admitted to Bethlem Asylum, for throwing her children out of the window.

Mr. James Berry (1852–1913) was a real hangman at the time, and the description of a man being decapitated while hanged is true. The methods, weights, and even the material of the rope are all factual. He also used to visit "especially nervous" prisoners in their cell. Everything about the cell at Newgate has been described, and taken from his memoir, which I have referenced at the end, including the description of decapitation.

Amelia Dyer (1837–1896) is another real character mentioned in the book, although you may not have realized it! In keeping true with the era, I have referred to her by one of her many (known) aliases— Mrs. Harding—a pseudonym she is known to have used. She is believed to be, even by today's standards, the worst serial killer ever in U.K. history.

Amelia Dyer was a prolific baby farmer, who would advertise in local newspapers to adopt and nurse a baby, in return for a fee from the child's mother. Oftentimes this was a lump sum, which was preferable to her, as it meant she could discard of the child quickly, without any repercussions. However, she also kept many children who were paid for on a "weekly" basis, or with an extortionate lump sum fee. Eventually, she murdered the babies, initially by starvation, and later—when she realized she could speed up the process—by suffocation, thus pocketing the money that would otherwise have been used to look after the child. Often, the fee paid by the mother was not adequate enough to cover the cost of looking after a child, and the mother was well aware of what would happen to her baby once she handed him or her over. However, there is one famous case that spanned across the newspapers in England in 1896. A governess handed her child to Dyer for safekeeping and spent four years trying to get her baby back. Dyer tried to convince her another child was hers, and finally told her he had been adopted out. The name of this poor governess is not mentioned in any historical records, and I can only presume this was to protect the identity of a middle-class woman who broke social convention.

She never got her son back, and she never found his body.

I have taken liberty with this poor, unknown character of history, and based the chapter concerning the woman on the road on her torment. I cannot imagine the pain of this mother. There are numerous accounts of hundreds, if not thousands, of girls and women alike giving their babies up in the manner in which she did. Adverts in the newspaper, that while innocent to the unsuspecting reader, read like a coded message to these desperate women. Women who found themselves pregnant with an illegitimate child, out of work, no money. They had no way to survive; even orphanages at the time would not accept children born out of wedlock. Employers would not offer jobs to women who were pregnant, or who had children. There was no welfare. Many workhouses turned them away. They had little in the way of options.

Although many women knew that in adopting their baby out they would never see them again, extensive research into this subject indicates that there were an equal number of naive, innocent women who had no idea the person looking after their children was intending to murder them.

However, not *all* baby farmers were disreputable, but the term eventually came to be used as an insult.

It is widely believed that Dyer killed upwards of four hundred children, but was only found guilty of the murder of one. She hanged at Newgate Prison in 1896.

The worst part of this for me, as a mother myself, is not Amelia. It is the fact that she was *not* the only one. Through my research, I have found dozens, if not hundreds, of women executed in the nineteenth century for the dubious trade of baby farming.

Dorothea Jordan (1761–1816) was a real person, the mistress of William IV for over twenty years (at that time, he was known as the Duke of Clarence). Although they loved each other, royal policies forced the king to marry someone of his own social standing and stature; Mrs. Jordan, after all, was simply an actress. She and William had at least ten illegitimate children during their time together. After their relationship broke down, William IV gave her custody of their daughters (not of their sons; he kept those), and gave her a reasonable yearly stipend. However, to keep receiving this money, he ordered her never to return to the stage. When her son-in-law got himself into debt in 1814, she broke her promise to William IV and returned to the stage. When he received word of this, he regained custody of her daughters and took back her yearly stipend. To avoid creditors, she fled to France, where she died in abject poverty, alone, in 1816. She is known to have had a number of lovers, and at least one other child from another relationship. Mr. Stanbury is a fictional descendant of hers.

Dr. Tuke (1827–1896) was a real English physician and expert in mental illnesses. He came from a long line of Quakers, and his great-grandfather William Tuke, and his grandfather, Henry Tuke, co-funded "the Retreat," a place that today still treats people with mental health problems. It is located in Lamel Hill, York, United Kingdom.

Lady Stanbury, aka "Anne," is a fictional character inspired by accounts of real, aristocratic women at the time, and what we know today as "postnatal psychosis." Infanticide (i.e., the killing of a child by his or her own mother) is a real (and still continuing!) problem that plagued the nineteenth century, and affected mothers across all social classes. The socioeconomic issues at the time, the great divide of poverty, and medicine and psychiatry all being in their infancy led to many of these mothers being locked away, "guilty but insane" for their crimes. Some of them indeed were hanged. Yet many were cured and released.

The **hypnosis session** I have described is based upon a real session, which can be found in the books referenced at the end.

REFERENCES AND SOURCES

Bacon, G. *On the Writing of the Insane: With Illustrations*. London: John Churchill and Sons, 1870.

Berry, J. *My Experiences as an Executioner*. London: P Lund & Co, 1892.

Bly, N. *Ten Days in a Mad-House*. New York: Ian. L. Munro Publishing, 1887.

Bramwell, J. M. *Hypnotism: Its History, Practice and Theory*. London: Rider & Co, 1921.

Broussais, F. J. V., Cooper, T. *On Irritation and Insanity*. Columbia: J. M. Morris, 1831.

Bucknill, J.C. *Notes on Asylums for the Insane in America*. New York: Arno Press, 1876.

Bucknill, J. C., and Tuke, D. H. *A Manual of Psychological Medicine*. London: John Churchill, New Burlington Street, 1879.

Bucknill, J. C. *The Care of the Insane and Their Legal Control*. London: Macmillan & Co, 1880.

California, Commission in Lunacy; Wilkins, E. T. *Insanity and Insane Asylums*. Sacramento (Calif): T. A. Springer, 1872.

Chase, A. W. *Information for Everybody*. London: Taylor, 1869.

Clark. *Hand-Book for Attendants at the Asylum for the Insane*. Toronto: C. Blackett, 1881.

Earle, P. *History, Description and Statistics of the Bloomingdale Asylum for the Insane*. New York: Hovey & King, Printers, 1848.

Esquirol, Jean Etienne Dominique. *Mental Maladies. A Treatise on Insanity*. Philadelphia: Lea and Blanchard, 1845.

REFERENCES AND SOURCES

Gale, C., and Howard, R. *Presumed Curable: An Illustrated Casebook of Victorian Psychiatric Patients in Bethlem Hospital.* University of Michigan: Wrightson Biomedical Publishers, 2003.

Goddard, H. H. *The Criminal Imbecile: An Analysis of Three Remarkable Murder Cases.* New York: The Macmillan Company, 1915.

Goldberg, J. A. *Social Aspects of the Treatment of the Insane, based on a Study of New York experience.* New York: Columbia Press, 1921.

Gunn, J. C. *Gunn's New Domestic Physician.* New York: Cincinnati, 1857.

Haslam, John. *Observations on Insanity.* London: J. Hatchard, 1798.

Heidenhaim, R., Wooldridge, L. C, & Romanes, G. J. *Hypnotism; or, Animal Magnetism; Physiological Observations.* London: Paul, Trench, & Trubner & Co. Ltd., 1899.

Ireland, W. W. *The Mental Affections of Children: Idiocy, Imbecility and Insanity.* London: J. & A. Churchill, 1898.

Kerlin, I. N., Walter, E. *The Mind Unveiled.* Philadelphia: Hunt, 1858.

Krafft-Ebing, R. Von (Richard). *Text-book of Insanity, Based on Clinical Observations for Practitioners and Students of Medicine.* Philadelphia: Davis, 1904.

Maudsley, H. *Physiology and Pathology of the Mind.* London: Macmillan & Co, 1867.

Mercier, Charles Arthur. *Sanity and Insanity.* London: Walter Scott, 1890.

Mercier, Charles Arthur. *A Text-book of Insanity and Other Mental Diseases.* New York: Macmillan, 1914.

Napheys, G. *The Physical Life of Woman.* Toronto: Maclear & Company, 1871.

O'Donoghue, E. G. *The Story of Bethlehem Hospital from Its Foundation in 1247.* New York: E.P. Dutton & Co, 1915.

Packard, E. P. W. *The Prisoners' Hidden Life.* Chicago: The author, A. B. Case, printer, 1868.

Packard, E. P. W. *Modern Persecution or Married Woman's Liabilities.* Hartford: Published by the Authoress, 1874.

Royal Medico-psychological Association Handbook for the Instruction of Attendants on the Insane. London: Bailliere Tindall & Co, 1885.

Sane, P. *My Experiences in a Lunatic Asylum.* London: Chatto & Windus, 1879.

Savage, G. H. *Insanity and Allied Neuroses.* Philadelphia: Henry C. Lea's Son & Co, 1884.

Savage, G. H. *The Use of Sedatives in Insanity.* London: Macmillan and Co, 1886.

Savage, G. *The Influence of Surroundings on the Production of Insanity.* Journal of Mental Science. 1 (1), 529, 1891.

Savage, G. *The Harveian Oration on Experimental Psychology and Hypnotism.* British Medical Journal. 2 (1), 1205–1212, 1909.

Savory, J. *A Companion to the Medicine Chest.* London: John Churchill, 1836.

Spurzheim, J. G. *Observations on the Deranged Manifestations of the Mind, or*

Insanity. Boston, Marsh: Capen & Lyon. Tuke, S. (1813). Description of the Retreat, an institution near York, for insane persons of the Society of Friends: containing an account of its origin and progress, the modes of treatment, and a statement of cases. Philadelphia: Issac, 1833.

Tuke, D. H. *Insanity in Ancient and Modern Life: with Chapters on its Prevention*. London: Macmillan and Co, 1878.

Tuke, D. H. *Illustrations of the Influence of the Mind upon the Body in Health and Disease*. Philadelphia: Henry C. Lea's Son & Co, 1884.

Tuke, D. H. *Sleep-walking and Hypnotism*. London: J. & A. Churchill, 1884.

Tuke, D. H. *A Dictionary of Psychological Medicine*. London: J. & A. Churchill, 1892.

Tuke, D. H. *Reform in the Treatment of the Insane: Early History of the Retreat, York; its Objects and Influence, with a Report of the Celebration of its Centenary*. London: J. & A. Churchill, 1892.

Wehman, H. *The Mystery of Love, Courtship and Marriage, Explained*. Wehman Bros, 1890.

Wetterstrand, O. G., Petersen, H. G. *Hypnotism and its Application to Practical Medicine*. New York: G. P. Putnam's Sons, 1902.

Wyman, M. (1877). *The Early History of the McLean Asylum for the Insane; A Criticism of the Report of the Massachusetts State board of health*. Cambridge: Riverside Press.

Wynter, A. (1875). *The Borderlands of Insanity: And Other Allied Papers*. New York: G. P. Putnam's Sons, 1877.

The
MEDEA
COMPLEX

Rachel Florence Roberts

ESSAY BY
RACHEL FLORENCE ROBERTS

When my son was born in 2011, I had no idea that the experience would inspire an entire novel. And I'm glad it did, because it saved me—in more ways than one.

Postpartum depression. Two words. One condition. More than I could ever imagine. I spent months convinced that something awful was going to happen to my baby. I was terrified to go near him, but petrified not to. I didn't know what was the lesser of two evils—if I touch him and he dies, is that worse than *not* touching him and he dies anyway?

How could I protect him? Well. Much to the horror of my fiancé, I turned our apartment into a clinical experiment in sterility. I was a nurse, after all—I *knew* just how harmful and *sneaky* those pesky little germs could be. I knew they liked to move around the world, happily spreading their dirty Armageddon to everyone and anyone—and I knew just *how* they liked to travel.

On people.

In those first six months, probably half a dozen people were allowed into our apartment. I made them take their shoes off at the door. Then I made them go into the bathroom and wash their hands. Entering the living room, they were to rub their hands with alcohol gel, supplied within the lovely little dispenser I had bought especially for this purpose.

And they had to do it while I watched. Yes—no gel on your hands (and thirty seconds of rubbing!), you aren't holding the baby.

And don't even *think* of coming within one hundred feet of my home if you have a cold, or have sneezed within the last year.

Yes, I actually turned people away—especially well-wishers who sounded a bit "croaky" on the phone. One day, my mother phoned to express her disbelief that I hadn't taken my baby to the supermarket more than once in six months. I merely shouted at her and hung up, wondering how on earth I'd managed to survive all these years with such an obviously negligent mother. I was thankful—at that point—to be living in Malta, three thousand miles away from my family in the U.K.

It meant nobody could visit unannounced.

Instead, I continued to do the research needed to keep my baby safe. Yet, ultimately, it was this very insanity that saved me.

It didn't take too long to recognize that I had a problem—in the form of postpartum depression. Of course, many—if not all—new parents worry about germs, but it wasn't merely a concern for me; it was an utter conviction. I truly believed that something terrible would happen to my child. My own mother burst into tears one morning because I wouldn't let her hold him: I'd had a dream the night before that someone had dropped him in the kitchen, and his head had cracked open like an egg. I literally saw death coming for him everywhere, and in everyone. Including myself. There were times when I was just as frightened to be near him as not to be—I had mental images of throwing him off the balcony.

Looking back, I do wonder if I didn't have a touch of postpartum psychosis—oh, I wasn't hearing alien voices in the sink, but it was quite clear to me that these thoughts and fears were probably not normal. Ultimately, I visited a couple of local doctors who diagnosed me within minutes (postpartum depression), threw some pink pills at me, and sent me on my way.

Common practice in my home country—the U.K.—in such situations is to refer the new mother to therapy. I couldn't believe that these "doctors" prescribed medication so quickly without knowing me, my circumstances, or my background medical history. Not one of the several doctors I approached during this time asked me whether I had any history of mental health issues. As far as I was concerned, they were positively incompetent and I threw the medication in the bin (which I later learned was banned in the United States, Canada, United Kingdom, Japan, India, Ireland, Australia, and even its country of manufacture—Denmark).

I knew I needed to speak to someone, but I didn't know where to turn. So I sat on the balcony and cried, hating myself for moving to a country where I was completely misunderstood. Suddenly, I hated everything about Malta and wished I'd never moved to a place where I had no family nearby, no friends. I felt utterly, terribly, alone.

My next step was to go online. If the doctors couldn't help me, I needed to help myself. I spent weeks researching everything about postpartum depression.

Some of the articles terrified me. I started to worry that I might actually be "mad" and not merely depressed. And even if I wasn't mad, what if someone thought I was? I started to panic, told myself that I should never have gone to a doctor in the first place. What if, after I left, they thought about it a bit more and decided I wasn't fit to be a mother? For a short while, I flinched every time the doorbell rang, half-convinced that it was someone from the local mental hospital coming to take me away. I started to research not only postpartum depression, but mothers throughout the ages who had had their children taken away from them, or who were locked up. The more I delved, the further my own paranoia took me—all the way back to the nineteenth century.

I read.

I breast-fed, and I read.

And before I knew it, I was pregnant again.

Albeit this time, with a slightly more . . . unconventional baby. A more literary one.

A novel.

A story about a woman, who may or may not be crazy; who may or may not lose the thing that means everything to her. I sat on my balcony and asked myself whether I had it in me, whether I could actually write a book.

My husband was the first person to believe that I was capable. Not only of being a mother, but of becoming an author.

Ultimately, it took over two years for my postpartum depression to completely go away (without medication), but the research and writing process really did save me. It calmed my thoughts and diverted me. It answered my question.

I wasn't mad.

I was just a mother, a normal woman who loved her child more than anything.

QUESTIONS FOR DISCUSSION

1. At the beginning of *The Medea Complex*, Dr. Savage states that: "Men will forgive what women will not." This is a very sweeping statement—however, it is evident throughout the novel that Dr. Savage holds some strong opinions about women in general. Yet, when Edgar is charged with murder toward the end, Dr. Savage is very quick to assume he is guilty. Was Dr. Savage so blinded by his own preconceptions and biases? Was he negligent in his care of Anne? Or was he simply a man with good intentions who was, unfortunately, a product of his time? Do you think his opinions and theories ultimately contributed to the tragic ending?

2. What did you think of the servants' attitudes? Why were they so disrespectful toward Edgar? Do you think they truly did hate and resent him, or were their actions misinterpreted by his current state of mind?

3. What role, specifically, do you think young Betty had to play in the novel as a character? What did she bring to the novel?

4. Much of the story is based upon lies, deception, and miscommunication. What do you think may have happened if both Edgar and Anne had simply been open and truthful to each other from the beginning?

5. Does Anne have a conscience? How is she able to reconcile the idea

that being responsible for others' deaths is not only acceptable, but justifiable? Do you think, at any point, she feels guilty for what she has done? Why do you think the author decided to allow Anne to go unpunished for her deception?

6. At the end of the novel, Beatrix says that while she is no longer unable to judge Anne, she will continue to stand by her forever. Why does she feel this way? Is it because she herself is complicit in the entire plot, or is it because of the loyalty she feels because of her history with Anne's mother? Is there a point, in someone's behavior, that we could, or should, simply stop loving them? Is Beatrix right or wrong in remaining silent toward the end of the novel?

7. Is Anne a murderer? After all, she never actually spills any blood with her own hands. If she was ever found out, do you think she could, or should, be charged with murder? If so, of whom? Is withholding the truth that could set someone free a moral offense?

8. Do you think that sacrificing another child—one who is almost certain to die at the hands of a baby farmer—for your own means, is ever justifiable? What else could Anne have done, rather than go to such extreme measures?

9. Why was the justice system so lacking on behalf of Edgar Stanbury? Do you feel he was offered a fair trial? Was there enough evidence to ultimately send him to the gallows? Would the outcome have been different if he had been born into a different social class or had a more competent lawyer? Was it ultimately a failure of the court of law that sent Edgar to his death?

10. Edgar's last thoughts are "You bitch" and "I love you both." What does this ultimately suggest about his character? Do you think, at the end, he truly understands the level of Anne's deception, or does he remain ignorant of her actions? Is it possible to continue to love someone, no matter how badly they treat you? If he had gone to his death with anger and resentment in his heart, would that have added to or detracted from the emotional turmoil within the novel?

11. Anne fakes puerperal mania (modern-day postnatal psychosis) for her own means. Would you feel differently about her character if she genuinely suffered from the condition and had, in fact, killed her own child? If so, how and why?

12. The woman on the road claimed that she put her baby out to "nurse," and had no idea that the baby farmer harbored untoward intentions toward her child. Do you truly believe she was not aware of the danger she placed her child in? As Anne herself mentions at the end of the novel, the newspapers at the time were full of such reports of horror. And if the woman *had* put her child out with the sole intention of never seeing him again, what impact would this have upon your opinion of this character, and the fact that Beatrix left her on the road to die?

13. Considering the subject matter of the novel, does it surprise you to learn that the author was inspired to write this book while suffering from postnatal depression? Does it change your understanding of the story to realize that many of Anne's thoughts came from the author's state of mind at the time of writing? Did this bias the novel's outcome in any way? Were you also surprised to learn that much of the novel's content is based upon true people and real historical events?

14. Was the ending of the novel expected? Was it satisfactory? Did you feel as if you were quite firmly on only one character's side, or did you feel you understood them both? Or neither? Do you feel pity for Edgar's side of the story, or Anne's? Was there a passive character and an active character? Why do you think this is? Do you think that both their individual personalities were shaped by their upbringing and fathers' influences?

Photo by Xposure Studios—Fiona Kelly

Rachel Florence Roberts was born in Liverpool. She was inspired to write *The Medea Complex* after suffering from postpartum depression, following the birth of her son. *The Medea Complex* is inspired by true events that occurred toward the end of the nineteenth century, and is Rachel's first novel.

CONNECT ONLINE

rachelflorenceroberts.com

facebook.com/rachelflorenceroberts

twitter.com/rachelfroberts